False gods: the ecstasy

by

Cy Black

First Published in 2013
by Dragon Press LLP
Longbourne, Epping Green, Herts, HG13 8NE

Book cover artist: Gwenaneiry
Book cover subject: Gianlorenzo Bernini's Pluto and Persephone

CreateSpace Edition

ISBN-13: 978-1481233552

ACKNOWLEDGEMENTS

To my children, my true loves, for putting up with me during the process of writing this book.

To my mother, for a lifetime of love and devotion.

To Bertie, for being my life-saver.

To Antoinette, Millie, Julian, Camilla, Martell, Virginia and Rory for being true friends at crucial times.

To Coles, Joe, Min, Jonathan, Claudia, Nici and Humphrey for their belief in this project, and all of their help and extraordinary encouragement.

To Gwenaneiry, the young, talented Welsh artist who did the drawing for the book cover.

To Jane, Eva, Amal, Helen and Theo for their kind efforts.

To London, for its beauty, diversity, tolerance, parks and inspiration.

Sources for the Rumi quotations:

The Rumi quotations in chapter one, chapter eleven, chapter twenty and chapter thirty are taken from 'The Essential Rumi' translated by Coleman Barks and John Moyne, while the rest of them are taken from 'Rumi, Gardens of the Beloved' translated by Maryam Mafi and Azima Melita Kolin.

Cy Black

Cy Black never wanted to be a novelist. Cy Black was a dyslexic investment banker, but there was a story that would not give her any peace until it was told. This is the first book of that tale. The second is on its way...

For J,
my prod to remembrance.

False gods: the ecstasy

CONTENTS

I cannot think of any need in childhood as strong as the need for a father's protection.

Sigmund Freud

False gods: the ecstasy

Chapter One - Love at first sight

*The minute I heard my first love story
I started to look for you, not knowing
how blind I was.
Lovers don't finally meet somewhere
They're in each other all along.*

Rumi

Natasha Flynn stands, staring, fixated. A giant hand smacks her in the face, the instant her soul's eye locks with the soul's eye of 'the other', across a gigantic debt-trading floor, in the heart of the City of London. The multitudes of this infested floor melt away, as she loses herself in a wordless communion that spans all millennia, captivated by the terrorizing recognition of coupled lifetimes past, and coupled lifetimes to come. Time distills into the pinprick of presence that is NOW. All before, all after, all present, conspire only to this moment, NOW. On this grim, grey, gargantuan trading floor, Natasha is flattened by the fleeting comprehension of the monumental fact of infinity. Her breath, blood and heartbeat stand in suspension, with the sheer shock of such occurrence. Yin and yang prepare for battle and bliss.

'The other?' Sebastian Butler: thirty-four years old, six-foot four, close-cropped, dark brown hair and bright green eyes; long lashes. His perfect, male Y-shaped frame stands, frozen to the spot. His expression betrays a shock as profound as Natasha's, for his wide eyes are fixed on hers, and his mouth slightly parted, as if spellbound. He is wearing impeccably tailored trousers of midnight blue, with his shirt tucked in, just above his black leather, gold buckled belt. His fine silk tie, adorned with an exquisite duck-egg blue and lemon yellow tessellated pattern, is set in a plump,

half-Windsor knot, just beneath his chin. The stark whiteness of his crisp shirt, accentuates his light tan; the colour
of Jasmine tea. On first sight, the man is as pristine as his
Berluti, handcrafted, black leather lace-up shoes.

Sebastian Butler; sleek as an otter. Many a female onlooker would have had an impulse to admire him. This
female onlooker was enveloped with the desire to stroke
the back of his elegant neck and devour him. Sebastian
Butler: arrogant, rich, egotistical; as accomplished in the
sports arena as on the trading floor. He exudes the self-
assurance of a man who, quite simply, gets everything he
wants, peppered with the pathos of a man who gains little
sustenance from all that he has. In him, the evidence of
their exchange suggests, Natasha has found her soul mate.
A soul mate currently immersed in the feast of power,
money, ego and the ludicrous hearts of women, or the
hearts of ludicrous women, they taste much the same.

The NOW that all time has conspired to? Thursday the
eleventh of August 1994 on a dirty, grey, low-ceilinged,
four-hundred workforce strong debt-trading floor, in the
heart of the City of London. This place is far removed from
the natural light that barely penetrates the paltry windows.
The light that illuminates this workforce is an artificial,
spitting and stuttering light, which emanates from the vibrating neon strips above, and pulsates from the plethora of
computer screens all around, as they relentlessly splutter
the bright, ever-changing digits of capitalism, and the sec-
ond-by-second news flashes of the global populace, to this
particular corner of the planet. The food that feeds this human energy-drome is adrenaline; slowly and painlessly
slaughtering those it fuels. Four-hundred people, wired, on
perpetual alert, fight or flight, jerky, jumpy, hyper people,
feeling terribly powerful as they shift monstrous amounts
of money all over the world, to earn obscene sums of lucre
for their bank accounts; offshore.

For Natasha to clock her 'other' in such a 'now' perplexed and amused her. Her 'other' was not perplexed or
amused. He was just starving. The engorged ego of Sebas-

tian Butler, demanded more fodder than the staple of adrenaline. His ego craved to feed on a more rarefied dish, to gorge itself on another's passion blood, in a quest to recall what it was to feel. Poor, rich, Sebastian Butler, sadly destined to stalk suitable female hearts, from which to suck vital juices, to further nourish his insatiable ego run rampant. Sebastian was not thinking 'soul mate'. Sebastian was thinking 'supper!'

The dish? Natasha Flynn: twenty-three years young, five-foot ten, long, luxurious Titian hair and luminescent white skin. The gob-smacked girl had just a smattering of red-brown freckles, speckling the fine bridge of her neat nose, and dusting the top of her soaring cheek-bones, to add a touch of quirkiness to her beauty. She was long-limbed, poised and slender, with catlike, olive green eyes the sparkle of which hinted at a quixotic intelligence. She had a heart-shaped face that seemed, perpetually, to sport a bright, teeth-flashing smile, as arresting as the white sail of a yacht cruising the Mediterranean in August.

Natasha Flynn: the investment bank's striking, overexcited, highly ambitious, recently-recruited graduate trainee. Our hapless heroine had just found her challenge: this sleek creature wants to play. She fast concluded such game, to be far more fun than bond maths. With just one look, our protagonists' trade was, instantaneously, accomplished. The details of their immediate and eagerly embraced bargain, would be subconsciously and verbally communicated in the coming weeks. It would take the coming years to complete the mechanics of execution. Let the games begin!

"Hello you."

Sebastian spoke these first two words very quietly, as he fixed Natasha with terrifyingly penetrating, jet-black pupils. His expression was so intimately intense that the image of the snake Kaa, from Disney's adaptation of 'The Jungle Book', sprang to our heroine's mind. The eyes Natasha stared into now, were just as dangerously hypnotic. Uninvited, unflattering, mental images aside, the man's focus was so ferocious that Natasha was held hostage by it.

The ravenous Sebastian seemed intent on gaining swift and immediate control of the new plaything placed before him. Indeed, his expression could easily be classified as ridiculous, but for the fact that, the time it took to make such observation was the time it took to become mesmerized.

These eyes did not possess finite pupils. These eyes led to another place. The longer Natasha stared into them, the more infused she became with a strange and vital energy. Simply, her heart was in her mouth and she was buzzing from head to toe. The man's alertness was so extreme that Natasha felt to blink would put her at a disadvantage. Grinning broadly, the tall Sebastian stooped and extended his hand. Star-struck, Natasha, wordlessly, slipped hers into it and they shook hands, slowly, as he introduced himself, "Sebastian Butler, Vice President."

With this simple touch, a powerful flood of familiarity flowed into Natasha, of such strength that she felt utterly fearless before him, and she replied, teasing coyly:

"How do you do, Sebastian Butler Vice President?"

He gave her a censorious smirk for he knew, all too well, that 'Vice President' had not strictly been necessary, on either of their parts. Emboldened, she continued.

"Natasha Flynn, graduate trainee, attached to the fixed income division."

"So soon?" he asked incredulously, as he fixed her with sceptical gaze.

A quizzical look traversed Natasha's face, before she fast realized that Sebastian was dispensing a dose of her own medicine. Obediently, she lapped it up and, with eyes downcast and hand held on heart, she declared:

"Deeply."

"My, my, how easily your passions are aroused Miss Flynn, I do believe you will find yourself most at home on a trading floor."

Natasha flinched for, as if to prove his point, a thunderous roar of deep-throated male cheering exploded from a large bank of Trading Desks to her right. It was as if the traders in question had just witnessed a home goal. With a room so packed with indistinguishable screens, maybe they just had? As the raucousness ebbed, Sebastian smiled, sagely, before reluctantly releasing her hand. He then straightened his back and tipped his head to one side, then the other, to stretch out his neck. Natasha watched with strange fascination, as his sinewy jaw muscles rippled under freshly-shaven skin. Sebastian gave a giant yawn, and then allowed his arms to fall to his sides as he let out an impressive lungful of breath. Relaxed now, he grinned happily, put his arms behind his back and grasped his left wrist with his right hand, to adopt that open pose so common with kings and princes.

He proceeded to look over Natasha's head, haughtily, as he scanned the enormous room, the continuous murmur of which was louder and more sustained than a gushing gully after heavy rainfall. There was much for Sebastian to observe, for the trading floor was packed with row upon row of shoulder to shoulder young men, with the rare shock of an attractive female to patronize personnel and decorate the scene for male management. Those hunched at desks frowned in deep concentration, captivated by the colourful charts, the flashing numbers and the continual stream of words, that flickered across their multiple screens in the dominating towers of computers stacked up in front of them. Nearly all of their vast number had one, or more, chunky black telephones wedged between shoulder and jowl, while they engaged in skilful, often heated, negotiation. At times, the noise of the conversing collective was deafening and, more often than not, expletive. Natasha had her back to the rumbling throng as she stood before Sebastian. She was hesitating, captivated by his handsome face. She was not sure if he had finished talking to her yet. For more than a minute she hovered in front of him, hoping he would say more. She was not to be disappointed for, soon enough, Sebastian leaned forward and confessed, quietly:

"Anyway, I know exactly who you are Miss Flynn. I found out all about you…"

"You did?"

A bolt of shocked excitement shot through her, for Sebastian's proximity, and his declaration, had set her pulse racing. He continued:

"I certainly did Natasha... how could I help but not?"

She was overwhelmed, but determined not to show it. It took her longer than she would have liked to goad daringly.

"Why Sebastian, how quickly you resort to flattery. Have you no restraint?"

"Restraint is needfully observed by those who cannot afford to indulge in excess. Oh, and of course imposed on those who are either criminal... or insane."

Sebastian then looked up, at nothing in particular, to think about what he had just said. A subtle smile spread across his lips. It was clear he was rather thrilled with his riposte. Having spent a moment dwelling in self-satisfaction, he added authoritatively:

"All I can assure you Miss Flynn, is that I do not belong to the former category." He paused, no doubt savouring the precise extent of his wealth, before challenging, "As to the whether the latter categories apply, well, you will have to work that out all by yourself."

Natasha laughed, nervously, as she watched a manic glint traverse Sebastian's green eyes. A cold shiver ran down her spine and the hairs on the back of her neck and forearms prickled to attention. In that instant, she felt as vulnerable as a wildcat trapped by an impecunious taxi-dermist. He held intense eye contact, and then nodded once as if in acknowledgement of their developing understanding. Finally, Sebastian clapped his hands and began to survey the expanse of the trading floor, once again, as he recounted casually, "I do believe Edward informed you that you will be joining my Global Credit-Trading and Sales Desk for several weeks. You will learn all about the joys of our highly interesting, not to mention rather profitable, business. You will start with us a week on Monday. I am off sailing at the weekend, hence the delay, however..." Sebastian then set his white-hot attention back on Natasha, "I am certain that you possess enough stamina,

Miss Flynn, to last one more week broking futures with the exquisite Innes and her enchanting team."

He spoke with unconcealed mockery. Clearly, he viewed his own Desk to be vastly superior to the one on which she was currently working. He then continued in a hushed, suggestive voice, "Natasha, before I go away, I think it is important we have a little 'tête-à-tête'. I believe you would find it most advantageous if, prior to your joining us, I were to brief you on the salient points of our business model."

The prospect of an imminent 'tête-à-tête' with this astonishing man, was almost too much to bear. Natasha nodded eagerly. Sebastian lifted his right index finger to his top lip, as if in studied thought, before he continued, quietly, "I was thinking, what about joining me for lunch in the Directors' dining-room? We can... umm," his expression became playful again and he leant forward, emphasizing each word as he spoke, "get... to... know... each... other?"

Natasha's slanted eyes, for a moment, looked completely round. She blinked, as if playing for time, and then replied, guilelessly:

"Well why not? When were you thinking?"

"Is there ever a time so satisfactory as the present, Natasha? Please, follow me."

"Errr... OK... errr... just give me just a minute." our heroine stuttered.

Natasha barely had time to relish the extent of her exhilaration. Action was demanded, immediately. She took the thirty-metre dash back to her desk, frantically fumbled underneath it for her handbag, and then darted back to Sebastian's side, in a heartbeat. The physical exertion, combined with her excitement, made her blood pump so fast that she could hear her pulse pounding in her ears.

"All set!" she declared, breathlessly.

Smiling with smug satisfaction, Sebastian spun on his eye-wateringly expensive heels, hooked his suit jacket off the back of his chair and twisted his shoulders around, to put it on, as he strolled, casually, over to the exit. Politely, he held the glass door open for Natasha before following her through to the internal lift-bank. In a flamboyant fashion, Sebastian pressed the nearest button to call a lift and, as if Fate herself conspired to sustain the tantalizing flow of spontaneity, the doors to the lift directly in front of them, obligingly, slid open, "PING!" They exchanged a thrilled glance and stepped inside. The doors closed, "PING!" Sebastian pressed the dull chrome button for level-nine, and its boarder lit up yellow. The upward acceleration was so powerful, and Natasha so exhilarated, that her tummy began to flip wildly. She was on her way to lunch with a very important man and she had already lost her appetite!

Standing next to Sebastian, in silence, Natasha began to experience the most extraordinary sensation. All mental fogginess was swept away. Lethargy, doubt, anxiety, fear and self-pity were obliterated. Instead, a majestic, certain sun of consciousness dawned, resplendent. It shone unobscured to illuminate the most beatific landscape of 'being' imaginable; but there was more, Natasha's vital energy essence seemed to expand, exponentially. She felt as if she was being stretched out like chewing gum across all creation. Well, this rather gigantic office building at the very least! In short, 'Natasha' was annihilated. Now that concept only served to mark the epicentre of pure radiating force. Indeed, inexplicably, for these brief moments, she was a very sun. "PING!" They had arrived. SNAP. SHRINK. Natasha was Natasha again. Sebastian motioned for her to exit. She stepped out to discover a colossal, high-ceilinged glass atrium the size of at least three netball courts. The floor was of polished white marble, and the room so infused with light that it made her squint. This place was overwhelmingly impressive, even if her expression was not. Natasha gave a quiet gasp. She had never visited this part of the bank before. She had not known such splendour existed in this enormous, dog poo brown, rather ugly office building. Such floors must be reserved

FALSE GODS THE ECSTASY

for the bank's Directors and demigods - oh, and of course for clients, so easily forgotten.

Sebastian then led Natasha diagonally across the spectacular space, "click, click, click, click, click, click, click..." The harsh, penetrating sound of her high heels hitting the unforgiving surface, made her wince with embarrassment. Somehow the racket made her feel foolish and unprofessional. Sebastian's muted footsteps played a discreet base to Natasha's tottering treble. When her heels finally sank into a royal blue, thick-piled carpet, the embarrassing clamour was silenced, and she gave a soft sigh of relief as they continued, at a pace, down a corridor. Along the walls, giant, bold pieces of abstract art were displayed in which rich hues abounded: purple, orange, yellow, red, gold, blue, turquoise, green and silver; even the blacks had fathomless depths. Natasha had never appreciated art so intensely. Was this just part of this new man's effect on her, or simply the stark contrast to the scruffy, dark, drabness of the Debt Floor?

Light, colour, and all that was Sebastian Butler left Natasha feeling intoxicated. With each step, with this man, she was massaged by the cosy, warm, safe sensation that wealth is so adept at producing in those whom do not possess it. She was jolted from her reverie when Sebastian stopped, abruptly, outside a nondescript door marked with a neat narrow sign that read: Directors' Dining-Room. He opened it for her and they entered a moderately sized room. There were approximately a dozen tables covered with white tablecloths, formally set with highly polished silverware, and glasses that were so clean they winked glints of sunlight, as if for attention. The simple room was distinguished by a wall of floor-to-ceiling windows, which commanded the most striking views over the spectacular City of London. Natasha felt like gasping again but refrained, not wishing to appear like some hick who had never left her hometown.

The dining-room was empty. It was still only quarter to twelve and this was an early lunch, even by City standards.

Sebastian led her to a table for two next to one of the gigantic windows. For several moments they stood and admired the majestic, sparkling, cityscape beneath them. Suddenly, there was a demure cough. Natasha turned to find a waitress patiently holding out a chair for her, and she shot Sebastian a look before taking her seat, while he smiled at the girl and then took his own. He rested his elbows on the table and folded his hands beneath his chin as he grinned, almost coyly, at Natasha before setting his eyes squarely on the young waitress. She had short, copper-tinged, blonde hair but there was something suspiciously unnatural about the colour, as if she had had a rinse put through, to elevate it from the dull blonde it probably was without. It did catch the eye, however, but possibly not for the right reasons. The awkward girl wore the generic white shirt and black skirt of a waitress, but the skirt looked tight to the point of discomfort. Her smile was pretty though, and she addressed Sebastian with genuine warmth.

"Good day, Mr. Butler. So lovely to have you dine with us again."

"Good day to you too Donna, and thank you."

The girl then gave Natasha a curt nod of acknowledgement, before handing her a stiff, white menu card. It displayed the date at the top and three different choices for starter, main course and dessert. The typescript was embossed, intricate and black, while trimmed with a sliver of gold. Indeed, the menu was smarter than a wedding invitation from the Royals. When Natasha began to read it, she found that most of the dishes were richer than senior bankers, and more elaborate than the script in which they were typed. Bashfully, Donna handed a second card to Sebastian. When he thanked her, Natasha was convinced she saw the girl blush.

"Can I get you any drinks sir?"

"Natasha, tell me, shall we be good or bad?"

She giggled. Donna glared at her. Then Natasha ventured, with a touch of naughtiness, "Can't we be both?"

"Oh, I am sure we can manage that my dear." Sebastian

replied, before smiling with approval at the spirit of his new plaything. He then turned to order matter-of-factly, "A bottle of still mineral water and two double vodkas, with fresh orange juice and ice, please Donna."

The newly sullen waitress nodded tersely before leaving the room. Alone now, Sebastian leaned forward as far as his size allowed which, in such bright daylight, was a little too close for Natasha's comfort. Reflectively, he placed his chin on folded hands, once again, and began to inspect her face, meticulously. His studied scrutiny made her blood pump through her veins so vigorously, that she feared she too would flush pink, just like Donna. Thank God, Natasha was to be spared such a fate for, impulsively, he looked away, pushed his mouth into a pout, and then cast his gaze, lackadaisically, around the empty room. He soon tired of eyeing the barren dining space and turned to revisit the breathtaking view, while Natasha studied the flash menu card in silence. When Sebastian set his attention back on Natasha, its brief absence only served to accentuate its strength. Suddenly, the atmosphere between them became so dense, full of some kind of almost tangible energy, that she felt like a human-shaped slice of fruit suspended in clear-set, celestial jelly. Mesmerized, Natasha listened as Sebastian began to talk in a measured voice.

"Natasha, please, allow me to tell you a little bit about myself." He straightened his back, looked down at the tablecloth, toyed with one of the heavy silver knives, and then sighed deeply, before continuing in earnest, "I am such a fortunate man Natasha. Fortunate in many ways of course, but most specifically, fortunate in the way in which I have been blessed with a divine circle of what I choose to describe as... intimate friends."

Natasha's uninhibited glow of pleasure fast contracted. She leaned back in her chair and narrowed her eyes with concern. She did not like the direction in which this conversation, so quickly, was heading. Sebastian just laughed out loud, his eyes full of merriment, before expostulating:

"Oh Natasha, please don't disappoint me with such a

prosaic reaction." Our heroine smarted. Sebastian elaborated, indulgently, "Natasha, please don't get me wrong. I am a happily married man, with two adorable children. I love my wife, very much. Isabel is a truly wonderful person. Believe me, I could never be without her." Natasha smarted harder. Sebastian was married with children. Entirely unaware that these recent revelations had just inflicted a sharp stab and twist into Natasha's guts, he continued in tones that sought to convince:

"The real point is this; does marriage really have to mean the end of close friendships with all women, other than your wife? To believe that a married man can never again be close to any other woman is ridiculous; not to say depressing. I love women Natasha. I enjoy female company so much more than that of men. I need... I have, several close female friends, the dearest of them I choose to refer to as 'intimate', that is all I am talking about." Sebastian was speaking slowly, with affection and assurance. Slightly comforted, Natasha continued to listen without further judgement. Besides, she was still feeling mortified having been accused of being 'prosaic'. He elaborated, "Natasha, please rest assured, there is no reason for you to feel threatened. I just refer to my female friends, all of whom mean the world to me. My wife is a very important, and busy woman. Often, if she is travelling or away, I might have dinner, go to the theatre, or perhaps a party with one of my feminine companions. I call them my Walkerettes. I walk out with them don't you see?"

At which point Natasha could not help but interject:

"Let's hope walking out with one of them, never leads your wife to walk out on you, Sebastian."

Unperturbed, he looked at her, firmly, before continuing, "Understand this, Natasha, my wife would never leave me. These special friendships would give her no cause. They are not dull sexual liaisons. They are so much more important than that. Though I term them 'intimate' the most physically 'intimate' we ever get involves some harmless cuddle and, please understand, I would never leave my wife. Why would I? I love her so very much, and I have everything I could possibly want."

On this emphatic assertion, Sebastian paused and pouted. Natasha watched him intently, as he began to look around the perfectly-set dining-room, once again. He then looked out over the captivating skies of London, all metal and glass a-shimmer in the sunlight, as he pondered 'having everything' he could 'possibly want', and he looked a trifle bored by it. Sebastian's eyes then drifted back to rest on Natasha, to remind him that he had not strictly told the truth about having 'everything' he 'could possibly want'. Thoughtful, he cocked his head, fluttered his eyelashes and, with renewed fervour, continued:

"Natasha, do you not agree, it is such a tremendous, and rare, gift when one comes across a person with whom one 'clicks'?"

Natasha nodded.

"Everything rare is highly prized Sebastian."

"Well you do agree then, I knew it!" Looking so much more cheerful, he went on, "Surely, it would only be an ingrate, or an idiot, who would give up such a gift just because he is married?" Impulsively, Sebastian reached across the table and took her hand in his. Staring intensely into her startled eyes he whispered, "Natasha, it is impossible not to notice the extreme nature of our 'click'. I confess I have never had such a strong and immediate connection in all my life." With eyes still locked, he challenged, "Can you deny it?"

Sebastian's eyes darted from left to right as he searched Natasha's open face, urgently seeking some sign of her tacit collusion with the innocence of his 'click' to 'intimate friend' policy: Natasha just stared at him, star-struck. The very moment they had found each other across the trading floor this morning, Natasha had known this 'click' to be unlike any other. The more she stared into the glistening blackness of his pupils, the more she was increasingly sucked into an unfamiliar and spellbinding zone that seemed to kiss infinity. The same sensation that she had experienced, momentarily, in the lift began to burgeon from her, with frightening force. Inexplicably, she was gone, blissful and lost to sense. Natasha could only shake her head, minutely, in answer. This tiny reaction was all he required. He let go of her hand, laughed joyously, then shrugged, with relief.

Just then, Donna came into the room carrying a round silver tray with their drinks. Her unwelcome interruption was torturous. Impassive, she put the ice-packed glasses of vodka and orange juice onto the table before pouring them each a glass of mineral water. She then slipped the tray underneath her arm, while she snatched a furtive glance at Sebastian, before looking straight ahead, as she inquired, softly, "May I take your order madam, sir?"

Without taking his eyes away from Natasha, for a moment, an ebullient Sebastian declared:

"Donna, I am going to leave myself entirely in your more than capable hands. Only one course for me please. Just bring the best kitchen has to offer."

Donna hesitated, unsure how to respond to such licence, and shifted from one foot to the other as she fiddled with the rim of her tray.

"I'd really rather you choose Mr. Butler, you know, just in case like." she replied, tentatively.

"Well at least recommend something?" Sebastian persisted, looking directly at her now.

"Of course Mr. Butler, of course... I must say the Dover sole looks very tasty."

"Dover sole it is then, perfect. Thank you Donna." Then he questioned, "Natasha?"

"That sounds lovely, I'll have the same please. Some sautéed spinach on the side perhaps?"

"Why not!" Sebastian exclaimed, with excitement, before he added, "So Donna, there you have it!"

"Thank you sir." she replied, before quickly bustling out of the room.

As Natasha's eye followed her, she noticed that her generous bottom was almost breaching the back seam of her snug skirt. Oblivious, Sebastian quickly resumed:

"Natasha, I am drawn to you. I was so powerfully drawn to you the minute I first saw you on the trading floor. It was three-and-a-half days ago now, but I have been watching you ever since, desperate to catch your eye. I can't believe you didn't even notice me! Well, until this morning that is... I can't explain it, there is just something there. Something here." Sebastian wafted his hand back and forth between the pair of them, as if to illustrate precisely where 'here' lay. Natasha nodded, fatalistically. He then stared back out of the window to peruse the dazzling cityscape, once again, as he narrowed his eyes and said, with tired resolve, "I love my wife, Natasha..."

Sebastian was mid-sentence, when Natasha decided that she had heard quite enough of this man telling her how much he loved his wife. Feeling mischievous, she interrupted, "I thought your wife's name was Isabel?"

Sebastian started, shocked by her boldness. He stared censoriously at her.

"Now, now Natasha, don't be catty, not when we were getting on so delightfully well."

Natasha contracted her brow in concentration.

"What was it Shakespeare once wrote? 'The lady doth protest too much'?" Circumspectly, Sebastian looked at her, as she continued, "Well, please forgive me for saying so, but I think 'the gentleman doth profess too much'. In short, Sebastian, if you said how much you loved your wife less, I would be inclined to believe you more."

Suddenly, he was crestfallen. Natasha had struck a nerve. Instantaneously, a dramatic change swept over him. If he had been a chameleon he would have switched from a scaly neutral green, to shocking crimson with bright turquoise spots. All of his confidence, dare she say arrogance, wilted before her eyes. Natasha was bemused to detect that the man was almost shaking. Almost? In fact he was. From the start, Natasha suspected that Sebastian had performed this little speech before. Now, however, it was obvious that he was not practised at fielding critical interruptions.

In some long-forgotten, back attic room of Natasha's mind, a cold-light called Reason feebly filtered through the splintered shutters of her impressionability, to illuminate the ludicrousness of the situation she now found herself in. Tragically, this insight was as foreign to her now, as was daylight to the Debt Floor. And so it was, when an older, married man began to pay the young Miss Flynn highly inappropriate attention, the girl just felt heart-flutteringly flattered, and gut-wrenchingly grateful. Had the foolish young woman any self-respect or sense, she would have extricated herself from this engagement somewhere around the moment the word 'intimate' was first uttered. Instead, Natasha was far too dazzled by the older man who had said it, and too busy smarting from his gibe. Worse, the silly girl had started to flirt, coquettishly, challenging the man's true feelings for his wife. Now the offender trembled before her, all she felt was protective. Most disturbingly, it was in this dubious situation that Natasha discovered herself to be the happiest she ever had been. Sitting in the Directors' dining-room, waiting for Dover sole, Natasha found herself, indiscriminately, pouring all of the powerful joules of her love into a man she had just met and, in so doing, the salt of herself dissolved, effortlessly, into an ocean of omnipresent, omniscience to leave Natasha bathing in spiritual bliss.

The man's shaking really had to stop, however. Fortuitously, as Sebastian fast absorbed Natasha's high-amperage adoration, his self-verification was completely restored and he did just that. The abashed, overgrown, sharp-suited child was banished. When Donna burst into the room brandishing plates of steaming, delicious-smelling white fish, she was to be spared Sebastian's trembling, and her crush happily preserved. Soon, the fragrant food, prettily garnished with lemon lilies, was placed onto the table. Donna left, for a moment, only to return with a silver dish of spinach, oozing slimy chunks of garlic. She served them each a mound, with a silver-serving spoon, before inquiring:

"Can I get you any more drinks sir?"

"Two more of the same please Donna." Sebastian ordered, without reference to Natasha, before taking a deep glug of his drink. When the waitress had left, he leaned over the table and, with a look that married slyness to shyness, he spoke with assurance, "No Natasha, I will say it, just one more time, just for you: my wife is one of the brightest, most remarkable of women and, yes, I love her very much."

"No Sebastian, I will say it, just one more time, just for you: in my experience, one doesn't have to say something so often, if one means it."

"Well, perhaps, Natasha, your experience is not as vast as you presume?" he suggested, as he scanned her face searching for a reaction, before adding ambiguously, "And 'perhaps', I do love my wife just as much as I profess?"

Immediately, a reaction was secured and Natasha's mouth burst into a thrilled grin, for Sebastian had spoken this second 'perhaps' with rhetorical emphasis and, oh, how eagerly did our young heroine hang all of her hopes on that single word, for 'perhaps' it meant there was a chink in this man's heart just wide enough for her to enter.

"Go on Sebastian, say it one more time, just for me, and I promise I'll believe you." she dared, boldly.

Sebastian did not say it one more time. Sebastian just said, "Meow."

This day the terms of their engagement were laid down over the lunch table. The logistics of happening hovered, mirage-like, between them, patiently waiting to manifest over time. As they stared longingly into each other's eyes, of one thing they were certain: they were both hook, line and sinker in love.

When Donna returned with more drinks, Sebastian shifted the conversation to neutral ground. He reminded Natasha that he would be sailing off the Côte d'Azur next week. He told her how he was to spend nine days on his yacht with family and friends. He would leave the girls behind, of course, they were far too young. He then mentioned the party planned for his thirty-fifth birthday, and how much fun it would have been if Natasha could have joined them. Sebastian went on to tell her how enthusiastic he was about the prospect of her working with him and his team. Natasha was interested to note that he appeared to love his team, nearly as much as his wife. She also noticed that he spoke with as much enthusiasm for credit-trading, as he had done for his 'intimate' friends.

Sebastian's enthusiastic talk was at times hijacked by unintended silence. At these junctures Sebastian and Natasha just stared at each other, indiscreetly holding hands. Inane grins would spread across their faces, for minutes at a time, only to be evicted by their giggles when they realized just quite how ridiculous their effect was on each other. So many smiles, so much laughter, the pair simply could not believe their luck at having found one another. The conversation ebbed and flowed, while elemental happiness celebrated itself in their glows.

Lunch ended, at last, and Sebastian and Natasha returned to the trading floor. The time was approaching for the spell of their togetherness to be broken. Sebastian bravely rose to the task.

"Well Miss Flynn, it was a pleasure dining with you today. Tomorrow is my last day in the office. I am back a week on Monday. I sincerely look forward to having you on board when I return."

"Mr. Butler, I greatly enjoyed a delicious lunch, and a most enlightening conversation. I cannot begin to tell you how interesting I found the intricacies of your market. Please allow me to thank you for sharing quite so much with me."

Sebastian raised his eyebrows at Natasha's discreet jest. With eyes alight and hearts thumping, they mutually acknowledged that the time had come for them to separate. Even the thought of so doing was unbearable for an unfamiliar, stubborn, gravitational pull sought to join them. They hovered close together, perplexed by this strange force sensation, before laughing with embarrassed wonder as they tried to conquer the attraction that tugged so at their souls. Sebastian, the seasoned investment banker, knew they were making a spectacle of themselves. He also knew it would take no time before an alert colleague would notice this unusual interaction. It must come to an end.

"Right." Sebastian said, with a definitive nod.

"Right." Natasha echoed.

They looked at each other, for one more moment, inexplicably enraptured. Then, with determination, Sebastian ripped his eyes away and set them on the bright yellow, digital-display clock pulsating from a black rectangular block high up on the wall. It was almost three o'clock. His face darkened and Sebastian repeated, as he stared down at the dirty carpet with stern resolve, "Right."

He then broke away and, sombrely, strolled back to his desk, picked up a black leather folder, tucked it under his arm, and left the trading floor. Just like that, he was gone. Natasha stared after him, transfixed. An agonizing wrench stirred in her torso, as if a clawed hand had just delved down her gullet to collect her intestines, stomach, lungs and heart, then ripped the lot out; ouch. Was that really just vodka they had been drinking? Natasha could not move. She was still standing by the back-to-back rows of Sebastian's sales and trading teams' desks. She could not stay there, staring down at the carpet like some weirdo for long. She had to move. Out of the corner of her eye she saw one of the traders flick his attention upon her, with suspicion. He jabbed the young guy, who sat next to him, in the ribs who, in turn, looked over to watch the new girl behaving oddly. Finally, Natasha was spurred to act. With head down, she strode back to the Futures Desk. She must be more careful going forward. A female trainee returning from a three-hour lunch with a good-looking Managing Director, did not look good. As she approached the Desk her heart sank for inquisitive faces tracked her every move, meticulously. Everyone was thinking the same: where the hell had she been? Natasha clocked the people present. She was more than relieved to note that Innes Plattenberg, the head of the Desk, was nowhere to be seen. The only way she could handle this was to brazen it out. Without Innes there to challenge her, she could pull it off. Avoiding further eye contact, and not even acknowledging how late she was, Natasha reached for her swivel chair, pulled it out and sat down with a bump. She picked up 'Yield Curve Analysis; The Fundamentals of Risk and Return'. She opened the three-inch thick book and started to read from the point where she had left off.

Disgruntled colleagues' attention still rested on her. It seemed to burn into the top of her head. Natasha held her nerve and tried to focus on her book. She could feel the silent exchange of unimpressed opinions, all around. She almost cracked and blurted out some guilt-ridden explanation but, fortuitously, fate remained allied and the telephone lines began to ring, demonically. The traders dived upon them and soon they were swept up in a wave of intense negotiations, price-discovery and trade-execution. The market went ballistic, shouts, cheers and curses filled the stuffy air. The striking new girl became invisible.

Natasha Flynn read about 'time value for money' and the 'curvilinear relationship between bond prices and bond yields'. It was hard to concentrate. The trading floor was so noisy, and the vodka she had drunk at lunch-time made the maths more challenging than it should have been. Besides, it was too late to study 'the fundamentals of risk and return' for the risk was already on: Natasha had fallen madly in love with a married man...

Chapter Two - My little mouse

My heart saw Love
Galloping alone towards the desert
and, shattered by love's majesty
fell in love with Love.

Rumi

By seven o'clock the next morning Natasha was back at her desk. She felt restless and fidgety. She had woken, with a surprising jolt, at five forty-three. She had been too full of excitement to go back to sleep, so she had decided to go into work early. Now, following her second double espresso, she was so wired it was impossible to concentrate. Her head just kept spinning around to check each and every person as they arrived on the trading floor, hoping to spot Sebastian. It was making her dizzy. More and more men kept arriving, in quick succession, with pale faces, puffy eyes and blank, fatigue-filled stares; much like her own state of appearance. Most had lips puckered, poised to take sips of scalding coffee through slits sliced into plastic lids, so keen were they to stimulate alertness. Pink or white newspapers were firmly clamped under arms, or rolled tightly and brandished like some sort of baton. Shiny shoes glided across the worn, peach-tinted carpet, while gruff grunts and mumbled 'good mornings' of perfunctory greeting were, continually, exchanged as employees made their way to their desks. At this time of day, smiles were as scarce as girls.

Natasha watched the early morning ritual; transfixed. Newspaper after newspaper was thrown, or slammed down, onto desks, while swivel chairs were waltzed into position, so that neat male bottoms could wiggle into occupancy. Eye-catching gold or silver cufflinks were, ceremonially, adjusted as necks, shoulders and backs were stretched out before computer screen buttons were flicked, one after the other, to fire-up the multi-coloured Reuters, Telerate and Bloomberg live-feeds. Flickering, bright digits

35

and words cascaded onto screens with fresh market pricing
and news, to be instantly devoured by curious eyes, in the
hunt for pertinent information that could precipitate a trade
to produce a profit, or inspire one to prevent a loss, before
the main markets opened.

By seven-twenty the trading floor was almost full and a
succession of confident, authoritative, male voices from the
bank's research department, started to crackle over the
'hoot n' holler' summarizing important political, credit,
economic and interest rate news. The low hum of the Debt
Floor was rising and, by now, several shots of caffeine had
transformed tired minds and eyes to full alert. Natasha interspersed people-watching and head-swivelling with
studying the shifting graphs of the contracts of the Futures
Market trading. Our heroine's ignorance remained supreme, for the only intelligence she could decipher was
how desperate she was to see Sebastian; an urge more
compelling than a nicotine craving. Worse, at this embry-
onic stage in her career, it was difficult for her to distract
herself for, as yet, she did not actually have anything to do.
Natasha had just been instructed to spend some time on the
many different Trading Desks, in order to comprehend the
complexity and diversity of the business, and to meet and
impress the powers that be. If none of the Desk Heads
wanted to take her on, permanently, when the three-month
graduate-training programme was finished, Natasha could
kiss goodbye to her well-paid job just as quickly as she had
embraced it.

In short, for now, she had no clients to call, no products
to sell and no sales targets to achieve. She was just collecting the best graduate starting salary she knew of, to sit like
a sponge and soak up, currently, unintelligible information.
With no immediate purpose, or structure, to her day, Natasha had far too much time to dwell on, and seek out, the
mysterious man who had so enchanted her. Consequently,
she spent a full hour of this Friday morning pretending to
finish her book on bond maths while frolicking in unfamiliar feelings of jubilance. When Natasha, finally, clapped

eyes on Sebastian, at eight-thirteen, her steady elation was jolted to ecstasy: each subsequent glimpse she managed to steal, was as invigorating as it was exhausting.

Joy aside, Natasha knew she was in dangerous territory. The man who was making her feel this way was not only a big boss, but he was married. Sebastian was already, emotionally, genetically and financially, invested with another woman. In the circumstances, where could the love she felt ever go? Stubbornly, such thoughts continued to plague her. Natasha could only resolve not to get involved. She would allow herself to daydream only. What harm could a crush, even such a strong one, really do? She would satisfy her desire to spend time with him via the proffered role of chaste 'intimate friend'. Natasha may not be able to control her feelings, but she must control her behaviour.

After all of that coffee, Natasha needed a pee. The lavatory was at least thirty-five metres away, so a trip there almost qualified as an excursion. She stood up, straightened her skirt, picked up her handbag and made for it. Sebastian spotted her movement, in an instant. Their eyes locked and he started to walk, briskly, towards her. When they met, they grinned at each other. It would not go too far to say that they shone. Sebastian leant forward to whisper, urgently, under his breath:

"Can you escape?"

Natasha darted a look at the Futures Desk. It was pretty quiet and she calculated no one would notice if she were to disappear for ten minutes.

"Not for long." she replied.

"That's fine, come with me."

Natasha followed him. The lavatory could wait. Sebastian led her to a different lift-bank, which was at the other end of the enormous room. When they took the lift to the fifth-floor, she noticed that he was carrying something.

"Is that a video, Sebastian?" she inquired, with piqued interest. As he stepped out of the lift, he darted a bashful look at her and replied:

"Maybe..."

Then he looked straight ahead, and escorted her down a corridor, much narrower and less impressive than the one yesterday. Soon enough, he stopped outside an unmarked door. He opened it, and they entered what appeared to be a meeting-room. Immediately, Sebastian went over to the gigantic television set in the corner, which had a video recorder tucked underneath. Just like the dining-room, this room had a full wall of floor-to-ceiling windows, but with less spectacular views. Bright, golden sunlight flooded into the room and onto Sebastian's gorgeous face, as did endorphins into Natasha's brain. Quickly, he bent down, inserted the video, and then fiddled with the buttons on the remote control while drawing the blinds, before coming to stand next to Natasha in the semi-darkness.

Suddenly, an image of Sebastian as a young man, walking purposefully across a green field, flashed up onto the screen. He was wearing a brown leather flying jacket, light blue jeans and goggles. He had just come to a halt next to a canary yellow biplane. Elegantly, he swung one of his long legs onto the bottom-wing before springing up onto it and crouching, in order to avoid hitting his head on the top wing. He made his way to the pilot's seat, leaned across it, took his weight on his arms either side and then hopped over, to ease himself down into it. Sebastian must have been in his early twenties, maybe even Natasha's age. The feeling this image promoted in her was just as familiar as the live version. His eyes now rested on her, and he explained, with a helpless shrug:

"I wanted you to see this. Don't ask me why. I just felt compelled to show it to you."

This was not the same man that Natasha had had lunch with yesterday. There were no prepared speeches, no mention of intimate friends and no macho language about trading. Today, Sebastian looked like the young boy on screen: vulnerable but putting on a brave face. How he could imagine that an amateur video of his having a flying lesson, many years ago, could possibly be of interest to anyone astounded Natasha, yet there she was, entranced.

"The truth is, Natasha, I'm terrified of flying. I thought if I took lessons I'd overcome my fear."

"Can you fly now?"

"Fly?... I can do advanced aerobatics."

Not sure whether to be sceptical or impressed, she laughed and inquired, "Are you still terrified?"

"Utterly."

Staring into each other's eyes with eternal recognition the pair began to giggle and, if possible, Natasha fell in love with Sebastian a little bit more. He shrugged, shook his head then sighed, forlornly.

"Natasha, what are we to do?"

She smiled, softly, at this man, who made her feel so much of everything, all at once, and with deliberate misinterpretation, she took the opportunity to nudge them back to reality and suggested, "Rewind the video, go back downstairs and do some work?"

He smirked and, reluctantly, they did just that. When they stepped out of the lift onto the second-floor, Sebastian hesitated and then asked:

"Natasha will you let me give you a lift home this evening? You live in Notting Hill don't you?"

"Pembridge Square."

"I pass Pembridge Square on my way. Come over to my desk at five. It's Friday after all. I'll drive you home. Well, eventually, perhaps we'll take a little detour first?"

Oh my God! Another tantalizing, 'perhaps'! Immediately, Natasha felt sick with anticipation.

"How can I refuse Sebastian? London Underground is a sorry alternative to a personal chauffeur service." she replied with as much nonchalance as she could muster.

"Until five it is then." Sebastian confirmed, as Natasha walked through the door he held open for her.

He followed, then darted a meaningful look at her, before he ambled back to his desk, thoughtfully, still clutching the video to his chest. As soon as Natasha got back to the Futures Desk, Tom, a young American trader, eyed her curiously. He was in his mid-twenties and handsome in that dark, clean-cut, preppy fashion. As cute as Tom was, he lacked the edge that Natasha was usually drawn to: bright, sincere, easygoing and straightforward, not her type at all. Easygoing he may be, but right now he was about to become problematic.

"Natasha, please tell me I did not see you go off, then come back, with Sebastian Butler?"

Natasha flushed-red and she knew it. She was mortified. Tom laughed. Then, sensing he was on to something, he moved in for the kill.

"Hey boys, our little Miss Flynn is blushing crimson."

Immediately, Tom's glee caught the attention of the other three men sitting at the Desk: Chris, Fabio and Jason. They all turned to look at Natasha and see if the spectacle was worth witnessing. Fabio laughed then, smiling naughtily, he interjected in a thick Italian drawl:

"Natasha, I understand, I have that effect on most women in my vicinity. It is very predictable, they just have to come within a two-metre radius, look into my eyes and they are overwhelmed by the desire to fuck me! Naturally this can cause them to blush..." Fabio paused and watched Natasha attentively to see how she would react. She did not. Patiently, he raised his eyebrows to reveal his beautiful brown eyes, more completely, then he added, "My effect on you, Natasha, seems to have been a little delayed. I am comforted to learn that, finally, you respond to my charms. I had started to wonder how many times I must bring you lunch before you take proper notice of me?" Fabio then burst into laughter. Once he had recovered, he looked at Natasha, seductively, as he informed her, "In case you have not yet realized, Natasha, I would be more than happy to satisfy your every desire, so no more of this blushing."

The men sniggered. Fabio was the Italian stud of the Futures Desk, if not the entire trading floor. The moment Natasha had met him, only four days ago, she had fancied him rotten and he had been flirting, outrageously, with her ever since. Fabio had short, glossy, jet-black hair, deliciously fresh, tanned, olive skin and he was around six-foot two. It was clear he worked-out for his perfectly toned muscles protruded, ever so fetchingly, from his expensive, dark grey Italian suit to prove visible testament to his admirable self-discipline. Today, his shirt was so white it looked ice-blue and accentuated the lines of his defined jaw, prominent cheek-bones and firm, plum-coloured mouth, most effectively. Fabio had one of those noble, ever so slightly Roman noses that, for some reason, Natasha always associated with strength of character. However, Fabio's eyes were his most devastating feature. They were rich chocolate brown, speckled with brilliant flecks of gold, and smoulderingly eloquent. If you were a female lucky enough to be graced with their attention, without words, Fabio would communicate, 'I want to take you to bed right now and drown you in the juice of your multiple orgasms.... Please?'

Somehow a woman could tell, if she were to allow it, that this would be a fair assessment of the Fabio experience, though one hoped the drowning part was metaphorical! In short, if a woman with a pulse was ever the recipient of a 'Fabio special' she simply went weak at the knees and her tummy would somersault in acquiescent anticipation. Natasha was getting one of these right now and, though her head and heart were full of Sebastian, disturbingly, her loins were responding to the delectable Fabio's brazen sexuality. Surely, it was only a matter of time before her scatter-shot libido would take exclusive aim to correspond with the burgeoning sentiments of her heart? Fabio's flirtatious eyes continued to feast, hungrily, on her flustered discomposure yet, as tempting as he was, Natasha quickly looked away.

Though the guys on the Desk were well used to Fabio's flagrant self-satisfaction, when it came to his attractiveness to the opposite sex, today they were not going to allow him to steal all the limelight. Jason a quick-witted salesman from Essex, immediately, interjected:

"Shu' up you Italian git. Step righ' back an ge' in line."

"Hey guys," Tom interrupted, "Natasha isn't blushing

because of any of you bozos. She's blushing because I saw her returning with Sebastian Butler."

His name silenced them all. Slowly, and deliberately, they all turned to look at Natasha with aroused curiosity. Fabio was taken aback. He pouted with exaggerated disappointment before inquiring:

"Why Natasha... am I not rich enough for you?" Defiantly, he looked at her before assuring, "Trust me, when I am as old as he, I will be richer, and in better shape, but maybe you are not the patient type?"

Our heroine knew she must put an end to this conversation, and now, for they were all enjoying it far too much, at her expense.

"Boys, boys, boys, don't get over excited, and yes, Tom did see me with Sebastian Butler, but the only reason I blushed is because I've agreed to join his Desk in a week's time and I have not yet had a chance to tell Innes. I don't want you loud-mouths to let the cat out of the bag. Innes needs to hear it from me. Besides, it was you lot who told me how fierce she can be."

Innes Plattenberg was the only woman on the trading floor who headed up a Desk. By all accounts, she was a formidable opponent. Natasha did not relish telling her that she had been invited to sit with another team. The Debt Floor's big global boss, Edward Sanford, had informed Natasha on Wednesday that Innes had been impressed with her, and was considering offering her a permanent position. She did not want to screw-up such a possibility, just in case she needed to take Innes up on the offer that had not yet, but she hoped might, come. Then Chris, a fat forty-eight-year-old Englishman from Surrey, shot Natasha a look laden with foreboding, and muttered, "All I will say to you, Natasha, is this, 'Out of the frying pan...'"

All week, Natasha had detected alcohol on Chris' breath after lunch, but he had worked at the bank for over fifteen years, so when he leaned forward to say more, she paid attention. His light grey, slightly watery eyes, darted from left to right to check who was in earshot before he continued, "Innes is child's play compared to the way that wanker operates. At least with her, you know where you stand. In business, Sebastian's as slippery as an oiled-up snake, and his reputation with women makes Fabio look like a queer."

When Fabio caught Chris' comment, he thwacked his solid upper thigh in outraged protest. Laughing, even more loudly than before, he expostulated:

"Hey, hey, Chris I heard that. Let me tell you, when I am as rich as he, it is Mr. Butler who will look like the man who bends over and wiggles! Look at me! Am I not so much more handsome?"

Fabio held out both his arms to look over one bicep, then the other, in turn, nodding with approval as he did so, before he started to chuckle mischievously as he contemplated a future of infinite riches and perpetual philandering. Natasha rolled her eyes at him, before quietly saying to Chris, "Thank you for your concern Chris, I do appreciate it, but really, there's no need to worry about me. I just want to learn about the products he trades. He was telling me he has the most profitable Desk on the trading floor, high margin and all that."

"Well I'm not sure about that, but it's up there I guess…" Chris conceded, reluctantly.

"As you lot have already taught me: 'high margin' good, 'low margin' bad. Oh yes, and what was the other one? 'Buy low', 'sell high'. See, I'm getting the hang of this stuff already." Natasha jested, as she continued to pump out a smoke screen for the benefit of the boys.

Chris grunted, unamused. He picked up his telephone, shoved it to his ear and began to dial. Clearly, he had heard enough. Natasha did not think he was convinced for a minute. She looked over at Tom, then at Jason. Thankfully they too had lost interest. Tom was on a call, and Jason had become fixated on his screens and engrossed in a calculation. Finally, she looked back at Fabio. His eyes were still bright, and he was blowing her kisses. He then raised his eyebrows, hopefully, as he clutched his crotch, suggestively. Still holding, if not massaging, himself Fabio leaned towards her to whisper with gravitas, "You just let me know when, Natasha. I wait. Unlike you, I am patient."

"Fabio, you're gonna to need to be." she replied, unequivocally, before flicking her hair, dramatically, to terminate the conversation.

Natasha then turned her attention to Bloomberg. She was still learning to master this most indispensible of financial market tools, and she decided to spend the rest of the morning in that endeavour. She prayed the guys were not too suspicious about Sebastian though. She must be invisible when she left with him later.

When a white plastic carrier bag was dumped onto her desk at twelve thirty, Natasha jumped. Truth be told, she had been falling asleep, so at least the shock had woken her up. When she looked up in confusion, she saw Fabio's beautiful face grinning down at her. It seemed he had brought her lunch; again.

"You just let me know when, Natasha." he said gently, as his solid body leaned over her.

Fabio then took his time to straighten up before, slowly, he strutted back to his desk.

"Thank you Fabio." Natasha shouted after him, before fast clarifying, "For the salad, not the offer!"

When five o'clock struck, Natasha burst out of the ladies room having touched up her make-up, in preparation for her lift home. As she walked towards Sebastian, it felt like butterflies were performing advanced aerobatics in her tummy. Indeed, her excitement was so extreme, it was as if every single one of her bodily functions was in suspension. Her breath was tight, and her heart barely seemed to beat. The only things that appeared to function normally were her legs, for they carried her briskly in the direction of Sebastian. As Natasha approached, she could see his tall figure pacing up and down. He looked restless. Business was still in full swing and the chairs on his bank of desks were packed to capacity with Sebastian's highly dedicated - in product and attitude - team. Most of the men were still locked in concurrent conversations on their telephones. Only the odd sporadic cackle punctuated the intensity of the atmosphere, to hint at the imminent end of a long working week. When Natasha came within ten feet of the Desk, many of the men turned their heads, with interest, and continued to watch her out of the corner of their eyes. Sebastian must have sensed it for, immediately, he locked eyes with her. Purposefully, he darted his glance to the nearest exit. In a flash, Natasha understood. Subtly, she veered course to make it look as if she had been heading in that direction all along. The keen observers soon lost interest. There was no currency in a trainee leaving the office for the day.

As Natasha nervously waited for a lift, and for Sebastian, she reflected how fortunate it was that his miniature fiefdom was situated smack next to an exit. Then, with a sudden stab of disquiet, she recalled what Chris had said about him, and her brow contracted. Could he have chosen such a spot with deliberate calculation? As soon as Natasha felt Sebastian's presence by her side, her unpleasant consideration was blasted to oblivion. She beamed brightly and, once again, on perfect cue they heard a cheery, "PING!" Giggling with the novelty of this repeated string of coincidences, Sebastian and Natasha stepped in. The spontaneous choreography of their departure had been utterly seamless and, Natasha hoped, invisible.

As soon as they left the office building, they were greeted by sunshine, and an active breeze that skirted skin and tousled hair. They breathed soft sighs of relief, while smiles creased their faces as they started to acclimatize to the unimaginable joy of being next to one another. It was a glorious afternoon blessed with weather that would have instilled a spring in the stride of the most lacklustre individual. As for Sebastian and Natasha, they were on fire.

They took the short stroll to Sebastian's car park, in silence, enjoying the weather and their proximity. When they arrived, they turned into the darkness and down the oil-stained, concrete ramp to the car park attendant's booth.

Inside, a small black man, with a mischievous grin, leapt off his stool as soon as he spotted Sebastian. He lifted a set of keys from a hook on the tan corkboard to his right, then did a collected jog to go and get the car, while staring at them over his shoulder with keen interest as he flashed a toothy smile. Natasha hoped the man's cheerfulness was endemic to his character, rather than a betrayal of his knowledge of Mr. Butler's habits.

Almost immediately, a purring black Porsche 911 rolled up. The attendant left the engine running and hopped out. Discreetly, Sebastian passed the man a brown note, for his trouble, and his grin extended to the tips of his ears. Sebastian dismissed his gratitude with a single wave, before bending down to open the passenger door for Natasha. As soon as she got in, her nose filled with the heady-smell of leather and, in a flash, Sebastian was by her side.

When they roared out of the car park, Natasha's unsettling concerns could not keep up. Why had she been fretting anyway, she was just getting a lift home? Sebastian drove very fast through the narrow backstreets of the City, but Natasha did not object, in fact, she revelled in it. With the continuous stop-start of city driving, she experienced one vicious accelerating lurch after the other, to promote so many shots of adrenaline to spurt into her bloodstream, that she found herself collapsing into uncontrollable fits of giggles. Chemical it may have been, sophisticated it was not. Sebastian concentrated hard, effortlessly slicing through the building Friday afternoon traffic, and thrilling Natasha all the way. It was not until they hit Embankment, and the rippling blue-steel-grey of the River Thames dazzled them with starbursts of white light, that Sebastian broke the relaxed silence and chimed, cheekily:

"Pembridge Square wasn't it?"

"That's where I live." Natasha replied, in a tone that expressed her non-commitment to an imminent arrival there.

Sebastian smirked. Knowing the game they each played, finally, he broke the impasse:

"Well I think it's far too glorious just to go home, don't

you? Why don't we go for a quick drink first?"

Natasha's throat constricted with excitement, at the prospect, and she replied, as calmly as she could:

"Why not?"

"Great! A drink it is then. I know exactly where I want to take you."

In record time, they reached the Fulham Road and the car was soon parked under a thick green canopy of gigantic plane trees. The pair got out, crossed the road and stepped into a narrow fronted, cocktail bar called, Le Shaker. It was only five-thirty and, save for the barman polishing glasses, the bar was empty. It seemed more than appropriate that they should have the place to themselves. The way they were feeling, they thought they deserved the world.

Anyone familiar with this establishment will know there is only one comfortable seat in the house: the small red-velvet sofa positioned directly in front of the door. This is where Natasha sat, with Sebastian bang next to her. Having made it to a drinking haunt, alone together, they were disproportionately thrilled with themselves. Sebastian gave a massive sigh, as if to release all of the tension he had accumulated throughout his lifetime. With both hands sitting on top of his long thighs, and his fingers drumming impatiently there, he inquired:

"Natasha, what can I get you to drink?"

"Vodka and orange please."

Sebastian caught the barman's attention and ordered two of the same, before he shot a quick glance at her, smiled, and then gave a bashful shrug. For a moment, Natasha thought how his evident nervousness seemed to be so incongruous with his fine broad shoulders. She grinned at him and waited, for she knew not what. The drinks were quick to arrive, along with a wooden bowl, piled high with giant vegetable crisps: potato, carrot, beetroot and parsnip. Natasha started to graze as the barman receded, inconspicuously. For several minutes, the only sound in the bar was her soft munching until, suddenly, Sebastian made a bold announcement, as he stared pensively at his knees:

"Natasha, I have decided to personally appoint myself as your matchmaker. It is my mission to find you a fabulous husband." he looked up, to find Natasha's jaw grinding to a halt, mid-chew, before continuing, "Preferably someone fabulous from my circle. Once I have done so, I can, innocently, get to spend stacks of time with you. What do you think?"

He looked at her encouragingly, as if genuinely excited by his plan. Natasha started to chew, again, trying to finish her mouthful as quickly and quietly as possible. She swallowed with an audible gulp.

"I thought your idea about having a drink was better." she replied, with a deadpan expression.

Natasha's reply seemed flippant yet, in truth, his proposition hurt. Sitting next to him, she could not envisage ever wanting to marry anyone else. Sensing her disquiet, Sebastian qualified:

"Seriously Natasha, it's a wonderful plan. You see we have a problem. I am married, but I am in love with you. I don't even know you, and I am in love with you. If I were single, I would have already proposed to you by now."

Then Sebastian thought, for a moment, before continuing gravely, "My only option is to content myself with finding you happiness with another. You are far too dangerous for me to have as an intimate friend, if you're not married off. I am decided."

"Well Sebastian, thank you for informing me, that *you* have decided it is time to marry *me* off. How very considerate." she replied, while trying not to scowl.

Natasha hoped that her tone was teasing, however, her guts were churning in a potent whirlpool of conflicting emotions. Heaven: Sebastian loved her too and she had not imagined any of the extraordinariness between them. Hell: he was married and had resolved to marry her off to someone else. Natasha's boundless joy elevated her to the heavens (led by her wrists), while her grief grappled with her ankles (one for each of his children) and fixed her fast to the floor. The result was the emotional equivalent of a fully taut, torture chamber's rack. She felt herself begin to split. Impulsively, Sebastian reached forward to take Natasha's hand in his. Gently, he began to examine it, carefully opening it up and stroking the length of her tapered fingers.

"Natasha, you have beautiful hands. You have the hands of an artist." Laughing now, Sebastian looked at her and shook his head. His expressive eyes delved into hers, "What the hell is someone with hands like this," he lifted one up, to display it to himself and to her, "so obviously the hands of an artist, doing in investment banking?" Then he thrust his head forward and accused with mock severity, "How the hell did *you* end up on a trading floor?" Sebastian looked comically exasperated, the whites of his eyes lighting up their little corner of the bar. He shook his head from side to side in disbelief, before taking several grateful glugs of his drink, only then to instruct the waiter, "Two more of the same please."

It was Natasha's turn to widen her eyes. Two double vodkas, in quick succession, on an empty stomach (colourful crisps hardly counted) were surely asking for trouble. Sebastian continued.

"This is all your fault. It's quite evident now that you should not be in banking at all. If you were doing what your hands tell me you ought, painting pictures or some such, if you were doing that, then we would never have met. If we had never met, then I would not be presented with this impossible dilemma." He stopped, as if exhausted by his own conjecture. His train of thought had not ceased, however, for he began to chuckle to himself. Sebastian turned to stare, adoringly, into Natasha's eyes while he continued to fondle her hand, but lightly now, as if it were his personal, delicate appendage, "Come to think of it, I've already spent several hundred thousand pounds on art this year, and it's only August! If I'm honest, we would probably have met anyway, in the galleries or the auction houses." He then paused, in deep thought, before downing the rest of his drink and adding softly, "I guess, some things are just meant to be..."

CY BLACK

Sebastian then fixed Natasha with a stare so intense, it touched her soul. She blinked in wonder at their Fate, as his words ricocheted inside her head, 'meant to be, meant to be, meant to be...' He had not finished, and continued:

"The art world, banking, what matters the backdrop? I have a feeling we were always going to end up here. Here, just like this. Sitting on a sofa, in an empty cocktail bar, feeling like we've known each other since time began. Here, alone, together, not wanting to be anywhere else in the world."

At last, Sebastian was spent. A wave of resignation washed over his elegant features and, for a moment, he looked like the unhappiest man on the planet. Natasha's hand, passive to this point, suddenly gripped his with certitude as she reassured:

"Sebastian, please don't look so forlorn. Everything will work out; somehow."

In the ensuing silence, in this secluded, intimate space, Sebastian and Natasha held hands, tightly, as they tried to assimilate the phenomenon of their extraordinary effect on each other: this unexpected, miraculous discovery of someone whom, effortlessly, made the other feel complete to the point of bliss. It was almost too divine even to comprehend. It was certainly too painful to cope with the circumstances in which one of them was found.

The meditative spell was lifted when the waiter returned with more drinks. Sebastian let go of Natasha's hand. The physical disconnect was an abrupt shock for each. Their truncated energy fields struggled to attain wholeness in their new isolation, like distressed silver blobs of mercury idiotically darting around, as they urgently seek like blobs with which to re-bond. Natasha reached for her glass and took a big gulp of the sweet drink, while a hole the size of Jupiter erupted at her core, to promote a feeling of pure terror. Then Sebastian lifted his vulnerability-filled eyes, and looked earnestly into her face, as if to implore her to be kind with him, his heart and his family for, by now, she must realize her devastating effect. Natasha just stared at him, with devotion. Then, with eyes locked, he lifted his glass to toast, with forced abandon, "To Natasha's new husband... I think I may have just the man." Sebastian then stood: the investment banker recovered, "Well my darling one, I think it's time to get you safely home before my resolve to behave honourably caves-in. Any more drinks this evening would be reckless."

Natasha nodded, then got up. Immediately, she felt dizzy and overwhelmed by the sloshing feelings Sebastian had engendered in her. He soon paid the barman and they left. He drove the ten-minute drive back to Pembridge Square, in five. They said nothing. Too much had been said already. The car screeched around the corner and into the square as Sebastian enquired:

"What number?"

"Twenty-six please."

Almost before Natasha had finished speaking, they had pulled up outside. The property was a large, white stucco fronted, ramshackle old villa that had once been a magnificent family home. It had since been unceremoniously chopped up into twenty-two small flats, studios or bedsits. Natasha had recently rented one of the bedsits, on the uppermost floor, and she was forced to share a bathroom and lavatory with two others. The arrangement was not ideal, but the room was pretty and full of light. What is more, the area was perfect for the house was only a short walk from Notting Hill Gate tube station and the central line, which got her into Liverpool Street Station, in less than twenty minutes. When she considered the money she spent on clothes, she knew she could not afford anything better in a safe, central London area; even on an investment bank's graduate's starting salary. Besides, she had figured that with the hours she would be working, she would only be sleeping there anyway. The engine was still running when Sebastian turned to catch her eye.

"Sadly, my darling one, it's time to say goodbye."

"Thank you Sebastian, for the lift and the drinks."

"I'd much rather be going on holiday with you."

"I'll be there with you in spirit, Sebastian. I promise. By the way, I hope you have a very Happy Birthday."

Natasha leant over to kiss him lightly on the cheek; a position from which it was hard to recover. Then he declared, petulantly, as she moved to leave:

"I miss you already!"

"Stop it!" Natasha scolded, yet his words made her brim with delight. Reluctantly, she got out of the car, slammed the door and walked up the crumbling outdoor stone steps to the paint-peeled front door, only the dull brass doorknob and letterbox of which recalled its former grandeur. Natasha dug around in her handbag for her keys and then let herself in. When she glanced behind her, she found Sebastian leaning across the passenger seat and watching her, intently. He waved goodbye, then revved the engine in a further farewell, before roaring off.

Sebastian was gone. The hole was back. It seemed to gape at the very heart of Natasha's soul. As if his sudden departure had prompted her spirit to lurch after his and take her at her word. The unfamiliar sensation made her feel nauseous and dizzy. She must be imagining things. She had to get a grip. Pulling herself together, she went inside, shut the door behind her, crossed the grand hallway and began to ascend the sweeping staircase. The golden sunlight flooded in through the magnificent sash-window on the half-landing, only to highlight the threadbare scruffiness of the red carpet that had seen better days. With each floor Natasha climbed, the ceiling height and staircase proportions tapered to increasingly modest proportions. With each step Natasha took, she felt equally diminished. Tonight, the effort to walk up to her room seemed disproportionate to the task, for a dead weight pulled at her limbs and at her heart and she groaned, despondent:

"Shit, I'd forgotten how sticky-tarmac heavy Sebastian-less reality feels."

Chapter Three - **Fabio & Fibonacci**

It was Monday morning and Natasha was sitting at her desk. She had been free of Sebastian's presence for two days now and, thankfully, her cognizance had normalized. What is more, she knew she would not see Sebastian for the rest of the week. Having spent all weekend reflecting on what had occurred last Thursday and Friday, Natasha could now recognize just how weird and extraordinary their interaction had been. Even so, it was difficult for her to understand exactly what had happened. All she knew was that the events of that two-day period had possessed an inevitability and power with which she was unfamiliar. It was as if she had been unwittingly, and forcibly, sucked into a drama where she knew the dialogue spontaneously by heart, and she was the star, acting opposite a co-star, she knew even more completely than the script. What Natasha did not know was how it would play out, and who, or what exactly, was directing its course. Replaying the scenes, again and again, she had drawn her own conclusion: the director of this new play must be that feared and fathomless chap called Fate. Never before had she been so helplessly governed by such force of personality!

Natasha's state of mind continued to oscillate between joy, at having found a man who, unconditionally, so delighted her, and despair, due to the circumstances in which he was found. Knowing that there could be no future with Sebastian, her sensible course of action should have been never to see him again, and so slam the door tightly shut to such immense temptation. Yet how could she do so when they worked together? She kept reminding herself that over three thousand people had applied for the thirty-odd places on the bank's graduate-training programme. She had been bloody lucky to get one at all, and there was no way she could betray herself by forfeiting such an immense career opportunity. Natasha was left with one avenue open to her: self-control. Sebastian must remain a good, although already inappropriate, friend.

CY BLACK

Having condemned her heart to the fate of not being allowed to love the first thing in the world it was leaping out
of her chest to so do, she resolved to distract herself by focusing on the job. There was much to absorb in this new
world of finance, and Natasha was being paid a fat salary
to decipher the unfamiliar jargon and culture of this trading
floor, as soon as possible. One thing was obvious: in this
place patience was at a premium. Natasha had to become a
contributing member to the bottom line; and fast. Consequently, for her second week on the Futures Desk, she
decided to learn all she could, while working up the courage to tell Innes that she would be moving to Sebastian's
Desk the following Monday.

Surprisingly, one of Miss Flynn's most fascinating days
was spent sitting next to the flirtatious Fabio. She learnt
that he was a brilliant mathematician and that his job was
to proprietary trade in the Futures Market. In effect, the
bank gave him a chunk of their balance sheet, with which
to play, in order to produce a profit. He would buy and
hold a contract, or an option on it, (go long), if he thought
the price would rise, or sell one or other without owning it,
(go short), if he thought the price would fall. Then, when
he deemed it to be the right time, he would close out the
reverse trade to lock in an immediate profit. When Fabio
had finished explaining this very simplified version of how
he spent his days, Natasha arched a fine eyebrow.

"In short, Fabio, you get paid, rather well I imagine, to
play in a market casino with leveraged deposit holders'
money?" she questioned, haughtily.

Fabio shook his head from side to side, as he tut-tutted,
as swiftly and precisely as a ticker tape machine, in outrage
at such an ignorant suggestion. He proceeded to look at
Natasha in mock horror, his beautiful long-lashed eyes appearing not unlike a pair of shiny conkers, in proportion
and colour. He then spoke slowly, rolling his tongue luxu-
riantly around every syllable in a deep, musical voice as he
admonished her, "Casino, Natasha? Did you learn anything
about math at school? Highly informed decision making by

me, combined with my sophisticated understanding of market behaviour and of the instruments I trade - with tools such as Chartism at my disposal - hardly equates to playing in a casino!" Though Fabio was scolding her for her impudence, all Natasha could do was cross her arms over her lower stomach as it convulsed with a wave of lust: the sound of his voice, the view of that face, his intelligence and passion. Our heroine was flummoxed by her intense physical reaction, for she thought she was in love with Sebastian: how confusing! Oblivious to his disturbing effect on her, Fabio continued:

"Probability!"

He said this word with so much reverence that it seemed magical. For a split second, Natasha instinctively understood that all of the manifestations of the cosmos were explained by it.

"Pro-ba-bil-ity." Fabio then repeated, as if to give Natasha ample time to appreciate the profound wisdom contained there, before he elaborated, "In a casino, Natasha, the odds are forever stacked in favour of the House, over time, one will always lose money."

Fabio was looking directly at her now, with a very serious expression. He was pointing his finger in her face as if to warn her, urgently, of the perils and stupidity of gaming. He then relaxed his muscular shoulders, rested back in his chair and, with a lavish gesture, he threw his elegant arms outwards, with palms up-turned, as if in thanks to God for himself, as he exclaimed:

"I..."

So pleased with this concept of self was he, that he jerked his hands a little higher into the air to punctuate his point, before continuing:

"I, on the other hand, have been trading futures for this bank for over four years now. My trades are rigorously risk controlled and, on a dollar risk weighted basis, sixty-three percent of the time I produce a profit, of varying magnitude. In short, I consistently make money: a lot of money."

He studied Natasha's face, with burning intensity, as if

to check whether she was suitably impressed or, indeed, to discern if she had actually grasped the impressiveness of his boast. The 'sixty-three percent' success rate part, not the 'a lot of money' part, for Fabio, along with the rest of the men in the front office, had long known, to their advantage, how quickly girls were impressed by 'a lot of money'. In fact, in that regard, Fabio's success rate was less than a whisker away from one-hundred percent.

Our heroine was humbled, while Fabio seemed satisfied, for he went on in more detail about the various methods he used to trade his market. Natasha fast discovered the fascinating world of technical trading, or 'Chartism' as it could be known. As he began to explain it, he conjured up a second magical word, which he uttered, with almost the same degree of reverence that he had used to utter 'probability': "Fibonacci!"

He then leaned back in his chair and smiled, in sublime contemplation, for several moments before continuing, "Please Natasha, allow me to tell you all about Fibonacci. At the very beginning of the thirteenth century, a highly gifted Italian mathematician named Leonardo of Pisa, now more commonly known as Fibonacci, wrote a book called Liber Abaci in which he revealed, among other things, a fascinating numerical sequence that he had discovered with the help of many rabbits."

Fabio then reached for his pen and drew a cartoon sketch of a large eared rabbit, closely resembling Bugs Bunny, on his trade blotter - evidently there was no end to this man's talents! He then wrote down a row of numbers, in a very neat hand, until the top line of the page was filled with them: 1, 1, 2, 3, 5, 8, 13, 21, 34, 55, 89, 144, 233, 377, 610, 987, 1,597... Once Fabio had finished, he flicked his attention back onto Natasha and smiled, warmly, with encouragement as he said, "Now, Natasha, look closely at this sequence of numbers, then I want you to tell me something very interesting about it?"

Natasha looked at Fabio. Natasha looked down at the numbers. She frowned, for a few seconds, before her face lit up, and she fired back in answer, "Each number in the series is the sum of the two preceding numbers?"

Fabio beamed.

"Of course they are!" His brawny shoulders then shook with a chuckle before he added, "But Natasha, I expect a little more from you than that. Look again."

Helpfully, he passed her his calculator, leaned back in his seat, crossed his heavy arms and grinned. Natasha stared back down at the numbers and, feeling under pressure, she frowned harder. Quite frankly, having spotted the pattern she was not sure what Fabio expected from her. She looked back at him, quizzically, for a little help. He grunted gently with disappointment before giving a resigned shrug.

"OK, OK, Natasha, you told me that you did not study math to degree-level, so I give a little help." He turned down the corners of his kissable lips before he requested, entreatingly, "Please, do not disappoint me a second time." Then tapping the business calculator he had just handed her, Fabio looked sternly into her eyes as he revealed the word that would salvage her, "Ratio."

Now he had said it, Natasha was cross with herself for not thinking of it. If Fabio had not been so bloody gorgeous, she was quite sure she would have worked it out all by herself. Anyway, following his prompt, she was off dividing each number by the one that preceded it, in fast succession. She worked quickly, and started to jot down a new series of numbers above the sequence Fabio had transcribed, putting each number in between the two numbers that she had used to calculate it (accurate to three decimal places): 1, 2, 1.5, 1.666, 1.625, 1.615, 1.619, 1.618, 1.618, 1.618, 1.618. By the time Natasha had written 1.618 down for the fourth time, she began to giggle. Fabio then rested his big hand on hers and grinned at her and he patronized.

"Enough now Natasha, I am sure, even *you,* can spot the pattern by now."

"Oh Fabio, you're too kind." our heroine replied, with cheeky sarcasm.

Fabio just chuckled, happily, while a bright light danced in his beautiful eyes and he flashed his sparkling white teeth at her in a wide smile. He went on to explain that Natasha had just discovered 'The Golden Ratio' for, as she had just demonstrated, the ratios of consecutive numbers in Fibonacci's sequence quickly converge to repeat, endlessly, the mysterious number 1.618. This ratio was sometimes referred to as the 'divine proportion' because it replicated itself throughout Nature, science and art. Indeed, it was the veritable spinal cord of all creation. Fabio was alight with inspiration as he described how this 'Golden Ratio' unfolded again and again, to define proportions as diverse as the distances of the branching on trees, the leaf arrangement along stems, the veining of individual leaves, the flowerings of an artichoke, the petal arrangement of a flower, shell spirals, wave curves and even the family trees of bees, cows and of course the rabbits with which Fibonacci began.

Natasha's mouth fell open. She was dizzy with discovery. Her mind raced. How had she not known of this inspirational phenomenon before? Why had no one ever told her? Was this not the first thing a maths or biology teacher should impart to their class? Fabio just continued to dazzle her as he expanded on the extent of the ratio's omnipresence throughout the natural world, to encompass and dictate the skeleton formation of animals and humans, the proportions of chemical compounds along with the geometry of crystals. Wow!

Fabio then explained, with great excitement, how the men of finance employed this ratio to market data chart analysis: Fibonacci Fans, Fibonacci Arcs and Fibonacci Retracements. All were regularly and successfully referenced, to predict the probable future behaviour of efficient financial markets, the Futures Market most certainly qualifying as such. Natasha questioned:

"If so many market participants all referred to the same methods of prediction, are not the consequent market movements just a self-fulfilling prophecy?"

Fabio just smiled, charmingly, and then shrugged: if his use of such methods consistently made him money, why should he care? It was his job to exploit self-fulfilling prophecies, not to correct them. He had a point. While Natasha listened attentively to Fabio demystify some of his trading methods, meticulously, she was struck by how appropriate it was to learn of this 'divine order' now, at the very moment when her life's events seemed to be being dictated by an intelligence beyond herself. Oh, and how compellingly appropriate to have learnt it from the possessor of such perfect human proportions as Fabio! As Natasha marvelled at the passion that flowed from him, she was tempted to get out a measuring tape to proof Fibonacci's Golden Ratio on him right away!

How much Natasha liked Fabio this day, perfect proportions and lustful longings aside. His enthusiasm for the subjects about which he spoke, filled him so fully there was no room left to accommodate his habitual arrogance, shameless flirtation and extreme self-satisfaction. Today, all Natasha could see was a gorgeous, inspiring young man passionately describing his fellow countryman's discovery, and grateful to share the joy of it with her. How his big brown eyes glistened with sparks of gold now. Although she could not stop thinking about it, not once did Fabio suggest casual sex, or even clutch his crotch. Awe aside, Natasha was a touch disappointed.

As the markets began to display greater volatility, Fabio fast excused himself to concentrate on his work. Natasha thanked him, gushingly, and then, reluctantly, returned to her temporary desk just two seats away. Now she was free to drift off into her reverie. The world was a miraculous place full of unfathomable mysteries, yet framed by a subtle celestial order, perceivable by those willing to seek out such fantastic possibility. For a moment, everything seemed less random and chaotic and a patience, to which Natasha was unaccustomed, swept over her. Even her craving for Sebastian was tamed, for time will unravel all and what is meant to be, 'meant to be, meant to be,' shall be so.

The rest of Natasha's instruction that week could not touch the impressiveness of Fabio and Fibonacci. As she studied the nuts and bolts of the Futures Market's business she discovered that, no matter how mathematically complex the products were, there was nothing fundamentally new in financial markets. The only way to make money was to buy something for less than one could sell. However, the distinguishing features of the financial markets seemed to be that they were global, more transparent and because the financial rewards were so high, they attracted some of the brightest minds in the world.

Market participants' wits were, perpetually, pitched against hundreds of thousands of other clever brains, all pursuing the same goal and accessing the same information - at a hefty price - in order to achieve it. A virtual, global Olympic Arena of intelligence, alertness and competence where Olympian rewards were to be had for the best of those who competed.

Well, once upon a time, for as long as the Chancellor of the Exchequer was masturbating over the City of London's tax receipts, that was the theory...

By the end of her second week, our heroine had learnt that she had chosen to work in an elaborate, highly pressurized, mathematically sophisticated, global market, but what a market it was! Every time the Desk erupted into a vortex of brightly flashing dealer board lights and frenetic price action on computer screens, it was met with the immediate attention of all present to stimulate gruff shouting, arm waving, sweating brows and fraying tempers. It would only be a matter of time before impatient altercations would fill the trading floor. Natasha would watch, mesmerized, as the men flared up with intense shots of adrenaline that made their faces shine and their starry-eyes pop out, while they were called upon to perform competently, with cool-heads, under immense pressure.

Often a man would spring to his feet, while on a call, unable to contain the fierce energy that coursed through his tense frame. Some would be driven to pace up and down, for as far as the long, black, spiralling telephone cords would allow, while they conducted several discussions, on different lines, at once. One day, Natasha witnessed Fabio deal with four separate conversations, concurrently, without even breaking into a sweat. He traded hundreds of millions of dollars worth of different contracts, all at the same time, lining up the best bids or offers while having to monitor the different counterparty limits set by compliance. Each one of his conversations demanded complete concentration and total precision. As he executed all of his trades perfectly, a serene, almost celestial, calmness spread across his beautiful face, like sunshine.

Natasha paid particular attention to Chris and Jason on their client calls, for she knew she was destined to end up in sales. The men were on the 'phone all day long making or taking one call after another, lucky if they got the chance to nip out for lunch. Natasha would observe their blank stares, compulsive leg shaking and the tight tension in their jaws as they, urgently, waited for a client's instruction. All trading parties would be primed for action, impatiently waiting for 'the green light' to close, and every one of them highly stressed and anxious, in case the market were, suddenly, to move away and they would be forced to start pricing all over again, or worse, lose the trade entirely. At last, visible relief would brighten serious brow when the client came back with the desired decision to precipitate a victorious: 'Done!'

If Essex-boy Jason was particularly pleased with a profitable trade, a further adrenal shot would be self-administered, as he would punch his fist up into the air, triumphantly, to make his rigid body jerk forward, aggressively, in celebration. Following the fierce jolt of fulfilment on the close, he would then sit back down and, distinctly, recount all trade specifics with the trading party in confirmation: the contract, the size, the currency, the price, the time, the trade date, the settlement date and be sure to detail any agreed deviations from the norm. Then, another line would start to flash and he would do something similar all over again, and again, and again: next, next, next, next, for eleven hours a day, five days a week. Often, every detail of every trade would have to be remembered if there was not the luxury of time to record, clearly, the tens and hundreds of millions worth of dollars, yen, sterling, Swissie, francs or lira that had been dealt.

Frantic, barely-legible scribbling was scratched all over trade blotters in the hope that frenetic, financial shorthand could be decoded, when sufficient time allowed, to write out trade tickets correctly. The tiniest mistake could cost millions, along with your job. Once completed, trade tickets were stuffed into trays that were frequently emptied by girls from the 'back office'. The 'back office' was the place where all of the agreements made by the people from the 'front office', with counterparties from all over the world, would then be translated into action. Once the instructions of a trade were fed into the settlement systems, trillions of dollars, in every currency on the planet, would be wired to the correct settlement accounts. Only once the money had arrived in the Clearing House would the financial instrument that had been dealt, be released. This process, one of the most common forms of settlement, was known as D.V.P. or in full, Delivery Versus Payment. What an expression! It reminded Natasha of the unwritten rules of a whorehouse. The abode of the oldest profession in the world and here, the wisdom of it was implemented by the men of high finance, whose forefathers most likely learnt it there long ago.

During the most frenetic market sessions, those seated would dissipate excess energy by jiggling one leg, or even both, up and down in a successive shaking motion. This irritating habit was endemic on the trading floor. At the zenith of activity, the forward propelling impatience of the collective was so powerful that Time itself seemed bullied by it, for the hours were fast gobbled up and spat out in the commotion. Unlike in an Olympic Arena, however, here there was no adequate physical exertion to dissipate the flood of energy produced by all of those adrenal shots.

FALSE GODS THE ECSTASY

Natasha wondered what all these testosterone-packed men did with their accumulating aggression. Did they carry it home and take it out on their families? Did they go out to bars and clubs and drown it in drink? Did they pull young, naïve, drunken girls to shag it all away with a grunt and a roar? Or perhaps, it just lodged, unexpended, in pumping muscle, delicate tissue and vital organs to cause irritability, stiffness, aches, pains and, finally, some fatal illness.

It was several weeks before Miss Flynn was to witness the most natural outcome of so much stress and competition, for a physical fight broke out on the Foreign Exchange (FX) Trading Desk. Such scenes were not a common outcome but, when stress and spirits were at their highest, the threat of violence always lurked and, if ignited, the whole floor would go berserk as brave colleagues would attempt to break up the fracas or, on a bad day, join in. Our heroine observed this pressurized crucible of human stress with intense curiosity: fascination and fright commingled. The behaviour here was startlingly akin to that of apes vying for dominance in the wild. The endemic and excessive physical posturing, that had seemed so odd to her, at first, started to make sense.

For now, Natasha was just a captivated spectator. When the dealer boards were alight and the din on the trading floor deafening, she was irrelevant, insulated from the aggression, yet transfixed by it, as each day she would be reminded of the fragility of civility. Then, with vague terror, Natasha would wonder how cool her head would be when it was her turn to perform on three calls at once, to trade in tens, or even hundreds of millions of dollars worth of cash. The slightest error could cost a fortune or, more frighteningly, incur the wrath of every colleague. Woe betide the unfortunate who screwed-up, sacked or despised by all for the financial cost their incompetence had inflicted on the bonus pool. Would Natasha hold her nerve when one of those big burly bond traders, with no time for anyone and no manners to disguise the fact, was screaming at her in front of everyone for 'fucking up?'

For all of the action, sometimes the markets seemed to sleep. At such times a spell of fairytale lethargy would be cast on all of those paid so much, to sit and watch the markets' stillness, meticulously. How they would struggle to remain primed for a sudden resurgence in frenzied activity. The longer such periods lasted, the greater the number who would begin to slouch moodily over desks, suffering grim boredom as sullen eyes, surreptitiously, delved into 'The Sun' or some blokes' magazine, predictably depicting powerful cars, expensive yachts and multi-million dollar motor boats, along with a profusion of skinny, large-breasted, flesh-flashing blondes; for how else were they to remind themselves why they were there in the first place?

Yet, even at these times, all eyes would repeatedly flick-up to monitor computer screens for any material change. Each had learnt, to their cost, if they missed a single iota of crucial information, great losses could be incurred in a second, to precipitate greater consequences.

Men, men, men, there were men everywhere, quite a change from Miss Flynn's fatherless home and girls-only boarding-school. The ratio of men to women in the highly paid front office must have been nine to one, while in the poorly paid back office it was reversed. Where was Fibonacci's Golden Ratio now? The extent of sexist employment practices seemed to know no bounds, for it was blatantly obvious that the scant quantity of women in the front office were not only bloody clever, but invariably rather attractive as well, even if a hardness often took possession of their pretty features.

Natasha then remembered that she must inform Innes Plattenberg she was due to move Desks. Truth be told, she was rather in awe of Innes. She had such poise, fierce intelligence and indefatigable self-control. Her slightly square, but attractive face, had impressive bone structure and her large, light blue eyes, though they lacked any sparkle, were as clear as a mountain pool, while Innes' repertoire of facial expressions seemed to be restricted to: light smile, intense focus and considered judgement.

However, it was Innes' self-discipline that drew Natasha's admiration most of all. When Natasha arrived at work each morning, around seven-fifteen, Innes would have already been at work for an hour. At noon, she would head for the gym with a kit bag slung over her shoulder that was nearly as big as she. Innes would then swim fifty lengths, everyday, and return with a slightly flushed, squeaky-clean complexion having picked up a salad for lunch, on her way back to the office. She would then eat at her desk, working all the while.

Apparently, she never left the office before seven at night, except on Friday when she would leave at five in order to travel down to her country house in Hampshire. This rigorous self-discipline would be employed day after day. Innes would only vary it when she jetted all over the world to meet the most important clients. Natasha felt weak just witnessing the woman's schedule. When she cheekily questioned Innes as to whether she had any vices, Innes just smiled and, for the first time, Natasha detected a glint of guiltiness in her eye, when she confessed:

"Sleep. I'm in bed by ten o'clock every night to get my full seven hours." Innes' expression softened as she leant forward to confide, with a hint of a glint in her mountain-pool blue eyes, "Oh and, of course, a good red."

In an instant, Natasha was even more gob-smacked, for what world had she entered where sleep now qualified as a vice? And as for red wine, surely everyone knew that it was good for you? Natasha took advantage of this candid moment with Innes Plattenberg, to advise her that she was due to join Sebastian Butler's Desk the following Monday. Innes had arched a single blonde eyebrow and commented:

"Sebastian's is a profitable business. Learn all you can while you are there but, please consider, there is a job for you here, if you so wish."

Natasha was both thrilled and relieved to have the offer of a permanent position, so quickly. If nothing else worked out, sitting next to Fabio all day was not such a bad backstop! When an exhausted, but satisfied, Natasha stepped out of the office, on Friday afternoon, she was overjoyed to be looking forward to such a promising lot. What is more, she knew that the next time she entered the building, she would be working with Sebastian. Frankly, she could barely wait.

Chapter Four - Keep it in the family

"Beep, Beep, Beep, Beep, Beep, Beep..."

A hideous piercing racket penetrated Natasha's consciousness at five-fifty a.m. to rouse her from deep sleep. Immediately, an adrenal shot was dispensed to prompt her heartbeat to thump so frantically inside her chest that her eyes sprang open, in shocked surprise. She stared through the gap between the blind and the frame of the skylight above her head, to find the sky was that fragile dove-white of first light.

"Beep, Beep, Beep, Beep, Beep, Beep..."

Irritated by the ugly sound, Natasha smacked the button on top of her alarm clock to silence it. For a brief moment the sweet illusion of peace resumed until, tweet by high-pitched tweet, Natasha became aware of the cacophony of birdsong that burst forth from the garden square beyond. The exhilarating sound recalled the significance of her own day. Monday had arrived, at last, and with it, imminent sight of Sebastian. A state of bliss that Natasha had forgotten existed returned to envelop her.

Inspired, she leapt out of bed to shower and get ready. By the time Natasha was dragging the brush through her wet, tangled hair she had decided what to wear: her beautifully cut, black Armani suit. She had not worn it to work since her first day. The minute Innes had spotted the diminutive length of it, she had frowned, most sternly, in disapproval. Natasha had vowed never to wear it again. Now, however, that she was no longer working directly with Innes, and since having learnt that it was the suit she had been wearing when Sebastian had noticed her for the first time, she was more than prepared to risk arousing Innes' displeasure, in the hope of courting Sebastian's approval!

It was three-minutes past seven when Natasha burst onto the trading floor wearing the afore-mentioned outfit with skin more luminiferous, hair more lustrous and a smile more brilliant than ever. She had that wild look in her eye as she scanned the enormous space seeking Sebastian's handsome face. The unimaginable occurred: she was there, but he was not. Natasha was stung by acute disappointment. Worse, she was sobered by her foolishness. She may well have spent the entire weekend imagining a feverish Sebastian waiting for her, with eyes as bright and breath panting like her own, but now the time had come, she suspected someone as important as Sebastian, would rarely arrive at work much before the morning meeting. Why, oh why, should it be any different today? Sobered, she huffed and resolved to get a grip on her burgeoning bunny-boiler tendencies.

Natasha then gritted her teeth and focused on the immediate problem. Seeing as Sebastian was not there to welcome her, with whom should she check in? Curiously, she eyed the few unfamiliar men who had already arrived. As was usual with traders, all of them were preoccupied with their computer screens and, consequently, oblivious to her presence. She was on the verge of going up to the friendliest looking one when, suddenly, he turned his head and caught her eye. She flashed a smile and the man cracked his face into a cheeky grin, before leaping up and wobbling over to her, at surprising speed. He thrust out his chubby hand and she grasped its dryness, gratefully, before shaking it firmly, as he spoke.

"You must be the new girl Seb told me about?"

"Natasha Flynn, how do you do?"

The man's face creased-up into a prune's worth of deep wrinkles that tracked a half-century of good humour. In a broad Essex drawl he introduced himself.

"Freddie Clarke, good ta mee' ya."

Freddie was a barrel of a man with a smirk full of devilment. His hair was iron-grey and he was rather short. He could only have been five-foot four and his girth approached half of his height, which made him remind Natasha of one of her favourite childhood toys called 'The Weebles.' These rotund little fellows were about two-inches high and almost as wide. The minute Natasha had seen Freddie walking towards her, the ancient musical ditty that had been used to market these endearing little characters, so successfully, had cheerily filled her mind: 'Weebles wobble but they don't fall down!' This recollection was responsible for the sentimental grin that Natasha bestowed on Freddie now, which only served to work to our heroine's advantage, for he could not help but respond positively to this pretty young girl's genuine smile. When Freddie had finally finished shaking her hand, he placed his other one, protectively, onto her back.

"Na, don't ya worry abou' a fing young lady, I'll take good care of ya." he reassured.

He then escorted her to a vacant desk three chairs behind his own. From that day on, Freddie took Natasha under his wing, and God knows how much a girl needed such a wing in this cutthroat, aggressive environment, even if Natasha did not.

She was soon to learn that Freddie Clarke was Sebastian's Head Trader and most trusted colleague. Freddie explained that Sebastian's Desk comprised of six sales people and four traders, all of whom reported, directly, to him. He told her how he would get her computer terminals hooked up to Reuters and Telerate - the crucial information services that are the life blood of the financial markets - "as soon as". Freddie then clarified that she would be "even more useless" until these live-feeds were activated. He expected it all to be "sor'id" (meaning 'sorted') by the end of the morning. Freddie then spoke to her about Bloomberg, that indispensable bond pricing, option pricing, bond cataloguing, news and messaging service.

"Well it's too bloody expensive to ge' for someone who aint makin' us any money, so you won't be ge'ing ya own righ', 'till we fink good and propa, if a' all. All righ'?"

Natasha nodded, in demure acknowledgement of her own uselessness, before Freddie consoled:

"Wo' I will do though is ge' ya yr own login and ya can share Matt's Bloomberg terminal. He's the salesman that sits on ya left but 'e's not in ye'. I'll intra duce ya when he ge's 'ere. In summary, ya on Reu'ers and Telera'e la' mornin' an' you'll av Bloomberg access on Matt's terminal, eva late afternoon or tomorra mornin'. Go' i'?"

Natasha was not sure if she had, but she nodded anyway. Freddie then excused himself so he could get his stuff together before he had to "scoot" to the morning meeting and he went back to his desk. Then, in afterthought, he picked up a bundle of papers from the top of his desk and came back to pass them to Natasha before explaining, rather hurriedly, that the sheets comprised the list of the Trading Desk's primary bond inventory. There was also a column that defined the Desk's specific axes (current market interest), namely: sell, buy, hold or neutral. Those marked 'sell' were the positions they wanted to shift "as soon as," the bonds marked 'buy' were the positions they were happy to increase "a' the ri' price," those marked 'hold' were the ones they wanted to hang onto, for now, while those marked 'neutral' were the ones where the Desk's view on buying or selling, was just that. Freddie instructed Natasha to familiarise herself with the lot by the end of the day before, finally, walking back to his desk. Then, in a burst of inspiration, he grabbed a book from on top of one of his screens and, without warning, he turned to throw it at her. Fortunately, Natasha had been paying attention and she was able to lurch forward and catch it, just in time, to prevent the heavy thing from slamming into her shin. Still recovering from fright, she straightened up and read the big book's title: 'Financial Market Analysis' by David Blake.

"I wan' ya to read tha' by lunch-time and then I wan' ya to tell me all abou' Floa'ing Ra'e Notes and wo' three and six month libor fixes at today, go i'?" Freddie smirked.

"What's libor?" Natasha questioned, clueless.

"Find ou'!" he barked, before chuckling so hard that he bent double. Nonplussed, she stared at him while the deep gravelly sound of his laughter resonated through her.

Suddenly, a loud voice bellowed out from behind Freddie. Her eyes darted to the source and, immediately, fixed on Sebastian. Captivated, Natasha listened to his strident command.

"Freddie Clarke please stop terrorizing our most recent recruit!"

Freddie's ears pricked, with keener interest than Natasha's, and he turned to greet Sebastian. He was upon them, in an instant, heartily patting Freddie on the back with a firmness that displayed genuine warmth yet, while engaged in this ritual of male bonding, Sebastian's eyes never left Natasha. Up close, his penetrating stare delved into her core. Natasha found herself flinch with the strike of his presence. The physics of her reality began to shift. Her mental alertness intensified, and her vision was boosted to high definition. Even the dull colours of the trading floor acquired a greater luminosity, while every atom of her being seemed to vibrate at a higher frequency as if in resonance with Sebastian's energy.

Oh, Sebastian!

Freddie lifted his face, to catch his boss' eye, and only then did Sebastian look down at his loyal Head Trader. Beaming, Freddie greeted him:

"Yo, Sebie, welcome back. How was the sailing?"

Freddie was grinning from ear to ear and his bright blue eyes were twinkling with merriment. Sebastian answered him with pensive sincerity yet, all the while, he continued to stare into Natasha's soul.

"Strange as it may sound my friend, I would much rather have been here."

Natasha blushed for she knew his reply was meant for her. Sebastian turned his attention back to Freddie, and chuckled in arrogant jest, before continuing:

"Oh, Freddie, you know the South of France in August." He did not. "Too much sun, too much food, too much wine and too many bloody boats. In the end, it all becomes a rather monotonous blur of self-indulgence..."

Unlike Sebastian, Freddie had spent all of the last week working bloody hard and, unsurprisingly, he reacted accordingly, "Oy, fuck off Seb."

The familiar colleagues laughed, good-humouredly, before Freddie added:

"By the way, Happy Birthday old man! I hope you had a goodun." Continuing to chuckle, all the while.

"Yes, I did, thank you Freddie," and, for a third time, Sebastian shot a look in Natasha's direction as he declared with deliberate passion, "but God it's good to be back."

Natasha's extreme delight was accentuated by Sebastian's evident reciprocity. The pair of them grinned like the Cheshire Cat. Unaware of their silent dialogue, Freddie spoke seriously to his boss.

"Well my boy, now you're finally a' work, aint i' time we go' dan t' some? Too much chit-chat mate, we've go' a mee'in' to take." It was Freddie's turn to place his hand on Sebastian's back but, due to the height differential, it would be more accurate to say 'hand on Sebastian's lower shoulder'. Freddie continued talking as he led him away, "There're a few trading positions we managed to lose last week and no' all of 'em to the stree' neva."

Sebastian and Freddie fast became absorbed in business matters. Natasha watched the unlikely pair from behind as they strolled off towards the meeting-room. The six men and one blonde woman, who had already been sitting at their desks, along with a couple of blokes who seemed to have materialized from nowhere, followed after them. All heads were held forward, as purposefully as a sprinter's, while hands clutched trade blotters that were covered in scrawls, with biros invariably jammed into binders or discreetly tucked behind pink ears.

In a flash, the chairs surrounding Natasha were empty. Still standing, she looked across the giant trading floor to discover that nearly all of the other people had disappeared too. The place was eerily quiet now. She sat down at the desk Freddie had just assigned to her, and looked down at the sheets. Then she took a look at the book. Where to start? Well that was easy, with coffee of course! Natasha stood up and dashed over to the breakfast room, at the far end of the trading floor, to grab herself a double espresso from the vending machine. When she returned, the trading floor was still almost her own. She sat down again and took a sip of her coffee. It was so revolting that her face screwed up with repulsion, before she recovered enough to eye the book, then the sheets of paper, once again. Where to start?

Tentatively, Natasha began to flick through the bond inventory page by page, her brow becoming increasingly tense with concentration. The symbols, acronyms and abbreviations were all double Dutch to her. She recognized the numbers, at least, if not their significance. Natasha resolved to read through every single line, slowly, to try and decode this unfamiliar financial language, however, each line remained stubbornly incomprehensible to her. She read them through twice but did not feel herself any the wiser. Fuck that! Defeated, Natasha let the papers fall to the desk then picked up the book. It was an inch and a half thick and, as she quickly scanned through its pages, immediately, she could see that it was technically daunting. She turned to page one-hundred and twelve and began to read about floating rate notes (F.R.N.s), as instructed. By the time she was studying the formulae to calculate the adjusted dirty price of an F.R.N. she had almost forgotten about Sebastian. Natasha soon learnt that LIBOR stood for the London Inter Bank Offered Rate. This was the interest rate at which major banks in London could borrow unsecured funds from other banks over the short term, in fifteen different maturities, ranging from overnight out to twelve months. LIBOR rates were fixed daily for ten different currencies and calculated by collecting the rates at which major contributing banks could borrow unsecured funds, in those currencies, for those maturities, in the open market. LIBOR was then calculated via a specified method that cut out the 'outliers' in order to achieve a representative rate of borrowing for banks in London on that day. Once the rate had been calculated it was fixed at 11 a.m. every morning. These LIBOR rates then became the daily benchmarks that were used to price loans, mortgages, bonds (including F.R.N.s) and derivatives. The 'floating' in floating rate notes, derived from the fact that, throughout their lifetime, the coupon, or interest rate paid on such debt instruments, kept refixing over current market LIBOR rates and was not 'fixed' like on a normal bond.

In short, LIBOR was crucial. It represented the current cost of cash. The whole banking business revolved around the cost of money. What is more, the valuation of all financial instruments relied on it, for it provided the discount rate at which the current value of all future cash flows was calculated, thus the present value or price of any security. Natasha had just learnt something vital. She was engrossed, so when a man's hand, suddenly, grabbed the book from her, then proceeded to chuck it into the waste-paper bin next to her desk, Natasha jumped in outrage. Simultaneously, her head shot up to confront the culprit. There stood Sebastian. His arms crossed casually across his chest as he stared down at her with a preposterously happy expression. Natasha's crossness, immediately, morphed into glee.

"Hello you." she said softly through a broad grin, before admonishing playfully, "And, by the way, Mr. Butler, I was reading that book. It's Freddie's book. He gave it to me with strict instructions. I'm sure he'll be most unimpressed if he thinks I just threw it into the bin."

Sebastian ignored her protest. Instead, he just stared at her, adoringly, for some time until he spoke, reflectively, while the corners of his mouth burst with contained excitement, "Hello you... I was telling the truth when I said it's good to be back."

His eyes glistened, captivatingly, their colour as deep as the forest greens of a peacock's feathers. Sebastian looked happy, healthy and refreshed. His face and hands were now the rich golden-brown of light maple syrup. His subtle tan suited him immensely. In an excruciatingly jolly mood, he finally addressed Natasha's rebuke.

"By the way Miss Flynn, I don't have books on my Desk, there isn't anything in there..." he pointed, theatrically, at the little black bin that contained the big white book before continuing, definitively, "that will teach you anything about this business. Our profits are not driven by theory. Our profits are driven by people. People and the strength of the relationships they manage to forge over the years." Sebastian shrugged his broad shoulders to concede a little, "Sure you need to understand bond maths, and of course you will, but while you're working with me, I never want to see your head stuck in a book again, understand?"

Natasha looked up at him blankly. To accentuate his point, Sebastian leaned forward, picked the book out of the bin and then, this time from a greater height, he dropped it straight back in, smiling crazily as he did so. Once it had landed with a heavy thud, he continued.

"While you are working with me, Natasha, you will learn about the real drivers on a trading floor."

Regally, Sebastian cast his penetrating gaze across the expansive room that, by now, had been repeopled. He motioned with his head to direct Natasha's line of vision.

"Look around you Natasha, look all around. Everyone sitting at these four-hundred-odd desks, every single one of them, knows how to price a bond. Every single one of them understands the time value of money and most of them can price an option too but, Natasha, concern yourself with this one question..."

Sebastian held his right index finger to the ceiling as he looked into her face with intensity.

"Why that fat man over there..."

Then Sebastian twisted his body around to point brazenly at a severely weight-challenged man who sat to his right about fifteen metres away. The large man looked as if he was in his mid-thirties. He had the whitest skin Natasha had ever seen. It was almost transparent. Incongruously, a thick, short, black bristled beard tufted from his blue-white skin. The black hair on his head was so wild it bore more resemblance to a mangrove swamp than to the man's patchy facial hair. Unlike the rest of the men working on the trading floor he did not wear a suit, instead, he wore dark brown corduroy trousers and an open necked shirt. He was captivated by the colourful electronic displays that danced on the computer screens before him. He had six of them all to himself. His eyes were on fire with focus as they darted all over the multitude of graphs, perpetually altering columns of prices and endless news snippets, without pause. Natasha had noticed him before, because he never seemed to engage in conversation with his colleagues, other than to trade or confirm a price. The man would sit all day long concentrating on his work, as if he were under some meditative spell, while rapidly consuming the contents of several take-away cartons over-spilling with an international spread of food.

Sebastian continued to ask the one question worth answering, "Why last year that fat bloke made himself four-and-a-half million dollars, personally, while that blondish guy over there, the one in the crumpled grey pinstripe..."

Now, equally shamelessly, he pointed to an older chap, probably in his mid-forties. The man was wearing gold wire rimmed spectacles and the greying pallor of his skin matched his dull ash blond hair. He seemed to repeatedly squint, as if distressed by the artificial light. He sat much farther away so Natasha could not make out his features clearly, however, she had noticed his upper body wince, the minute he had realized that Sebastian was pointing at him, as he asked her, "See him?"

Natasha nodded but looked away, for she felt ashamed to be staring at someone who, obviously, felt so uncomfortable with the uninvited interest he was attracting. Sebastian remained cruelly impervious.

"While that sad old man over there made less than three hundred and fifty-thousand dollars the same year and, unless he manages to boost his production significantly in the next four months, he's marked to get fired before bonuses are due?" Then Sebastian added, with cautionary menace, "They both understand bond maths, Natasha."

Sebastian was about to complete his first lesson to the young Natasha. No longer pointing at anyone now, he gripped the edge of Natasha's desk and, with princely eyebrows raised, he advised, "Natasha, study the behaviour and method of both these men, long and hard, and then if you can work out why that was the case, you will have learnt something worth knowing." Sebastian paused, for a moment, before dishing out a further valuable nugget of Machiavellian wisdom, "Natasha, the only reason any of us are here, is to make money. You can have all of the technical knowledge in the world, but unless you translate that into significant cash generation, it is only a matter of time before you get fired; end of story."

Having made this pertinent point, Sebastian lost all seriousness. His face relaxed into a playful grin and he shrugged his shoulders, dismissively.

"As for Freddie, Natasha, why he hasn't read a book in his whole life, so I can safely assume he holds no particular affection for them. There is no need for you to worry about Freddie, Natasha, you would be far more sensible to worry about me."

Telephone line one, of twenty or so, on the crumb-encrusted, grease-smudged black dealer board in front of Natasha, started to flash bright green. Sebastian spotted it, instantly. He sprang to his feet and, in one stride, he was back at his desk where an identical dealer board could be found. Quickly, he whacked the button to click into the call and fired, solemnly, "U.C.B."

Sebastian's expression was granite. Natasha was unaccustomed to his work persona, but this morning she was discovering a ruthless side to the man she loved. When he heard the voice on the line, however, his face softened, dramatically, and she recognized him once again.

"Bruno, how wonderful to hear from you!" he exclaimed. As soon as she heard the exuberance of his voice, Natasha concluded that he would be busy for some time. She seized the opportunity to go to the lavatory and spruce up. When she returned, Sebastian was still on the telephone but now, he was sitting in her chair with his feet propped up on her desk.

"Talk of the devil." he muttered, as she approached and, by the time she had reached him, Sebastian was holding the handset out to her, invitingly, "It's for you."

"Who is it?"

"Now that would be telling."

Sebastian remained seated while a bemused Natasha took the call. She propped herself up on the desk to echo the pose Sebastian had adopted earlier.

"Natasha Flynn, how can I help?"

"Oh, how I appreciate an obliging lady." a deep, incredibly well-spoken voice replied, before raucous laughter rumbled down the line.

Instantly, Natasha warmed to him. She was intrigued and decided to enter into the playful spirit of the dialogue. Sebastian watched her like a hawk.

"Why, kind sir, my only wish is to serve. Please enlighten me as to how I might do so, most effectively?"

"Oh, sweet lady, what music to mine ears, you cannot know quite how long I have awaited such tantalizing offer. But generous lady, my only pleasure will come from being granted licence to service you."

Then the deep voice boomed with a coarse cackle. Natasha almost blushed but, after taking one look at Sebastian's fierce expression, she managed not to. Instead, she teased, "Please, kind sir, I'm most uncertain as to the appropriateness of such 'service', for there is my reputation to consider!"

Natasha giggled as she stared at Sebastian, flirtatiously. The voice on the line seemed as amused as she, however, for some reason Sebastian did not, for he continued to stare at her, hotly.

"Oh, fine lady, as a gentleman I can assure you, your reputation shall remain intact. The 'service' to which I refer is of the 'silver' variety. In short, would you do me the supreme honour of joining me to indulge in some excessive gastronomic pleasures?"

The voice was so kind and the proposition so exciting that Natasha could not help but accept.

"Why sir I should be delighted for 'tis excessive pleasures that please me most."

She giggled again. Sebastian raised his eyebrows at her, censoriously, still unamused. Now the dinner-date was set the mysterious voice dropped the feeble, but fun, bawdy Shakespearean pastiche and, with hearty tones, he introduced himself:

"Bruno Monmouth, how do you do Miss Flynn? Sebastian has told me much about you." He then flipped back into the language of high romance to add, "May I inquire as to when I might have the pleasure of experiencing such a vision of true loveliness with mine own orbs?"

Natasha paused, as she tried to work out which night would work best, and then she questioned:

"Thursday?"

"Thursday it is." he answered, without hesitation, before inquiring, "Please give me your address and I will pick you up at six forty-five?"

"Thank you Bruno, I look forward to it, but I am afraid you are at an advantage for Sebastian has told me nothing about you," Natasha narrowed her catlike eyes at Sebastian, before declaring with forced conviction, "but, rest assured, I greatly look forward to getting to know you properly when we meet."

Our heroine was trying to tease jealousy from Sebastian and he knew it. He did not react, but just continued to stare at her, while his eyes were alight with the fire of mischievousness. Natasha looked down at her feet to escape their intensity and fiddled with the coiled, black, telephone line while she gave Bruno her address.

"Twenty-six Pembridge Square, flat twenty-one."

Bruno said goodbye and then, just before he hung up, he added a cryptic postscript with commanding gravitas:

"Dress warmly!"

Natasha put down the handset. Quizzically, she scanned Sebastian's face. He stared back at her, serenely, with a self-satisfaction that could rival Fabio's. Intrigued, Natasha broke the silence, and inquired, with genuine interest:

"Who is Bruno Monmouth?"

"Bruno Monmouth: six-foot five, dark hair, brown eyes,

handsome, intelligent, athletic, daring, titled and most importantly, single. In short, Natasha, perfect husband material, for a perfect young lady, and I could not help but notice that you both seemed to hit it off remarkably well."

Still oozing self-congratulation, Sebastian stood up. He stretched his long arms into the air, taking his time over this habitual ritual, before adjusting his belt, with a firm tug, as he added, in an off-hand manner:

"Oh, yes, and he's my first cousin."

Natasha stared into the distance as she absorbed this additional snippet of information. Sebastian had just fixed her up on a blind date with his first cousin. Then she recalled Sebastian's quiet toast in the bar, 'to Natasha's new husband'. She remembered his thoughtfulness when he had said, 'I think I may have just the man.' Talk about keeping it in the family! And now, on his first morning back, Sebastian was putting his peculiar plan into action. Natasha felt hurt that his feelings for her had not prevented him from pursuing such a project, however, she committed to play along with Sebastian's plot for, God knows, she needed something to distract her from her increasing obsession with the married man standing in front of her.

"Well Sebastian, I can't wait to meet him. He sounds gorgeous." she exclaimed, in a tone that dripped defiance.

Natasha then flung back her head, crossed her arms and sat down, in her recently vacated seat, with a bump. Her chair was still warm from Sebastian. Huffing, she leaned over to the waste-paper bin, picked out the large book then banged it down onto her desk. She opened it up where she had left off and, with a deliberately riveted expression, she began to read. Sebastian watched her little performance, patiently, without saying a word. Once she was settled, he leaned down behind her, placed his arms gently around her shoulders and whispered, with assurance, into her ear:

"Oh, he is Natasha, he is. How could I offer you anything less?"

Sebastian held this intimate position, for a moment. She could feel his warm breath brush the side of her neck. Involuntarily, she felt herself dissolve into him, at which point, Sebastian ripped himself away and disappeared. Three-hours of reading about the time value of money, yield measures, yield curves, duration, convexity and how to calculate the 'clean' and 'dirty' price of a bond, gave Natasha ample time to cool her temper. When Sebastian was back at her desk at twelve o'clock her heart leapt with joy. Without discussion, he suggested simply: "Lunch?"

Before she knew it, Natasha was standing next to him, in the lobby, waiting for a lift. Indeed, why had she been upset with him in the first place? He was only running with the plan of which he had informed her, after all. He was just trying to prevent the pair of them from acting on the powerful feelings they felt for one other, in order not to jeopardize his marriage. There was nothing wrong with that, in fact, it was a most responsible course of action. What is more, Bruno sounded fascinating.

"PING!" They stepped into the lift and, as it descended, her mind went into overdrive. In truth, Natasha could not imagine an offence Sebastian could commit that would cause her to forfeit one moment of time that she could spend with him. Now she came to think about it, setting her up on a date with a tall, dark, handsome, available, rich relation was bloody considerate. By the time the lift had reached the ground-floor, Natasha's mood had been elevated to cloud nine: "PING!"

"Natasha, follow me, there's somewhere I want to take you." Sebastian said, softly.

That is precisely what she did. It was a spectacular summer's day and the bright sunshine warmed Natasha's back and comforted her face, while the light breeze blew her hair around, haphazardly. Soon enough, they had taken the short walk to a gigantic covered market.

"Well Natasha, here we are: Spittalfields Market." Sebastian announced, with affectionate fanfare. "It's so close to where we spend our days, but so very different. I just love coming here. I wanted to share it with you." As he spoke he sought eye contact, as if to seek her approbation.

"Thank you." she whispered, touched.

Sebastian seemed relieved. Only then did he walk under one of the massive arched openings and into the gigantic airy, high-ceilinged, covered market that so effectively facilitated the yellow sunlight to flood it, cheerfully. The sheer magnitude of the structure pulled one's attention skyward; to precipitate a gasp of appreciation, as one frolicked in its vastness. In this posture, they strolled silently, side by side, admiring the expansiveness of the space. Sebastian visibly relaxed, then he drew a deep breath, pulled his shoulders back and puffed out his chest, to stand even taller than before. Then he explained:

"Oh Natasha, I so love it here. Every time I come, it feels like I have escaped some oppression from which I didn't know I was suffering. It has such a liberating energy. It is so much more, so much more... creative?"

Sebastian nodded in answer to his own question and his energy field continued to expand. The bronzed man began to glow. Natasha struggled to rip her attention away from him, however, she forced herself to look around the scene in order to untangle the details of the place that so fascinated her Love. There were creative textile offerings, in every material and all varieties of colour, laid out for sale, draped over patterned, or dark velvet cloths that prettily masked the ugliness of the collapsible, metal stall tables beneath. The stalls were set up in several long rows and multifarious people drifted like floodwater down the wide aisles. They milled around in trance-like states, touching, viewing and tasting all that was openly displayed. A man was singing a sad ballad with which Natasha was unfamiliar, while he strummed its slow chords on his guitar. The sound reverberated in the grand space to define a mood of deep longing.

Then Natasha's nose filled with the enchanting aroma of hot spices, originating from the little kitchen trailers where food, from all over the world, was being prepared, swiftly: Indian, Lebanese, Greek, Chinese, Thai. Natasha wondered if the fat bearded man was scoffing from such take-away cartons, at this very moment, as he sat at his desk mesmerized by electronic screens. The steaming, hot dishes proffered themselves with warm inviting colours and delicious smells, tempting passers-by to indulge in their exotic flavours for lunch.

They turned the corner to amble slowly down another wide aisle. Here they found hoards of cardboard boxes, stacked high with scruffy, dog-eared second-hand, hard-back books. In the next aisle, Natasha paused to study the intricate, artistic designs that decorated quirky handmade lamps, bookends, ashtrays, eggcups and side-tables, ideal for brightly cluttering any home. Then they moved through the picture stalls, which displayed scenes of nudes, ranging greatly in size and quality. Natasha admired some of the more tasteful ones, while no one could ignore the virtually pornographic ones that Sebastian stopped to study with a disbelieving grin. There were other pictures too: land-scapes, still life and country sporting scenes, depicting fox-hunting, horse-racing, fishing and shooting. The art was not necessarily of the highest quality but, in aggregate, it managed to enliven the most reluctant aesthete.

Natasha then noticed the array of private shops and res-taurants that supported the high roof to enclose this market space. The shops sold clothes, large canvases of quality art, rugs, antiques and even some African artifacts. The brim-ming restaurants fed the hungry City-workers and queues were developing outside the most popular establishments. Here, one could choose from an even more international spread of food to include: Spanish, Japanese, French, Pol-ish and Russian. This image feast was a great tonic for Natasha following the hours she had spent staring at words, numbers and formulae on screen or page. Suddenly, the possibilities of life multiplied before her with each new sensory stimulus. She had only devoted a few hundred hours of her life to the visual depravation of a trading floor, while Sebastian had devoted more than ten years of his; no wonder this audio, visual and odorous patchwork of expe-rience provided him with such joy.

Natasha looked at him again. She was certain, he had changed colour. Yes, he had been tanned after his sailing trip, but now his skin seemed lit from within, as if ignited by a spiritual luminosity. Then our heroine's nose twitched, in happy recognition, and she grinned like a thrilled child, for she could smell pancakes. Sebastian drew them to a halt in front of a makeshift kitchen stall, where an old man was dribbling a ribbon of batter onto a big, round, dark brown, piping hotplate. Then he declared, with boyish enthusiasm:

"Let's have pancakes!" While holding his arms wide open, at which point, the old man flipped over the one he was making, as if to tempt them further as Natasha chimed:

"I love pancakes."

"Me too and I've not had one in years. In fact I am going to have two. I'm ravenous."

"Well, why ever not? I would not wish to stand between a man and his appetite."

"Pancakes it is then!"

Sebastian asked the man, sweating behind the hotplate, if there was anywhere they could sit, to be directed with a jerk of his head to some garden furniture nearby.

"I'll send a girl over." he added gruffly.

Satisfied, they went to sit down.

"Pancakes in Spittalfields Market, with Natasha, oh, what fun!" Sebastian exclaimed.

Natasha eyed him cautiously. He was still looking far too pleased with himself, and she inquired, suspiciously:

"Well Sebastian, I must say you are remarkably jolly today. Is this the effect of turning thirty-five, or are you really so fond of pancakes?"

"No, Natasha, and don't play dumb. You know exactly why I am so bloody jolly today. Do you just want to hear me say it?"

"Say what?"

Natasha's eyes widened, with anticipation, while her pretty mouth struggled to suppress a joyous smirk. Sebastian stared at her, accusingly, from under raised brows. Without uttering a single word, the steeliness of his expression sharply communicated this one: behave! Enjoying herself immensely, Natasha tilted her chin down and wiggled her head, from side to side, to indicate that she attended his reply. Sebastian fast relented and blurted:

"Have it your way Natasha" before he paused, and then allowed three little words to escape, through a helpless sigh, "I love you."

Hearing these three little words from this one big man made Natasha's heart detonate with joy! Sebastian continued to delight her as he repeated:

"I love you. I love you. I love you. I am so bloody jolly today because you make me feel that way."

"Moi?" Natasha goaded.

"Toi!" Shaking his head he recalled in disbelief, "I was sitting in the sunshine on my favourite sailing boat, in one of my favourite places, surrounded by my favourite people and all I could think of was you."

Sebastian studied her, for some time, as if trying to decipher why she had such a powerful affect on him, before he confessed, in defeat, "The only place in the whole world I wanted to be, was with you. That, my dear, is insane. You, my dear, are driving me insane."

Natasha swallowed whole this heartfelt compliment, for which she had so successfully angled. The feast was so satisfying that by the time the young, bored, blonde waitress lolled over to their table, Natasha did not want to eat. Clearly, Sebastian craved more tangible sustenance than love, for he ordered two pancakes, as he said he would, along with a bottle of still mineral water. Natasha just ordered a double espresso. Only once she had promised to share Sebastian's lemon and sugar pancake, was the sullen waitress allowed to leave, with the stern instruction to bring two forks.

As soon as she was gone, the couple leaned over the table to clasp each other's hand in a knot of fingers. Their eyes locked. Helplessly, Natasha's increasingly predictable soul journey began. She was sucked into the awe-inspiring ubiquity contained in the blackness of Sebastian's pupils.

He too seemed to reap the same spiritual fix from Natasha, for the pair of them became stupefied by heady bliss. The external world was ignored, merely a superfluous stall-cloth, existing only to present the priceless truth to be discovered in each other's gaze. Never before had Natasha played such a scene. Until now, she had believed the image of 'mesmerized lovers' only occurred in cartoons, yet here she was, transfixed by a man she had met just over a week ago, by a man she had not even kissed properly, by a man who was, tragically, unavailable.

Their intense communion was broken, only when the waitress returned with a laden tray. She put the food and drinks onto the table and then left without a word. Natasha downed her coffee while Sebastian poured them each a glass of mineral water, before tucking into his bulging chicken and asparagus pancake. Natasha began to look around, to find the market was more crowded now and there was an increase in rowdiness. Long lines were starting to form outside some of the restaurants and a more familiar City vibe of impatience was developing. Soon bored by everything but Sebastian, Natasha turned her attention back to him and probed:

"I do hope you are not just toying with me Sebastian?" He stopped chewing, for a moment, and looked at her, questioningly. Natasha continued, "It's just sometimes, I get this vision of you as a mad scientist, dressed in a white coat, picking up a little mouse, viz. me, in order to enact some bizarre psychological experiment."

"I wonder what could possibly have given you that idea, Natasha?"

"Possibly the fact that you declare love for me at lunchtime, having engineered a date for me with another man this morning - a relation no less!"

"Hmmm," Sebastian sounded before finishing his pancake in pensive silence. He then leaned back in his chair, wiped his mouth with the paper napkin and smiled, contentedly, as he nodded with approval, "yes, my little mouse... I like that. You, Natasha, can be my little mouse."

Natasha did not appreciate him embracing such an image of her, so readily, and she sought to caution him.

"Please, remember, Sebastian, cats have been known to choke on mice."

"Well then, is it not just as well that you cast me as a scientist, not a cat, Natasha?"

Realizing she had screwed-up her warning, Natasha huffed with displeasure and chose to ignore Sebastian's impertinent question. Instead, she took a long gulp of her water, as if to wash back down the ill-considered words that had been so disloyal to her intention. Then the charmless waitress arrived with Sebastian's pudding and cleared his plate. For the remainder of lunch, Natasha was more guarded. They shared the sweet pancake in calm silence.

Finishing up, Sebastian paid and they walked back in the direction of the office, indiscreetly, arm in arm. As they crossed the blustery expanse of Exchange Square, he stopped to break away, and made an announcement:

"Well my darling one, I'm off to my club now to have a quick steam."

Taken aback by his abrupt plan for departure, Natasha tried to control her disproportionate reaction.

"Enjoy." she replied, expressionlessly.

Then she quickly looked away. With arms crossed, head bent and eyes fierce, she began to walk back to the office, alone. Painful feelings welled up inside her. It was as if something precious had just been snatched away from her. Sebastian did not move. He just watched her strangely diminished figure descend the wide outdoor steps that led off the square and back to Broadgate Circus.

Natasha's mind was whirring out of control, and her unaccountable emotional distress had caused a fat lump to lodge in her throat for, despite Sebastian's exquisite love declaration, the minute he had grasped the 'mouse' image something had changed. Was this really all just an amusing game to him? She remembered their 'intimate friends' conversation, in the Directors' dining-room. Natasha was certain that he had played that scene many a time before, but today, confounded by bliss from just looking into each other's eyes? Could there really be any point or pleasure in such pursuit, unless he felt as heavenly as she?

Her head ached now; too much ecstasy, too much sugar and now this doubt and confusion. By the time Natasha had reached the office, she had committed to thinking no more of Sebastian. Instead, she was determined to read the rest of that fascinating book about finance, which Sebastian had forbidden, in order to gain a thorough understanding of bond maths and the credit markets by five-thirty! No, really, she was just fine. Or was that FINE: Fucked-up, Irrational, Neurotic and Emotional?

Chapter Five - The blind date

It was six-twenty on Thursday evening. Natasha had just stepped out of the shared shower, which was situated half a landing down from her bedsit. She wrapped a fluffy white towel around herself, before grabbing another one to put her hair up in a turban. As she walked back to her room, leaving damp footprints on the red carpet as she went, her thoughts turned to what she might wear for her date with Bruno Monmouth. Strangely, she was rather excited and, unsurprisingly, quite nervous. She had never had a blind date before, let alone with the cousin of the man with whom she was in love. Bruno's words 'dress warmly' kept echoing in her head.

What on earth did he have in mind? Summer was still obligingly in evidence, and though it was beginning to get chillier at night, it could hardly yet be described as cold. What on earth is a girl to wear on a date in late summer, when the firm instruction given was to 'dress warmly'? As she pondered this dilemma, her mother's words came to her rescue, 'Layers dear, always wear layers to be prepared for extreme temperature variables.' Her mother was especially fond of this homespun adage on family ski trips. With this advice at the forefront of her mind, she opened her wardrobe doors to survey her options.

Natasha wanted to appear 'feminine', avoid the sin of looking 'tarty', yet achieve a potent dose of 'tastefully sexy' while managing to dress warmly at the same time. Natasha soon determined that such a feat was more daunting than the Black-Scholes' option pricing model! She shot a glance at her bedside clock. It was six twenty-five. Natasha had to get a move on. Decisively, she extracted a pair of close-fitting chocolate jeans, a fitted, brown, cream and raspberry patterned Moschino silk top, and a pair of cocoa-coloured Prada kitten heeled sling-backs, with cream piping, from her wardrobe. She laid her outfit out on the bed. Then she provided the 'warmly' component by pulling out a cream, cashmere polo-neck jumper from her chest of drawers before, once again, scrambling in the bottom of her wardrobe to find a, slightly crushed, Prada handbag that matched her shoes. Having done so, she unwrapped her hair and gave it a vigorous towel drying, before brushing it, as she eyed the displayed ensemble with approval.

Once dressed, she blow-dried her hair before applying some make-up, always a little more heavily for the evening. Finally, she stuffed her little handbag with essentials, picked up her cashmere jumper and, just as she was checking herself in the full-length mirror on the back of her wardrobe door, the intercom sounded. He was early. Hesitantly, Natasha answered, "Bruno?"

"The very same." his friendly voice replied.

"I'll be down in just a minute."

Quickly, she grabbed her handbag and bolted out of the bedsit. Immediately, doubts began to creep into her mind and she wondered, what on earth she had been thinking to agree to this date in the first place. What did Bruno actually look like, anyway, and where was he taking her? Worse, would he just remind her of Sebastian? Made light by her nervousness, along with the excitement of the unknown, Natasha floated down the three-flights of stairs, as airily as a dandelion seed's gossamer parachute. In no time, she was stepping out onto her top front step and flashing her white teeth in welcome as she exclaimed:

"Bruno!"

Natasha had made a pact with herself not to check him out, straight away, for such an approach would be too obvious, and embarrassing, instead, her plan was to look him straight in the eye, then assess him, discreetly, later on. True to her word, she stared into Bruno's handsome face.

"Natasha!" he boomed, with equal fervour.

Immediately, it was evident Bruno had no qualms about checking Natasha out, for his eyes noted her every detail, with great conscientiousness. His shameless audacity did, however, afford her the luxury of giving him the once over. To each it was clear; they liked what they saw, and Bruno stated, or perhaps overstated, in a hearty baritone:

"My cousin told me that you were 'stunning' Natasha and, by God, he was right!"

Self-consciously, she looked down at her pretty shoes for she felt uncomfortably 'on show.' What is more, she'd been caught off-guard to find that Bruno wearing full-leathers and carrying a motorbike helmet. He just looked so big, so broad and so black. All of a sudden, Natasha felt unusually shy and girly. She fought her embarrassment and looked up at this big, grinning man, once again.

Sebastian had described Bruno as he was: six-foot five with short dark hair and handsome, in a square-jawed 'Thunderbirds' fashion. His brown eyes were soft and kind yet, despite all of his bravado, they appeared to betray an intrinsic shyness, for he could not hold direct eye contact with her for any length of time, or maybe that was just because he was too busy staring at her body?

Anyway, she liked him at once. He exuded the energy of a person who is open, fun, kind and just plain decent. Natasha had been to university with equally posh boys, however, they were of a younger generation and more interested in going to raves and taking drugs than they were in charming girls. Natasha's male contemporaries were more likely to open the door for their drug-dealer than for their girlfriend. Bruno, on the other hand, was in his late-thirties and his manners were so impeccable they seemed to hail from an old war movie. Natasha would have cast him as the decorated, dashing officer who spoke with a plum in his mouth, habitually displayed extreme physical daring on the battlefield, and yet exhibited great sensitivity to women, while effortlessly exuding an intoxicating sexuality, all the while: in short, a rather compelling package. Well, Natasha was to learn more about that later. Besides, Bruno was a man who just made a girl feel 'safe'. A quality that was to prove to be somewhat misleading by the end of the night!

Without a word, Bruno placed his large hand onto Natasha's waist and escorted her down the front steps to his monster motorbike, before smiling kindly.

"I have a fabulous surprise for you this evening Natasha but, there is one condition, you must not ask me any questions until the surprise has unravelled!" he then announced.

He looked at her, quizzically, to see if she would comply. Her face was full of light as she marvelled at this extraordinary leather-clad man. Without hesitation, she answered, enthusiastically, "Deal!"

Bruno grinned. He instructed her to put on her jumper then he took off his leather jacket and passed it to her and told her to put it on as well. He then relieved her of her handbag and shut it away, safely, in a compartment in the main body of the motorbike. Finally, he handed her the spare helmet and Natasha teased, with preposterously questioning eyes, "Put it on?"

"Gosh, Sebastian was right when he said you were bloody bright." Bruno joked in mock amazement.

Still chuckling, he put on his helmet and then mounted the bike before Natasha clambered on behind him. As soon as Bruno had donned some worn leather gloves, he started the engine and, with a bone-rattling growl, they sped off. He carved through the traffic of West London, at ridiculous speed, while Natasha felt the intense buzz of the engine's vibration from head to toe. She concluded, very quickly, that Bruno's instruction about not asking any questions was rather redundant for this mode of transport, though exhilarating, made conversation impossible. All Natasha could hear was the engine's deafening roar and the thumping of the wind. In sore need of a windbreak, she found herself tucking in behind Bruno's broad back to rest her helmet-wearing head on his shoulder. How immediately physical they were. It felt so natural, yet so odd, to be clutching a strange man, determinedly, around the waist so quickly, however, Natasha's very safety depended on this clinch. What a cunning method for a man to get a cuddle, without the tedious preliminaries of small talk!

As she held his bulk and felt his warmth contrast strongly with the blustering wind they moved against, Natasha rediscovered just how swiftly ease could be established between a man and woman. She began to relax into Bruno and enjoy their closeness. Sitting on this motorbike, happily holding this man, prompted our heroine to reflect on the pitfalls of being single and trying to find a boyfriend worth having. So often, when she liked someone and he liked her back, the linear confines of initial fact-finding conversation would, unintentionally, cascade into a stagnant pond of grave misunderstanding, or worse, a reservoir of perceived insult. Oh, how regularly did the lonely, shy and damaged use words as weapons to protect themselves from any available source of love, intimacy and trust. Natasha sighed as she, silently, thanked Bruno for saving her from herself, for she had not held a man like this for a very long time. It felt good. It made Natasha think of her ex-boyfriend and an unexpected pang of emotion inconveniently pounced, as soon as she realized just how much she missed him. Had she been too hasty in her decision to finish with him? How programmed are we not to appreciate what we have, until it is lost. She blinked away threatening tears. Shockingly, on the back of a speeding motorbike, wrapped around a big bloke, Natasha was struggling to prevent the unthinkable: an emotional breakdown on a blind date!

Appalled, she determined to snap out of her morose, mental meanderings. Instead, she forced herself to focus on the exciting evening ahead. Where were they going? What were they going to do? Well, she knew food was involved, and 'excess' if she remembered correctly. At least the 'dress warmly' riddle was now solved yet, despite Bruno's clear instruction, she had failed to dress warmly enough, and already deprived him of his jacket.

After twenty minutes or so of racing up the M4, Bruno took the required exit then, expertly, slipped around several roundabouts. The smaller roads turned into even smaller lanes and he continued his skilful, intimate embrace of the more challenging curves and bends, the sharpest of which caused the bike to angle, so much so, that the road felt far too close to either one of Natasha's kneecaps for comfort.

She could not imagine at what speed they were travelling but, suffice to say, it was bloody fast. Truth be told, it was thrilling. What on earth had come over her earlier; low blood sugar no doubt, or was she just premenstrual?

They were now driving down a small, sunny, country lane, where the hedges were so high that you could not tell what lay beyond. Bruno had reduced the bike's speed to a bumpy crawl, just before the lane turned into a rutted, dirt track. Clearly, he knew the route intimately. Soon they were presented with a wooden five-bar gate that led into an enormous field of open pasture. Adroitly, Bruno dismounted the bike then opened the gate to wheel the heavy vehicle through, while Natasha shuffled her feet along the dry ground, in an effort to help. He then closed the gate, got back on the bike and was whizzing them cross-country, in the blink of an eye. After the long hot summer, the field was so rutted that the pair of them were flung all over the place. The indignity of being so violently bumped up and down, while clutching onto an equally wobbly Bruno, made Natasha laugh out loud. Whatever would happen next? In no time, they pulled up next to a wide, rippling river. They both got off and Bruno removed his helmet. Our heroine noticed that his hair was slightly wet with perspiration. He ruffled his hand through it, before shaking his head from side to side, briskly, like a wet dog. Bruno's cheeks were ruddy, his eyes fierce and his breathing heavy now. He looked more dashing than ever. Natasha frowned, for she feared her hair would not recover from being squashed as prettily as Bruno's had. Quickly, she whipped off her helmet, flung her head forward and put her hands through her mane, in an effort to resuscitate some vibrancy. When she looked up, she discovered her date suppressing an indulgent smirk, as he comforted:

"Your locks still look perfect to me my dear!"

Embarrassed her vanity had been so apparent, she gave a wry smile, in silent apology, before she started to admire the rolling green, yellow-tinged landscape. The birds were tweeting, the grasshoppers clicking and the river splashing.

There was not a soul to be seen. Bruno had transported her to a peaceful English countryside idyll and it was beautiful. Natasha was charmed, and she inquired:

"Oh Bruno, it's wonderful here. Where are we?"

"We are in a rather private corner of Windsor Great Park. I hoped you'd like it." he explained.

"I love it."

"This is one of my favourite places Natasha, perfect to just get away from it all. I thought it would be fun to bring you here."

Bruno looked at her, hopefully. Natasha felt a stab of guilt. This was the second time this week that a man, from the same family no less, had thought fit to share one of his favourite places with her. Rather than feeling flattered, Natasha just felt ashamed. Had Bruno known of her feelings for his cousin, and Sebastian's plan for them, he would not have been in the mood to share this place with her at all. Natasha searched Bruno's attentive eyes. She wanted to connect with the real man behind the square jaw, black leather and bravado. This time he held eye contact.

"It is truly beautiful Bruno, thank you."

He nodded in gratitude. They stood side by side and stared into the blue, green, and steel rushing-colours of the fast-flowing river, for some time. Much of the remaining evening's mellow light bounced off its undulating surface, and billions of star-flashes of phosphorescence leapt up to offer a veritable banquet of soul-food for the depleted. Natasha suspected she ought to know which river it was, but she did not. Captivated by its ceaseless light-dance, she became convinced it must be the River Thames. She did not wish to shatter the poetry of the moment by exposing her crude ignorance, so she remained silent while discreetly turning to observe Bruno. He was as captivated as she had been. He stood wonderfully tall with his long, leather-clad legs, majestically supporting a 'Y' proportioned torso that was just as impressive as his cousin's, if not more so, for he looked fitter than Sebastian. This sudden vision of this fine man's silhouette against the evening's golden light, promoted a powerful undulation of desire to roll through Natasha. More than disturbed by her evident randiness, she fast averted her gaze to refocus on the river, and thoughts as pure as the water that flowed there. Bruno then coughed politely to re-engage, and then he flashed a dazzling smile at her before announcing, with an enthusiasm as torrential as the river:

"Natasha we are going to have a picnic."

"How wonderful."

She then glanced at the motorbike to try and imagine what type of picnic could fit in such a vehicle; a couple of 'Pret-a-Manger' sandwiches and two cans of coke perhaps? Well, what the hell, it was a charming idea. Natasha was on the verge of sitting down when Bruno commanded:

"Natasha, please wait a moment. Stand exactly where you are, close your eyes and don't move."

He then started to laugh.

"No peeking!" Bruno added, firmly.

"Your wish is my command."

Increasingly seeped in intrigue, obediently, Natasha shut her eyes and waited. First she heard him walking away. Then, for what seemed like ages, all she could hear was the sound of the river, a few birds chirping lazily, and the rattling of insects; no Bruno. For the first time, Natasha felt terribly vulnerable. What the hell was she doing standing in a field with her eyes shut, relying on a total stranger? She began to admonish herself for her stupidity. Could this be some horrible joke? Could it be possible that Sebastian had got his cousin to drop her off, in a remote spot, and abandon her there for fun? That would not be any fun at all, but it may ensure that she fell out of love with Sebastian! Becoming fretful, and annoyingly thinking about the wrong man, Natasha was about to open her eyes when, suddenly, she heard some rustling in the bushes. At least it was not the roar of a powerful engine! No, she was being paranoid. She must learn to have a little faith.

Comfortingly, Natasha heard more. It sounded like a heavy object was being dragged towards her. Nothing from

Pret-a-Manger was that heavy except for the furniture. It seemed she had underestimated Bruno. The dragging came to a halt next to her. She could hear his breathing, heavy now from his exertions. Then she heard the sound of light metal clinking, followed by a quiet creaking. Bruno was opening something, and he repeated, with strictness:

"No peeking Miss Flynn."

Natasha continued to wait, with eyes closed, for what felt like an eternity. At least this time there was plenty of action. She heard the clinking of plates and glasses, some rustling of what may be plastic, the clanging of metal, and then what sounded like a couple of match strikes. Finally, Natasha heard a very welcome 'pop.'

Ah, champagne, her favourite!

"Natasha, now you may open your eyes." Bruno announced, as if speaking to an excitable child.

When she did, the first thing that came into focus was a fine crystal champagne flute, full of bubbly the colour of honeycomb. Bruno was holding it towards her, grinning proudly as he did so. Eagerly, she took it and they toasted, happily, to elicit a delicate clink of such fine pitch that it paid perfect testament to the quality of Bruno's crystal!

"Cheers Natasha." he growled, huskily.

"Cheers."

Then they each took thirsty sips of their fizzing drinks.

"This is my favourite peach champagne Natasha. What do you think?"

"Bruno you spoil me, this is absolutely superb. As a matter of fact, my favourite cocktail is a Bellini and this is even finer, more delicate."

"And stronger may I add. Anyway I'm glad you like it, for had you not, I would have had to drink the whole bottle by myself!"

"In which case, you may well have preferred had I not liked it!"

"Not at all, not at all. I am driving, if you recall."

They laughed and continued to enjoy their drinks as Natasha turned her attention to the picnic. At her feet, she discovered a truly impressive feast laid out on a dark green and yellow tartan blanket. The more she looked at it, the more astounded she became by the meticulous presentation and quality. There were two Wedgewood, blue dragon patterned, bone china plates with diamonds of foie gras terrine surrounded by little crustless squares of golden toast. On several serving plates of the same design, she found quails eggs, king prawns and slices of smoked salmon, fully garnished with lemon, finely chopped egg yolk, egg white, onion, capers and parsley. She then spotted a large, intricately engraved, silver bowl brimming with glistening, black caviar that had the handle of a small silver spoon sticking out of its luxurious wetness. Finally, there were two enormous, light, white swirls of meringue topped with deep, purple-red raspberries and giant, juicy strawberries, all laced with a copious mound of whipped cream.

There was more. Next to the blanket was an engraved silver ice bucket, in which there was an open bottle of champagne, along with an unopened bottle of white wine and, snuggled next to that, a silver candelabrum holding three candles, the flickering flames of which danced prettily in the still, August evening air. She was awestruck by the scale of the feast laid out before her. Indeed, Natasha's own father had never made as much effort for her in her lifetime, as this candid stranger had done this night.

Bruno then knelt down and, using a small garden trowel, he started to dig a little hole. When he had finished, he began to stack the thick dry twigs, which had been sitting in a box next to the blanket, into a pyramid. Natasha looked on in wonder. Having prepared what was soon to be a little fire, Bruno looked up at her, with his big brown eyes, and explained, "What is on the rug is to start and to finish with. For our main course I am going to cook a Thai duck red curry. I hope you're hungry."

By which point Bruno was laughing with embarrassment for, now that everything was laid out, he suspected that he might have been a little too lavish.

"I'd better be!" Natasha fired, while trying to stifle giggles, before she failed to do so and the couple's rippling laughter rolled out across the meadow.

Infected by mirth, their eyes met and they exchanged a flirtatious glance. Bashful, Bruno looked away to refocus on the fire. He lit two waxy firelight cubes and put them underneath the wood, before he bent down and blew on the fledgeling flames to coax robust licks of yellow, red and orange fire to rise and make the wood take light. It began to burn properly, just in time, for the sun was about to set. Satisfied, Bruno stood, refilled their champagne flutes and then raised his as he toasted, happily:

"To our picnic, to our evening and to each other."

Natasha smiled and nodded, demurely, then they both took a sip of their champagne, before making themselves comfortable on the unoccupied corners of the blanket.

"Bruno, please tell me, how on earth did you managed to arrange such a feast in the middle of a field in Windsor Great Park?" Natasha felt compelled to ask, having examined the picnic at close quarters.

Bruno laughed, his face bursting with pride.

"Natasha, let's just leave it at this, I have a little chap called Jack who, on occasions, can be extremely useful." he confessed, modestly.

"You mean to say someone else did all of this for me? Surely I should be having dinner with him, if it is he who made all of the effort?"

"Not all of the effort Natasha!" Bruno objected slapping his thigh as he did so, before elaborating, "Everything you see before you, I chose, I bought, I prepared and I laid out. All of the details of this evening are mine. I packed our picnic into a large hamper and arranged for Jack to deliver it to an agreed location nearby, not so very long ago. I will also be relying on Jack to collect this lot when we're done." Then, looking more serious, he continued, "If, however, you still feel that I have not done enough to deserve the pleasure of your company this evening, then I am prepared, but highly reluctant, to call Jack and he can come and take over from here. What do you say?"

Natasha looked into the fire as if in deep contemplation. Bruno then cautioned, "Before you make your decision, Natasha, I feel duty bound to inform you that Jack is fifty-eight years old, of great use around an estate and happily married with two teenage children. So, what's it to be?"

Natasha paused, reflectively, before replying:

"Having been made fully aware of the facts, I am pleased to inform you Bruno, that I would be delighted to spend the rest of this fine evening with you, and leave Jack to his wife!"

"Fabulous!" Bruno exclaimed, before handing her a plate with a knife and fork wrapped in a navy blue linen napkin. "Please, do start."

And start they did. Clearly, Bruno was ravenous and he soon polished off his foie gras before tucking into the seafood. Once Natasha tasted the delicious food, the ensuing extent of her appetite surprised her. The caviar was particularly fine, and Bruno explained it was Iranian. Soon enough the champagne was finished and Bruno cracked open a bottle of Chassagne Montrachet. Once they had worked their way through their starters, Bruno went about cooking their main course over the open fire. Natasha was more than impressed to find that the curry with which she was presented, matched any she had enjoyed at the best Thai restaurants in London. Gosh, what a remarkably talented chef Bruno was.

During the course of this amazing evening, Bruno and Natasha ate like kings, drank like lords and chatted as compulsively as mothers at the school gate. Natasha was to discover that Bruno had not had a serious girlfriend for over six months. He felt that to be an exceptionally long time and he was more than ready for one now. He explained that he had split up with his last girl friend, because they had been dating for over a year and he knew he did not want to marry her. He clarified that it was not because he was not ready for marriage 'per se', but because he knew he did not want to marry that individual. Having realized that, he thought it only fair to let her go, so she could find someone who did. He was careful to explain, with eyebrows raised in grave concern:

"She was in her mid-thirties you know."

Natasha thought that very noble of Bruno, however, when she discovered the extent of his ex-girlfriend's heart-break (she was still to be found recovering at a Buddhist retreat in Bodh Gaya) she doubted that his ex held the same view! Then it was Natasha's turn to share her recent romantic history. She told Bruno that she had finished with her long-term ex-boyfriend from university almost a year ago and, to be frank, it had taken her that long to get over him. Yes, she had been the one who had ended the relationship, but that does not make it any easier you know. Why had she ended it? Well, after three years they had become greater friends than lovers and she was far too young, or maybe naïve, to give up on the dream of 'great lovers.' Natasha, much like Bruno, had wanted more. Yes, she had had the courage to give up something 'good', driven by the instinct that something 'great' was possible. And yes, she may well have underestimated just how hard it is to say goodbye to something 'good' when something 'great' has not yet, and might never, materialize. Yet she could not help but believe that something 'great' never came along, while one contented oneself with something 'good.'

"Am I making any sense?" Natasha checked, in earnest.

And, gosh, Bruno thought she was making perfect sense. Or at least that is what he told her. He too, was convinced that she had done the right thing, for now her ex-boyfriend was free to find someone who thought being with him was 'great' rather than just 'good.' In fact, what similar experiences they had had! What, he had been heart-broken too? Oh, so similar. Yes of course, of course it was painful, but certainly for the best.

"More wine?" he questioned.

"Oh Bruno, you spoil me." she replied.

Then Natasha tipped her glass towards him and Bruno topped it up until, soon enough, the bottle of wine was finished as well. As luck would have it, however, Bruno happened to have a second one, wrapped in an ice jacket, just in case. Was there no end to this man's foresight? Having covered the 'where are you currently standing on the romantic front', to mutual satisfaction (each of them so principled), the conversation fast moved on to careers. Natasha was to learn that Bruno had his own private equity fund, because he found it to be 'so much fun.' She soon deduced it was not financial need that drove Bruno to work as hard as he did. He just loved it. He had studied P.P.E. at Oxford then worked in corporate finance, for a few years, before starting his own company almost five years ago. As luck would have it, it was now doing 'remarkably' well!

Natasha then talked a little about her new job. How she enjoyed the challenge, but the early starts were punishing. She confessed that she was not yet actually doing anything, but she looked forward to getting fully qualified, so she could start to do the job for which she had been hired, and then discover if it was any 'fun' or not. As she spoke these words, Natasha realized just how much she wished that the only reason she went to work were because it was 'so much fun', for what an enchanted life that must be to live.

By the time they had finished the curry, all the natural daylight had vanished as completely as Natasha's mental faculties. The picnic had been demolished, and now the decadent scene was lit only by the flickering candlelight, the orange glow from the fire and the milky moonlight, cast by a sliver of a crescent moon, which crowned the velvet blackness of the night like an exquisite tiara.

Following much persuasion, and more wine, Natasha even managed pudding. Meringue and summer berries were her favourite, after all. By five-past eleven, moonlight, candlelight, too much amazing food, even more fine alcohol and Bruno, had all taken their effect on our heroine. Natasha gave a deep sigh and shifted her position to recline lazily onto her side at the edge of the blanket. She propped her head up on her hand and looked into Bruno's kind face. Artlessly, her pose only served to accentuate her slim waist and well-proportioned curves. Natasha may well have been oblivious to this fact, or to most things by this point, but the display of such curvaceous lines, prompted Bruno's sexuality to scorch as hot as the flames that warmed them. His eyes darted all over her physique, more attentively than traders do their screens. Natasha was tired and tipsy, while her green eyes had become long and narrow in her repose. Bruno, on the other hand, was becoming increasingly animated. His body was coiled like a spring, as if poised to strike. As the chill night air began to wrap around our couple, Bruno was inspired to wrap himself around Natasha. In an instant, he skilfully executed some swift ground manoeuvres, to culminate in his lying snugly behind our torpid heroine. Once positioned thus, he draped his heavy arm over Natasha's waist accompanied by some apologetic mumblings of "Just to help keep you warm." Then he tugged her into his body, assertively. This swift and successful enterprise made it clear that Bruno's faculties were in much better shape than Natasha's, as did the enormous, turgid erection bursting out of his leather pants and poking her in the bum!

The shock of this unexpected invader jolted Natasha from her languorous state. She froze, her eyes now wide with fright. Bruno held her tightly as he began to nudge his erect penis into the fullness of her bottom, suggestively. As surprised as she was, Bruno's driven, vital, sexual energy began to envelop her. Natasha was foxed to discover her shock fast metamorphose into animalistic lust. As Bruno's thrusts became more and more bold, without forethought or design, Natasha found herself, instinctively, begin to push back against his pulsating protrusion and, in no time, her genitals began to throb with want. It was evident Natasha had denied herself erotic pleasure for far too long, for she felt like she was ready to blow. Indeed, if Natasha had been a kettle, she would have been whistling louder than a gale force wind!

Bruno was most encouraged by her responsiveness and he gripped her ever more tightly. He began to nibble her ear as he continued to nudge his penis into her rhythmically. Natasha gasped, surrendering further to his passion. Bruno was panting now and he began to play with her ear-lobe, first licking, then biting it, to send shock waves of titillating electricity along her neck and around the base of her head. The consequent rushes were delicious. Bruno's hand was now pressed flat against her stomach to keep her tightly clinched to him. His thrusts had become more like the undulating rolls of a stormy sea and he was becoming increasingly breathless.

In a flash, he slipped his large hand under, then up, her top to grasp her breast firmly. Recklessly, he ripped her bra away and Natasha heard the delicate lace fabric tear. Flesh on flesh contact was achieved and Bruno began to squeeze and massage her breasts. Natasha trembled with the intensity of it. Her nipples were erect, crying out for attention. Her breath quickened to match his. Bruno peppered his massaging with forceful nipple tweaking, first one, then the other, to the point that touched pain. Natasha yelped but craved for more. Her vagina began to contract with longing, for it yearned to hold the large member that burrowed into her from behind. Her body began to writhe against Bruno, and her urgent urgings demanded she enjoy Bruno's gigantic readiness now!

Natasha's breathing was fast and shallow and her tummy muscles oscillated with the acuteness of her scorching lust. She arched her back against him, each inch of her flesh pining for his touch. The determined rhythm of Bruno's motion and the hot intimacy of his breath against Natasha's neck, continued to draw her extreme desire. Natasha wanted to rip off all her clothes and free Bruno's cock from its confinement NOW! Natasha wanted Bruno inside her NOW! Natasha wanted to push him to the ground and mount him NOW! Natasha wanted the wide girth of Bruno's cock to stretch the wet walls of her cunt and ride him vigorously until dawn: NOW!

As Natasha's long neglected sexual desires made their adamant demands for immediate satisfaction, her mind was seized by a torturous spin. How had she found herself in such a position? How had she come to be so hijacked by sexual chemistry a.k.a. Bruno? Did the three bottles of booze have anything to do with it? Either way, Natasha could not work out how Bruno, so quickly, had brought her to the point where she just wanted to rip off his clothes and fuck his brains out! But then again, what a 'compelling package' indeed, Natasha would defy any woman to resist! So much for making a woman feel safe. As Bruno's teeth teased her earlobe, his hands grasped her breasts and his penis pounded into her bottom, it seemed nothing could be further from the truth!

Despite her arousal, stubborn, confused thoughts of resistance continued to plague her. She had made no conscious decision to have sex with this man, this night. She was not in the habit of sleeping with a man she had just met. She did not want to fuck someone she hardly knew. How could she possibly have sex with Sebastian's first cousin? She could not do this. She did not want this. How was she to extricate herself from this sexual fervour? After all of the effort he had made for her, the last thing she wanted to do was offend him. How was she to extract herself from this clinch with some degree of elegance? If it all went horribly wrong, how the hell was she going to get home? As Natasha's foggy mind raced, as swiftly as her pulse, Bruno continued to successfully stimulate her body and it continued to crave full penetration NOW! Suddenly, Bruno pushed Natasha down onto her back. He climbed on top of her. They were off the blanket now and Natasha could feel the cool grass beneath her. She felt the deep primeval draw of mother earth. Bruno was kissing her forcefully, the weight of him crushing her made her feel even more desirous. His strong hands continued to stroke, then grasp, her breasts. Natasha could feel his erection throbbing beneath the leather. Bruno slid his hands underneath her back and undid her damaged bra. He pushed her top all the way up, to expose her alabaster breasts to the night. He gasped at the sight, then lunged down to take one of her nipples into his wet mouth as he pinched the other one, hard, between his fingers. Natasha's desire was accelerated. Her resolve to resist was obliterated by her pleasure. Craven, she brought his mouth to hers and began to kiss him as passionately as he kissed her. She cradled his head lovingly between her hands. He still tasted of the sweetness of the meringue. Lips devoured, saliva lubricated tongues intertwined while Bruno's feverish hands explored Natasha's body. Suddenly, his hand was fiddling with, then undoing, her jeans. He shoved them, along with her knickers, far down her soft white thighs to expose her engorged, red-pink sex. Gently, he began to stroke and probe her clitoris, taking his time to tease juice from her. Delighting in the slippery wetness that was so fast concocted, Bruno thrust two of his fingers up into the warm silkiness of her. He gasped, with exquisite pleasure, when he discovered more sweet syrup lodged there. He pulled his fingers from her to take them into his hungry mouth. He sucked them, adoringly, to taste her, moaning with happy approval as he did so. At last, he returned to stimulate her excruciatingly sensitive female button. He played more with her there, delicate and teasing at first, then boldly thrusting his fingers back into her to draw even more sweet juice, to lubricate her cunt to perfection. She was so wet now, yet Bruno was relentless. Mercilessly, he dominated her clitoris, until she could have cried out with the itching intensity of it: MORE, MORE, MORE, MORE and then, and then, and then, and then, at last, with a raspy gasp of exquisite relief, Natasha came and came and came, her cum flowing as freely as the river. Natasha's upper thighs became drenched with her secreted delight. The wetness of her legs glistened, enticingly, in the darkness, to reflect the inviting warmth of the fire's ochre light.

Bruno was beside himself with passion. Natasha's exposed, glistening pussy, begged deep penetration. Frantically fumbling, gasping all the while, Bruno undid his leather trousers and shoved them down over his toned bottom. Finally, his enormous erection was released and it reared up to be admired. Natasha was dazzled by it. With fast and shallow breath, Bruno looked down at his impressive, throbbing cock and lined himself up to penetrate her. The moment when his fat penis would slide into Natasha's silkiness was less than a second away. The wet walls of her vagina ached to be filled and stretched by him. She felt the impossibly soft skin of his penis' helmet touch her impeccably lubricated labia. Oh, how much she wanted this! Oh, how much she craved this! Yet, as much as she did, suddenly, Natasha became stricken with panic. She could not allow this. She could not sleep with her boss' cousin on their first date. How could she ever look at Sebastian again? Throbbing genitals aside, this had to stop: NOW!

In a decisive twist of fate, Natasha pulled her face away from Bruno's kisses and, concurrently, pushed him away from her, determinedly, with both hands.

"Bruno! Stop! I can't sleep with you!" she screeched.

So much for elegance...

The only person more astonished than Natasha was Bruno. In his highly sexually aroused state, a perplexed Bruno drew away from her, groaning with disastrous disappointment. He remained on top of her with, his arms either side of her head supporting his weight. In this posture, Bruno looked down into Natasha's flushed face. It was brushed by the flickering of the candles' flames. In this meager light, Bruno searched her eyes in profound confusion. When he saw them fraught with fear and shame, all at once, his countenance softened and his pupils dilated with compassion. There was a long pause. Bruno collected himself following such an abrupt turn of events. With a forlorn sigh, he finally rolled off Natasha to lie on his back, on the cold grass. After several seconds, he elevated his bottom, pulled up his trousers, and sternly put himself away for the evening. Bruno then sat up and looked down at Natasha, who was still lying on the ground in silence. Slowly, she began to dress herself.

"Really Natasha, don't worry. I don't want to do anything you don't want to do." he reassured her.

Ashamed that she had allowed things to get so far advanced before making her feelings clear, Natasha looked, apologetically, into his kind eyes.

"I am so sorry Bruno. As much as I am attracted to you, and as much as I want to, it's just too soon."

He nodded with the understanding of a - slightly disgruntled - saint, and then muttered:

"Sebastian did tell me you were full of surprises."

Natasha covered her mouth, in embarrassment.

"I'm so sorry." she mumbled.

Bruno managed a smile.

"Really, no need to apologise, Natasha, it's all my fault. I'm so attracted to you, that I'm afraid that I behaved in an ungentlemanly manner."

Natasha was still lying on the blanket staring up into the midnight blue, star-speckled sky, as she tried to reorientate. An understanding, but rather crestfallen Bruno, slowly, stood up before wandering over to a clump of vegetation. He turned his back to Natasha, dropped his trousers and took a pee. As she admired his beautiful bottom from a distance, strangely, the only thought that went through her mind was, 'I hope someone else's picnic isn't hidden in those bushes'.

And so it was that the tidal wave of Natasha and Bruno's strong sexual chemistry crashed, unfulfilled. When he returned, Bruno was ever chivalrous and he attempted to dissipate the copious foam of awkwardness left in its wake, as he methodically refilled their glasses before making a final toast: "To us!"

Natasha smiled softly at him, with gratitude.

"To Bruno. Thank you for a wonderful evening and, even more so, for your rare understanding."

Having packed up, Bruno dragged the much lighter picnic hamper away, to hide it in the previously designated spot. Then the pair headed back to London and, in a flash more dazzling than Bruno, they were outside Natasha's home. Despite the exhilarating ride, Natasha was tired now and her hands were frozen. Once she had unlocked her front door, she turned to say good night. Without word, or warning, Bruno grabbed her in his arms and, if possible, kissed her even more passionately than he had done in the field. Clearly, the motorbike ride had re-stoked his testosterone levels. Holding Natasha firmly by the shoulders, he looked at her, meaningfully, and said, "Good night Natasha, I can't begin to tell you how much I enjoyed this evening."

"Me too." Bruno kissed her, more gently, one last time and then, reluctantly, let her go and started to walk down the steps. Natasha was quick to cry after him:

"Bruno, your jacket!"

"Keep it. I'll call you at work tomorrow." Then he added, through a smirk, "I've got the number."

Natasha flashed a smile and then waved him off, before making her way up to her bedsit. She was exhausted: physically (not enough sleep), chemically (too much alcohol) and emotionally (too much Bruno). She checked her watch to discover that it was almost one o'clock. Quickly, she calculated that she would get five hours sleep; not great, but doable.

Chapter Six - **A feeding frenzy in TRUTH**

Beyond belief and disbelief
lies the vast expanse of ecstasy
where the mystic lays his head
on the cushion of Truth.

Rumi

When Natasha awoke the next morning, she was surprised to find that she did not have a hangover. Once again,
she was grateful to Bruno; this time, for supplying such
fine quality alcohol. As she stretched, yawned and blinked
the sleep from her eyes, an instinctual anxiety clutched
stubbornly at her chest. What was that about? Natasha felt
so out of sorts this morning that she almost missed the
morning meeting, even though Freddie had told her that so
doing was simply 'not an option'. It started at seven-thirty
yet, when Natasha dumped her handbag on her desk and
grabbed her trade blotter, the time was already nudging
that. When she shot through the meeting-room's open door,
she was more than relieved to find that the meeting had not
yet started. However, her sloppy punctuality drew disapproving glances from several of those present, for such a
close call, from a junior, was most impertinent.

All of the chairs were taken, so Natasha was forced to
sidle up against a patch of wall next to Matt. She shot a
look to her left to find another salesman, called Oliver,
standing the other side of him. The men were both, lazily,
slumped against the wall, with legs crossed at the ankles
and arms folded defensively in front of them. Their mouths
were set in stolid scowls and their overall demeanour was
one of begrudging belligerence. Natasha scanned the room
to find that everyone else's eyes were as bleary as her own
and the general mood sluggish and sombre. The fact it was
a Friday probably contributed to this fact for, everyone
knows, Thursday night is the City boys' 'big night out on
the piss.' Natasha assumed the whole lot of them was horribly hung-over.

Everyone there was male, except for a platinum blonde woman called Keri. She was probably half a dozen years older than Natasha and she appeared to be in better shape than the men. She was pretty, with her hair cut short in a striking bob and a heavy fringe. When Keri was stressed, however, Natasha had noticed that she was prone to a high pink-colour that infected her looks, somewhat, with the hint of country bumpkin. Her laugh was infectious though, so it was hard not to like her. Like Freddie, she hailed from the East End. Keri was always deferential to the men in the team, in fact, to everyone on the trading floor, so when Natasha learnt that Keri was not a graduate, but had managed to progress to the front office from the back office only a year ago, she was not surprised. This feat was no easy task and Natasha suspected that the kind-hearted Freddie Clarke might have had something to do with the girl's elevation. Well that, and the fact she worked like a dog.

Suddenly, Sebastian walked into the room. His eyes alone were bright and alert. He stood at the head of the black, elongated, oval boardroom table. His expression was inscrutable. As soon as Natasha saw him, she identified the root cause of her anxiety. Last night she had almost fucked his cousin, the man billed to rescue her, yet with just one look at Sebastian her heart split with a longing more compelling than the tides for a full moon. Had they been alone together, Natasha would have simply squealed with glee. Ah Sebastian, her heart sang from the rooftops. Oh Bruno, her shame uttered from the gutter.

Suddenly, Sebastian fixed Natasha with a stare so fearsome that it scorched. She had only ever seen him employ such a countenance while trading; never before had she been the recipient. It struck her with admonishment so merciless that Natasha felt like squirming. Did he know what had happened last night? Was he angry? Was he jealous? As the traders and salesmen looked at their boss with expectancy, Sebastian managed to rip his gaze away from Natasha to stare sombrely down at the pristine coral carpet - no filth and coffee stains allowed in meeting-rooms.

Calmly, he collected his thoughts, the ones not about Natasha, and then, in an instant, he held his head up with the poise of an emperor to conduct the meeting and said:

"Good morning."

Not attending a reply, he stared at the floor again and began to pace up and down as he summarised the preceding day's business-activity in minute detail. He informed the assembly of the sizeable bond positions they had bought, or sold, the quantity and the Libor level at which they had traded. Sebastian emphasized the most profitable trades with a view to replicating them, as long as the window of opportunity existed to do so. He then flagged attractive basis swaps and identified a couple of bonds where the option or convertible component was currently mispriced. He urged the company to attempt to source more of these bonds from their clients, so they could swap out the derivative component to create synthetic floating rate notes and, in so doing, monetize the arbitrage.

The jargon he used, and the degree of detail, was intensive and relentless. It was becoming a little more familiar to Natasha, but she had to concentrate hard to work out the meaning of so many unfamiliar words and speech structures. Sometimes, like now, her tired mind just relinquished the effort necessary to make sense of it all and her thoughts drifted off to Sebastian, once again, while butterflies played havoc with her unfed, alcohol-soaked tummy.

Natasha's concentration was retrieved when the voice of the live version of the man she was thinking about, shifted up a gear in volume. Now Sebastian was informing his team members of the results he expected from each and every one of them that day. As he did so, his eyes were liquid bright and his determination more penetrating than acupuncture. When he was done, the atmosphere in the room had been transformed to one of buzzing alertness.

Satisfied, Sebastian handed the meeting over to Freddie. Freddie's dialogue was more anecdotal. He added colour to current market sentiment and conditions. He identified banks (houses) or brokers who had specific axes (interests to sell or buy a specific bond or do a specific combination of trades) and explained where the Desk's appetite fitted in with that market interest. He mentioned a couple of trades he wanted to execute of which Sebastian had not spoken and, finally, he told them about the trades on which he was working, but had not yet closed. When Freddie had finished, each and every sales team member outlined the significant trades they had done the day before, and the important ones they were currently working on closing, as soon as possible.

Natasha's head was dizzy with the sheer quantity of detail it was expected to absorb. Nearly every word spoken was important information that should be retained. So much unfamiliar jargon, spoken so quickly, and for so long, seemed to be the most condensed communication of intelligence that she had ever been expected to memorize. She scrawled down notes on her dealer pad, with no confidence that they would ever be of any use to her.

This meeting happened every morning, whether Sebastian was there or not. When the markets were especially active, they would have two or more meetings a day. This was the forum used to ensure the team communicated efficiently and worked together, with focus, on one common goal: the making of hundreds of millions of pounds worth of money for the bank, in the hope of taking a few million home for themselves at bonus time. It seemed, when there was enough money to play for, human beings were capable of great focus, discipline and productivity. Over time, it would become equally evident that, when there was this much money to play for, financial market participants were capable of great skulduggery as well.

Finally, the morning meeting was concluded and the 'troops' marched back to their desks. As Natasha followed them, she realized that she must still have been pissed when she woke up, for the longer she stayed awake the worse she felt. So much for quality booze! Before starting to scrutinize her computer screens, Natasha turned her attention to a more immediate priority: breakfast. Dumping her pad on her desk, she briskly walked the two hundred yards, or so, to the breakfast room to find a healthy queue, of rather unhealthy men, helping themselves to sausages, bacon and eggs. The couple of women, who were there already, helped themselves to juice, yogurt and fruit. Although as many women are as partial to sausages, bacon and eggs as men, it seemed that such women did not work here. Natasha took her place in the line and began to shuffle down. Like all of the activities on the trading floor, it seemed to possess the same curious forward momentum. She soon helped herself to a glass of orange juice then grabbed the fattest butter croissant she could see for, by now, she was craving starch to absorb the mildly nauseating alcoholic-residue sitting in her stomach. She gave the vending machine coffee a miss. It was just too disgusting to tolerate, especially this morning.

When Natasha returned to her desk, she discovered that Sebastian was sitting in her chair, waiting for her. He was leaning back with his hands behind his head, legs crossed and feet propped up, in front of her computer. He was not wearing his jacket now, just a sky-blue, cashmere round neck jumper, over a white shirt and a blue and pink striped silk tie. His green eyes were wide, and sparkling with devilish anticipation as he welcomed, through a suspicious smirk, "Good morning Natasha."

He then yawned, extravagantly, before springing up in front of her like a jack-in-the-box. Sebastian placed his hands behind his back and leaned forward, until his face was less than an inch away from hers. She felt overwhelmed by his physical proximity. He was glaring at her with an invasive intelligence-seeking look, as if to probe the very pores of her skin. Natasha felt horribly self-conscious. He knew. She just knew he knew. Could Sebastian really fathom her very thoughts, or had he just spoken to Bruno? Had the pair of them laughed at her sluttish, yet awfully gauche, behaviour? Sebastian held his intrusive posture, to Natasha's great disquiet, and questioned, rather menacingly, "Late night was it my dear?"

"Good morning Sebastian and, in answer to your question, I'd say 'moderately'." Natasha nodded once, in agreement with her fair assessment of her bedtime. Then she began to fret, for she feared she must be looking rather rough, to have provoked such a question in the first place.

"Well young lady, I can't say it looks 'moderate' from where I'm standing." he commented, a little cattily Natasha thought, before continuing, "In fact, I suspect there was nothing in the least bit 'moderate' about last night."

Then he just stared at her, with eyes so full of accusation that she nearly blurted out, 'I'm sorry!' Natasha held back her ridiculous impulse, however, but it was too late. Sebastian had just read the sorry dissertation of guilt scrawled across her face. Smiling cynically, he tilted his beautiful head to one side and asked, curiously:

"And how was Bruno, Natasha?"

She refused to be made to feel guilty. She had done nothing wrong. Feeling slightly incensed, she answered with razor-like precision:

"Oh, just as suitable as you promised Sebastian."

With that, Natasha plopped down into her seat and started to switch on her computer screens with great zeal. In any case, she had to escape from the hot, dazzling searchlight of his interrogation. Reluctantly, Sebastian sauntered back to his desk. When he sat down Natasha was delighted to note, out of the corner of her eye, that his legendary focus seemed to have deserted him. For the first time, Sebastian was looking distracted. Now he sat fidgeting behind her, Natasha felt so restless she could have screamed. She had to get out; time to go and get a proper coffee. She stood, picked up her handbag and, just as she was on her way out, the entire team was on to her. Orders came in thick and fast:

"Mine's a large cappuccino." Freddie shouted.

"Make that two." Matt added, curtly.

"Double espresso; short." Oliver slipped in from the right, and then Ed requested, with pointed politeness:

"Natasha, mine's the same please."

Finally, Keri asked, sweetly:

"And another cappuccino, if it's not too much trouble."

Left with little option, Natasha mumbled back:

"OK guys, OK guys, they're on their way."

Natasha soon joined the bustling throng of suited, serious-faced, predominately male City workers as they swarmed over the polished, litter free, stone pavements of Broadgate, like a colony of industrious ants. It was only ten past eight and the light was still fresh, unlike Natasha this morning. Many of these people were just on their way to work. This second wave of suits worked in financial disciplines that demanded a less penal alarm call: corporate financiers, lawyers, personal bankers, logisticians and computer programmers, to name but a few. Splashed sparingly amongst them, one could find some of the most senior figures of the trading floors. These rare specimens were so important that they could keep their own hours. It was a category Mr. Butler had the privilege of joining, when it suited him. Basically, if one made enough money in this business, few were brave or foolish enough to interfere with your method.

Dodging through the human traffic, Natasha dropped down the outdoor staircase into the round well at the heart of Broadgate Circus. She skirted the side of it and went into her favourite coffee shop. Here, not only was the coffee very good, but the charming Italians were very quick at dispensing it. Immediately, she thought of Fabio. After all of the lunches he had bought her, she decided she would get him a coffee too. Besides, she missed his banter. Apart from Freddie, they all seemed much less friendly on Sebastian's trading Desk.

Thankfully, by the time Natasha was on her way back to the office she, finally, felt 'all in one piece' even if it was a reconstituted piece. Indeed, the more she thought about Sebastian's comments earlier, the more enraged she became. It was he who had set her up with Bruno in the first place, so who was he to stand in judgement? If Sebastian coped this badly with her going on a date with a man he wanted her to date, then how the hell was he going to cope with the marriage he planned to broker to the same man? It was ridiculous. Natasha wanted to laugh out loud, at herself yes, but mostly at Sebastian.

When Natasha sauntered back onto the trading floor brandishing a carton filled with hot, cardboard cups, she was no longer reeking of guilt, but of coffee. Not that Sebastian was there to notice. She handed out the drinks to her colleagues then, as soon as she was back at her desk, she was bombarded with screwed up balls of banknotes chucked at her in payment. Matt took the time to pass her a ten-pound note by hand, as he advised, sardonically:

"Take that darlin', you sure aint earnin' wo' I am."

Followed by hoots of laughter from the rest of the Desk. Natasha was mortified to note that even Keri joined in. When she unscrewed the balls of money and counted the cash, she discovered that she had been paid thirty-five pounds for coffees that had cost her less than sixteen. Coffee runs were not all bad then, but as she tucked the notes into her purse, she could not help but lament how everyone on this Desk was more than happy to remind her, and often, that she was just a 'cost to be carried'. Truth be told, Natasha was still recovering from the heated, one-sided exchange she had had with Freddie yesterday, following a big hit he had taken on a trade. As Natasha downed her espresso, Freddie's harsh words returned to haunt her:

"Oy, Natasha, do you have any idea wo' it's costin' me to have you si''in' there at that desk like a bloody lemon? Do you have any comp-re-hension of wo' Bloomberg, Telerate and Reu'ers are chargin' us? Just maintainin' your compu'er systems and the floor space you take up, costs me a fuckin' fortune!"

She had been so taken aback by his unprovoked tirade that she had just stared back at him, open mouthed, until he had been charitable enough to enlighten her.

"'Bout half a million fucking bucks a year, that's wo'! And guess wo'?" Natasha had not been foolish enough to

117

attempt a reply, for Freddie had been on a roll and the fury that fuelled him had nothing to do with her, and everything to do with the money he had just lost and the stress of the expenses the Desk carried daily. Natasha was just the weakest link and, on a trading floor, that meant vulnerable to attack. Freddie had then continued to do just that.

"Si''in' in that desk righ' now, we could hire a bloke who'd actually be making us six mill' a year. Instead, we go' you!" At which point his lip had curled, and he had pointed his fat finger, accusingly, in Natasha's face before repeating, as if there had been any room for doubt:

"You, who's just fuckin' si''in' there, an' costin' me bucket loads!"

When Freddie had finished, Natasha had watched how his furious crimson-face, made his fired-up eyes look an even prettier blue. And to think, he was the one who was supposed to be looking after her! Natasha shuddered and then remembered she must give Fabio his coffee before it got completely cold, besides, she needed cheering up. She stood, and then took the thirty-metre stroll over to his desk to place the small white cardboard cup on top of it, as she leant forward over his shoulder to whisper softly into his neat ear, "For you."

In a flash, Fabio turned to look up at her and, on sight, his scrumptious face lit up. Inspired, he flung his hands into the air and exclaimed happily:

"Ah Natasha, so you have not forgotten me? I hope you know, I am still waiting... and not for coffee."

Natasha just flashed the whites of her eyes and gave him a flirtatious smile, before she put her hands behind her back and flounced off. By the time she got back to her desk, she noticed it was almost eight forty-five. Only nine more hours to go! She frowned for, despite her shocking hangover, she knew she must commit to some productive course of action. Then, suddenly, with that very thought, and perhaps in atonement for yesterday, Freddie's gruff voice came to her rescue, "Oy Natasha, get yourself over 'ere, I've go' somethin' tha' 'ull make use of ya."

Obediently, she made her way to his desk and stood beside him to wait for his instruction. Freddie, however, just continued to stare at his screens and ignore her. After several minutes, she realized that her mere presence was not enough to engage this man's flighty attention, so she cleared her throat and inquired, politely, but wilfully:

"Freddie, how can I help?"

Finally, his gaze landed squarely on her. His round face was not red and angry today, but instead its friendly self. He smiled warmly up at her, compulsively jiggling his left leg up and down, as was his habit. He pulled up a swivel chair next to him then tapped its maroon upholstery with a flat hand. Natasha sat down and Freddie handed her several sheets of paper that had condensed spidery scribbling all over them and said, "Take a look a' vis."

Natasha did so. It looked like a list of bonds, for she recognized coupons and maturity dates. Freddie continued to grin cheekily at her, as if his outburst yesterday had never happened. If only Natasha could forget about it as quickly as he... Freddie then asked cheerfully:

"Na, do ya know 'ow t' work an Excel spreadsheet young lady?" Natasha nodded. "Great, 'ere 's a load o' stuff we bough' yesterday and I won' ya to inpu' all of these babies into our systems. Go' i'?"

Again Natasha nodded, this time rather tentatively, as she looked down at the sheets of paper. She saw odd symbols, numbers and fractions in odd places, assemblies of letters that bore no relation to words, and the only words that were used, were used in entirely unfamiliar contexts. Freddie watched this new girl's face and its storm of expressions, as clouds of confusion, doubt and bemusement passed over her pretty brow. Thankfully, he just smiled and said, encouragingly, "Don't look so worried Natasha, it aint as bad as it looks. I'll show ya wo' means wo', where i' goes and ge' ya star'ed, it's a piece a cake, ya'll see."

Freddie explained that all of the funny letters were 'Bloomberg tickers' (shorthand identifiers for the bonds on the Bloomberg system) and, as suspected, all of the numbers and fractions, were the bond coupons, and the dates, the bond maturities. All Natasha had to do was put the information, exactly as it appeared, onto the Excel spreadsheet. As for the notes, they may not make any sense to her, but the traders knew exactly what they meant and she just had to add them in the 'comments' column, 'ver batum'. For a moment, Natasha wondered why Freddie seemed to be able to pronounce his 't's when saying Latin words, before she was forced to start paying attention as he began to show her, which cells, required what information. True to his word, he sat with her as she entered the details of the first four bonds. The job was as billed: easy, but utterly boring. One just had to be very precise with the details. Once Freddie was satisfied she understood, he left her to it, assuring her that it was the best way to familiarise herself with their product. Natasha was conscientious and quick at the task, but the longer she had to do it, the duller it became. To think what these men got paid to do stuff like this! As she toiled, she was aware that Sebastian's seat remained stubbornly empty. The space seemed to beg his presence as desperately as she. He must be in meetings. He seemed to have so many of them.

Time passed much more quickly now she was engaged in a tangible task. Soon enough, Natasha was hungry. It was already twelve thirty-five. She stood up and stretched out her stiff muscles. There was a lot of sitting down in this job. Natasha then asked Freddie if she could pop out to grab some lunch. His reply was unforgiving.

"Have you finished?"

"Nearly." she replied, meekly.

"'Nearly' ain't 'nearly' finished enough. You can go ou' and ge' ya lunch when you've finished. I need tha' information printed ou', like yesterday, so ge' to i' girl."

Freddie's abrasive manner led Natasha to conclude that he could do with getting some lunch himself 'like yesterday', however, she kept her thoughts to herself and got on with the job. By five-minutes past one, she was done. She printed out the updated spreadsheet, as fast as she could, and handed it to Freddie on her way out. He shouted after her, in thanks, "This better be righ' young lady, 'cos if i' aint, and you aint 'ere to fix i', then I aint 'appy."

Natasha answered him with supreme, if utterly unfounded, confidence, "It's right Freddie, see you later."

She waited in the lobby, impatient and famished.

"PING!"

The lift doors to her far right opened, and out stepped Sebastian. He raised an eyebrow.

"Where are you going?" he inquired, nonchalantly.

With irritation, Natasha noticed that Sebastian was entirely composed.

"To get some lunch." she replied, abruptly.

The severity of her tone surprised Natasha, while his answer surprised her even more.

"Wait, I'll come with you."

Without waiting for a response, he went onto the trading floor to grab his suit jacket, from the back of his chair, and then returned to stand next to her before a second lift had arrived. As they waited expectantly, the effect of their proximity began to work its invisible magic. Soon enough, Natasha's earlier itch of irritation was soothed by the balm of Sebastian-induced bliss.

"PING!"

They stepped in. Standing next to Sebastian made the ragged, hung-over Natasha feel more revitalized and refreshed than any two-week stint at an Aman resort, and this was a damn sight cheaper, or so she thought, for Natasha had not yet learnt that the most expensive payments are never made with money.

"PING!"

As soon as they were outside, he broke the silence.

"What about a curry in Brick Lane?"

Sebastian's proposition appealed immediately, but Natasha was concerned that Freddie would be expecting her back at her desk, any minute, no doubt with several corrections to make, so she asked, "Shouldn't I get back quickly? Freddie thinks I'm just popping out for a sandwich."

Sebastian looked at her, condescendingly.

"Now Natasha, Freddie works for me." This statement in itself, seemed revelational enough for Sebastian, however, Natasha still remained hesitant. He elaborated, to humour her, "Freddie can hardly tell me off for keeping you out for a long lunch now, can he?"

With the facts that accompanied Sebastian's professional power so expressly spelt out, Natasha's persistent doubts were swatted to oblivion. Relieved of such cumbersome companions, she was quick to catch up with him, for he was already on his way to Brick Lane. The day was most dull. The sun was blocked by slow-moving clouds and everything looked flat, tired and grey following the brilliance of the last few weeks. Today, Sebastian was the only bright thing in Natasha's sight, and the weather made a curry seem like a rather comforting idea. They walked, briskly, to arrive in Brick Lane in less than ten minutes. In no time, Sebastian was holding the door open for her at his favourite Indian restaurant. They chose a discreet red-velvet upholstered four-seater booth at the back.

Just like on Monday, as soon as they sat down their eyes locked and they became strangely spellbound. Preposterous grins spread across delighted faces and, instantly, they dived into that astonishing zone of elevated consciousness that neither of them could understand, nor resist. The waiter's presence wafted over, no more than a breeze on which to cast their orders, without reference to the menu: chicken tikka massala for Natasha, and lamb passanda for Sebastian. They decided to share a pilau rice, a plain naan and a saag bhaji. Then Sebastian requested:

"Oh yes, and two Tiger beers please, very cold."

Throughout this process, the lock of our lovers' stare was broken only twice. Once, in the service of accuracy, when Sebastian tore his eyes away to specify "very cold" and secondly, in the service of courtesy, when he turned to say "thank you". Even for these brief lapses of his undivided attention, Natasha found herself rippling with resentment. In short, she could not get enough of him. Natasha was feeding. Gorging on a fodder that seemed the source of her very self. She was off. Here with him, she was invincible. Here with him, all was attained. Here with him, TRUTH was discovered: all else exposed as illusion. There remained a mute awareness in the core of Natasha's heart, of the existence to which she was born. She held a distant recollection of Nature, beauty, music, colour, smells, tastes and strong affections. She could still recall the cruel terrors of abandonment, injustice, suffering and pain. Yet ensconced HERE, she could laugh transcendentally at it all. HERE is all there is. HERE is all that matters. HERE is all there ever was.

Just as every conceivable colour of light is the composite of white light, HERE the kaleidoscopic range of human emotions, instantaneously, collides to create BLISS. HERE the material world is exposed as a prism, the temptations of which just fragment souls and separate them from, THIS. THIS: the source that spews all matter, fabricates spacetime and ignites life before, over time, inexorably tugging everything back home again to THIS, over and over, ad infinitum. Clearly, Natasha's bizarre Sebastian-induced experience had made her a proponent of the unpopular oscillating Universe theory, however, at this moment in time, Universe formation was not her primary concern.

Instead, Natasha's soul just screamed with joyous delight and jubilantly celebrated the glory of all creation for, momentarily, it had the privilege to dwell HERE. HERE: that sacred place where all are liberated from the brain-forged barbed-wire ball of thought: relentless, rusted, ensnaring and ripping at soft tissue, in order to hinder and frustrate the journey to THIS. For in the vastness of HERE mean-spirited, curmudgeon Thought, gets such an attack of agoraphobia that he becomes mute. With his silence comes his death, and the sickening see-saw of incessant judgements, rightly, lies derelict. HERE, Thought is laid to rest without mourners, for his contemptuous children, Fear, Anger, Hate, Doubt, Envy and Greed, die with him, to be unceremoniously slung into a mass grave, and their recent

Rule of Evil Tyranny, annihilated. THIS, HERE with HIM. Natasha is SOARING. YES, YES, YES, higher and higher, more and more. Natasha becomes a spiritual python, disengaging her jaws of self to swallow HIM whole. HE becomes part of her. She will forever digest HIM with all this spiritual fire. She will forever replenish HIM with all this spiritual fire. Possessed of HIM her soul flame ignites: incandescent.

HE in she. She in HE.

She is HE. HE is she.

One heart.

One soul.

One love.

UNION.

Natasha stares into Sebastian's eyes, spellbound; captivated by the vision of his eternal, omniscient, omnipotent, ubiquitous soul. Her spirit SOARS, SOARS, SOARS, and then, suddenly, SATED. Violently, she pulls back to wrench herself away from this particularly powerful fix of Sebastian. She must manufacture a safe landing strip, before she is propelled from this planet entirely. She is as high as a kite; reeling and verging on nauseous. What the hell just happened? Sebastian watched her with interest as she struggled to regain some separation of self. Disappointed to have lost her, he switched his mode of engagement. Coyly, Sebastian leaned forward, to take her hand in his, and he began to fondle it idly, while he spoke to her, adoringly:

"Oh Natasha, Natasha, Natasha, you have such beautiful hands. You know I shall play with them forever, and never tire of so doing."

Their hands became intertwined. The edges of Natasha's self started to dissolve, once again. He reached for her other hand to complete their circle of engagement. Natasha looked down at them, so snugly held in his. With this physical connect, she was no longer soaring, uncontrollably, instead, she was gliding, serene and ecstatic.

In this intimate space, Sebastian finally said, what he

had been waiting to all morning, "You know, Natasha, you can fuck my cousin if you want to."

The crudeness of his suggestion wounded her deeply. No amount of hours spent on a foul-mouthed trading floor could have prepared her for this verbal violence. Pensively, Sebastian continued. Natasha listened, shocked and numb.

"Sex has never been my motivation, Natasha. You really are welcome to indulge in that pastime with Bruno. My darling one, what I'm really interested in is mind-fucking."

Natasha swallowed hard as she stared, hopelessly, into his eyes and wondered, 'Why so cruel?' Sebastian's energy flow had frozen, yet he continued to torment her.

"Bruno can have your body, if that's really what you want to do with it. Leave the kissing, the fondling, the slobbering and the fucking to him."

Sebastian was remote now, and snarling with distaste at the gross lack of refinement such activities possessed. He still toyed with Natasha's hands, while his snarl twisted into a grimace, as he contemplated such acts between his cousin and his Love. If Sebastian's energy flow had frozen, Natasha's heart had frostbite. It hurt so much that she feared it was approaching a gangrenous state. Fortuitously, before her most vital organ decomposed, Sebastian's expression began to melt. He became strangely inspired.

"Natasha, I want your mind. I want your heart. I want your soul." Before imploring, with desperate urgency, "Please leave those for me, only?"

"Oh Sebastian, you must know, by now, that you command them all?" our heroine whimpered back, despondent.

The permission Sebastian had just plopped into their ocean of Oneness, continued to promote an eternal, radiating ripple of bewilderment throughout Natasha. Her eyes questioned, silently, 'Why do you want to hurt me?' Yet, Natasha knew why. Her Love's ego was enraged and he was driven to punish her. Punish her for making him fall in love with her. Punish her because she had come along when he was married and, most specifically, punish her because she had behaved like a slut last night with Bruno. Sebastian may well have orchestrated the date, but that was not enough. He had not orchestrated the pace of Natasha and Bruno's physical intimacy. They had done that all by themselves with the help of some peach champagne, and two bottles of Montrachet. It seemed Sebastian was determined to regain control and get ahead of their sexual trajectory. By granting Natasha permission to sleep with his cousin, he was clawing back power. Clearly, Sebastian was far more comfortable with his enslavement to that lord, than he was with his new enthralment to love. Cruelty was a small price to pay to recover control. Natasha checked, in a weak voice, while still smarting from his brutality:

"Did Bruno tell you?"

"I haven't even spoken to him. I didn't need to."

Natasha looked away. She was right. He must have sensed everything. She felt violated, yet she wanted to re-assure him at the same time, and she explained, "Sebastian, you know I didn't have sex with him, don't you?"

"Arbitrary lines in the sand, my dear, arbitrary lines in the sand."

Appalled, she objected:

"No Sebastian, no, there is a difference."

"Is there?"

As Sebastian looked searchingly into her eyes, Natasha was lost for words. Indeed, what could she say? All she knew was that this lunch had somehow gone horribly wrong. Sebastian had just given her graphic permission to sleep with Bruno. Worse, he had implied that having done as much as she had done last night, she might as well have gone ahead and slept with him there and then. How could he know so much anyway? It freaked her out. Well, if Sebastian's aim was to tame their love with sexual complexity then she could only but try to help him, and herself, in the process. Besides, maybe he was right? Maybe if she went out with Bruno and gave him a chance, she would have a hope of circumventing a full-blown affair with the man sitting in front of her? As she continued to stare into his questioning eyes, Natasha made her bold decision: she would do exactly as Sebastian had suggested. She would go out with Bruno and she would have brilliant sex with a kind, gorgeous, boisterous and available man. Surely, it was worth a try?

Finally, Sebastian had said what he needed to, and Natasha was resolved to date the cousin of the man whom she loved beyond comprehension. When the food arrived, Sebastian was quick to change the subject. For the rest of lunch our lovers discussed aspects of the business, almost like normal colleagues, yet they were not, and now the plot was poised to thicken, Fate's grip on their destinies inched tighter. Once lunch was finished, Sebastian paid and they left. Solemnly, they walked back to Broadgate. Just before they were about to get there, in a rush of impulsiveness, Sebastian grabbed Natasha by the hand and pulled her into a sheltered doorway. He wrapped his long arms around her and, wonderstruck, she hugged him tightly. His nose, cheek and mouth nuzzled into her soft hair, while she burrowed her face into the fine wool of his suit jacket. She could hear his heartbeat, as Sebastian's eloquent lips spoke of his tragic torment, "Natasha you're driving me mad."

Agitated, he paused and Natasha could feel the emotions rupturing inside him, before he mustered the strength to continue, "A minute does not pass without a thought of you. A moment does not pass without your image in my mind. My peace is destroyed. My concentration lost. Natasha I'm married. These feelings are tearing me to shreds." He then placed his forehead against hers and, with eyes closed, he entreated, "Natasha, please just get out of my head?" Sebastian was clutching her as he spoke, so quietly, she could barely hear him, "I love you, Natasha. I don't want to, I don't understand it, but I do."

In this passionate clinch, our confounded lovers became lost in adagio. It was the sound of rainfall that drew Sebastian and Natasha back to real-time. Still in each other's arms, they turned their heads, to rest cool cheek on cool cheek. Silently, they stared down at the glossy, blue-black pavement to watch the downpour splatter each and every inch of it. On impact, each raindrop became the discrete centre of a multitude of radiating circles of miniature waves, each interfering with the other raindrops' profusion of circular ripples, to create a hypnotic pattern of dynamic, geometric, watery beauty. Slowly, they braced themselves to separate. At last, a dishevelled Sebastian released Natasha. She was disturbed to catch him wipe away a glistening tear, from one of his bewildered eyes.

When they, finally, walked back onto the trading floor, it was two-thirty and their metamorphosis, from distraught passionate lovers to neutral colleagues, was complete. When Freddie saw with whom Natasha was, he held his tongue, while other pairs of eyes darted over to note: Sebastian and Natasha had returned from a long lunch, for the third time. Natasha sat down, guiltily, at her desk. Sebastian made a call. Soon enough, Freddie walked behind her to mutter, disdainfully, under his breath:

"'Righ' i' wasn't.'"

Natasha winced. As she had feared, Freddie was cross with her. True, he could not tell Sebastian off for keeping her out late, but he could take it out on her, for allowing it. The bright green light on Natasha's line began to flash. She hit the button to click into the call.

"U.C.B."

"Can I speak to Natasha Flynn please?"

Immediately, her tone softened.

"Bruno?"

"Is that you Natasha?" he questioned, before adding, "I didn't recognize your voice. You sound so different." He then paused as he became accustomed to this more sober version of his recent date, before jesting cheekily, "So, is this Natasha 'the working girl?'"

"I don't believe any sensible lady would own up to that definition of herself."

He gave a whoop of laughter and continued, in earnest:

"Natasha, seriously, what are you doing tonight?"

She thought, for a moment, and then realized she had no

plans. The last three weeks had sped by so quickly, and she had been so tired, that she had neglected to make any social engagements. As she became aware that Sebastian's ears were pricked, Natasha confessed:

"Actually, Bruno, nothing at all."

Bruno was quick to reply, "Well you are now! I've been invited to a party in Kensington. Will you come with me?"

Natasha remembered her recent resolve and she replied, with as much enthusiasm as she could muster:

"Bruno, I would love to!"

Sebastian's brow darkened.

"Brilliant, I will pick you up at eight. Besides, lots of banking folk will be there. You'll have fun. Sebastian and Itzy might even join us. Dress code: cocktail." Bruno declared, utterly oblivious to the prime plot.

Sebastian and Itzy? Oh no, Natasha could not face that, not today. She added, with forced joviality:

"Can't wait Bruno and remind me to return your jacket." Then, remembering his habitual mode of transport, she inquired, hesitantly, "Will you be on the bike?"

"Absolutely, can't stand traffic jams!"

"Super..." Natasha remarked, apprehensively, as she tried to imagine how she would fare on the back of it clad in cocktail-wear. She hung up. When she turned to glance behind her, Sebastian was gone.

CY BLACK

Chapter Seven - **Lucasta Chatworth**

Natasha had opted for a 'little black dress', but not too 'little' in an attempt to preserve her dignity on the motor-bike-ride to the party. It was a sexy, silk-cotton mix, strappy number, which showed off her back and was fitted around the waist, before flowing out into a full skirt that ended about four-inches above her knee. Natasha looked into the mirror then carefully brushed her hands down her front to get rid of any creases. She eyed her image with pleasure, for she looked glamorous, had honoured the dress code and had done so in an outfit that would not split when she mounted Bruno's bike. She had cracked it!

Natasha then, with some effort, located the handbag that matched her Jimmy Choo black satin, sling-back shoes. Once she had done so, she struggled to stuff her house keys, lipstick, mascara, powder compact and purse into the tiny thing before, at last, she managed to snap it shut. She was ready. Natasha looked in the mirror to check her appearance, one more time, to find that her eyes looked particularly dramatic tonight, and they seemed to stare back at her, as if in challenge. She feared she had overdone her mascara, but it was too late to do anything about it if she had, for the intercom had just sounded.

"I'll come straight down." she gushed.

"Perfect."

She fetched her embroidered cashmere cardigan, and Bruno's black leather jacket, from on top of the bed then left to negotiate the stairs in her gorgeous, but impractical shoes. As soon as she opened the front door, she found Bruno standing at the bottom of the stone steps looking exceedingly dapper. He was dressed in a cream jacket, an open-necked pink shirt and navy blue chinos. He was staring up at her in wonder, as he gave a soft gasp, before complimenting, simply, "Natasha, you look beautiful."

"You look pretty hot yourself Bruno, but thank you."

Natasha grinned warmly at him as she walked down the steps, slipping her cardigan on as she went. Bruno beamed.

130

Gallantly, he offered his arm to escort her to his bike. Once again, he insisted that Natasha wear his jacket before he passed her the spare helmet with apology-filled eyes as he consoled, "It really isn't very far, and your locks look lustrous enough to survive the affront."

Natasha gave an awkward smile, for she was ashamed that Bruno must think her so vain. Then the pair of them donned helmets, climbed onto the bike and scooted off to the party with a loud, vibrating vroom. Oh shit! What a complete idiot! She had not cracked it at all! Hot-blood rose to Natasha's cheeks and her mind and stomach churned with torturous embarrassment. The stupid girl had completely neglected to take into account the effect of swift motion on her full skirt. How could she not have thought of it? While both of her arms were forced to clutch Bruno around his waist, her skirt was at liberty to be lifted by the forceful wind and, fitfully, dance up and around thus, intermittently, exposing everything it was designed to conceal.

Our heroine had never been short of attention but never before, nor since, did Natasha receive as much as on this night. All ears in west London must have bled, from the thunderous cacophony of car-horn sounding, piercing wolf-whistling, loud clapping and rowdy male cheering in appreciation of the sight of relentless flashes of Natasha's exposed, black g-string-clad bottom, suspender belt and stocking-wearing long legs. The masculine excitement was such that it was a wonder the silly girl was not lynched!

Following the longest short journey in the world, Natasha and Bruno finally arrived at the party. Natasha leapt off the bike, more swiftly than a philanderer dismounts his adulterous lover when chanced upon by her husband. Still red-faced and beyond humiliated, Natasha removed her helmet and ruffled her hand through her hair, as she attempted to regain some composure. When, finally, she was brave enough to meet Bruno's eye, she found him standing, demurely, next to his bike with his helmet tucked neatly under his arm. It was obvious he was trying his hardest to stifle a burgeoning smirk. Natasha just dropped her chin to her chest and stared down at her beautiful shoes, as she passed Bruno the spare helmet and requested, almost inaudibly, "Please, just say nothing."

Being the true gentleman he was, Bruno did just as he was asked. Indeed, he never even referred to Natasha's public humiliation again. Instead, he offered her his arm, as if nothing so hilarious had ever occurred, and took charge.

"Righto Natasha, please come with me."

Silently, she slipped her arm into his and he led her up the external flight of stairs to the large sage green front door of a grand six-story, white stucco fronted, terraced house in Palace Gardens Terrace. As soon as they entered, the awful memory of wolf-whistles, shouts, laughter and all of that honking, was thankfully overridden by the drone of opinionated adult voices, competing to be heard. The party was as packed as Fabio's biceps.

Standing in the wide hallway was the host. He was almost as tall as Bruno and impeccably turned out. He had short, dark hair with an unremarkable, but kindly, face and he looked to be in his mid-forties. The man roared in welcome as he greeted Bruno, as boisterously as a Labrador. Eventually the pair of them saw fit to take a brief break in their hearty back slapping, just long enough, for Bruno to introduce Natasha Flynn to Hugh Blackmore with pride. As soon as Bruno had done so, a wave of new arrivals flowed into the house, and Hugh suggested that they give their coats to the attending Filipino, before going in to join the rowdy party.

Obligingly, Bruno and Natasha got rid of the leather jacket and entered the grand drawing-room, where Bruno was quick to help himself to two glasses of champagne from a circulating silver tray, carried by a young, pretty Filipino girl with a peaceful smile and rather sleepy eyes. He passed Natasha a glass then continued on through the room to penetrate the heart of the hurly-burly. The noise was deafening, and the fact that the ceiling height must have been at least eighteen-foot only served to increase the racket. The room was massive, with walls of deep saffron, on which several fine, life-sized portraits in oil, set in heavy gilt frames were displayed. Natasha assumed the subjects to be Hugh's ancestors and their presence gave a formal, not to say stiff, air to the room.

The enormous windows overlooked the wide cherry-tree lined street, and had lavish, cream and gold, taffeta drapes with burnt-gold tasselled tiebacks. An arch, supported by classical white ribbed pillars, led from the drawing-room into a dining-room, of equal scale, where a bar area was to be found. Rows of glinting wine glasses, champagne flutes and whisky tumblers were lined up on a white tablecloth in front of a profusion of bottles. Behind them, two young men, dressed in white shirts, black bow-ties and waistcoats were flamboyantly mixing cheerful multi-coloured cocktails. To the rear, French windows led onto a paved patio and a sixty-foot lawn beyond.

As Natasha looked around the impressive room and its occupants, suddenly, Bruno no longer appeared to be a relic from an old war movie. Indeed, in this assembly there were several laughs louder and more booming than his, voices just as plummy and a couple of men just as tall, broad and earnest as he. It was evident that Bruno was in his natural habitat, and the quantity of intense interest he generated in the females gathered in this luxurious enclosure, only confirmed this to be the case. Unmistakably, Natasha's date was exuding that magnetic, seductive aphrodisiac labelled: ELIGIBLE BACHELOR. The effect of which was so alluring, in this company, that Bruno was spontaneously bombarded by flurries of immaculately turned out ladies, who compulsively gushed high-pitched greetings. These women eyed Natasha and her outfit, more greedily than the extensive audience that had applauded her immodest flashes all the way here!

Each forensic examination of Natasha by these predators, and the information they garnered there, was meticulously, mentally catalogued under the heading: most effective methods to attract Bruno Monmouth. This repeated scanning of Natasha by the array of circling, twittering females, began to display some ritualistic predictability that included all, or some, of the following component parts: FACE CHECK, accompanied by an excessively enthusiastic greeting on introduction, followed by frigid air kissing before a slow, FULL LENGTH FIGURE CHECK would be executed, while some seemingly innocent question would be put along the lines of, "So how long have you known Bruno?" or "Where did you meet Bruno?" or, at its worst, an accusatory, "I've never seen you before!" Natasha would then give a polite response, as these women would shamelessly study her HAIR, SKIN (several times), DRESS, SHOES, HANDBAG, WATCH and JEWELLERY with inquisitive eyes that darted as swiftly as neutrinos. At last, these invasive ladies would settle their attention back onto Natasha's FACE. Then they would fix their expressions, uncomfortably, in a fake smile before executing some 'hair flick' or 'quick pirouette' to culminate with the presentation of their back to Natasha, and their heaving bosom to Bruno, in order to attempt full captivation of him - the only thing they were ever interested in, in the first place!

Thankfully, Bruno was as competent at handling women who had designs on him, as he was at handling his motorbike. Fortunately, for Natasha, he did so to her advantage. Time after time, the chivalrous Bruno gently outmanoeuvred these women in order, successfully, to maintain Natasha as the centre of his focus. It was all rather dull and unpleasant for her, however, she was most touched by Bruno's subtle social cleverness and sensitivity to her position. Finally, even Bruno had had enough of all of the failed attempts to catch his interest, and he gallantly offered Natasha his arm and suggested:

"Shall we go into the garden and get some fresh air?"

Natasha smiled with relief, and Bruno led her out of the French windows, collecting two more glasses of champagne on the way. Once on the patio, they both enjoyed several lungfuls of invigorating evening air, before Bruno looked at Natasha apologetically and explained:

"I'm afraid, Natasha, I know far too many people here. I do hope you're not too bored by it all?"

"I think you mean women?" Natasha teased, before consoling, "Really Bruno, it was kind of you to invite me."

"Kindness had nothing to do with it. Simply, I wanted to see you far more than I wanted to come to this party, but I had already committed to it. I thought I'd to kill two birds with one stone and all that."

As Bruno was speaking, more people spilled onto the patio. Natasha was relieved to find that they were not all single women heading in their direction. She could not help but notice one couple in particular. The young woman was exceptionally beautiful. She had long, thick, glossy black hair that stretched almost to her small waist. She had generous magenta lips and a ghostly pale flawless complexion. Her eyes were large and dark, with black lashes curled as extravagantly as a cow's and she must have been at least Natasha's height. She was very slender, yet without becoming angular and bony. All in all, the young woman had a rare air of exceptional elegance.

The woman in question had noticed them too, and she gazed aloofly in Bruno's direction. Clearly, they knew each other, however, instead of stampeding over to greet him breathily, the woman just smiled sadly with acknowledgement, before turning her attention back to the tall, handsome silver-haired man with whom she was. Gosh, now Natasha was looking at him properly, the man was even better looking than the girl was beautiful. Natasha suspected that he was in his early-fifties. His steel-coloured hair was shot through with streaks of blue-white, while his eyes were an astonishing bluebell colour, which was most dramatically set-off by his deep mahogany tan. The man's gorgeous face had a bold, regular structure, with high cheek-bones, and a nose an aristocrat would covet. When a face held such a nose, yet boasted a decent chin, the effect was devastating.

Bruno soon noticed, with concern, that Natasha's attention had been diverted. Quickly, he moved in between her and the couple she had been admiring, then dipped his head and whispered into Natasha's ear, confidentially:

"Tragic, tragic..."

Bruno had certainly managed to regain Natasha's undivided attention with his hyperbole. Subtly, he encouraged Natasha to edge away from them. When they were a little farther away, Bruno looked around, innocently, to detect if anyone was in earshot, for he would never be so gross as to be caught discussing another guest in public. Satisfied it was safe, Bruno said in a quiet voice:

"That girl over there, the good-looking one?"

Natasha nodded, minutely, in acknowledgement, knowing exactly to whom he referred. He went on.

"Still recovering from a nervous breakdown. Broken heart, apparently, along with another little problem." Bruno paused as he surveyed the company again, to check if anyone was listening. Comforted they were not, he continued, incredulously, "Fell madly in love with my cousin, would you believe it?"

Natasha's form stiffened rigid, more alert than a fox that could smell the approaching stench of a pack of hounds. His name was out of her mouth, before she had even captured the thought of him.

"Sebastian?"

"The very same."

Now she was hungry for details about Sebastian, the gorgeous older gentleman was fast forgotten.

"They had an affair?" Natasha spluttered.

Bruno threw his head back and laughed out loud, so ridiculous seemed Natasha's suggestion.

"Good God no. Sebastian is a happily married man. He would never entertain such a thing. No, it's so much more tragic than that..."

Surreptitiously, Bruno bent down to impart the flesh of the happening directly into Natasha's ear, "They used to work together, at his old shop... poor girl..." He shook his head from side to side with compassion as he contemplated the memory of it. He continued, "Poor dear girl, got it into her head that he loved her. They were only ever good friends you know, but somehow she lost the plot entirely, wrong end of the stick and all that. Completely lost it..."

Natasha's eyes shone and her head nodded, in encouragement. Bruno's eyes were still darting all around, to ensure no unwelcome listeners could overhear his secret uttering. Feeling secure, he looked into Natasha's dilated pupils before adding, with eerie excitement:

"She even showed up at his home once, banging on the front door and screaming the house down... it was four o'clock in the morning, or some such ridiculous hour..." Natasha was gripped. Bruno elaborated, "Inconsolable the poor girl was: screaming, sobbing, hitting and scratching at Sebastian, rambling and raving about their 'love'. He couldn't make any sense of it at all... poor Itzy had to call the police she did, before Sebastian got hurt..." Bruno did more compassionate slow head shaking, then carried on, "Arrested she was, 'disturbing the peace', well, once her family found out about that little humiliation, they packed her off to Il Convento the very next day. Lucky for Sebastian, what?" Here, Bruno could not help but laugh, lightly, before he became studiously serious again, "Apparently her 'love' delusion was connected to a rather unhealthy cocaine habit. Poor girl, she had such a bright career ahead of her and so pretty to boot..."

It seemed Bruno had finished, for he tailed off here. Natasha, however, was on her own fact-finding mission, mentally cataloguing the information garnered under the heading; Sebastian's effect on women.

"When did this all happen?" she pressed.

"Oh, I'd say it must be well over a year ago now. She was at Il Convento for six months. Well, that was the end of her career in banking."

"Are they still in touch, Sebastian and she? Did they ever make up?"

"Good God no. After that display? Itzy wouldn't stand for it, and quite frankly Sebastian didn't have the stomach for it. Come to think of it, thank God they couldn't come tonight, after all. Gosh, that would have been awkward."

Another morsel of news: Natasha would not see Sebastian tonight. She did not know if she was relieved, or not, for she had prepared herself for the possibility. Natasha had no idea how she would react to seeing him with his wife but, for now, she was not to find out. Thoughtful, she took a covert look at the pale-faced beauty, once again, as she inquired, with a far-away look in her eye:

"What's her name?"

"Lucasta Chatworth."

Natasha allowed the name to settle into her consciousness, slowly, to see what it felt like. Can the essence of someone, of this someone, be gleaned from the unique vibrations held in the sonic pattern that has defined them for their lifetime? 'Lucasta Chatworth.' Natasha repeated the name again and again in her head, hoping the sound of it could agitate some instinctive truth regarding the actual events that had occurred between this woman and her Love. What sequence of events could have extracted such an extreme reaction from Lucasta Chatworth? Did this beautiful, contained young woman, really reach such a pitch of delusion all by herself? How unsuccessfully had she walked the tightrope of 'intimate friend' for, surely, she must have been at least that? Somehow, the version of the story that Bruno had been fed, did not ring true.

Moving on, Natasha returned her attention to Bruno, and asked, "So what does she do now?"

"Shag her psychiatrist, from the look of it!"

"That handsome chap is a shrink?"

"He's not just a shrink, Natasha, he is the top shrink at Il Convento. Aren't there some rules about that? Not taking advantage of your patients and all that?"

Bruno wasn't really asking a question, just thinking out loud. Natasha threw the older man another look, and then pursued her inquiry, "Seriously, what does she do now?"

"Oh, she wrote some slushy romantic novel, drawn from the fantasy love she thought she had had with my cousin, I fear." Bruno contemplated this information before bursting into sardonic laughter and adding, "Doesn't say much for Il Convento does it?"

Even Natasha managed a smile before Bruno became serious again and said, "Couldn't bring myself to read it, not my bag at all, and I know Sebastian never did. Itzy wouldn't have allowed it... can't blame her."

Bruno was still shaking his head solemnly, but it was clear he was tiring of the depressing subject. Bruno's character seemed to tend towards joviality and, it seemed, he wanted to return to that space now, for he dropped the discussion with a sigh, before his face beamed, once again, with the cheerfulness of a sunflower.

"Come on Natasha, let's go back inside and grab one last glass of champagne, before I take you out to dinner."

Natasha smiled at Bruno then nodded for, suddenly, she felt the chill in the air and her glass was almost empty. Gently, he took her hand and drew her back into the warmth, light and laughter of that large house. Resolutions and suspenders aside, Natasha knew she would not have sex with Bruno this night. Following the revelations about Lucasta Chatworth, her head was far too full of Sebastian, to even think of allowing Bruno to enter her body.

Chapter Eight - The flash fish & chippy

It was eleven forty-five on Monday morning and the name 'Butler' had just flashed, in bright orange, on the Bloomberg screen. Natasha's spirit pogo-sticked with delight. Matt was not at his desk, so she quickly bashed the little rubber button that took her straight into Sebastian's message: 'You, me, lunch 12.'

Natasha, immediately, typed in her reply.

'Where?'

Fast, to receive his.

'Outside Brasserie Rocque.'

'Done.'

The unexpected prospect of spending time alone with Sebastian, so imminently, was almost too much to bear. Amphetamine-snorting butterflies started to tickle Natasha's insides, and it took her all of her time to control the impulse to flap her hands up and down with glee. Well, that was until Freddie approached.

"Oy, Natasha, here's something I wan' ya to do for me." he muttered, quietly.

She deleted Sebastian's message, in a heartbeat. Natasha was terrified Freddie's request might prevent her from meeting her Love on time. Freddie was already hunched down beside her, with elbows leaning on the top of the desk. Being a short man, this position was not as uncomfortable as it sounds. In his hand he held a pile of papers, a sight that was becoming a predictable precursor to Freddie asking Natasha to perform some boring task. She braced herself and looked up at him, to catch the neon strip lights reflecting off his ice-blue eyes. Today, Freddie was full of smiles and Natasha gave him one of her best. Indeed, it was natural to smile at Freddie, as long as he had not just lost a bucket load of money and was screaming his head off at you. She inquired, sweetly, "How can I help?"

Freddie gave a deep, rascally chuckle, "Hurry the fuck up and get F.S.A. qualified, so you can start making us some bloody money!"

Natasha was becoming increasingly familiar with Freddie's goading, and she gave him a long-suffering smirk, before delivering a gibe proof reply.

"How can I help you, this morning, Freddie?"

"Yeah, yeah, yeah... seriously Natasha, when ya doin' yur exams?"

"Next week, I'm off to Switzerland with the other graduate trainees to start the formal training. I think we take the exams towards the end of the full eight-week course."

"Eight fuckin' weeks? I'll be retired by then!" he growled, grumpily.

Natasha held his gaze, steadily, while she waited for him to work his way around to the point of his visit. This took some time, for Freddie began to grumble more about "the pointlessness of graduates" and not knowing "what the hell they were smoking?" Not the graduates, but Personnel who insisted on recruiting them. Finally, he got around to the reason why he was there.

Natasha anxiously watched the time tick by, as Freddie explained that the sheets were the record of the sales people who had sold large blocks of European, dated, subordinated bank debt to their clients, which was due to mature in the next few years. He wanted her to focus on blocks of "twenty-mil plus" and get the sales people in question to check if their clients still owned them and, if they did, did they want to sell them back to the Desk and, if so, what was their target price? Then Freddie wanted Natasha to compile the results on a spreadsheet for him by close of business tomorrow. Huffing with the tedium of having to explain stuff to a novice, Freddie thrust the pile of papers into Natasha's hand then strutted off, giving her just enough time to escape for her longed for rendezvous.

The minute Natasha set her beady eyes on Sebastian, standing outside Brasserie Rocque, she was catapulted to the heavens. As soon as their eyes met, he gave a strict nod in the direction of the sculpture, The Fulcrum, that depicted five, soaring, rusted sheets of metal and stood at the mouth of one of the entrances to Liverpool Street Station. Immediately, Natasha understood his concern. Instead of approaching him in this public place, she just glided past him, indifferently, and headed in the direction indicated. Soon enough, once she was out of Broadgate Circle, Sebastian subtly fell into step with her. Natasha thought it odd to become, so quickly, practised in the art of discretion and, in this case, valour had no part in it. They did not speak, but instead just walked, briskly, away from prying eyes.

After several twists and turns, Sebastian took a left down a narrow cobblestoned street, always a precarious surface on which to stroll for a girl handicapped by high heels. The lane was lined with tiny shops, from which sombre-faced shopkeepers sat and watched silently, or loitered in front of their premises, some of which were barely more than alcoves. These shops sold cigarettes, magazines, international newspapers and drinks, while some offered shoeshine, reheeling and key-cutting services. All of them seemed to sell black umbrellas. Soon they began to pass little restaurants, and some dark bars that were already filling up with red-faced, fat-bellied, beer-swigging men, even at this hour.

Sebastian came to a halt outside a discreet entrance with an open door that led to a narrow flight of stairs. He beamed cheerfully at Natasha and indicated, with a flourish, that she should enter. Unquestioningly, she did so and began to climb the narrow wooden staircase. At the top she found a small Georgian landing with rather damaged, highly varnished, wooden floorboards. An old-fashioned curled-hooked coat stand, stood naked in the corner. Sebastian opened the door that was next to it, and they entered a charming little restaurant.

All the tables were covered with white tablecloths and fully set, while pretty yellow flowers filled, to bursting, the simple white vases that were placed at the centre of each. The sunlight that spilled into the room, through the generous Georgian windows, seemed to lend an intense, rich buttercup-yellow to the enchanting hue of the floral displays. On sight, the young hostess, hovering behind a narrow podium next to the door, greeted Sebastian by name. She then showed them to a table for two, next to a large sash-window. Once they were seated, the attentive girl handed each of them a large, black, leather-bound menu. When Natasha studied the limited selection of dishes, she discovered that this quirky place was in fact a posh fish and chip shop. She loved fish and chips; she was just unaccustomed to paying twenty-three pounds for them. Feeling famished, Natasha was quick to order:

"Haddock and chips please, with peas; not mushy. Oh, and a bottle of still mineral water."

"I'll have the same please." Sebastian added without even bothering to open his menu. He then rolled his eyes at Natasha as he commented sardonically, "What easy customers we are..." before requesting in afterthought, "Oh, and two double vodkas and orange please."

When the waitress left, Sebastian reached across the table, to grasp her hands in his. Holding them, tightly, he sought intense eye contact.

"Oh Natasha, Natasha, Natasha..."

She just stared back at him, giddy with happiness. Squeezing her hands, with greater pressure, Sebastian began his light-hearted lament.

"You don't understand. What am I to do? I altruistically supply you with my cousin, to preserve my sanity and my family, then what happens? There am I on a grouse shoot with Bruno, and all he can do, all bloody weekend, is bang on about how brilliant you are. You, in my ear, and in my head, all bloody weekend!"

Sebastian was laughing at the phenomenon of his enslavement, and at the irony that Bruno was unwittingly serving that force. By the time the drinks arrived, his eyes were alight with wonderment. When the young girl placed them on the table, Sebastian reached for his and took a big gulp. Natasha watched him with concern and took a little sip of hers, out of politeness. Emboldened, Sebastian leaned forward until their faces were eye to eye, no more than two-inches apart. Staring at her, a little wildly, he spoke with mock accusation, "You... Natasha Flynn... the very woman I am supposed to be forgetting about..."

Sebastian's passion, combined with the proximity of his forehead, eyes, nose and lips, made Natasha's spirit spiral beyond the stratosphere. The desire to merge was overwhelming. Sebastian put his smooth brow against hers and closed his eyes. Natasha shut hers too and, in the blackness, she felt his mental energy fire up the synapses of her brain, as if electrocuted. Natasha was flying, executed to bliss. The intensity of this hit made her eyes open in fright, to find Sebastian's open as well and staring into, and beyond, hers. It was as if each silently explored the eternal self-essence that dwelt in the other's soul, for what Natasha stared into now, was more familiar to her than herself. Suddenly, she felt an impulse to kiss as inexorable as vertigo. She lifted her chin so her mouth moved towards his and, just before their lips were about to touch, Sebastian wrenched himself away, disengaged his hands and thrust himself back into his chair. Natasha was left hanging, hankering after the fulfilment of a moment that had, torturously, just receded. Sebastian and Natasha's self-control had just been, dangerously, tempted.

Some more people began to arrive, to rescue our lovers from such potentially perilous privacy. Sebastian took another swig of his drink, wiped his lips with the back of his hand, and then began to fidget uncomfortably. He looked rather bemused by it all. Trying to look anywhere but at Natasha, he pouted as he stared at the floorboards, dejectedly. By now Natasha had recovered a neutral position and she took a larger sip from her vodka. After a moment's contemplation, and from a safe distance, Sebastian then confessed, calmly, "My God Natasha, what you do to me. One whole weekend with none of you, when so much was spoken about you, was simply a living hell. By this morning my heart was aching so much, I thought I was having a cardiac arrest."

Enraptured, she reached forward to take his hand, as she

summed it up, "I guess it's official: we're in love, it hurts, and we haven't got a clue what to do about it."

They both looked rather lost, as they considered their inconvenient situation. They felt hopeless and elated, all at the same time. Delighted that Sebastian seemed to be as smitten as she, Natasha turned her mind to the unpleasant subject that had troubled her ever since Friday evening.

"Speaking of love Sebastian, tell me, who is Lucasta Chatworth?"

When Sebastian heard the name, his eyes began to dart around the room. The little restaurant was now almost full with fellow diners, while Sebastian remained strangely reticent on the subject of Miss Chatworth. He gave Natasha's hands a quick squeeze, before letting them go and allowing his arms to fall down by his sides. Then, as if on cue, their lunch arrived. The pretty waitress placed the steaming food onto the table, and the golden battered fish were so big that they overhung, each of the plates, at both ends while the hand-cut chips were fat and crisp, and the peas a brighter green than Sebastian's eyes. Even though Natasha was starving, and the food looked mouthwatering, she refused to be diverted. Once the waitress had left, she eyed Sebastian suspiciously and, stubbornly, questioned again: "Lucasta Chatworth?"

Sebastian just looked down, hungrily, at his food. He then took a deep breath, as if to collect his thoughts, while he picked up the half-lemon, which was tightly wrapped in muslin gauze, and squeezed its sharp juice, evenly, along his length of haddock. Natasha maintained her expectant expression and waited, patiently, for his slow-coming reply. He proceeded to cut a chunk of fish and half a chip, before popping the lot into his mouth. Thoughtfully, he began to chew. Natasha waited sternly. She was not going to allow Sebastian to gloss over his history with Lucasta Chatworth, as easily as the unsightly floorboards had been made pretty with a thick coat of varnish. Natasha wanted the full facts, as ugly as they may be.

Once Sebastian had finished his mouthful, he looked at

her dispassionately then, slowly, repeated the name of the woman in question, "Lucasta Chatworth." As if by so doing, he could invoke some satisfactory memory of her, and the whole sorry affair. Natasha nodded, severely, and only when he engaged in the subject, did she begin to eat.

Pensively, Sebastian began, "Bruno told me he had seen Lucasta at the Blackmore's party. He said he had touched upon her unfortunate history. He also mentioned how inquisitive you were on the subject."

"Can you blame me? Sebastian, what really went on between you two? The woman certainly did not look as unhinged as the story Bruno related to me would suggest."

More relaxed now, Sebastian shook his head, slowly, from side to side, just like Bruno had done. Then, at last, he embarked on the sad story.

"Natasha, it was a long time ago... we used to work together." he explained.

"I thought it was only a year ago?"

"More, almost two." Sebastian paused to take another mouthful of his lunch and chewed it slowly before continuing, "You don't really know yet Natasha, you have only just started in this business, and you certainly haven't been put under any pressure to date but, take it from me, working on a trading floor is unforgiving, and some personalities just don't prove robust enough to survive it."

Sebastian took, chewed and swallowed another mouthful before he explained further.

"Lucasta and I sat next to each other. We were in just after seven, and often worked twelve to thirteen-hour days. You really get to know someone when you sit next to them for that many hours a day, five days a week..."

He paused, before adding with a touch of regret:

"Or I thought I knew her."

Sebastian was staring into space now, conjuring up the days he was describing, in his mind, and lost in the memory of them. Then he snapped out of it and became animated as he began to elaborate, "It was an exciting time in the City Natasha. Money was for the taking and we were all as high as kites on the buzz of our own success. Cocaine was all too available and the ethos was simply 'work hard, play hard.' I guess sometimes it just got out of hand. My God, the excess of it, we were even doing Charlie at work. Often on a trip to the lavatory you could find the tell tale smudges of powder residue left carelessly on top of the cisterns; disgusting snorting it from there, when you think about it. But, by God, it was a time of tremendous fun, if you could stand the pace, sleep deprivation and the pressure." His expression darkened as he added mournfully, "Clearly, Lucasta could not. She was a little too fond of the old Charlie, and it just distorted her perspective."

Having described the backdrop to Lucasta's fate, Sebastian took another bite of his food. It seemed he was enjoying his lunch far too much, to allow the telling of a sad tale postpone the consuming of it. Having, finally, finished chewing he looked pensive before conceding:

"Certainly, we liked each other, and yes, we did spend a lot of time together, but where she got it into her head that we were involved in some passionate love affair, I really can't imagine."

Natasha remained unconvinced and, stubbornly, delved further, "Surely, you must hold some responsibility for Lucasta believing such a thing? You must have given her some encouragement?"

Sebastian was getting bored with this interrogation.

"If you are wondering whether I behaved with her, as I behave with you, you could not be more wrong."

Oh, how Natasha wanted to believe him. Sebastian then smiled at her as he took one of her hands in his, once again, and spoke with certitude.

"Never did I say I loved her. Never did I have a burning need to see her, and never did I tell her as much. Lucasta was not you, and it was never anything like this."

Hungry for faith in him, her demeanour softened. With a relieved smile, Sebastian admitted:

"Sure we were very close friends. Sure we had the odd cuddle, but, Natasha, that was the extent of it."

147

"Did you ever sleep with her?" she questioned, boldly.

"Never."

Natasha believed him. Yet still she could not help but wonder, out loud, "Why did so little, produce so extreme a reaction from such a woman?"

Sebastian had had enough. With conviction, he summarised the whole sorry affair.

"She was yearning for the intimacy that was lacking in her life and I was there. We spent lots of time together, professionally, and she simply came to imagine things that just weren't true. All of her obvious attributes aside, Lucasta was of a fragile psychological disposition. She took too much coke, and she lost it. End of story."

Sebastian had finished. He wished to move onto a new subject. Then, echoing Natasha's earlier words, he inquired, mischievously, "Speaking of love, Natasha, tell me, how is Bruno?"

"You should know that better than I, having spent the entire weekend with him," she retaliated, before pausing to add softly, "and, anyway, you know it's not love."

"Not for you perhaps... By the way, Natasha, how long do you plan on keeping him waiting?"

"What do you mean?"

"You know exactly what I mean."

Natasha was cross. Was nothing sacred? She snapped, defensively, "Look Mr. heartbreaking, matchmaking, married man, I don't think that's any of your business."

"Now, now, temper, temper. You can hardly blame me for being curious. So when are you seeing him again?"

"I have no idea." she answered, grumpily.

"Well, after the way Bruno was talking about you this weekend, Natasha, I'll put a bet on that you will hear from him before the end of today."

"Can't wait." she said, flatly.

Then it occurred to Natasha, that whilst Sebastian had successfully managed to negotiate the Lucasta Chatworth hurdle, she had just fallen flat on her face over the Bruno Monmouth one. In fact, just the raising of the subject had destroyed her mood. All Natasha wanted, was to be free to love Sebastian. She was beginning to feel increasingly trapped by the complexity of her romantic position.

When lunch was finished the pair of them strolled, unenthusiastically, in the direction of the office. When they got to Finsbury Circus, Sebastian suggested they separate. Natasha nodded. His caution made sense. Then, impulsively, he inquired, softly, "Do you want a lift home?"

Natasha nodded meekly, unable to resist.

"Meet me at the car park at six." he instructed.

Natasha smiled in answer, and then slowly made her way back to work, alone. When she got to the office, Sebastian was not there. When she got back to her desk, she found a garish yellow post-it note stuck to her computer screen, which read: Bruno called 12.47. Sebastian had been right.

Chapter Nine - **Bruno gets lucky**

It was Thursday night and Natasha was getting ready to go to Bruno's house, for the first time. He wanted to cook dinner for her. Bruno loved cooking. Natasha had already seen him on Tuesday, when he had taken her out to a quirky restaurant in Kensington where all of the waiters were gay, a fact that only served to accentuate his masculinity. They had enjoyed good food, fine wine and each other's company, while Bruno had given her some sound advice regarding her career. He reminded Natasha that he had done a stint in the industry himself, straight after university. As much as Bruno had been sure to emphasize the importance of reputation, punctuality and professionalism, he could not stress enough how vital it was to secure a good mentor to "show one the ropes" and "watch your back", and that was exactly how the conversation had turned to Sebastian. If Sebastian had had to listen to Bruno praise Natasha all weekend, it was Natasha's turn to listen to Bruno wax lyrical about Sebastian that evening. He could not speak highly enough of his cousin, and Bruno seemed to be very impressed by Isabel too, for he described them as the "perfect power couple". Bruno even congratulated Natasha on having secured such a successful, decent chap as Sebastian as her mentor, going as far as to say, "Natasha, you can't go wrong with Sebastian. By God, if I had found such a mentor in my early days, I may well never have left the business."

The more Bruno had praised Sebastian, the more guilt-ridden Natasha had become. The fact that Bruno did not have a bad word to say about anyone, made Natasha think her own and Sebastian's behaviour even more duplicitous. Bruno played saint to their sinners. It was becoming increasingly clear that Natasha must rid herself of her feelings of loyalty to Sebastian, once and for all. The only true commitment he had made was to his wife. Natasha, on the other hand, was a free agent. Bruno was handsome, funny and single. She was attracted to him and they were just starting to spend time together to get to know each other. There was no shame in that. By the end of Tuesday night, Natasha had determined to fall in love with the decent Bruno and quash her addiction to his more complicated, married cousin.

These were the thoughts that continued to ricochet in Natasha's mind, as she got ready to spend another evening with Bruno. Being ever the gentleman, he had insisted on picking her up and was due to arrive in less than ten minutes. Following the motorbike debacle last Friday, Bruno had even been considerate enough to insist that he pick her up in his car. Clearly, he was not expecting her to be wearing trousers. Natasha was determined not to disappoint him. Tonight, she had chosen a figure hugging, black-velvet, halter-neck dress that finished halfway down her thigh, to flash lots of leg and she was taking extra special care with her make-up. Indeed, Natasha wanted to look as ravishing as possible, for she suspected that the time had come to allow Bruno to ravish her.

As Natasha sipped her way through a glass of champagne, she wondered precisely how long a girl was expected to survive on hand holding, cuddling and kissing alone. By the time she had finished her second glass of champagne, she was convinced that she had survived quite long enough. It had been almost a year since she had had sex, surely, that was long enough to get over an ex? By the time Natasha had finished doing up her black suspenders, she had decided that tonight was certainly the night! With the silent formulation of that intention, Natasha's tummy began to somersault in anticipation and she was disconcerted to find that lustful throbbing had been prompted down below. The force and strength of this spontaneous physical reaction, only confirmed that our heroine had made the correct, and long overdue, decision.

When the doorbell sounded, Natasha told Bruno she would be down in a jiffy, and then she grabbed a chilled bottle of Bollinger from the fridge and dashed down the stairs. As soon as she opened the front door, Bruno looked up at her and gasped on sight. Natasha grinned with delight, for is there ever a compliment more eloquent than that? Vivified by her appearance, Bruno leapt up the flight of stairs, with the immediacy of a vampire, then offered her his arm and escorted her to his open topped 1961 midnight blue Jaguar E-type roadster. With a hint of G-force Natasha was sped off to Bruno's South Kensington home. In a thrice, Bruno was parking in the beautiful, white stucco fronted terrace, Pelham Crescent. Once he had done so, he begged Natasha's patience while he put up the roof, locking the canvas down, silver rivet by silver rivet. Natasha just listened to the ticking of the engine, as it cooled.

Once she was inside Bruno's impressive home, he suggested she make herself comfortable in the elegant drawing-room before he disappeared. A gas fire was roaring and its colourful, flickering flames transformed the slightly Spartan atmosphere into a more welcoming one. Natasha sat down on the large brown leather sofa and looked around the room with curiosity. Undoubtedly, it was architecturally a marvellous space, however, the presentation left no doubt that Bruno was a bachelor, for never had Natasha seen a home so lacking in a woman's touch. Apart from the bare necessities, the place was barely furnished. There were bookshelves set in alcoves either side of the fireplace that burst with old books, a solid walnut coffee table in front of the sofa and behind it, set back at either end, there were two rather ugly modern standing lamps that had sprawling, black, electrical leads. There were also several squat towers of box files dotted in random spots about the room and, finally, a completely incongruous giant red beanbag slumped next to the enormous front window. That was it. As for the expanse of wall space, it was empty, save for a grand oil painting of a fox-hunting scene in an ornate gilt frame above the fireplace. Bruno soon reappeared with two champagne flutes, held by their stems, in one hand and a rattling silver ice bucket in the other. He put everything down onto the coffee table before taking the bottle from the bucket and deftly opening it with a pop. When he poured the honey-hued liquid down the side of one of the flutes, Natasha noticed that he was holding a bottle of vintage Dom Pérignon. She smiled to herself, for she was starting to get used to being so bloody spoilt by this warm-hearted man.

"Just a minute." Bruno declared.

Then he left the room, oddly taking both glasses with him, only to return, but this time with a bright red strawberry bobbing up and down in each.

"I seem to remember, summer fruits are your favourite."

Natasha was so thoroughly charmed by Bruno's consistent, inspired generosity, that on the spur of the moment, she decided it was about time for her to be equally so. On a mission, she stood up and, with hips rocking, she walked towards him. Bruno held out her drink, but she did not take it. Instead, she just stared into his eyes and slowly enfolded his waist in her elegant arms. Having secured his undivided attention, she lifted her radiant face to plant her soft, red lips onto his mouth. The sensation was so sweet and tender that Natasha gave an involuntary moan. Encouraged, Bruno groaned slightly then he slipped his slippery tongue into her mouth. Natasha followed his lead and they began an explorative, teasing, gentle French kiss.

Bruno still held the champagne flutes, so any response was somewhat impeded. Precisely because of this, they were forced to savour the sweet innocence and intimacy of the moment, before Natasha had a better idea. Disengaging, she looked, naughtily, into Bruno's gentle eyes as she relieved him of the champagne flutes. Taking a sip from hers on the way, she put them onto the coffee table before returning. Natasha then reached up to place her hands on Bruno's shoulders, before tracing her forefinger down his shirt line, until she reached the first button that was done up. Pouting provocatively, she began, teasingly, to unbutton his crisp, white shirt. Once she had undone two, she tilted her head and began to kiss him on the side of his warm, soft neck. He smelt deliciously of clean male and, if she was not mistaken, he was wearing Jill Sander, an aftershave that made her double up with longing. Bruno's strong hands began to caress her body, roaming up and down her ticklish sides, enticingly brushing the sides of her breasts on the way, with inquisitive probes, before moving to her rump and forcefully massaging her full bottom. Having breathed in several lungfuls of Bruno, Natasha pushed his shirt from his muscular shoulders, while he continued to touch her body all over and start to nibble hungrily at her neck. Not wanting to be distracted from her mission, Natasha placed her forefinger onto Bruno's mouth, with strictness, to command his stillness. Bruno obeyed and his breathing became more and more ragged, as his level of excitement increased. Natasha started to trace the tip of her tongue down his neck, to work her way to the top of his broad shoulders. With diligent adoration, she began to cover each and every inch of them with swift, sweet kisses, until her lips started to work their way to his hairless, pectoral muscles and chest. Natasha worked hard to cover all of his body with light teasing kisses, moving her head down, relentlessly, as she did so. His skin smelt so clean and delectable, and it was so silky soft, that she nuzzled the tip of her nose against it, affectionately, as she continued to kiss him all the way. By the time she had passed his tummy button, she was kneeling on the oak floor before him. Bruno's hands were massaging her head, tantalizingly, to send shock shivers of electricity down her spine. Natasha lingered her oral affections on his solid six-pack, while she began to undo his belt-buckle and the top button of his trousers, before finally unzipping his fly.

Bruno's heavy penis was already starting to stir, to make his boxers bulge impressively. When Natasha, inquisitively, slipped her hand into the slit of his magenta silk boxer shorts, she found him erect, pulsating and eager. She took Bruno's turgid penis firmly in her warm hand and drew its length out like a manual snake-charmer. She found herself give a moan of appreciation at Bruno's impressive, ever-ready member before she, gently, inserted its turgid tip into her mouth. She then began to teasingly suck, lick and play with its helmet. Bruno gasped with the intensity of his sexual arousal and his cock became as hard as industrial rubber. She took a firm grip at its very base and began to move her hand up and down rhythmically, lubricating the action with her saliva as she continued to suck, lick and tease his cock's velvet-soft helmet. Bruno's animalistic groans were testament to his pleasure, as Natasha started to take his penis more and more deeply into her mouth and throat, to then move her head up and down on his giant member, her inspired tongue forever stimulating its length, with increasing pressure.

Bruno was beside himself with arousal. He almost yelped, when he stopped massaging Natasha's head, instead, to clamp it, firmly, in between his big hands. Bruno then started to control Natasha's rhythm and dictate the depth his cock was thrust into her hot, hungry mouth. The back of her throat was filled with him now, and he began to pull her head in and out, in and out, in and out, in and out, as his penis repeatedly plunged into her mouth. Bruno was so big, he kept pushing beyond her gagging reflex, which just surrendered to his manhood, pliantly. On and on and on, Natasha gave him the deepest blow-job, while his strong hands controlled the rhythm all the way.

Intermittently, she would break off to focus on teasing the silky end of his penis with her tongue, until Bruno begged to plunge himself back into her mouth, once again. Natasha was dizzy with his desire for her. Again and again, she would tickle the sensitive skin at the very end of his penis with the tip of her wet tongue, before returning to the repetitive penetrative pumping in and out of her mouth. His well-endowed cock seemed to expand, ever farther, with the stimulation, to fill her throat more and more fully. In, out, in, out, in, out, in, out, Bruno was panting uncontrollably now, grasping her head ever more firmly, as he repeatedly plunged himself into her mouth, in, out, in, out, in, out, in, out, until, finally, Bruno approached the apex of his pleasure to gasp hoarsely in warning:

"Natasha I'm going to come, I'm going to come."

She just continued to serve him in this pumping labour of love, nodding her head, minutely, to give permission, yet still working Bruno's beautiful sex to distraction with her mouth. His breathless, groaning frenzy, along with Natasha's devoted motion, became increasingly ferocious and frenetic until, at last, Bruno's body stiffened rigid and, crying out with ecstasy, he began to shudder, as wave upon wave of release was ejaculated into Natasha's warm, silky mouth and his salty viscous cum gratefully swallowed down, gulp after gulp until, at last, the copious flow of Bruno's potent sperm was spent. He emitted haunting, other-worldly moans, all the while, as if transported by the intensity of his orgasm until, finally, he was sated.

Fondly, Natasha licked all the remaining fluid from the tip of Bruno's impressiveness, before kissing the end of it, affectionately, then gently putting him away. Natasha, slowly, brought herself to her feet only to notice, for the first time, how sore her knees were. Standing in front of him now, Natasha gave a coquettish smile, before reaching for, then taking a sip of her champagne. From the way he was looking at her, Natasha was not sure who was more impressed with her performance.

"You taste nearly as good as your Dom Pérignon." she giggled, before fishing the strawberry out of her drink and popping it into her mouth.

Bruno continued to stare at her with undisguised wonder. Finally, he managed to say, through a smirk:

"I am so glad that madam approves of the refreshments this evening."

"More please... of everything." Natasha entreated, as she tilted her empty glass towards him.

Flattered, Bruno chuckled before pouring her another.

"Natasha you divert me delightfully, however, I think it is about time I fed us don't you? Are you hungry?"

"Starving."

"Good. Please make yourself comfortable. Most of it is prepared, so I shouldn't be long."

Bruno then took Natasha by the nape of her neck, to

give her a lingering kiss on the lips, before leaving to go downstairs. Natasha made her way towards the sofa and sat down. Her whole body was tingling with desire, as she sipped her divine drink and stared into the orange and yellow flames that danced, fitfully, before her. Her mouth still tasted of strawberry and she continued to sip on her exquisite champagne as she became increasingly mesmerized by the flames. In what felt like no time, Bruno was back and carrying two plates. He put them down onto the dining table, which had already been set, before lighting the three candles that sat in a candelabrum at the centre of it. Having created the romantic setting, Bruno pulled out a chair for Natasha and announced, with ceremony:

"Dinner is served."

Once the pair was seated, Bruno looked into Natasha's eyes and said, sincerely, "May I say it is a real pleasure to get to know you better, Natasha?"

"Thank you, and it has been a delight to get to know you too, Bruno."

They smiled at each other then raised their glasses and drank to pleasure. As soon as Bruno had put his glass back down, he went on to give details of the forthcoming courses with pride.

"Natasha, we are to start with a duck liver mousse, accompanied by celery, apple, honey and walnut salad, with lightly toasted walnut bread then, to follow, we have grouse breast draped in bacon with winter vegetables and roast potatoes." Bashfully Bruno added, "The bird is from the shoot last weekend. Gosh, it was a fantastic day. I'll have you know our party took a bag of over one hundred and eighty brace! Please forgive me for saying so, but Sebastian and I were probably the best shots in the field, so I think it safe to assume that the bird you will dine on this evening was, most likely, shot by one of us."

She smiled tightly. So much for forgetting about Sebastian, at the very mention of his name, her heart contracted with yearning. Beaming, Bruno continued, utterly oblivious to her disquiet.

"Finally, Natasha, for pudding I will serve homemade ginger and orange ice cream with crispy brandy snaps."

Natasha was beyond touched by the effort Bruno kept going to, in order to impress her, and she forcibly ousted the intrusive Sebastian from her head.

"Oh Bruno, you spoil me." she scolded, flirtatiously.

"Natasha, may I accuse you of the same? Long may it continue..."

Natasha chuckled guiltily, for she knew exactly to what he referred. She then looked at the food, thrust her fork into the light mousse and tasted it: exquisite. With each delicious mouthful, and with every cascading giggle Bruno extracted from her, Natasha goaded herself into falling in love with this good-looking, talented, considerate man. In the circumstances, how difficult could it be?

By the time the delicious feast was finished, the candles were mere inch-high flaming stubs. Our heroine's mouth still felt cold from the gasp-making ice cream, while her heart was warmed through by Bruno's bonhomie. Most satisfied, she placed her napkin onto the polished table, and stood to clear the plates. Bruno rose too, but only to stroll around the table and tuck in behind her. She could feel the firm bulge in his trousers pushing into her. He leaned over her, took the plates she had just picked up, and put them back down. Next, he took her left shoulder then spun her around to face him before, in one fell swoop, he effortlessly swept her up into a fireman's lift and carried her over to the sofa, while Natasha squealed with as much excitement as a child being twirled around by daddy. He then threw her onto it before jumping on top of her. She could not stop giggling, and she kicked off her shoes with wild abandon. Bruno started to ravish her, kissing and caressing her insatiably, to the point of bruising. His force just made Natasha's excitement more extreme, as her hands explored his fit muscular form. Well, this was a fuck-sight more fun than clearing up!

Bruno's weight bore down on her, as he continued to kiss her with feverish passion. Natasha struggled to match his force, as she moaned with primal want. Bruno had gone and done it again, for all Natasha wanted to do was fuck his brains out! A determined hand shot up her skirt and Natasha found herself squirming with desire. With both of his hands Bruno forced Natasha's fitted dress all the way up her body, to hook it over her breasts in a roll of velvet. Her bra, knickers and suspenders were all on show against her white flesh. In a rip tide of intention, Bruno whisked off her black lace knickers, and then flung them across the room. Natasha just laughed, happily, through her kisses, at this big man's bold molestation. Forcibly, Bruno spread her legs and inserted his finger up inside her hot velvet softness. Beside herself with arousal, Natasha's vagina went into spasm. Already, she was dripping and Bruno's highly accomplished sexual skill coaxed more and more slippery lubrication from her. Bruno then began to focus all of his attention on stimulating her clitoris. With his fingers he drew juice from inside her, to slide it all over this most sensitive zone. Natasha began to quiver wildly, anchored only by the weight of Bruno on top of her. Her body began to writhe and undulate in exquisite sensual agony.

Their passion was hotter than flame. Natasha longed to be filled by him. Her lust shot to fever pitch, as Bruno relentlessly played with her increasingly engorged clitoris. Natasha could wait no more. Frantically, she unbuckled his belt, undid his trouser button then unzipped his fly. Bruno could not have been more turned on, for his large cock sprang out from his pants to greet her. Bruno's manhood was throbbing and free.

Quickly, he pushed his trousers and boxer shorts down his long thighs, with one hand, while still, vigorously, playing with Natasha's sensitive lubricated sex, to make her ache for him. Then, with one powerful thrust, Bruno's wide girthed member penetrated her, to stretch her to perfection. Natasha cried out to be so full of him. The walls of her vagina began to convulse, repeatedly, around his cock as he started to thrust his impressive length and width into her.

The couple's cascading moans seemed to derive from

Purgatory, so unholy were their sounds of erotic pleasure. Bruno ploughed his gorgeous cock into Natasha again and again, deeper and deeper, faster and faster. The pair began to pant, as Bruno's thrusts approached crescendo. Natasha bit her bottom lip, as the tip of her nose began to tingle and itchy rings of constriction formed around her wrists and ankles to herald imminent orgasm. They were now wrapped so tightly around each other, it was as if they had become fused: separate flesh and blood sealed by the slimy perspiration of their writhing bodies, until he muttered, urgently, "I'm going to come Natasha, I'm going to come."

Natasha stopped all motion and then, with firm intent, she panted her instruction, "Yes baby, yes, but not inside me, I'm not on anything."

Forbidding his release into her secret warmth, tipped Bruno over the summit. He ripped himself out of her and, immediately, began to ejaculate his copious load. Spurts of white cum splattered all over Natasha's exposed tummy and her black lace suspenders. The sight of his viscous spunk potently shooting forth, prompted Natasha's hovering orgasm to hit and she yelped like an injured dog, as her violent vaginal orgasm was released, to make her tremble, from head to toe, with the strength and intensity of its waves, as juice squirted from her to make wet her upper inside thighs. For some time, the quivering couple lay fixed in a tight clinch, oblivious to the mess of sex locked in between their hot sweaty bodies. In a state of complete relaxation, Bruno seemed to weigh twice as much. His weight squashed down on her until, finally, he flopped off to lie on his side, close next to her. Natasha's sex continued to tingle from its recent joy. Smiling, she looked into his handsome, flushed face and lifted her hand to stroke his soft ruddy cheek, as she muttered, affectionately:

"Bruno, once again, you spoil me."

He smiled, with deep contentment, and replied, "As you do me, Natasha, as you do me. Long may it continue..."

Chapter Ten - Make a date

"Brrr, Brrr, Brrr, Brrr, Brrr, Brrr, Brrr, Brrr..."

It was late. Who could be calling at this time? Curious, Natasha answered the 'phone: "Hello?"

Immediately, without a sound, she knew it was him. Natasha flopped down on her bed and emitted a whimper of relief. At once, his consciousness began to envelop her, as if the telephone line could transport his thought waves into her room as easily as his voice. Even in silence, his essence kept Natasha profound company. She could not speak. Eventually, Sebastian did.

"You didn't keep him waiting long then."

Instantly, her face and ears were swept up in a burning scorch of unqualified shame. Sebastian said no more. Natasha scrambled for an excuse, but what could she say? Instead, she chose to ignore his comment and ask the question that had plagued her ever since Freddie had announced that Sebastian would not be coming in to work that day.

"Where did you go Sebastian?"

After an interminable pause, he spoke.

"I couldn't face you today."

His voice was quiet, desolate. Natasha was shot straight through her heart. Spontaneously, full tears sprang up in her eyes. Why were his words so unbearable to hear? She was supposed to be falling for Bruno, yet here she was crying because of Sebastian. Natasha began to question what had prompted his call. Had Bruno told him? Had Bruno called Sebastian, straight after he had dropped her home last night, to boast of his sexual conquest? Surely, such a man was not capable of such a thing? Was that even the point? Natasha wiped away her tears with the sleeve of her fluffy bathrobe. Still, Sebastian said nothing. His silence was terrifying. It felt as if he was rummaging around in her mind, grasping each and every memory image at will, to study one after the other with disconsolate disappointment. Sitting in her own bed, in her own home, at eleven thirty-five on a Friday night, Natasha felt more exposed to Sebastian than she ever had done before. It seemed like the strength of their freaky psychic connection was increasing by the day. Now she came to think about it, considering the images available for his perusal, following last night, it was hardly surprising that she felt so devastatingly exposed. At last, she broke the silence, as if to divert him from his invasion of her mind.

"I didn't think I would see you, or even get to speak to you. I leave for Switzerland on Monday for two weeks..."

"You think I don't know that?"

"Sebastian, it was torturous. When Freddie told us that you weren't coming in today, I felt sick."

Sebastian even managed to chuckle, as if he had tired of feeling morose, and he accused:

"Serves you right Natasha Flynn..."

"What do you mean?"

"For keeping me awake all night with your sexual misadventures..."

Inexplicably, Natasha found herself apologizing for the very thing that she had spent the last two weeks persuading herself did not qualify for contrition.

"I'm sorry Sebastian." She paused, forlorn and confused, before she ventured, "Did Bruno tell you?"

"No Natasha, he didn't. Once again, he didn't need to. Unfortunately, I have every sordid scene indelibly singed onto the film reel of my sorry recollection. You make a lunatic of me my darling one. I never believed this type of connection was even possible..."

Natasha could feel Sebastian's pain. Sincerely, she repeated, "I'm sorry Sebastian."

Sebastian continued to try and process this peculiar phenomenon, before elaborating, "Thanks to you Natasha Flynn, last night I virtually got fucked by my first cousin." He then paused, before adding sarcastically, "It is an experience I would not recommend, I can tell you!"

Natasha sighed with relief, for Sebastian was becoming more like himself, so much so, that she even dared to jest:

"Well, I'm afraid I cannot concur with that view."

"Enough!" he barked back, outraged.

They were both quiet again, but this time their sadness had gone. Bizarrely, Natasha's teasing compliment to Bruno seemed to have salvaged their connection via their shared, sick sense of humour. Like consciousness started to unfold and merge. Twin spirits began to resonate, and unsavoury recollections of sexual escapades were eclipsed. After an unfathomable time in communion, Sebastian broke the enchanting spell and asked, "Are you free tomorrow night?"

"Maybe, why?"

"We're going out. I want you to take me to one of your trendy nightclubs."

Natasha chuckled. The thought of this spoilt, sophisticated, older man queuing up at a rave in Kings Cross with a bunch of jiggling, drugged up 'hoodies', wearing jeans and flash trainers, seemed beyond absurd; yet it delighted her. Most of all, she was thrilled that she would get to see him before leaving for Switzerland; but how could he propose meeting her on a Saturday night? Natasha provoked:

"What about your wife? Will she be joining us?"

"Now, now Natasha, I don't think you're in any position to take the moral high ground, do you? Besides, Isabel leaves for a business-trip tomorrow so it'll be just the two of us. Unless of course you want to bring Bruno along, just in case you haven't finished slobbering over him yet?"

"I don't slobber." Natasha asserted, defensively, before adding, following a thoughtful pause, "Really though, would that be sensible?"

"No, I think it would be a shocking idea to bring Bruno, or Isabel for that matter."

"Seriously Sebastian, you and me, going out alone to a club, would that be sensible?"

"Sensible? Sensible? Natasha, after what I went through last night, indeed ever since meeting you, I don't even know what sensible is any more. My feelings for you are not sensible. The experiences I have when I am with you, or away from you, defy all sense. In such circumstance, how do you expect me to behave sensibly? Please, tell me that?"

Natasha sighed deeply and then said, with profound resignation, "If I knew how to control any of this, Sebastian, God knows I would."

Silence.

He was the first to speak.

"I'll pick you up tomorrow, at nine. Good night, my darling one."

Then he hung up. It was done, and Sebastian was gone. She had not planned to go out alone, at night, with her boss, but the arrangement to do so, had just been made. A date was all set for tomorrow night, and Natasha had not prevented it.

Chapter Eleven - The first kiss

There was a dawn I remember
when my soul heard something
from your soul. I drank water
from your spring and felt
the current take me.

Rumi

Natasha was standing next to the only proper window of her bedsit, fidgeting nervously, as she waited for Sebastian. It had just gone nine o'clock, and the suspense was making her feel sick and light-headed. She kept standing on tiptoes, as she strained to peer over the high, wide ledge of her windowsill to see if his car had arrived. The exercise was pointless because, unless one actually clambered inside the window's alcove to sit on the windowsill itself, the window afforded no view of the road beneath. Natasha was just not thinking straight.

In fact, tonight, she was so thoroughly excited that she could barely draw breath. This only served to exacerbate her light-headedness. Well, that and the fact that she had not eaten a thing since breakfast. What was it about joy that slaughtered the appetite so? Come to think of it, Sebastian was the best diet she had ever known for, since meeting him almost a month ago, she had lost nearly three-quarters of a stone without even trying. As for tonight, Natasha's energy was vibrating at such a love-induced high frequency that, if Sebastian did not arrive soon, she feared she was in danger of disappearing altogether!

Suddenly, Natasha started, for she heard the deafening roar of a monstrously powerful engine. It must be him. Without a thought she grabbed her coat and handbag, then bolted out of the front door and down the stairs at a gallop, with no care or concern for her sure-footedness for in her mind's eye she was already safely held in his arms. When she was almost at the bottom, she could hear the distant buzzing of her intercom spilling down from her bedsit.

Clearly, Sebastian had displayed greater poise on his arrival, than she on his. When a beaming Natasha flung open the front door, Sebastian flinched slightly, for he had been expecting her voice, not her person directly in front of him. As soon as he adjusted to this reality, he dissolved into a glow as luminous as Natasha's: the pair of them as spontaneously phosphorescent as randy fireflies.

There they stood, smiling and shining, brightly, captivated by the miracle that was each other. Now he was here, Natasha found no rush to fall into his arms, for all urgency had been suffocated by the ecstatic elixir that, instantaneously, enveloped her. Suddenly, aware of his shameless adoration of his Love, Sebastian looked down at his feet with embarrassment. He was wearing what looked like a brand-new pair of blue jeans, with a chestnut-brown leather belt, and white cotton Polo shirt underneath his brown leather flying-jacket. Dressed like that, and still staring at his shoes, while shuffling his feet, Sebastian looked half the age of the man whom Natasha had met at work. In fact, he looked as excruciatingly shy and vulnerable as a teenage boy on his first date.

Natasha was then struck by the realization that this was, in fact, their 'first date'. The words had not been said, but that is exactly what it was. Now Sebastian was standing on her doorstep, waiting to take her out, there was no disguising the fact. Was he so bashful because he knew what he was doing was wrong? Natasha was far too full of joy to spend any time moralizing, instead, light-footed she reached up to kiss him gently on his cheek before turning to close the front door behind her. Then, with the innocence of carefree children, they held hands and walked down the wide front steps. Sebastian had brought the Porsche. No wonder she had heard its growl upstairs when he had arrived. It was parked directly outside. He opened the passenger door for her and, once inside, that increasingly familiar, distinctive aroma of expensive leather filled Natasha's nostrils. As soon as Sebastian was sitting in the driver's seat, he turned to her and inquired:

"So my darling one, what's the plan?"

"We're going to The Cross."

"Where?"

"The Cross, it's a nightclub in a grungy part of Kings Cross but the music is brilliant and an old friend of mine, Jazzy, is D.J.-ing there tonight. We used to date a while back. He was kind enough to put us on the guest list. Are you up for it?"

Sebastian was smiling circumspectly. Was he having second thoughts? He looked ahead, clutching the leather-covered steering-wheel, with both of his hands, before looking back at her.

"Natasha, I can't wait to meet your ex-boyfriend; a disc-jockey no less!"

"I think this whole evening is a long stride outside your comfort zone Sebastian, are you sure?"

"I'm game. Let's do it."

"If we end up chatting to Jazzy though, please don't say anything about the ex stuff, it was years ago and when I finished it, it didn't go down well."

"If I can't mention it, then why did you tell me?"

"Because I trust you." Natasha said unquestioningly yet, as soon as she had, she was not so sure if she did. Moving on, her face brightened and she explained, "We don't want to get to The Cross until around midnight, so we've got a few hours to kill first."

"Do we have to kill them Natasha?"

"No, we could always enjoy them instead."

"Well, I suggest we do precisely that. Why don't I take you to Blakes for dinner first?" before he added, in after-thought, "That's if they'll let me in dressed like this."

"That sounds fabulous."

Their evening was set. Sebastian started the car, and the extreme power of the roaring engine made everything inside hum, as they accelerated off to South Kensington. By the time they had arrived at Blakes, Natasha was as high as a helium balloon released off the top of K2!

Once Sebastian had borrowed a tie from the cloakroom

attendant, a hostess led them to a table for two at the back of the restaurant. They were in highly jocular spirits, simply happy to be alone together with an uninterrupted evening stretched out before them. During the course of the dinner, neither work, Bruno nor Isabel were mentioned once. They just held hands and stared into the fascination of each other's eyes, as they drank amazing wine, ate fabulous food and laughed their socks off, over nothing in particular, until their cheeks ached from such prolonged merriment. By the time Natasha was sipping on her double espresso, she had decided that Blakes was as sleek, sophisticated and black as her Lover's Porsche and, no doubt, just as exorbitant.

It was after midnight, when they finally arrived at The Cross. There was an enormous, scruffy, jostling queue rammed in between high, metal, gridded barriers, which stretched at least sixty metres from the matt black, double doors of the club entrance. The individuals, whom comprised the queue, busied themselves chewing gum, or the inside of their mouths, while posturing with some neck or shoulder stretches, or sometimes more elaborate peacock-like shows of 'attitude'. Just like on the trading floor, there was a lot of jiggling and jaw grinding, but here the activities were drug, not stress, induced. Every now and then a sporadic shout burst out from the kettled-in crowd, or sometimes the odd whistle of sheer animalistic exuberance.

As Sebastian and Natasha walked towards the unruly throng, they looked at each other with eyes wide in alarm. This feral crowd could not have been more threatening, following two-and-a-half hours cosseted in the luxurious surroundings of Blakes attended by an oleaginous waiter. Sebastian and Natasha were fast jolted into the state of hyper awareness that potentially dangerous situations always provoke. It was strangely exciting to be rattled so. Sebastian began to take further note of his surroundings, showing the whites of his eyes, even more, as he scanned the area, intently. It was just an urban wasteland most of which had, for now, been employed as a makeshift car park.

Though Natasha had said nothing when Sebastian had parked his flash car nearby, she did fear for its safety and wondered if the wheels would still be there when they returned. With a strict flick of her head, Natasha indicated that Sebastian should follow her. Brazenly, she flounced past the fenced-in queue, straight up to the several thickset black bouncers who controlled the doors. She smiled, broadly, at the grim-faced, beefy men and said, breezily:

"Hi guys, we're on Jazzy's list."

The tallest of them puffed his chest out, much like a threatened bullfrog, then he slowly swaggered towards her. His legs were so muscle-bound that his inner thighs had to roll around each other, in order to achieve forward motion. Having made it, he grunted moodily:

"Name?"

"Natasha Flynn, plus one."

His thick-skinned brow crimpled in concentration while he scanned the list attached to his black plastic clipboard. Finding nothing on the first page he flicked over to the next, then the next before locating the stated name. He looked at Natasha, suspiciously, then gave a surly nod. The whites of his eyes were urine-yellow and his dark skin pocked from unhealthy living. He bent down, laboriously, to unclip the brass end of the maroon plaited rope that served as a barrier. He gave a curt flick of his head to indicate that they could enter then, in a surprisingly smooth, friendly voice, the giant bouncer addressed the two pretty young blondes standing behind the podium with the cash tills, "Two non-paying guests, Jazzy's list."

Both girls acknowledged him, obediently, with vacant nods and Sebastian and Natasha waltzed through to slip into the dark, hot, smoky, thumping environment of The Cross. If the queue outside had been packed, inside the people were as crushed as scattered road salt under the passing tyres of a juggernaut. You could almost hear the grinding of bodies as they pushed past each other. Here, the music was pounding so loudly that it made the club's floor vibrate, ferociously enough, to penetrate the soles of their

CY BLACK

shoes and permeate their bodies and organs with base beat. The incessant, internal thumping rhythm cleared Natasha out so completely that she became just like a drum: empty but for the reverberating tribal beat. They pushed their way down crowded, low-ceilinged corridors, past rocking, teeth-grinding clubbers with black, giant pupils, so dilated that their irises had disappeared altogether. All these haunting faces were washed shiny with sweat, while their hair was made soaking wet from the same. Clearly, ecstasy was the drug of choice here and, as these club-goers tripped on it, their souls fled to leave a disturbing, diabolical absence behind their eyes. Sebastian and Natasha pushed on and on, staying glued to one another, as they navigated their way through tunnels until, finally, they stepped under an arch that led onto the main dance floor. The vibration here was even more intense, for this room held the most powerful loud speakers in the club. They gently shouldered their way to the centre of the floor, and began to rock their bodies to the rhythm. The giant D.J. box towered above them like a sacred altar. Natasha's handsome ex-boyfriend, Jazzy, was working the decks, mesmerically, buoyed by the adoring, drugged-up crowd. Affectionately, Natasha looked up to catch his eye. Jazzy spotted his striking ex-girlfriend soon enough and, without smiling, he gave a curt nod and a quick pursing of lips to acknowledge her arrival. She flashed this musical heartthrob a genuine grin of gratitude but, right now, Jazzy was too consumed existing in a god-like state as he manipulated, paced, delighted and distressed the five-hundred plus crowd.

The bass, the heat, the flashing red, green, blue and white lights, along with the heaving energy of the room, swept Natasha and Sebastian away and they danced in a tribal-like trance deep into the night. In this thumping, packed, Kings Cross nightclub, our lovers found an unlikely space to forget everything that made it so difficult for them to be together. All they were aware of was being next to one another, on a hypnotic musical journey of pounding, peaks and troughs. Natasha was satisfied to note that, for 'an old' bloke, Sebastian danced remarkably well, even if a little overenthusiastically. When she noticed the trend-setting Jazzy check out her tall, new companion, with curiosity, before delivering a tacit nod of approval in her direction, Natasha was ashamed to admit that she felt proud and relieved, all at once.

In time, Natasha and Sebastian became wet with sweat themselves, even without the aid of a couple of ecstasy tabs. Natasha could feel rivulets of the stuff running down her back. Even her hair was beginning to become soaked. Sebastian reached forward to touch her arm, gently. Immediately, she looked up at him. The music was too loud to talk, so Sebastian just flicked his head towards one of the exits, as he took Natasha's hand. Devotedly, she allowed him lead her off the dance floor and through a small arch that led to a narrow balcony outside. It was packed too, and covered with a blood-red canvas awning. The fresh night air hit them full on and, gratefully, the pair inhaled deep gulps to replenish their oxygen-depleted bloodstreams. Miraculously, Sebastian spotted a solitary red plastic chair by the balustrade, squashed between two tables that were jammed with different parties, each of which were smoking, drinking and talking loudly above the music. Playfully, he pulled Natasha over to it before, promptly, sitting down. She just stopped dead in her tracks, surprised by this lapse in manners. When their fired-up eyes locked, all became dangerously clear, for Sebastian slowly patted his thigh with the palm of his hand as he commanded softly:

"Sit on my lap, Natasha."

Without pausing to consider anything so pedestrian as consequence, Natasha did so. They stared, deeply, into each other's glistening eyes, bewitched; each as fatally fascinated by the beauty of their spiritual reflection, as was Narcissus by his face. They were still wet with salty perspiration, the beads of which glistened like brilliant sequins on face and lip. With each exhalation their hot breath left dragon-like trails in the black night that mingled together with every puff. Their white faces had an ethereal brilliance, as if catching the sunbeams of each other's happiness. Still lost in the deep, captivating pools of their pupils, their lips were no more than an inch apart, just like that time in the flash fish and chippy when they had been so dangerously tempted. Just like then, an inexorable force pulled their mouths to one another's, fuelled by profound spirit longing. Now though, the will to resist this elemental tug was doubled up with exhaustion and about to throw in the towel. Quietly, Sebastian uttered two tiny words that would change everything, "Kiss me."

Not one conscious thought occurred in our heroine's mind for, in an instant, her lips were on his; fused. The day of surrender had come and it was beyond heavenly. Their lips were air-locked. More compelling than fluid to salt, their tongues sought each other's, to roll, coax and play in the most rapturous kissing conceivable. Natasha's slim arms were draped adoringly around Sebastian's broad shoulders, while he protectively encircled her waist. Ecstatic, they retreated into their brand-new world: exquisite, perfect peace rediscovered. If such a thing as soul exists then theirs, in this, unite as inextricably as their dragon breath had done only moments before.

Hours passed, in a time warp of essential spiritual intimacy. Eventually, beyond intoxication, our couple took pause. When their lips disengaged and they looked into each other's eyes, it was a rebirth. They rested their brows together to delight in a celestial communion of minds. Here they stayed, spellbound, each stunned by the enormity of this monumental happening. This extraordinary confirmation of 'the other' left each of them undone, cruising willless on an eternal ocean of euphoria. Eventually, souls sated, they slipped back into continuum and, at last, Sebastian gasped:

"Let's get out of here. I want to be alone with you."

It was five forty-five in the morning. They left The Cross, blissful and gripping each other, tightly, around the waist, unable to separate, as they took the short stroll back to Sebastian's car.

All four wheels were intact: unlike the pair of them.

Sebastian drove like a demon through the empty streets of the seediest parts of Kings Cross. It felt obscene to feel so joyous, in such a car, when surrounded by so much evidence of human misery and despair. In several revs of the powerful engine, derelict squats with filthy walls and smashed, or boarded up, windows were abandoned. The staggering drunks, wandering hookers and slumped drug-addicts were soon left behind, and the coarse graffiti and street debris of broken bottles, crushed beer cans and Styrofoam take-away rubbish was no more. As they relentlessly travelled west the grimy filth, and guilt from witnessing it, was left behind.

The streets became cleaner, emptier and brighter. London was bathed in the unearthly English-mustard yellow of the street lamps' sodium glow that so effectively obscured the twinkling stars. By the time they had reached the Bayswater Road, twilight was itching to pounce. Imperceptibly, this intensifying indirect sunlight bounced off the upper atmosphere to be scattered beneath, soon to assume the ascendant illumination of this eerily beautiful cityscape. The roar of the engine was the only sound, each other's soul the only company. Sebastian raced on, before taking an abrupt left turn at such speed that, without the steering-wheel to steady her, Natasha nearly fell on top of him. The black car zoomed down the pink-red road that sliced through the varied greens of the mature trees and dew-dripped grass, to the very heart of Hyde Park.

Suddenly, Sebastian took another sharp left, straight into the car park, just before the bridge that crossed the Serpentine. With a gravelly screech, he came to an immaculate stop at the South East point, in front of the majestic Serpentine Lake. Swans, geese, ducks, moorhens and seagulls were lazily stirring on the still steel-white-light streaked lake. An exhilarated Sebastian turned off the ignition then turned to stare at Natasha, with dewy eyes full of hope. Her inspired face was sublime and radiant.

"Oh Sebastian, how clever of you to bring me here."

she gushed rapturously. "This is one of my favourite places on earth." He smiled at her, the light in his eyes brighter than a moonbeam. Pointing with excitement, Natasha continued, "Look, look over there." Sebastian dutifully looked in the dictated direction. "Yes, right over there, that's where I was born"

Sebastian looked quizzical.

"Hyde Park Corner?"

"Almost; the Lanesborough, in fact. It used to be a hospital... In the old days."

"St Georges." Sebastian interjected, knowingly.

"Exactly, how did you know?"

"Don't forget, you are talking to a Chelsea boy who was living in London well before you were even thought of."

"Well, I have just always loved it here, thank you for bringing me..." she paused before recalling, "Oh Sebastian, I remember the very first time I came here. I must have been five or six years old. It was late summer. I was with my big sister in the back of my mother's boyfriend's gigantic Rolls Royce. We rolled around on the large, slippery, leather seat with every turn. We couldn't stop giggling with the sheer space of it - no one gave a damn about seat belts in those days. He was called Eli (my mother's boyfriend) he had no time for my sister or me, but he was in love with my mother. He only tolerated us to gain favour with her. Come to think of it, they were all like that...

Anyway, to shut us up he bought each of us a bar of Cadbury milk chocolate, the size of a breeze-block. Well, I guess it worked, because we did not make a squeak, we just sat in the back and gorged ourselves until we felt sick. Then he parked in this very car park, just over there, before we took a walk around the lake.

Even though I felt completely sick, I remember hating him and loving this park, his car and the chocolate." She trailed off pensively, for a moment, before adding, "Why am I telling you my childhood secrets?"

"Why not?" Sebastian questioned, "After last night, Natasha, you're my adult secret."

To make her widen her eyes, in horror, and splutter:

"Adult Secret? Oh please Sebastian, that sounds like a soft porn channel."

Sebastian laughed lightly, just before Natasha's bad joke was superseded by the brilliance of dawn; for the crimson peak of the sun's distant disc had just poked over the black-muddy-brown silhouette of the Knightsbridge skyline, flushing the sky with slashes of red and orange to mark the birth of a new day. It was done. Daybreak had arrived and, this night, Sebastian and Natasha had kissed properly for the very first time. In the light of day, the consequences of the forbidden line they had breached began to niggle. Sebastian took a deep breath. Then he looked to the skies, reached for Natasha's hand and muttered, while shaking his head in disbelief, "Boy, do the gods have a sense of humour..."

"Ha ha..." Natasha expressed, in staccato.

He caught her eye and, with one look, they both acknowledged the difficulty of their circumstance. Natasha then stared, hopefully, at the sheer brilliance of the low red-orange risen sun.

"It'll work out Sebastian. Somehow our love will work out." she said, at last, with calm assurance.

Chapter Twelve - Freaky psychic interference

"Beep, Beep, Beep, Beep, Beep, Beep..."

Natasha's hand flailed out to arrest the usual culprit that so disturbed her. In the ensuing silence, the grim pout and frown that had dominated her face since waking, relaxed. She was lying in her warm bed, tucked under her crumpled, white cotton duvet. She gave a laboured starfish-yawn, with arms and legs extended as far as they could reach, making her back arch like a cat. As she came around, she began to blink her bleary, elongated eyes, to shift the sticky sleep that coated them. Only then did she begin to look around to notice that her blind was still drawn over the little attic window above her head.

Alarmingly, Natasha soon realized that she had absolutely no idea what time, or even what day it was. Propping herself up, she checked the offending clock. It read: 18:33. Having discovered the time, Natasha needed to work out the day of the week. Of course, it must be Sunday and, with that established, the preceding evening's sequence of exceptional events, cascaded into her mind, like a row of toppling dominos. An enormous smile spread across her face as she recalled that she had spent most of last night blissfully ensconced in Sebastian's arms. Her chest tickled, for her heart was aflutter with the memory of it. Having stayed awake all night, her Love had dropped her home this morning, a little after eight, before driving out to his country house in Gloucestershire.

Natasha must have slept for more than ten hours solid. No wonder waking up was hard work. Following such a marathon of unconsciousness there was not a drop of adrenaline left in her system. Having run on the stuff for the last several weeks, the lethargy that possessed her now, was both unfamiliar and unpleasant. Dozing still, Natasha's mind dwelt on the memory 'domino' of her lips pressed against Sebastian's. In an instant, she was snatched from her deadened self, and her soul began to somersault with sheer joy, as Sebastian's beautiful face burst into her consciousness, more majestic than the sunrise of this very morning. She was swept away by the force of his disembodied presence. Despite her heavenly, ditzy happiness, her more practical nature began to tap, persistently, at the door of her bliss, to remind her that she was due to leave for Switzerland first thing tomorrow morning. It was also quick to remind her that she had a date with Bruno in less than an hour's time.

O.M.G! Natasha had to pack, shower and get ready; immediately. This urgent call to action, worked its magic for, instantaneously, she was flooded with a fat shot of adrenaline and, quickly, she got out of bed. Now, her heart was racing for more than just Sebastian. As for her somersaulting soul, well, she just had to get on without it, for she had far too much to do!

Natasha pulled her bashed-up suitcase from underneath her bed then began to pack. She hated packing for, having boarded since the age of nine, and having been the daughter of a mother who always wanted to get away (fortunately with her children and not, like so many of her friends' mothers, away from them), she felt she had spent far too much time doing so already and, of course, it was always so much worse if one was not going anywhere fun, like now. Switzerland was fine if you were going skiing, but Natasha was not. In fact, Natasha already knew what she would be doing most of: missing Sebastian. With the happy thought of him, she was reminded, once again, of Bruno's imminent arrival. To her surprise, Natasha managed to pull it off for, when the doorbell sounded, she was ready with the bulk of her packing done. She could finish the rest later. Once she had told Bruno she would be straight down, she quickly stuffed her things into her bag. Her hands were shaking and she felt completely wired. Natasha was about to spend the evening with Bruno, having spent all of last night enraptured in his cousin arms; how confusing...

Bruno was in an exceptionally buoyant mood this evening but even he, in all his innocence, commented that Natasha seemed a little distracted. He drove her to Tootsies to "grab" a quick hamburger because he thought it "highly important" that she get an early night, so she was on "top form" for her trip tomorrow. Over dinner, Natasha's emotional malaise persisted, to such an extent that Bruno began to make excuses for her. He was fast to conclude that she must have been feeling under pressure, because she was about to embark on the intensive, graduate-training programme. Eagerly, she acquiesced to Bruno's analysis and apologised for being such dull company. Indeed, Natasha would have acquiesced to anything - and would do so later - in order to avoid confronting the truth: she was in love with Sebastian, yet she was dating Bruno and, unfortunately, he was falling for her.

While Natasha sat opposite a perfectly delectable, intelligent, handsome, attentive man she felt treacherous and stupid for being semi-present. She may be there in person, but her soul had fled with Sebastian that morning. She squirmed with discomfort, due to the disconnection between her true feelings and her current position. Natasha then began to wonder why fate had conspired to place her in such a thankless situation. Indeed, this evening it seemed to her that the gods did not have a sense of humour, instead, they were simply rather cruel.

When Bruno's hamburger arrived, it was almost as perfect as he. Natasha realized just how hungry she was, and tucked into her chicken burger, with relish. With each mouthful, and with every sip of a remarkably good red wine, she slowly began to relax, and feel less insane and god-abused. She spoke little, ate and drank much and, contentedly, listened to Bruno's bombastic chatter as he told her all about the "utterly thrilling" shooting weekend he had just come from, before going on to insist that Natasha "simply must" join him on the next one.

Indeed, it was all starting to go jolly well, and Natasha even found herself giggling, until Bruno mentioned Sebastian. She started like a spooked horse as soon as she heard his name. Bruno explained that Sebastian had had lunch with him, this very day, and that they had spent the afternoon shooting together. He became thoroughly inspired when he described quite how superbly his cousin had shot. It soon became apparent that Bruno could not compliment Sebastian's skill at killing enough.

"And to think Natasha, Sebastian told me he had not had a wink of sleep all night long! Something about some 'magical party' at a 'secret location' in London. Can you believe it?" he yelped, in good-humoured outrage.

"Gosh!" she spluttered, as she tried to summon a convincing look of surprise, when all she felt was rather sick.

Listening to the good-natured Bruno accolade Sebastian so gushingly, pricked her guilt, mercilessly. She glugged down the fabulous red, as fast as she could, trying to drown the moral scruples that so afflicted her. Unwittingly, Bruno continued to make Natasha writhe when he exclaimed:

"I told him Natasha, in no uncertain terms, if such an evening of debauchery makes him shoot so bloody brilliantly, then I'll be damned if I'm not joining him on the next outing!"

Bruno began to laugh, so much that his shoulders heaved up and down until, finally, he slapped his hand, definitively, onto the table to give a loud bang. He then lunged forward and, looking earnestly into her startled eyes, he said:

"You can come too if you like. It all sounded most intriguing, and, God, did he look well on it. Why, Natasha, I barely recognized him."

Whacked by the irony of it all, she winced. Most frightening was Sebastian's uncanny stamina. Natasha had spent all day sleeping and struggled to wake, while Sebastian had driven to Gloucestershire, lunched with friends and shot bloody brilliantly all afternoon. Just contemplating such feats made her feel weak.

Bruno paused and was staring blankly at the table before he added, seriously, in afterthought, "Not sure what Itzy will think when she finds out though, she won't like the sound of it one bit..."

"Maybe she won't find out?" Natasha ventured.

Her question only drew hysterics from Bruno until, at last, he managed to collect himself enough to reply:

"Clearly, Natasha, you have never met Itzy! Itzy has a habit of finding out about absolutely EVERYTHING! Sebastian hasn't got a hope in hell of keeping such a scrumptious secret from her."

The way Bruno said EVERYTHING made Natasha gulp, nervously. Isabel sounded like a frightening force. Natasha was relieved when Bruno changed the subject. He projected as to how excited she must be about her trip. Indeed, how thrilled she must be to have secured a place on the coveted graduate-training programme at U.C.B. in the first place.

"What an exciting time this is for you Natasha. This is just the beginning of, what I have no doubt will be, a phenomenally successful career in a highly lucrative industry. Well done you!"

With that Bruno poured Natasha her fourth glass of wine, and then raised his.

"To Natasha!"

"Oh, thank you Bruno."

"I know I have not known you long Natasha, but I can tell you this now, I will miss you while you're away."

Bruno's sensitive brown eyes sought Natasha's, as if seeking some encouragement. Natasha flashed a shy smile then looked away and reached for her drink.

"It's not for long Bruno." she muttered, dismissively.

It was only nudging nine when they finished dinner. Bruno paid and drove Natasha the short distance home. He parked his gorgeous E-type roadster outside her house. Ever the gentleman, he opened her door for her, and then escorted her up the steps to her front door. When she inserted her key, Bruno made it plain that he wished to grab more than just a hamburger this evening. He was standing snug behind her with his big hands on her hip bones and pulling her peach bottom, firmly, into his groin to introduce his enormous erection. Bruno then gave an animalistic grunt and, the moment the door opened, Natasha virtually fell through it from the shock. She only just managed to save herself from falling flat on her face, with a little help from the randy Bruno. By the time she had turned around to face him, he had already closed the front door behind him. He stared at her, determinedly, with that unmistakable look in his eye of a man on a mission, while his jeans bulged impressively in front of him. Without word, or invitation, Bruno simply took Natasha by the hand and, with her in tow, he galloped up the three-flights of stairs, as fast as a man is able while brandishing a monster erection! Breathless and shell-shocked, Natasha was, suddenly, in front of the door to her bedsit. She opened it, in a rather fumbling fashion, and as soon as she had done so, Bruno picked her up and carried her across the threshold, before deftly slamming the door shut with his foot, then throwing her dramatically onto the bed. By the time she was bouncing up and down, she was laughing hysterically and, soon enough, a panting Bruno dived on top of her, taking care to preserve his manhood in the process.

The bedsprings were creaking and Bruno's mouth was on Natasha's to silence her giggles. Impatiently, he ripped open her coat, pulled up her top then dragged her bra down in order to expose her pert white breasts. Feverishly, his mouth sought one of her rose-pink nipples and he began to suckle on it, hungrily, as he pinched the other one to make it erect, before lavishing his oral attention on it next. Having feasted on both nipples, Bruno nuzzled his head, affectionately, into her bosom to his heart's content, as he whispered, "Natasha, I've wanted to do that all night long."

Then Bruno kissed Natasha, again, with a passion that was almost suffocating, before breaking away, once more, which was fortunate for it allowed her to breathe.

"Remind me next time, no more of this eating out. Having to behave in public when all I wanted to do was ravish you was sheer torture. I think I was craving my B.J. aperitif. A man can fast get used to that you know?" Bruno then resumed his kissing before he stopped to add, with a startled expression:

"No wonder I did all the bloody talking, I could barely contain myself!"

Natasha laughed, so touched was she by the extent of his ardour. Being picked up and flung around was always a sure way to improve her mood and, God, Bruno was brilliant at it. As she lay underneath him gently stroking his soft clean hair, her heart began to melt towards this sincere dynamo of a man, while her genitals began to pulse lasciviously. Natasha began to kiss Bruno, as passionately as he did her, enjoying the weight of him bearing down on her and his long arms squeezing her as tightly as was legal.

Natasha could not fathom how readily her body responded to this large man's embraces, for she was already the fortunate beneficiary of her extreme arousal, while her mind stubbornly chose to punish her brutally. Each of Natasha's sensual peaks of pleasure, and with Bruno there were plenty, was accompanied by a discordant sound track of self-disgust that relentlessly played in her head while her heart contracted with its betrayal, and lodged itself tightly in her throat. Oh, why was she cursed with such a foolish, opinionated heart?

Bruno was insatiable tonight, probably because he knew he would not be able to have her for the next two weeks. Indeed, it was becoming apparent that Bruno was moving at a faster pace than was his habit and, let's face it, his habit was quite fast enough already. Even before Natasha had decided on her sexual strategy, regarding Bruno this evening, following her chaste intimacies with Sebastian last night, he was lying on top of her, in her bed, with his tongue down her throat and his hand up her knickers. Already, two of his strong fingers were inside her expertly whipping-up willing wetness. Simply, Bruno had disintermediated Natasha's distracted head, to deal direct with her libidinous vagina, that most ineffective gatekeeper of her chastity. Bruno required no verbal consent from Natasha, for he had just procured the wettest invitation from her sex to slide his throbbing manhood inside her, as soon as possible. Following a frantic trouser button and fly fiddle, and a fast shove of his boxer shorts and jeans down his muscular thighs, Bruno's impressive, pulsing penis was unleashed. With a single guttural grunt he slid his big cock into the lubricated, tight, inviting warmth of Natasha. She moaned with extreme pleasure as Bruno's ever-astonishing member stretched the walls of her contracting vagina to capacity. By the time Natasha was crying out with the sheer cunt-clamping pleasure of being fucked by such a stud, she had finally worked out the strategy she should have employed earlier: namely, she ought to have feigned fatigue at the front door, and not allowed him to come up to her flat in the first place! As much as Bruno moaned and groaned with ecstatic pleasure, having sex with him was not really fair, in the circumstances.

Even to a tipsy, emotionally perplexed Natasha, it was clear, by this point, that the best course of action was to proceed to mutual orgasm. The more aroused she became, the more appealing this solution. Soon enough her moans, cries and yelps reached a pitch that almost matched Bruno's. That was until it all went horribly wrong and, with a sudden violent bolt of invasion, Sebastian's disembodied presence pounced onto her: BASTARD. He was right there on top of, and inside her, spiritually overlaying Bruno. Worse, it was as if he was psychically attempting to usurp Bruno entirely. The man screwing her so delightfully, disturbingly, seemed to flip from Bruno to Sebastian to Bruno, second by second, with Sebastian's presence beginning to dominate. It was more than distressing to be hovering on the peak of an explosive orgasm, which had been instigated by Bruno, when Natasha was utterly captivated by Sebastian, in absentia. Like a bodiless, pervasive Cheshire Cat, Sebastian's eyes bored into her soul while his grin hovered, manically, between this copulating pair.

The more his phantom persisted, the more determined Natasha was to give Bruno an orgasm and get it all over and done with. He was working her fast and hard tonight, and she was almost squealing with excruciating arousal. Wanting to reach mutual climax, urgently, so as to be rid of

Sebastian's insane-making spiritual interference, she splayed both her hands across Bruno's toned, flexing, buttocks, and encouraged him to penetrate her, as deeply and quickly as possible, with each thrust, to help work him to orgasm; and boy did it work. Their breathing became more and more shallow, and their faces screwed up with their tangible agony, to herald climactic, joyous ejaculation. In a heartbeat, Bruno had pulled his length and breadth out of her, emitting a deep groan as he did so before, immediately, shooting sticky semen all over her pubis, tummy and semi-clad body with abandon. Oblivious to the copious spunk that was fast covering her, Natasha was transfixed by her own wipeout of an orgasm, which managed to obliterate Sebastian's grinning face, at last, with that white snow-curtain of mind-boggling, orgasmic, ecstatic release:

AAAHHHHHHHHH!!!

Finally, the rampant pair was done and Bruno collapsed heavily, in all of the sex muck, on top of Natasha. For some time, the gasping, shuddering, sweaty couple clinched each other tightly, in gratitude for their extreme erotic pleasure. Lying ensconced together, they drifted through that heavenly, carefree shoreless expanse that is post-orgasmic profound relaxation. It was a long time before Bruno stirred. Slowly coming to, he propped himself up on his elbows to check his watch. It was ten past ten. He looked, adoringly, at the languorous Natasha:

"Wow!"

She gave him a soft smile. Unsurprisingly, having just had an orgasm, and now free of Sebastian's stubborn image impregnating her consciousness, Natasha felt in much better shape. Whatever way one looked at it, she had fantastic sex with Bruno, even if she was in love with Sebastian. Natasha could not resist uttering their emerging leitmotif:

"Bruno, once again, you spoil me..."

Bruno bent down to kiss her gently on the lips, before he winched himself off and sat upright on the edge of the bed. His trousers and boxer shorts were still in a knot around his ankles. His penis, now drooping slightly, was still glossy from sex. He rested his elbows on his big square knees and looked down at the cream carpet, as if to collect his thoughts. Natasha just stared at him as she admired his strong back and defined arms. Bruno reached past Natasha to the duck-egg blue bedside table and grabbed the cubed-shaped box of tissues. Holding it, he pulled out several, then handed some to Natasha to clean up the mess that was all over her, before he began to wipe the sex juices off his tackle, meticulously. Then he compacted his handful of damp, used tissues into a ball, just as one might snow, before he lobbed it all the way across the room and straight into the gold waste-paper bin, next to her chest of drawers, to produce a satisfying thud.

Impressed with his aim, Natasha applauded. Bruno just turned to look at her and smiled, a little bashfully, before standing up to give an enticing flash of his pert buttocks. He then yanked up his boxer shorts and trousers, in one go, and did up his trousers. When he was done, he looked down at Natasha and smiled.

"Well gorgeous, I did make a promise to ensure that you got an early night, so I'm going to make a move now. Please call me when you get there tomorrow, just so I know you arrived safely."

"Not because you want to talk to me then?"

Bruno glared at her.

"You should know better than that by now, Natasha." She just smiled and nodded, as he leant down to kiss the languid girl full on the mouth, for the last time, before whispering, "I will miss you Miss Flynn."

Then he straightened up, made his farewells and left. Natasha remained on the bed, dozing, yet mindful of the fact that she had to get up, wash, finish packing, take her make-up off, brush her teeth and set her alarm for six a.m. for she had to be at Heathrow in time to catch the eight fifty-six flight to Zurich in the morning. Reluctant to move, she was forced to when the telephone began to ring.

"Brrr, Brrr, Brrr, Brrr, Brrr, Brrr..."

Natasha did not have to answer, to know who it was.

185

HE was in her mind already, as bright as the North Star on a frosty cloudless night in the mountains. Jubilant, she picked up the telephone and questioned: "Sebastian?"

He was silent, but Natasha could feel his presence as tangibly as she had felt Bruno' s body on top of hers, only minutes ago. Eventually, he spoke.

"I had to talk to you before you left."

No orgasm could compete with the sheer joy of just speaking to him. Natasha was swept away.

"Oh, Sebastian."

There was another long pause, for the communication that was occurring had nothing to do with crude speech.

"Did you have fun?" Sebastian questioned, in the tone of a father inquiring after his daughter's first tennis lesson.

Immediately, Natasha was back on his lap, in his arms with her mouth pressed to his in The Cross.

"Oh Sebastian," she gasped, "it was the most magical night I have ever..."

"No, I meant just now, with Bruno?" He interrupted, dispassionately.

The succulence of Natasha's love shrivelled up as swiftly as a garden snail chucked into a bucket of highly-salted water. Why was he being so churlish?

"Why do you ask when you were there, Sebastian?" she replied, curtly, for he had upset her.

The force of his presence still occupied her little bedsit, but his determined reticence was agonizing. Finally, he deemed it time to put her out of her misery and, in more sympathetic tones, he spoke.

"Trust me Natasha, this bloody boundless, space-time continuum conquering connection we have is equally disturbing for me. Most especially when you're fucking my first cousin."

There was no judgement in his voice now, just bemusement. For a long time, they stayed on the line dwelling on the extraordinary phenomenon that they experienced in relation to one another.

"It's OK Natasha, you have your fun with Bruno, be

Bruno's girlfriend. It's safer for both of us that way."

Natasha's heart felt squeezed to the point of pulp.

"I love you." he said, at last, almost inaudibly.

Then he hung up. With these three, quiet, little words Natasha became invincible. Well, certainly capable of washing, packing, make-up removal, teeth brushing and alarm clock setting. Despite only having woken a few hours ago, she felt disproportionately exhausted. Well, what did she expect after too much red wine and psychic interference from her soul mate, while screwing his cousin, not to mention a mind-blowing orgasm?

It was eleven thirty-eight when Natasha finally turned out her bedside light. As she lay alone, thinking about her current lot, and what the next two weeks held in store, she found herself looking forward to being able to take some distance from a life that, suddenly, had overtaken and overwhelmed her. The situation in which she had, so quickly, become ensnared, was not one she had ever wished for, or envisaged. Natasha was thankful when the oblivion of sleep, finally, came to claim her, and give her some reprieve from her horribly confusing feelings, and even more disturbing behaviour.

CY BLACK

Chapter Thirteen - **The condom conundrum**

The King who stole my heart
sent a message with a butterfly.
It said, "I am yours"
and a hundred candles
burst into flame.

Rumi

Natasha had been in Switzerland for four days now. Other than falling into a basic hotel bed at the end of a long day, or grabbing a quick nap on a coach journey, she had not stopped. The days had smudged into an indistinguishable blur of rushing along busy, grey streets, hurrying down endless, beige corridors and standing, wandering, or sitting in crowded offices or conference rooms. At every opportunity, the graduate trainees had been bombarded with bank blurb by the most senior U.C.B. bankers, or invasively probed by each other for detailed educational and personal information. In aggregate, the experience to date, had left Natasha somewhat wiser, but nursing a vague headache. The trip had not been enhanced by the fact that, the thirty-one graduates were being chaperoned by two wearisome young women from Personnel, called Kate and Sarah. Kate had startling ice-blue eyes, though not very large or prettily set, for they were a touch too close together. She had extraordinary, waist-length, thick, platinum blonde hair, which rested on the ledge of her tight-jean-clad bottom, which protruded, pertly, from the top of her exceptionally long legs. Kate's face was shamefully unremarkable, however, yet remained neutral enough to allow the bold bumps of her ample breasts, the flash of her blue eyes, the splendour of her hair and the athleticism of her physique, to cast a head-turning spell on most of the male graduate trainees. In fact, the minute a young English chap called Charlie had clapped eyes on her, he had observed:
"She's worth a squirt!" In a most lecherous mutter.
Kate's sidekick Sarah, on the other hand, seemed to

188

serve only as her foil, for the poor dear was tragically plain. She had mousy, thin, straight, shoulder-length hair, which managed to look a touch greasy for the entire trip. Her face was small with a pointed chin and her narrow nose stuck high up out of it, as if trying to get away. Along with her tentative small brown eyes and lipless mouth, one was left with the overall impression of a vole. Invariably, Kate and Sarah would be found standing close together and, in contrast, Kate was bestowed with an unwarranted beauty that would befit a goddess, or at least inspire a man to attempt an opportunistic act of copulation!

Although Kate and Sarah were far too dull for Natasha's tastes, she did begin to feel sorry for them, because the group of alpha personalities fast established that their primary purpose on this trip was to serve them. By the end of the second day, both of them were sulky and crestfallen, sheepishly scuttling around Zurich and repeatedly imploring their opinionated younger charges to stay together. Kate had all but abandoned her lavish hair flicking and, by now, must have sorely regretted handing out such conscientiously compiled itineraries on the first morning for, having done so, the graduates did not disguise the fact that Kate and Sarah had just made themselves redundant.

As Natasha began to get to know the other trainees she had to concede, liberal splashings of coarse humour aside, they were certainly an academically intimidating bunch. Most of them carried twice as many letters after their names as the number of languages they spoke: namely, three to five. Perhaps unsurprisingly, this group comprised some of the most self-confident, self-entitled people she had ever met. Anyone would have felt overwhelmed to be charged with such a group - Kate and Sarah did not stand a chance. As they all flitted around a dull Zurich, visiting several of the many U.C.B. offices in that location, Natasha began to realize just how revered U.C.B. was by the Swiss. The bank appeared to own much of the city and, the parts it did not own, were covered with its gigantic boastful advertisements. When the girls from Personnel were finally herding everyone into a coach, to leave for their next destination, Natasha was relieved. In just four days, she had heard quite enough uninspiring U.C.B. self-congratulation, eaten enough crustless, smoked salmon and cream cheese sandwiches, drunk enough processed orange juice, and heard quite enough about how grateful she should be for having been given the 'immense opportunity' to work for such an astonishing institution in the first place. She was certainly fed up with watching her fellow graduates staring into their futures, with eyes shimmering, as they visualized the immense wealth they were certain to amass for themselves, now that they were so blessed as to perch on the splendid springboard of U.C.B!

As soon as the coach started to roll on its way, Kate and Sarah began to puff themselves up with renewed self-importance before their trapped audience, for the timeliness of the itineraries they had handed out before, had just expired. From here on in, the graduates had no idea where they were going, or what they would be doing when they got there. It seemed, after their recent days of misery, the girls had learnt the truth of the adage 'knowledge is power', and now they gripped that lesson, as tightly as a stinging nettle, in order to prevent further self-harm.

Suffice to say, for the rest of the trip, all pertinent information was drip-fed. As expectant faces stared at her, the only intelligence that Kate deigned to provide, was that they were taking a three-hour journey to the next hotel in which they would stay to receive further intensive, academic instruction. Following a lumbering, increasingly winding, thoroughly sick-making drive, they finally arrived in a chocolate-box picturesque valley, in the depths of the Swiss September countryside. The valley was flanked by spectacular black-brown jagged mountains, the peaks of which were speckled blue-white with snow. A large, yellow sun was shining low over the westerly mountain ridge. It all seemed too perfect, and clean to be true, which was certainly a, long overdue, and most welcome contrast to our heroine's love life!

At last the coach ground to a stony halt outside a modern, low-built, characterless wooden block of an hotel. The sight was somewhat redeemed by the umpteen window boxes that covered it, which burst forth with a profusion of brilliant, iridescent flowers: pink, blue, yellow, orange, white, crimson and purple. The hotel sat alone without a village in sight. The only other structures visible, were two large residential chalets, set some distance apart, farther down the valley, each of which looked like they had been shut-up for now. Sarah gloated as she dripped drops of select information to her news-thirsty coachload. She informed them that U.C.B. owned the hotel, and that the only guests that ever stayed there were employees of the bank for conferences and intensive training courses, such as this one. Glee stole the tightness from her face when she shared this unwelcome slug of intelligence, the subtext of which was swiftly understood by all: in short, there was nowhere to go, no other guests to play with and no mischief to be had, or at least that is what she hoped for the ungrateful lot of them. Sarah ended with a vengeful flourish, "We will be staying here for nine days." and then she nodded her head once, defiantly, as a smile of satisfaction smudged across her little mouth.

Sarah's pale, freckled face grinned even more broadly, as she relished the graduates' voluble moans and groans of disappointment. The girl did not possess enough imagination to fathom that, if there was no fun to be had, several in this party would be sure to create some! While the group began to absorb the true limitations of the location, they started to scan their surroundings, as they put on coats and gathered their belongings, before shuffling down the aisle to get off the coach.

When Natasha was out in the sharp, cold air she was most enchanted to hear the scattered tinkling of heavy, brass cowbells for there were herds of the beasts everywhere, either black and white or brown and cream, grazing on the long, luscious, deep green grass that carpeted the valley. Once the driver had unloaded Natasha's suitcase, she wheeled it over the chunky gravel, with difficulty, then into the hotel. Having checked-in, a boyish, enthusiastic porter carried her luggage as he showed her up to her room. It was much grander than she had anticipated with a king size double bed, writing desk, chair and television. It was west facing with a large balcony that overlooked a superb mountain view. She tipped the porter and, as soon as he was gone, she slid back the heavy patio doors to step onto the balcony. She went over to the balustrade and rested her elbows on top, as she looked out across the majestic scene while taking great gulps of the freezing, pristine air. It was most invigorating.

Natasha felt at one with the world, and she marvelled at the extreme beauty of the peach-red sun as it threatened to set behind the mountain ridge. Already, brilliant slashes of ripe-pomegranate red were streaked across the baby blue sky and a ghostly, silver-white, waning half-moon, subtly, sobered the vibrancy of the heart-stopping sight to seize one with a cool serenity. The birds chirped robustly, the cows mooed contentedly and Nature's music was delicately percussioned with the random, carefree tinkling of cowbells; like a field full of wandering wind chimes. Natasha was so joyously overcome by the exceptional beauty of it all that, naturally, her mind turned to her Love.

"Sunrise with Sebastian, sunset in solitude."

With that thought, Sebastian's presence permeated her whole being, to delight and contradict her all at once. If she had not known better, it was as if he was standing next to her and witnessing this remarkable spectacle with equal rapture. Natasha was jolted back to the time-strapped moment, the minute she heard the pounding of trainers scrunching on the gravel path beneath. She looked down to spot two young men bobbing up and down, vigorously, as they covered the ground at surprising speed. One of them was wearing a frog green and white tracksuit, while the other was in an electric blue one, with two white stripes down the legs and arms. On closer inspection, she could see that it was Emmanuel and Klaus, two of the European graduates on the course with her. She had not yet really spoken to either of them, but she knew they were a few years older than she, for they had both done postgraduate degrees before joining the bank's graduate-training programme. They certainly looked manlier than her English male counterparts, who still brimmed with boyishness.

Indeed, Emmanuel was exceptionally handsome in that French, olive skinned, fit fashion and she could not have helped but notice his mesmerizing eyes. They were the turquoise-colour of the Caribbean. He was not as tall as Natasha's usual taste, however, his princely proportions certainly atoned for that. Indeed, Emmanuel would have looked as hot in trunks on a sun-drenched beach as he looked in a business suit. Let's face it, either outfit was a marked improvement on a frog green tracksuit. Soon enough, they were halfway across a field full of cows for a pre-dinner run. Klaus' and Emmanuel's exemplary conduct, quickly reminded Natasha of her less admirable plans. She was due to meet her new friend Maria in the bar in forty-minutes time. Natasha knew, full well, that she would not be taking a run before dinner but she was determined, at least, to manage a shower.

Refreshed, Natasha was now sitting comfortably on one of the big, brown, felt sofas in the bar, next to Maria de Feria, with a cold glass of vodka and orange in her hand. The place was filling up and, from the look of their pink cheeks, it appeared that Charlie and Ollie had been drinking there since they had arrived. The atmosphere was positively electric, for Kate had just made a surprise announcement (she was getting the hang of this): Edward Sanford, the dashing Global Head of Trading and Sales, (and also the very man who had hired Natasha) was due to join them, that very evening, where he would give a welcome pre-dinner speech, and then some preliminary academic instruction the following morning, before returning to London.

Natasha's new Spanish friend, Maria, was a pretty, petite brunette who was no more than five-foot five. She had shoulder-length, dark brown curly hair and a wide, full-lipped mouth that was forever smiling to flash large, dazzling white teeth. Maria had been recruited in Madrid and she had not yet met the legendary Sanford, nor even visited the London offices. She seemed overjoyed at the prospect of meeting the Global Head of Trading and Sales viz. God, as far as the Debt Division was concerned. Maria shimmered with excitement as she questioned Natasha, enthusiastically:

"Oh Natasha, Natasha, tell me, tell me: what is Edward Sanford really like? Is he as good-looking as they say? Is he as clever?"

Passionately, Maria leant forward to touch her knee, as she peered intently into Natasha's face. Our heroine was unused to such tactile behaviour and she automatically flinched when Maria's hand made contact. Not wishing to offend her warm-hearted new friend, she allowed Maria's hand to retain its position, and she determined to adjust to these Spanish ways. Gauging Maria's hunger for information, Natasha smiled, wickedly, then, with teasing evasion, replied, "Well, I don't know your type, of course, Maria so I am not sure if you will think him attractive." Maria just scrutinized Natasha's face and nodded eagerly to encourage her to divulge some specific details, "Well, what I can tell you is, he is never short of female admirers and as for clever? Bloody. When he interviewed me, his mind was quick, precise and highly stimulating."

Maria's generous brown eyes were wide with shocked indignation. She began to tap Natasha on the knee, several times, as if to scold her, before she started to shake her head from side to side in disapproval. She then instructed Natasha, in her charming, thick, Spanish accent, "OK, OK, he is clever, but what does he look like? You have not told me the most important part Natasha! Not good enough!" Natasha giggled at Maria's impassioned performance. With conviction, the girl went on to implore, "Natasha please tell me: how tall is he, what is the colour of his hair, describe me the colour of his eyes? Is he thin or fat? Is he muscular or wiry? And the *voice*, the *voice*, how is his *voice*?"

Here Maria broke her round of interrogation to roll her large brown eyes, extravagantly. She then snatched her hand from Natasha's knee, made a delicate fist, pulled her shoulders together and, with her fist placed passionately on her chest, she exclaimed breathlessly:

"Ah, the *voice,* Natasha..." Just dwelling on that concept and staring into space seemed to thoroughly enchant Maria, before she finally snapped out of it and looked directly into Natasha's eyes to impart a cherished secret, with gravitas, "The voice of a man, is the most important thing of all."

There was something about the way Maria had said 'man' that made Natasha want to meet the one of which she had been thinking; immediately. Delighted with her new friend's dramatic nature, she nodded in agreement, for she found the girl's observation to be quite true. In fact, she liked this bossy creature, immensely, and she was forced to wonder how such a colourful personality came to be in a Swiss valley, waiting to embark on an intensive course in bond maths.

"My, how demanding you are Maria! Well if you insist, I will do just that." Natasha conceded, with a chuckle. She then placed her hands in her lap, looked up and concentrated, in order to conjure an image of Edward. Having grasped a picture of him, in her mind's eye, Natasha met Maria's hungry gaze and began to describe the man in question. "Edward Sanford: well he is around six-foot one, so not so tall and more on the wiry than the muscular side, however, he has so much presence that I always remember him as being much bigger than he actually is."

Maria was listening keenly and nodding with satisfaction, as Natasha continued, "Edward's eyes are exceptionally quick and brown, much the same colour as your own in fact, if a little less golden, and he has short, dark hair with a slightly kinked fringe that makes him look boyish, even though he must be in his mid-forties. He has an acutely penetrating gaze, however, he is prone to breaking eye contact, but I think he just gets bored quickly, and moves on from the subject under discussion, before one has finished discussing it." Natasha paused and looked to the heavens, once again, to refresh Edward's image before continuing, "His face is on the narrow side, but his cheekbones are high, and his nose is strong and straight. His upper lip is slightly curled, which can make him appear a little cruel, if he chooses, but when amused, he has a conspiratorial smirk that makes you feel uniquely special, when he bestows it on you. Oh and, of course, the *voice...* the *voice.*"

Natasha mimicked Maria's impassioned annunciation of the word, and her new friend's eyes squinted playfully back at her to be sent up so, "Maria, I can assure you, you will not be disappointed by his voice, for it is as rich and warm as Italian chocolate fondant, oozing dark runny goo. As for his articulation, it is as precise and unforgiving as that of the most educated Englishmen."

Maria flapped her arms with delight before beginning to shower praises on Natasha.

"Oh Natasha, thank you, thank you; so well described and so much better than before! I can see him clearly now. Tragically, he sounds exactly like my type. Is he single, is he available?"

"Available? Apparently. Single? No. Married for yonks, with oodles of children."

Maria looked crestfallen and confused.

"What do you mean? Available? How so if he is married with so many children?"

Natasha stared, questioningly, at Maria, unsure as to whether her naïvety was for real.

"Sadly, Maria, too many married men are carnally available. It is rumoured at work that Edward is one of them."

Maria looked most disappointed, for she was frowning and staring down at the floor. Natasha could only attribute her new friend's reaction to her Catholic sensibilities. Wishing to cheer her up, she adopted Maria's affectionate body language and she leant forward, to place a hand on her knee as she consoled, "It is only a rumour. I could be doing the man a horrible disservice. Lots of people spread horrible things about people who seem to have it all. Maybe the disturbing rumours are merely due to others' jealousies?"

Maria raised her head and looked into Natasha's eyes then, with a clap of her hands, she dismissed the subject and, just like that, she was all bright smiles, once again.

"Can I get you another drink, Natasha? Same again?"

"Yes please." she answered, eagerly.

It was not long before the slightly tipsy young women were herded into the dining-room, along with the rest of the trainees. They sat next to each other at one of the long tables, all of which were covered in light pink tablecloths. Four tables were arranged in a square formation, and set for thirty-five diners. Steve Hughes, the head of Personnel, and Edward Sanford stood at the centre of one, locked in serious, hushed dialogue. Once everyone was seated, Steve piped-up and introduced himself, before saying a few words of welcome. He then handed over to Edward Sanford, so he could deliver his speech. Natasha had not met Steve Hughes before, and she was not impressed. He went a long way to explaining Kate and Sarah's lack of dynamism, for like attracts like, and the three of them seemed cut from the same dull cloth.

Edward soon rescued the room from Steve's cloying company, when he launched, vigorously, into an inspiring speech, pacing up and down as he did so, with an electric energy that seemed to charge the assembly. Maria looked star-struck for one, indeed, apart from the pair of them, there were only three other female graduate trainees on the course, and they seemed equally smitten with Edward's performance. He was quick to draw bursts of empathetic laughter from all present, as he alluded to his own invincibility, a plethora of his accomplishments and to the highly impressive calibre of every single one of them. He went on to offer advice on how to navigate the Swissness of U.C.B. in order to achieve one's objectives, continuing to flatter the capabilities of his audience, shamelessly, all the while. Edward then inspired, each and every one of them, to push themselves beyond their limits, before spurring them on with the daunting challenge: as soon as the course was completed and their honeymoon period over, all surplus fat would be cut, so they must be sure to evolve into a piece of core muscle of U.C.B.'s profit centres or, sooner or later, they would be out of a job. Edward then singled out Natasha, as he fixed her with his piercing eyes.

"If you are as good as someone at U.C.B. thought you were then, rest assured, the road of your future is paved with gold."

Natasha squirmed, for how embarrassing was that? Finally, Edward concluded his vivifying speech with a heartfelt, "Good luck."

Immediately, the room was filled with thunderous applause and foot stamping, along with low-level multiple mutterings of "Hear, hear." At least Maria was not as easily rabble roused. However, on a second inspection, Natasha was concerned to note that her friend's eyes shone a little too brightly, as she brazenly beheld the legend. Following a rich three-course dinner, most of the party moved back into the bar. Natasha and Maria were waiting patiently to be served when Edward Sanford materialized to Natasha's right. He stood close next to her as he, ritualistically, adjusted his solid gold cufflinks, before darting one of his beguiling, conspiratorial smiles in her direction.

"Can I get you to drink?" Edward inquired.

Natasha flushed, with the unexpected proximity of this charismatic man.

"Oh, thank you Edward, that would be lovely. A glass of champagne please."

Apart from a few handshakes, Natasha had never been this close to Edward Sanford for any length of time. Indeed, she had hardly seen him since her final, and decisive, interview over eight weeks ago. He was even more attractive close up. Not wishing to exclude Maria, Natasha stepped back to introduce her to Edward, formally. Maria was agog and she gushed with praise for his speech. He was clearly flattered, and Maria's darting, bright-eyes studied his face and form, meticulously, while they had a brief, intense conversation. Edward offered to get her a drink too, and Maria requested the same. While he was commanding the barman's attention, Maria moved in close to Natasha, and then leant forward as she whispered, into her ear.

"They are not rumours."

Maria then pulled away and, discreetly, tapped her wedding ring finger, as she gave a nod in Edward's direction. Natasha was not sure what she meant but, when Edward turned to pass her her glass, Natasha noticed a light circle where his wedding band would have sat, on his otherwise tanned left hand. This evening there was no ring there. Maria had noticed.

It was not long before Edward turned his attention to Natasha, again, while Maria wandered off to join the two graduates Natasha had seen running earlier. Edward started to engage her in conversation. He was standing so close to her that she could feel his breath on her face. It smelt of cigars. Natasha felt slightly overwhelmed to find herself the sole focus of Edward Sanford's piercing intelligence. Their body language would have been more appropriate had they been sharing intimate secrets, and not talking about his initial thoughts regarding the quality of the graduate intake this year. An unlikely rescuer arrived in the form of Steve Hughes, for he came up behind them and placed one of his hands on each of their outside shoulders. Nervously, Steve excused himself to Edward, for interrupting, before turning to Natasha and introducing himself. Natasha felt more than flattered that the Head of Personnel had made such an effort on her behalf. Suddenly, she felt ashamed to have judged him so quickly. It was only when Steve began to fumble around in the breast pocket of his jacket, to then produce an envelope, that Natasha realized there was more to his intrusion than uncommon courtesy. He soon presented it to her, right in front of Edward, before announcing:

"Natasha, I'm under strict instructions to give you this."

She took it, and looked at Steve, quizzically, while Edward's face betrayed even greater curiosity. Smiling creepily, Steve enlightened the pair of them:

"It's from Sebastian Butler. He said it was important."

The way Steve said Sebastian Butler, made it seem as if he revered him as much as the Swiss revered U.C.B. Steve then apologised to Edward, once again, before slinking off. Edward looked at Natasha with deeply suspicious eyes. Natasha was stumped and looked at him with a startled expression. In no time, Edward broke the silence:

"Well, Natasha, aren't you going to open it? How can one resist such intrigue for a moment longer?"

Natasha then thought of Steve Hughes. She had been right first time. Only a prick would have set her up in this situation. Did he really have to reveal that Sebastian had sent her a private communication right in front of his, and her own, big boss? The lengths some people will go to for attention! What on earth was she to do now? Natasha fought off a blush as she replied with borrowed nonchalance, "Oh, it can wait."

Edward persisted, undiverted:

"Important, Mr. Butler said, no?"

"Why Edward, what could be more important than enjoying a conversation with the very man responsible for hiring me?"

He understood precisely what Natasha was up to, but chose to indulge her stubbornness, besides, he would get the truth out of Sebastian when he got back to London. Natasha continued to avert a difficult situation.

"You promised me in my interview, not so very long ago, that one day you would tell me all about the wonders of heli-skiing in Zermatt."

Edward raised one eyebrow, censoriously, for several seconds, then finally relented for, like most powerful men, he enjoyed talking about himself, especially to pretty young women, far too much to resist Natasha's cue, and he soon launched into tales of his winter sport daring. He described how impossibly exhilarating it was to leap from a helicopter and fall into deep, virgin snow. He told her how when one stood on the peak of an unskied mountain, well, one absolutely owned it. No words could begin to describe the sheer exhilaration that possessed one: the adventure, the pioneer spirit, the excitement and the eerie haunting peace of it; well, once the chopper had fucked off, of course! Then to swiftly plough your blades through fluffy, spring powder to create perfect geometric spirals down the untouched mountainside, until tears start to streak from behind goggles with the sheer speed and brilliance of it all. He went on to exclaim, "I can assure you Natasha, as far as experiences go, un-bloody-beatable!"

She listened attentively and soon worked her way through her drink, only to be handed another. It was fast becoming apparent that Edward found Natasha nearly as tantalizing as heli-skiing for, in no time, she found herself squashed up against the wall. She did notice, however, that following the message from Sebastian, Edward had moderated his flirtatiousness for, though she felt trapped, his face no longer brushed quite so close to hers. As Natasha listened to him describe one of his favourite sports, with great passion, to her shame, all she could think about was the mysterious message from Sebastian. She forced herself to pay close attention, only to find that Edward made her laugh so much that her cheeks began to ache. Sebastian aside, Natasha had to concede, Edward really was an astonishingly talented raconteur. Finally, creepy Steve returned to suggest, tentatively, that Edward join him to circulate. Having spent the last forty-five minutes, in animated dialogue, with just one of the thirty-one graduates, Edward knew he was as cornered as Natasha had been. Reluctantly, he excused himself and bestowed one of his best smirks on Natasha before, impulsively, touching her lower arm and leaning forward.

"Natasha, I do hope you get all you wish for." he then whispered into her ear.

Strangely, Edward's kind words made Natasha's throat

engender a fat lump. Then, in a flash, he was across the room presenting his broad back to her, as he set about enchanting some fellow graduates. Our heroine just swallowed once, before leaving the bar. The minute she turned the corner she bumped straight into Maria. They both giggled, with shocked delight, at the happy collision, and then they each took a step back, to look at each other properly, as Natasha asked, with genuine interest:

"Hey Maria, what did you think of Edward?"

Her friend's face, suddenly, turned comically cross.

"I did not like him at all." Maria snapped.

Recalling Maria's expression every time she looked at the man in question, Natasha struggled to reconcile her response and inquired:

"How so, Maria? It appeared as if you liked him a lot."

"No I did not. Had he, on the other hand, paid me even half of the amount of attention that he paid you then, certainly, I would have liked him very much indeed!"

The girls burst out laughing and, once again, Natasha found Maria to be delightfully entertaining.

"Was it really so bad Maria?"

"It was worse."

Natasha smiled, affectionately, yet still she yearned to learn what was inside the envelope. Quickly, she excused herself, and told Maria that she would join her in the bar in few minutes time. In the blink of an eye, Natasha was locked into a lavatory cubicle and putting the loo seat down, in order to sit on top of it. Immediately, she took the white envelope out of her bag and held it to her heart like a precious present for, to her, that is what it was. Only this morning her Love must have held it in his hands and now, written inside were sentiments that encapsulated a slice of his recent consciousness. When Natasha turned the thing over to open it, she was puzzled to discover that the envelope had not even been sealed, for the flap still had the shiny, plastic strip stuck to the adhesive that traversed it. How daring she thought, for a moment, before soon realizing, with a gush of disappointment, that Sebastian could not have written anything incriminating. Indeed, it shouted to Steve Hughes that he had nothing to hide. How dull, when all Natasha craved from him were incriminating sentiments! Still hungry for anything to do with Sebastian, she took the stiff piece of paper out of the envelope to discover that it was, in fact, a postcard with a photographic image of the sun, on the verge of setting behind snowcapped mountains. Spookily, it could have been taken from her hotel balcony, only a few hours ago. She was bewitched. To have sensed him so tangibly there with her earlier, and now, to receive such an unexpected image from him, seemed more than extraordinary. Instantaneously, her skin sprang with goose bumps and the hairs on her forearms stood on end. Natasha turned the card over and began to devour the words, which were neatly written in fountainpen, blue ink.

We are thinking of you, and wish you the best for your trip to the land of the cuckoo clocks. We know where you are staying (did I get the view right?) so we can't imagine you will get into any trouble! Speaking of which, I visited a magical venue over the weekend, with a member of the team, and we got into lots of that. It was so fantastic that I have decided to make the excursion a regular Desk event. Get qualified, come back and be sure to join us next time. Important: my cousin awaits your call.   S

She read and reread the card, as if to take occupation in Sebastian's recent thoughts, even if the truth of them had been masked, a little ill Natasha thought, though she had to confess the Royal 'we' suited him. Each time she read the card she swooned, and each time she read the last sentence, her heart contracted with guilt. She had promised to call Bruno and she had not. She adored Bruno, but in this private moment just the thought of him, frustratingly, obstructed her worship of Sebastian. As she sat on top of the seat of an hotel lavatory, clutching and rereading a post card for a sixth time, she realized just how far gone she

203

was. By the time she had read, 'my cousin awaits your call' for the seventh time, Natasha knew she could not continue to deceive Bruno, any longer, for such a man deserved so much more than she was capable of giving him.

Finally, Natasha tucked the card, and her love, away before revisiting the bar. When she entered the room she was possessed of a beatific smile and, quickly, she found Maria sitting on the sofa in between Emmanuel and Klaus. Ollie and Charlie were close by, talking to, or rather drooling over, Kate. Natasha offered to get a round of drinks, and the momentum with which the orders were flung at her, turned out to be a harbinger of the night ahead.

Natasha was ecstatic following the correspondence from Sebastian and she did not need any more alcohol to enhance her mood, however, that is what she drank, and far too much of it. To become horribly drunk is never attractive, but to become horribly drunk with a group of people with whom you will be working, closely, for the next two months, and at the same bank, for possibly the next several years, is just plain stupid. Oddly enough, that is exactly what all those left in the bar, did that night. The trainees' appetite for alcohol, appeared to be as insatiable as their one for money.

It did not take long for the devastatingly handsome Emmanuel to begin to employ his French Martiniquean charm on Natasha. He was sitting close next to her on the chocolate brown sofa, with Maria on his other side. Maria was locked in conversation with Klaus while Emmanuel faced Natasha. One of his elegant ankles was resting on his knee, as he leant forward to rest his elbow on the other one, thus displaying a bulging crotch shot. Natasha's stare, however, could not leave his striking eyes, for they delved deeply into hers as he began to tell fantastical and terrible tales, in his alluring accent, encapsulated in a voice so bass that Natasha's very bones hummed with it. The sound hypnotized and seduced her, all at once. Oh God, Maria was right about the *voice* and how dangerous was Emmanuel's?

After much amusement, and more wine, for Emmanuel

made sure Natasha's glass was never empty, he began to share his childhood tribulations with his captivated audience of one. Oh, how astonishingly stoical was he, as he described how his parents had packed him off to France, at the age of five, to attend a monastic boarding-school. The more Natasha heard of his tale, the more choked she became, for how brutal was the regime he described: five a.m. wake-up calls and cold baths were the best of it, in that most un-Godly of institutions where 'men of God' presided over the suffering and abuse of innocents. How Natasha admired Emmanuel's courage and strength of character, as his other-worldly eyes bored into her heart, and he concluded in his all enveloping bass:

"Natasha, what does not kill you, makes you stronger."

This was Emmanuel's only judgement on his abandonment and stolen childhood. His fortitude and forbearance engendered such gushing empathy in our tipsy heroine, that she fell forward to clasp his hand. Holding it tightly, she stared into his hypnotic eyes.

"Oh Emmanuel, poor you." she murmured, breathlessly.

As Natasha did so, the depth of her heartfelt compassion caused her to spring a heavy tear, which began to roll down her delicate cheek, slowly. Emmanuel accepted Natasha's comfort in silence and, never breaking eye contact with her, he lifted his broad hand to stroke it away, gently. Still staring at her intently, he brought his finger to his mouth and licked off the minute amount of salty moisture with his eloquent tongue. As if the taste of her fluid were his invisible cue, sombrely, Emmanuel stood up and led Natasha, by the hand, out of the bar and then up the single flight of stairs to his hotel room. She was will-less, emotional, tired and drunk, and she followed Emmanuel less questioningly than a newborn duckling after its mother. He drew to a halt outside the heavy oak door to his room. He unlocked it effortlessly with the card-key and then slowly led Natasha inside and to the foot of the bed. Emmanuel turned to look directly into her glistening eyes, before cupping her face, gently, between his hands, as his stunning turquoise eyes penetrated the kernel of her heart.

Confusingly, Natasha felt that powerful vertiginous pull of sexual and soulful attraction. Emmanuel's hands slipped to the back of her head and, grasping the nape of her neck with quiet conviction, he pulled her to his mouth and kissed her with exquisite delicacy. Natasha could still detect the salt from her tear on his tongue, as she lost herself in the moment of acutely sensitive, intimate, oral sensation. The extent of her fatigue and inebriation quashed any measured resistance; instead, she just surrendered to the elevation of such delectable pleasure, with this most sexually sophisticated creature.

Emmanuel's kisses became more and more intense, until he gently pushed her back onto the bed before climbing on top of her, with great agility. He continued to kiss her all over her face, then on each of her closed eyelids, as he caressed her body, with such a seductive touch that it bewitched her. Natasha was swept away by his gentle, conscientious, celebration of her curves. Indeed, his kisses and caresses were the most accomplished Natasha had ever known. Utterly besotted by this beautiful man's sexual artistry, Natasha allowed him, gradually, to peel away each item of her clothing to expose her milk-white skin to his sweet mouth, inquisitive hands, and the cool moonlight that flooded in through the patio double doors.

With every new exposure of flesh, Emmanuel sighed with the appreciation and wonder of an artist. Natasha's only awareness, was of his attentive mouth on her flesh until she opened her eyes to find, to her surprise, that he had not only managed to remove all of her clothes, but all of his own as well. As they lay naked on the bed, his skin seemed so brown in contrast to hers, which glowed bright white in the moonlight.

Emmanuel's dark head began to move down her body, in minute increments, kissing every little sensitive piece of her on the way: ears, neck, collar-bone, shoulders, breast-bone, breasts, nipples, stomach, hip-bones and then tantalizingly close to her pubis. The flesh on flesh contact of his fit rock-solid body against hers was irresistible, and his satin skin even softer than Natasha's. The gorgeous, passionate Emmanuel simply soaked up the mystery that is woman with the thirst of the Sahara. Before his astonishing eyes and under his hot active mouth, Natasha felt beyond beautiful. Emmanuel was now luxuriating over her apple pert breasts. He kissed her each and every contour, for an eternity, before beginning to suckle and nibble teasingly at her erect nipples. Natasha was lying flat on the bed, ecstatic, as her hands ran hungrily through the thick glossiness of his cropped hair, while he continued to burrow into, and delight, her bosom to elicit gasps from our heroine worthy of the damned. Imperceptibly, Emmanuel now began to move minutely lower and lower and lower down Natasha's yearning body, lost in his kissing-worship of her all the way until, finally, he arrived at her exposed, pink, excited sex.

Emmanuel seemed seized by angelic inspiration, as he flicked out his silky wet tongue and pressed its hotness onto her clitoris. With both of his strong hands massaging her breasts, vigorously, he began to tease Natasha's clitoris, relentlessly, until she began to shudder violently with exquisite pleasure. Suddenly, his hot, strong, agile tongue was inside her vagina, darting in and out to drive her to distraction. Emmanuel's adoration of her body, his excruciating tenderness and his complete mastery of all female physical mechanisms, soon began to work their magic and explosively generate successive and dramatic lightning bolts of pleasure, that shot throughout her trembling body to promote orgasm galore!

Emmanuel's thirst was unquenchable, and he drank and drank and drank her sex juices, yet still gasped and worked on her for more. Natasha's acute, electric, arousal summoned a sliver of her sense and she managed to mumble, through sighs of deep longing:

"Condom."

For Emmanuel's highly accomplished art of seduction, was far too sophisticated, and clearly well practised, to risk full sex without one and, realistically, what woman could resist this? With that simple command, Emmanuel's gorgeous, flushed, wet face appeared smiling from in between Natasha's spread legs. He wiped the glistening, sweet wetness of her away, with the back of his hand, before pushing himself up from the bed. Now Emmanuel was standing naked before her, Natasha had the pleasure of witnessing the beauty of his tanned, defined, broad, breathtaking body as he strode across the room and into the bathroom. Natasha remained on the bed, her legs crossed with longing and her mind quite bewildered by her own restraint.

Emmanuel soon emerged wearing the white hotel bathrobe, only to leave the room. Natasha waited, impatiently, still electric with desire. He returned, soon enough, took off the robe, flung it onto the chair at the bottom of the bed, and then jumped on top of her. He started to ravish her, passionately, all over again. She pushed him back to look into those extraordinary eyes and, with a stern expression, she mouthed:

"Condom?"

Emmanuel's beautiful face broke into a grin.

"Natasha, I do not have a condom, but do not worry, one is on its way. Just, be patient." he uttered in his divine tones. What was it with gorgeous foreign men and patience? Natasha was not, and never had been. Sensing her disquiet, he laughed and then took her head, firmly, in between his hands as he instructed, sternly:

"Relax and enjoy. It won't be long. I promise."

Then he began to kiss each and every inch of her flesh, feverishly, once again. Natasha was too aroused and her brain too alcohol soaked, to question how a condom might arrive in his hotel room at this late hour, but she was soon to find out. As they moaned and writhed naked on the bed, locked in a passionate embrace, with their tongues down each other's throats, there was a loud knock on the door. Enthusiastically, Emmanuel leapt out of bed and dashed over to open it. When Natasha heard thunderous bursts of coarse laughter cascade into the room, she felt as if she had just been tasered. Dire dread plagued her, as soon as she recognized Charlie's cackling drawl as he slurred:

"Oy, you jammy bugger, if my cock was as gigantic as that, I'd be walking around the fucking Life Floor naked, not just opening the bloody door!"

Charlie's comment managed to provoke hoots of laughter from an appreciative audience, as he fast pushed past Emmanuel, to swagger into the room followed by a hysterical crowd comprised of Ollie, Klaus, Maria, Kate and Sarah. Natasha's hands sought to cover her exposed private parts, as her mouth fell open in shock. She was speechless. At least the fright had sobered her up. The uninvited nocturnal visitors were doubled up and clutching their sides, incapacitated by their smutty laughter. The chivalrous Emmanuel, quickly, grabbed his discarded robe and flung it at Natasha so she could cover herself. He then wandered over to Charlie with hands on hips, not caring who saw his tackle, for Charlie had been right regarding his phenomenally impressive asset. Emmanuel put his hand, firmly, on Charlie's shoulder and ordered:

"OK my man, the joke is over. Now get the fuck out of my room."

Still locked in hilarity, but sensing that Emmanuel meant business, Charlie chucked a packet of condoms onto the bed, and then allowed Emmanuel to lead him out of the room, with the same cool composure with which he had led Natasha in. The others were still struggling to control themselves, as they obediently shuffled out, after Charlie, with heads bowed; all except for Kate. Grim-faced and unsteady on her feet, she remained at the bottom of the bed. She had her hands on her hips, just like Emmanuel had done only moments ago. Kate was trying to look menacing, yet she seemed to be having some trouble standing up straight, as she slurred, "We look very poorly on this type of behaviour Natasha. It's simply not allowed."

Having emptied the room of all the others, Emmanuel returned. He soon captured Kate's undivided attention and, in between his piercing turquoise eyes and his gigantic dangling cock, the drunken girl did not know where to look as he admonished her, condescendingly, in the politest of delectably accented tones, "Kate, is this really the time?"

As Kate's eyes devoured the naked Adonis, she seemed incapable of preventing her gaze from dropping to, and then lingering on, Emmanuel's weighty penis. As she became increasingly mesmerized by its magnificence, even Kate was sharp enough to concede his point. With embarrassment, and peculiar reluctance, she too, finally, shuffled out of the room with head bowed. Emmanuel then looked at Natasha with beautiful apology-filled eyes. She stared back at him, still more than mortified. With eyes locked and their sombre faces lit only by the moonlight, it was as if the world had stopped turning. Suffice to say, their 'moment' had passed, and the unopened packet of condoms on the bed, remained so.

Chapter Fourteen - Calling it off

It was five-thirty on Monday afternoon, and Natasha was waiting for Sebastian outside the car park. She had not seen him for fifteen days now, and the imminent prospect of so doing made her feel excruciatingly nervous. Her head was spinning, her heart racing, and the palms of her hands were sweating so much that she had to keep wiping them on her skirt. She was, repeatedly, shifting from one foot to the other, like a small child made to stand in one place for too long. He should be here any minute.

Natasha had returned from Switzerland, late last night. Even now, she still felt poisoned from all of the alcohol. Every night after dinner, following eight hours solid of highly technical instruction, the trainees had congregated in the bar to bond, drink and unwind. Inevitably, they ended up drinking far too much. Though the trip had been professionally informative, it had been physically toxic. It was as if each and everyone one of them had been determined to milk the cow called Experience, until the last tug on her sore teat yielded only a dry moan of exhaustion, and a horrible hangover.

Surprisingly, following Natasha's night of public humiliation, no one ever mentioned it again. Even Kate did not follow up on the incident. The fact that Maria, and all the others left standing, had witnessed Kate and Klaus snogging in the bar later on, before then leaving together, may well have had something to do with that most fortunate fact. As for Emmanuel, he proved to be a gentleman, of sorts, and in the sobriety of the following day he had taken Natasha to one side. With head bowed in sincere contrition, and his beautiful blue eyes flashing at her, apologetically, he had confessed that he actually had a fiancée, whom he was due to marry in five months time. He managed to charm Natasha, yet again, by telling her how attractive he found her, and that he was really very sorry for seducing her because, in truth, wild horses - not to mention wild women - could not deter him from going ahead with the marriage, for the fortune his fiancée commanded was far too great to relinquish, under any circumstances. Natasha had had to admire Emmanuel's self-knowledge, if not his principles. Instead of pursuing further physical intimacy, the pair of them had become good friends. Indeed, for some reason, his ruthlessly candid cynicism made Natasha feel more peaceful than the valley in which they had been staying.

Suddenly, Natasha saw Sebastian approach and her heart leapt into her mouth. As he got closer, she could see he was grinning as broadly as she, and then, with the immediacy of an apparition, he was standing before her. He dipped his beautiful head and fixed her to the spot with his piercing eyes as he confessed:

"Natasha, I have not stopped thinking about you all day long. Miss Flynn, will you kindly get out of my head?"

"So it's not just me then?"

"You know damn well it's not Natasha."

His words transformed her into a star, sparkling in the heavens, all out flowing and self-perpetuating energy: bliss rediscovered. Gleeful to be together again they climbed, eagerly, into Sebastian's car. Natasha could not rip her eyes away from his face, for it had assumed a wondrous luminescence and she remarked:

"Look in the rear view mirror Sebastian!"

Sheepishly, he did as instructed. The image he caught sight of stole his breath away. Sebastian's eyes darted back to look at her, with excitement. Then Natasha gushed:

"Do you see it? Can you see how you're glowing?"

Sebastian checked his reflection again and his mouth fell open, slightly, in genuine astonishment. He then looked at Natasha, warily, before looking down at the steering-wheel and shaking his head from side to side.

"Natasha what the hell is going on with us?"

"You can see it! You're glowing more brilliantly than a camera flash. I've never seen it so intense."

"Well, if it means I am pleased to see you, then I already knew that..."

Then she questioned, with a puzzled expression:

"You have to admit, Sebastian, it's rather amazing, yet utterly terrifying all at the same time?"

"Much like yourself, Natasha, much like yourself." he replied, thoughtfully.

Sebastian started the car and, with an echoing growl of power, they roared out of the underground car park to race down the sunny backstreets. Sebastian drove even faster than usual, screeching away from traffic lights, and hugging bends at such speed that Natasha slid around on her leather seat. In less than twenty minutes, he was pulling up directly outside the striped, cream and racing-green canvas awning, in front of Blakes. Noticing that he had parked on a yellow line, Natasha cautioned:

"It's not six-thirty yet, you'll get a ticket."

"I'll take the chance, Natasha. If I get done, forty quid's a small price to pay for such convenience."

"Sebastian, are there not more admirable ways to spend your money than on an unnecessary fine?"

"Natasha, parking here was supposed to make things easy, not make you difficult."

Natasha dropped the subject, but his profligacy made her feel uneasy. Frowning, she wondered how many other consequences a man of such wealth was immune yet, as soon as she got out of the car, on her way to spend the early evening in such an expensive establishment, Natasha became only too aware of her hypocrisy and a sharp spike seemed to prick her in the solar plexus. Sebastian stepped back, to allow her to enter first and, as if sensing her silent concerns, he reminded her:

"You chose a career in investment banking Natasha, not social services. Get used to it."

Natasha just flicked her abundant hair and waltzed downstairs to the bar and restaurant, in silence. The room was dark and empty, as one might expect on a Monday at this time. Natasha heard the clicking of heels and she turned to find an attractive hostess walking towards them. She had glossy, striking red, shoulder-length hair and an ivory, heart-shaped face. Her full mouth was covered in red lipstick, and false eyelashes framed her far-away, grey-blue eyes. She wore a tight black polo-neck jumper and a short black skirt. Her appearance was as dramatic as that of an actress in full stage make-up. She smiled, affably, at them then offered to take their coats. Her voice was well-spoken and a little husky, while the lids of her large eyes were half-shut, as if the weight of her curled lashes were too much to support. This fact lent her that world-weary so-phistication, so common among metropolitan beauties working in hospitality, almost as if they are just waiting for it all to be over: whether that is their shift, or their life, was open to debate. Sebastian's eyes never left her, and he fol-lowed her hips, hungrily, as they rocked away to stow Natasha's coat. It was only when she was out of sight, that Sebastian took Natasha's hand, and led her to the privacy to be found at the back of the bar. They snugly positioned themselves shoulder to shoulder, thigh to thigh and hand in hand on the deep-plum velvet sofa. They were sitting to-gether happily now, without moral judgements or red-haired beauties to distract them. Squeezing Natasha's hand and flashing his emerald green eyes, Sebastian shrugged.

"So here we are again."

"Have we been here before then?" Natasha teased.

"Stop it."

"Stop what?"

"You know what." Sebastian darted, before filling his expansive chest, giving a deep sigh and continuing, "You... me... here... this... us... this fucking feeling, the same, again..."

Natasha felt complete serenity. It was as if their togeth-erness had always been inevitable. Suddenly, Sebastian became charged with incomprehension and expostulated:

"I just don't get it Natasha. You're not even my type!"

He looked flummoxed, and then fell back into the sofa as he declared with conviction:

"I like women with big tits! As for pale freckled red-heads, they have never been my preference... and then you

214

come along. YOU. You who strolled onto the Debt Floor and, with just one look possessed me. Worse, you thunderously plunder the interior of my mind to drive me to distraction. Natasha, it's as if I've lost all mastery of myself, and we haven't even had sex yet!"

Natasha was comforted for Sebastian's condition matched her own, and she inquired, censoriously:

"Yet?"

Sebastian looked at her, abashed. He seemed as shocked as she to have said it. Yet as they sat there, side by side, struggling to fathom their effect on each other, their eventual union seemed hopelessly unavoidable. Sebastian slumped farther back into the deep cushions of the sofa.

"Natasha, please, please tell me what's happening? Why do I love you? Why can't I stop thinking about you? Why can't I slot back into my old life?" He paused, took her hand in his and, with a fragile smile, spoke, "The simple one I had before you arrived to make it all complicated."

"I'm fucked if I can make sense of it Sebastian." After a pause, Natasha tentatively met his troubled gaze. "All I know is this: I love you. The feeling flows from me with a volition all of its own."

"I know Natasha. It's the same for me. I love you in a way I didn't know was possible."

A long silence followed, as they wondered at their predicament. The good-looking red-lipped redhead was back. Feeling ebullient, Sebastian ordered a bottle of vintage Krug, for he wished to spoil Natasha on her return. When the girl had gone, Natasha came out with what had been preying on her mind for the last two weeks.

"Sebastian, I'm going to finish with Bruno."

Sebastian stiffened. Natasha could see his mind computing the consequences of her chosen course of action. He looked at her, gravely.

"Is that really necessary, Natasha?"

"What do you mean?"

In a clinical tone, that murdered the natural cadence of

his voice, Sebastian explained, "Well my darling one, let's face it, your going out with Bruno is the best camouflage our love could have. Who could guess the truth, if you're Bruno's girlfriend?" Natasha frowned, disturbed. He continued to proselytize. "Think about it Natasha, if you continue to go out with Bruno, I will be able to see even more of you, whether my wife is around or not."

"Sebastian you're sick!"

"No, just practical."

"Your practical solution requires me to deceive, and continue to have sex with, your cousin; someone whom you are supposed to care about! Forget self-serving camouflage, I'm too fond of Bruno to use him like that." Sebastian's face was devoid of expression. Definitively, Natasha restated her intention, "No, I'm resolved. I am seeing Bruno tomorrow night and I'm going to end it."

Sebastian looked at her, with a naughty glint in his eye.

"Will you tell him about Emmanuel, or shall I?"

Natasha flushed. How swiftly the moral high ground crumbled under her this evening, as her wanton ways were fast exposed. Sebastian was grinning, tickled pink with power, "Were you not fond enough of Bruno, Natasha, not to have sex with another man? A Frenchman no less?" he inquired, softly, with raised brows.

Our heroine's moral high ground had just suffered a mudslide, to leave her squirming in soiled disrepute. Besides, what was wrong with Frenchmen? Emmanuel was absolutely gorgeous!

"You're not being fair Sebastian." she objected.

He persisted in probing her muddy maze of morality.

"Fucking Emmanuel is surely a greater betrayal of Bruno than chastely loving me, is it not Natasha?"

"Firstly, I did not fuck Emmanuel…"

"Not through want of trying, I hear…"

Natasha ignored him, for he was right. She continued:

"Secondly, it was you, not me, who said, 'and we haven't even had sex yet!' Such statements do not sit comfortably in the 'chaste love' camp. Finally, Sebastian,

Foolish she may well be, but her heart gave her no peace, for with each beat it pounded out two simple demands: love Sebastian, and do not deceive a kind man. When the buzzer sounded, Natasha flinched. Quickly, she grabbed her coat and handbag and then picked up the intercom.

"Bruno, hi. I'll come straight down."

When she opened the front door, gingerly, Bruno was standing on the top step and smiling broadly. He was wearing his leather jacket, as she would always come to remember him. He beamed with pleasure on sight of her and, with boisterous Labrador delight, he flung his arms around her, squeezed her, and then lifted her up. His warmth and vitality enveloped her.

"I've missed you Miss Flynn." he muttered.

Having hugged her long and tight, Bruno dropped her back down onto the top step. Still holding her, firmly, he looked, curiously, into her face.

"Two weeks away and not one call Natasha?" She was trapped and Bruno was determined. She looked at him sheepishly but remained silent. He pursued, "Did you get my messages?" Natasha looked down. Bruno continued, "I must have called at least five times." Still silent. "Did they really work you so very hard out there?"

"I'm sorry Bruno. I was distracted." Natasha managed, pathetically.

Finally, he released her. Bruno took her by the hand and led her down the steps to his gorgeous open-topped E type. He bent down to open the passenger door for her, and she climbed in. As soon as Bruno was in the driving seat, Natasha said, timidly, "Bruno, we need to talk."

He stiffened, and then gripped the elegant steering-wheel, tightly, with jaw clenched. He stared straight ahead with a blank gaze, for a moment, before lifting his chin to look down his nose, as he replied:

"That sounds ominous." Then he darted a wary look at her as he added, regrettably, "Shame, I had had other plans for this evening..."

Natasha smiled back before, spontaneously, reaching

over to plant a kiss on his handsome mouth. Mollified, Bruno started the engine and whisked them off to South Kensington. Sitting next to this tall attractive man, with the wind in her hair and the seductive hum of the classic car's engine in her ear, once again, Natasha wondered: what the hell she was thinking?

When they got to Bruno's home, he led Natasha straight down the stairs into the basement, where a large kitchen was to be found. There was an oak dining table at the back of the room, next to French windows that led straight onto the garden. It had already been, prettily, set with shiny silver knives and forks and canary yellow napkins. In the middle was a silver candelabrum, which Natasha was sure she recognized from the picnic, along with a cut-crystal vase, from which burst out five enormous sunflowers. Bruno motioned for Natasha to take a seat, while he fetched a bottle of Dom Pérignon from the tan American refrigerator. He returned with two flutes of champagne and, passing one to Natasha, he toasted:

"Welcome back."

"Thank you Bruno." she replied, earnestly.

Now there was an opening for Natasha to begin the 'talk', Bruno was as jumpy as a cat on a hot tin roof. No sooner had he taken a sip of his drink, than he sprang to his feet to return to the kitchen. With the press of a button, Chopin's cascading, delicate, elevating chords filled the whole basement, and Natasha was left to look around a kitchen of which any professional cook would have been proud. The music seemed to assuage Bruno's foreboding, and he began to look increasingly relaxed as he chopped some courgettes. Natasha even caught him smiling fondly at her. Clearly, he was in no hurry for the 'talk'. As Natasha sipped Dom Pérignon and listened to classical music, while she waited for a good-looking man to cook her supper, she had to confess it would be hard to concoct a superior scene of domestic bliss. What was she thinking?

The more Bruno cooked, the more contented he became. It took him less than twenty minutes to present

Natasha with a steaming, fragrant plate of king prawn and courgette linguine. He then lit candles, dimmed the lights and sat down. Once Bruno had topped up Natasha's glass, they began. Natasha ate the delicious food, in silence, and she wondered if now was the time to approach the subject she must confront. His dread of the 'talk' was tangible, for he too was uncharacteristically silent. Natasha could bear the discomfort no longer, but she did not feel ready to say what she must, instead, she buckled to blurt platitudes.

"This is superb, Bruno. You're such a talented chef and you make it look so easy. You just keep on spoiling me."

Bruno leapt at the small talk and devoured it for, if it lasted, he might be spared the serious 'talk' altogether. Smiling, most likely with relief, he gushed:

"Not at all Natasha, it is a pleasure and, seriously, the dish couldn't have been easier."

"I feel my turn to cook for you is long overdue, but I'm ashamed to admit, I barely know how."

Just like that, they were off in lighthearted banter, and each of them most relieved for the refuge.

"Is that allowed?" Bruno asked, quizzically.

"What?"

"A woman, who does not know how to cook?"

Bruno seemed more himself and, with wide eyes, Natasha retaliated, wryly:

"Oh I see, is that a woman's prime purpose in life?"

Bruno laughed, dirtily, then declared through a boyish grin, "No Natasha, a woman's 'prime' purpose in life is something that you're particularly good at." Bruno had managed to coax a flirtatious blush from the woman who was about to dump him. Emboldened, he flattered, "On second thoughts, perhaps you can get away with not knowing how to cook, for I suspect there are enough exceptional men only too willing to buy, or cook, dinner for you."

"Does that mean you're exceptional Bruno?"

"Abso-fucking-lutely!" he boomed, through the heartiest of chuckles. Natasha was alight with laughter, as she declared, from the bottom of her heart:

221

"Bruno, I could not agree more."

It was his turn to blush bashfully now. As Natasha worked her way through a delicious supper, it was as if she were waiting for the right moment, somehow, to arrive all by itself. Bruno seemed to sense that the 'talk' was on its way, for he began to shift around, uncomfortably, in his seat. When Natasha had swallowed her final mouthful, she knew it was time to bite the bullet. She placed her knife and fork neatly together, wiped her mouth, delicately, on the cheerful napkin then straightened her posture and looked directly into Bruno's sensitive brown eyes.

"Bruno, you know I said we needed to talk?"

The very big Bruno seemed to diminish before her eyes.

"That is a dreaded expression a man does not forget."

"Well, I think you're good-looking, fabulous, funny, charming and amazing in bed, but it's just that I don't think I am ready for a relationship at the moment."

Bruno looked away. A dark shadow began to possess his handsome features, as the implications of what Natasha had just said started to sink in. He was looking down at his food, intently now, as Natasha continued:

"As insane as it sounds, Bruno, I want us just to be friends. I'm not capable of offering anyone anything more at the moment."

Even Natasha was unconvinced by what she had said. Worse, she had just heard herself stray into that cruel and crucifying 'just friends' territory. Despite feeling relief having expressed what she must, now she had listened to herself, nothing seemed to add up, and of course she could not tell Bruno the real truth. Natasha just sat, silently, waiting to be rescued by his response. Bruno was as genuine and gentlemanly as ever, for he did not even challenge her inexplicable reasoning. Instead, he helped Natasha to fabricate an elegant exit. Reverting to detached, impeccable manners, he concealed his obvious upset behind a determined stiff upper lip and, with excruciatingly measured understanding, he began to speak:

"Natasha, I understand completely. Of course you have

just embarked on an immense career journey and the last thing you need, at this moment in time, is any form of distraction." Bruno had finished his food, by now, and he too placed his knife and fork neatly together. He then leaned back in his chair and met Natasha's eyes, before continuing to make it easy for her.

"Really, please don't feel at all bad. It would be a privilege to count you amongst my circle of friends." Natasha felt mean and foolish. Bruno continued with deliberate enthusiasm, "And do you know what Natasha? Do you know what?" He was looking at her with fierce eyes, as he nodded his head and began to praise her, only to make her feel more churlish than ever. "I have so much respect for you, to come here tonight and take the time to sit down and dine with me, and actually have the courage to look me in the eye and let me know exactly how you're feeling. Well Natasha, it is a rare woman who has the decency to do what you have just done now, and I thank you for it."

If ants had belly buttons then that is about as big as Natasha felt. 'The talk' had come and gone and Bruno had handled his disappointment like a saint. He filled Natasha's glass, again, then met her eyes.

"To our friendship." he toasted, with bonhomie.

"To our friendship Bruno." Natasha conjoined, meekly.

They both took a long sip of the divine champagne, before Natasha stood up to clear the table. She picked up the dirty plates and took them to the large butler's sink by the window while Bruno went to get a second bottle. The window overlooked the basement vaults of the house, offering a poor view but great privacy. It was dark outside. With head bowed Natasha rinsed the plates then bent down to load them into the dishwasher. Her pulse rate rocketed for, suddenly, Bruno's big hands were placed firmly on her hips. She stood bolt upright and turned around to face him, his hands allowing her hips to swivel through them as she did so. He clasped her bottom tightly now and looked into her face, with eyes so perplexed that they revealed the true extent of his sadness, for the first time. Natasha was struck

223

by the depth of the emotion she saw there. Her heart contracted at the sight for, regrettably, she had been the cause. As compassion filled her breast, Bruno's physical proximity prompted her libido to fill her loins. In an instant, her lips were on his. He clasped her head between his hands and they began to kiss with the desperation of the damned, simply swept away by champagne, Chopin, emotion and pheromones. Bruno's passion was on the ascendant and he forcefully pushed Natasha back against the kitchen cabinets. He kissed her ravenously as his body pressed against hers and his pulsing, erect member poked boldly into her tummy. Natasha could feel her sex throbbing with want and her stomach seemed to be somersaulting with the sheer intensity of her lust. With a single animalistic grunt, Bruno lifted Natasha up onto the deep evergreen, granite kitchen work-surface. Her bottom felt its chill, through her trousers, to contrast with the strong heat that emanated from Bruno's body, held against hers, as he became more and more worked up.

Now, her arms were draped around his broad, muscular back and her legs wrapped around his hips, so that she could feel his erection pushing into her genitals to arouse her further. They were kissing, passionately, as Bruno's strong hands roamed, adoringly, all over Natasha's hourglass figure to return, repeatedly, to stimulate her breasts. Natasha's vagina was pulsating deep inside her, as it longed to be penetrated by the large erection that pushed eagerly against it. The sexual urgency was tangible in this, possibly their final, act of copulation. Frenziedly, Bruno started to undo Natasha's trousers, and she his, in an equally frantic and fumbling fashion. Natasha was longing to hold this bountiful, boisterous man deep inside her, and she shifted her bottom from side to side, to help him rip off her trousers and black silk g-string. In an instant, her sex was open and begging for him, while her bottom felt the punishing coldness of the granite against her naked skin. Natasha's sexual arousal was so extreme she was already wet for him. With joy, she finally managed to get his trousers and boxer shorts off and, determinedly, she pushed them down his long, strong thighs. Bruno's pulsing penis was free, and with a single thrust he ploughed his readiness into Natasha's cunt.

In a divine moment, she felt the walls of her vagina ecstatically stretch to capacity. Bruno began to fuck Natasha like a man possessed, as the muscles in his buttocks worked over-time to repeatedly jab his penis in and out of her at a frantic pace. Natasha clasped his body close to hers, as she rested her chin on his shoulder and nuzzled her cheek into his. She could feel Bruno's jaw ripple from the effort of his swift, energetic exertions. She could feel her climax burgeoning, so overwhelmed was she with the size, heat, and virile force of him. He now clutched her tightly by the flesh of her hips and continued to shag her, with the frantic fervour of a dog stealing a quick fuck from a bitch in the park. Natasha held Bruno by his beautiful toned buttocks to help him drive his cock deeply into her, repeatedly, while her bottom kept slamming on the cold, unforgiving surface.

Faster and faster and faster they fucked and, with increasing desperation, Bruno's enormous, erect cock continued to lunge, frenziedly, into Natasha's engorged, wet cunt. Bruno and Natasha's breathing became more and more urgent, and their pulses were racing as sweat began to prickle through the flowering pores of their skin to promote a sex-induced sweat. As Bruno continued to work Natasha, rivulets of salty perspiration began to course down their backs, as their bodies yearned: more, more, more, deeper, deeper, deeper, harder, harder, harder, faster, faster, faster. Tonight, the pair was insatiable, gripped by a fucking fever: more and more, faster and faster, harder and harder. Tear at my hair while you violently fuck me! Until, suddenly, Natasha simply exploded with that mind-boggling exquisite release of vaginal orgasm: AAAHHHHHHHH!!!

At which very moment, an open mouthed and strained faced Bruno grabbed the base of his penis, to yank himself out, so as not to spurt his copious load inside her. Natasha was still reeling from the aftershocks of her orgasm and, in a heartbeat, she dropped down to kneel on the rough flagstone floor, where she grasped Bruno's manhood, assertively, then wrapped her warm mouth around the tip of it, to promote ejaculation galore. Clutching him by his pert buttocks, Natasha swallowed the shooting semen that spouted in spurts from his trusty cock. So turned on was she by the taste of him that she whimpered, and her hand found her throbbing clitoris and she began to masturbate, greedy for another orgasm, while she continued to swallow each new wave of viscous fluid that spurted from Bruno's inexhaustible cock until, at last, she plunged, once again, from the exquisite precipice of threatening climax to splash into a lake of pure, quintessential pleasure. Warm clitoral cum juices squirted all over Natasha's busy hand, and then dribbled down her soft inner thighs: BINGO! Yet again, she cruised the crescendo of ecstatic, mutual and copious coming: AAAHHHHHHHHH!!!

While Natasha's body was wracked with the spasms and aftershocks of orgasm, she continued to suck on Bruno's fountain of a cock, as if it were her only delight. Oh, how Natasha was tossed by the currents of gratitude, and buoyed by the waves of chemicals that blasted her brain to make her bond, with this man, at this moment, the sweet facilitator of such extreme sexual pleasure! She was relieved that her mouth was full for, had it not been so, she may well have blurted, 'I love you', as that was exactly how she felt and, really, in the circumstances, how confusing would that have been for both of them?

Finally, Bruno stopped spurting semen. He was still shuddering violently from the aftershocks of his urgent, explosive orgasm as, gently, he held Natasha's head to his penis, tenderly stroking her hair while she continued to kiss and worship his slowly deflating manhood. Having, finally, finished her adoration of Bruno's member, Natasha got to her feet and nestled into the soft cotton of his shirt, and the muscles of his broad chest, as the pair of them held each other in a tight clinch. Imperceptibly, in this embrace, the germ of sadness began to infect their hearts, once again.

Simply, none of what had occurred tonight, until they had had sex, had made any sense and, confused and despondent, Natasha whispered, `"I'm so sorry Bruno..."

Bruno huffed, lightly, and gripped her ever more tightly, as he nuzzled his face into her hair.

"Natasha can you come over tomorrow night and dump me like that again please?"

Yet again, Bruno had managed to extract a chuckle from a lost, foolish girl whose heart felt sad.

<u>Chapter Sixteen</u> - The invitation

The next morning a joyous Sebastian bounded over to Natasha's desk. She was sitting reading the bank's daily economic, political and expected market-numbers news summary, with stern concentration. She jumped with surprise, for she was still preoccupied by the preceding evening's events.

"You've done it!" Sebastian declared, with heightened enthusiasm.

Natasha looked at this tall man's beaming face, and was puzzled to say the least. Her expression was blank and unresponsive. Eventually, she managed to inquire:

"You spoke to him?"

Sebastian just shook his head, impatiently, clearly exasperated by the hung-over Natasha's slowness this morning.

"No, I can just tell."

"He was more upset than I had anticipated. I hurt him."

"Is that why you had to have sex with him? A consolation prize?"

God this was freaking her out! It was more than terrifying for Natasha to realize that her mind was no longer her own. Exposed, she glared at him crossly.

"Have I no secrets left?"

"Strangely, it would appear not."

Sebastian just reached across a dumbfounded Natasha and, presumptuously, took the piece of paper she was reading, right out of her hand. Absent-mindedly, he perused it, and then shrugged.

"Oh Natasha, stop worrying about Bruno. He'll be fine." Then he singsonged, nonchalantly, "I'm sure he'll have another beautiful woman on his arm, and in his bed, by the end of the week."

Natasha was unconvinced, and still troubled, as she stared blankly at her market screens.

"Hmm..." she sounded.

Sebastian had finished scanning the news-sheet and, suddenly, he startled Natasha by becoming ridiculously animated, as he grinned broadly, rubbed his hands together and declared, enthusiastically:

"And now for something much more exciting!" Natasha stared at him, not feeling in the least bit excited, as she wondered what on earth he was talking about. Sebastian's eyes were preposterously wide and shining with anticipation. Slowly, he spelt out the event that was so much more exciting than Bruno's heartache.

"I want you to come to my wife's birthday party on the 13th of October!"

Natasha was nonplussed. Sebastian shifted his head, jerkily, to one side, then the other, like a hungry sparrow suspiciously eyeing seeds scattered on a bird table. Even though he was gaining little intelligence from his studied inspection of the deflated Natasha, he seemed determined to engage her.

"That's two weeks tomorrow." Natasha remained disappointingly unresponsive to his inspired invitation, and he felt forced to elaborate further, "My friends are bored to tears with all my talk of a certain Miss Flynn and now, finally, they will have the opportunity to meet you for themselves. Even my wife's curiosity, regarding you, rivals that of a cat!"

Natasha did not know what to say or how to react. Sebastian was becoming more accustomed to this mute version of his Love, and he began to fill in the silences with a little less irritation.

"It will be so much fun! I can introduce you to all of the people whom are dearest to me, you may even get to meet my children!"

Quite why Sebastian was so excited by such a prospect remained a mystery to Natasha. She was not in the least bit excited, and thought the whole enterprise to be rather strange. Listening to him talk about his married life, and witnessing his excitement at the prospect of parading her through it, made her feel numb. Even though she loved him, at this moment in time, she was not sure if she liked him. Sebastian seemed to be playing 'wanton boy' to her

229

'fly' and she did not welcome the likely outcome of such a scenario. Finally, Natasha answered him.

"I do not want to come to your wife's birthday party, but thank you for inviting me. I think."

She then took back the sheet of paper he had taken from her, and began reading it again. Sebastian was crestfallen.

"What do you mean Natasha?"

"What I said." she replied without looking at him.

Sebastian's instinct was sharp enough to conclude that this was not the time for successful persuasion. Sobered, he swept away to allow her to finish reading the news-sheet.

"Oy!" Natasha's head jolted up to greet a smiling Freddie. "Now, a little bird tells me you're doing your F.S.A. exams in three weeks' time." Then Freddie just stared at her with a fat-faced look of interrogation.

"That's correct." Natasha responded.

"Fucking finally!" Freddie's barrel of a chest began to jostle up and down with spirited laughter, "Well my girl, you know what that means don't ya?"

"I finally get to do some proper work?"

"Forget fucking working. Now you've got to start producing, girl!"

"Isn't it the same thing Freddie?" Natasha ventured, more than a little confused.

"Who are you kidding? Everyone here wakes up and goes to work but, sad to say, there are some who may as well not have bothered! But you don't need to worry your pretty head about that Natasha, we're doing our annual cull, soon enough, and they won't be here for much longer."

For some reason, Freddie found such a prospect hilarious and he started to chuckle as if tickled pink. Natasha looked on, struggling to find any humour in such a thing. Finally, he recovered himself.

"My poin' is this, ya'd be sensible to ge' yaself some clients, young lady..." he explained, with greater composure. Natasha nodded in agreement. Freddie elaborated, "I had a cha' with Seb and he reckons, if ya pass yr exams, we can probably offer ya a permanen' position on the Desk, so i' makes good sense t' star' getting yr client list shaped up. We've got the banks well covered, but there aint no one on our Sales Team who's comp-re-hensively covering European and UK Corporates. It's a pretty crap account base, for libor product, but it could be the ideal place for ya to cut your teeth." Again, Freddie was laughing. Natasha was not. He continued, "Anyways, take a look at vis." He then passed her a printed-out Excel spreadsheet and explained, "Here are the top 200 UK Corporates. The ones in red we are already talking to, the rest are up for grabs. Ge' calling, find ou' how much money they've go' to invest, what they're buying, who they're buyin' from, and wo' their investmen' parameters are. Set up lots of mee'in's, and ge' ready to star' writing tickets as soon as ya qualified."

Natasha was thankful to have a defined task, however, she did not feel at all qualified to perform it. She was still attending training lectures every afternoon, but they were on financial theory and bond maths. Natasha did not have a clue about how the finance department of a company operated or, indeed, to whom she should be talking in relation to structured credit in the first place. Freddie must have sensed her bewilderment.

"Initially, you want to be getting the ear of the Treasurer." he explained, before continuing, "Once you're qualified and up for business, you want to be getting access to the C.F.O.s and C.E.O.s as well. Try and set up introductory meetings with them for next month, and you'll be surprised how much nicer these guys usually are, once they have met you; especially you Natasha. Go' i'?"

"Got it, and thank you Freddie."

"Oh, and go to my desk, Natasha, and take my copy of Euromoney. It has all the Treasurers listed in it, and even if it's a bit out of date, it's better calling up for someone who's left, than calling up not knowing who the hell you're calling for."

Freddie then walked away, and Natasha went to his

desk to retrieve the publication he had mentioned. She then began to make the calls he had instructed, and spent the rest of the day discovering the tedium and frustration of cold calling. Thank God she was calling from such a well-known bank for, once she explained that she worked for U.C.B. the people at the other end of the line were much more inclined to give her a fair hearing. Natasha did not leave her desk that day, except once, to run out and grab a sandwich. By six o'clock she had set up twenty-one meetings with corporate Treasurers, and she felt rather pleased with herself.

It was a tired but satisfied Natasha who, by seven o'clock, was sitting on her little sofa at home drinking a cup of hot herbal tea with her feet tucked snuggly underneath her. God knows, after the training course and then last night with Bruno, she needed an early night. Suddenly, the doorbell sounded, to make her jump. She put her cup down and walked over to the intercom to find out who it could be. "Hello?"

"It's me."

Immediately, Natasha's fatigue fled.

"Sebastian?" she squealed, with delight.

"Come down now, I need to see you."

Natasha forgot about her tea. Natasha forgot about everything. In a heartbeat, she put on her shoes, grabbed her suede coat from the hook by the door, flung her keys into her bag and then dashed out. She ran down the stairs, more excited than a pack of hounds leaping after a fox's scent. When she opened the front door, she found Sebastian standing before her with his hands clasped in front of him. Abashed, he rocked slightly from side to side and then looked into her eyes and said, simply:

"I had to see you."

Quickly, he averted his gaze, for a vague blush haunted his face. Natasha felt lighter than fresh cappuccino froth and, with a gasp, his name was out of her mouth.

"Sebastian."

He took one of her hands, and led her down the steps to

tug her off across the square to the local pub on the corner. Once inside, Natasha followed Sebastian up the stairs to the first floor, where he took her to a brown, studded-leather sofa at the back of the room, in front of the large sash-window. Natasha knew this preferred spot, for they had canoodled here once before. Sebastian indicated for Natasha to sit down, and then he reached inside his suit jacket to pull out a white, stiff, paper envelope before handing it to her and instructing:

"Stay there and read that, while I get us some drinks."

Then he disappeared. Natasha was in a daze and she looked down to see her name written, beautifully, in light blue fountain-pen ink, in a hand more elegant than Sebastian's suit. With apprehension, she turned the stiff, white envelope over and slipped the tip of her thumb into the corner of the flap, carefully, to ease it open. The envelope was lined with delicate, indigo blue tissue paper. Natasha pulled out a single, pristine, thick white card, of the finest quality, with a handwritten, untitled poem on it. She began to read, with great interest.

> *A spark of spontaneous passion*
> *Consumes in an instant*
> *Like moth to flame.*
> *The upheaval of lives*
> *The fraying of minds, all*
> *Thought obliterated by bliss.*
> *He reawakened; enslaved.*
> *She, dizziness disorientates; scared.*
> *"This man is too dangerous" she cries*
> *And dare not venture on,*
> *Let the cold steel of calculation*
> *Slay the glory of imagination,*
> *Oh, die you wayward heart*
> *Let bleeding Adventure lie dying.*
> *Goodbye dreams, goodbye mouse.*

> *Love S*

As Natasha read each line, increasingly, her eyes began to engender hot fat tears. Her heart seemed to crack and she felt powerless. Of course she should not 'venture on', yet an inexorable force kept pulling her back to this married man. Sebastian's poem was a wishful fantasy, for it bestowed the besotted Natasha with the strength to stop what was occurring between them. Natasha's collecting tears, mourned the hopelessness of her position and her inability to do so.

Quickly, she blinked away her sorrow, for Sebastian had returned with the ice-packed drinks. He was smiling sadly at her, tentatively seeking her reaction. When he sat down next to her, their eyes locked and they became, immediately, bewitched by each other's glistening, fathomless pupils. The world as they each knew it was swept away and they were home. As Natasha dwelt in this magical place of invincibility, she knew she must rally one last attempt to prevent the fate that seemed so inevitable. She would go to Sebastian's wife's birthday party. She would confront the truth of her true Love's life. He had a wife and two children, and his real life was with them, not with her. Fortified by the effect he always had on her, Natasha said, simply:

"I will come to your wife's birthday party."

Sebastian's expression was indecipherable, as he continued to explore the mysteries of her soul. He nodded once, in acknowledgement, yet Natasha was still overwhelmed by the intensity of his unbroken attention. Then staring deeply into her eyes, he lifted his glass and said:

"I'll drink to that Natasha." And they did.

Sebastian had got his way. Natasha had a poem to treasure, and a spectre of hope. Maybe, just maybe, the physical presentation of her Love at home with his wife and children, would be powerful enough to shatter the psychological manacles that held her, so enslaved, to this unavailable man.

Chapter Seventeen - Itsy's birthday party

Natasha was shivering, slightly, in the cool October evening air, as she stood on the front doorstep of Sebastian's terraced, white stucco fronted, Chelsea home. She was waiting for someone to answer the door. She held a gigantic bunch of white lilies that were poised to peak into the abundance of full bloom. She was so nervous that she felt sick, and her mind darted around in a panicked craze as the same question, persistently, presented itself: 'Why am I here?' The waiting was torturous and Natasha's heart, mind and hands trembled. She gripped the large bunch of flowers, more fiercely, grateful for their rich exquisite scent, for it helped to calm her. She felt very unsteady on her feet as if she was about to fall off the step and, for a moment, she felt foolish for wearing such high heels.

The sound of plummy male voices engaged in animated conversation, and the odd burst of raucous laughter, cascaded from this tall, white townhouse into the darkness all around her. As she strained to make out the words, she began to wonder if her bell-ringing would be heard at all. Impatient, Natasha reached for the doorbell again when, suddenly, she started at the decisive click of the latch. Her pulse raced, wildly, as the glossy royal blue door, slowly, began to swing open. Courteously, Natasha took a couple of steps back, but she was soon to discover that no amount of social etiquette was going to make this encounter comfortable, for the lady who stood before her, she knew, instantly, to be Isabel.

An eternal open-mouthed silence enveloped these two women the very moment they clapped eyes on one another. The striking young girl from work, a husband had already spoken far too much about, now faced the wife. With one look, both of them seemed to know everything. Natasha was the first to break the morbid spell and, mustering the warmest smile she could, she offered the lilies to the hostess, and declared, cheerfully:

"Hi, you must be Isabel. My name is Natasha, and I

work at U.C.B. with your husband. Happy Birthday."

Still open-mouthed, Isabel remained frozen to the spot. She just stared in silence at this beautiful, tall, full-lipped girl who was all dressed up, and standing on her doorstep, offering her a bunch of fucking flowers. As she absorbed the full extent of the threat, her face turned, increasingly, ashen and her eyes became as horrified as those of a startled deer, dazzled by the glare of approaching headlights. Clearly incapable of any adequate reaction, Isabel just started to reverse behind the door she had only just opened, until she disappeared, entirely, to leave Natasha standing on the doorstep still holding out her unaccepted gift. Natasha was flummoxed. The door had been left ajar, but she did not know what to do. How acute was her regret for coming here at all! Before she had the chance to collect herself and retreat she was, suddenly, swept up by several sets of boisterous couples that had just closed in behind her. Before she knew it, their excited momentum had driven her up the front steps and into the house.

There was no turning back for, as soon as she was inside, Sebastian spotted her. Instantly, their eyes locked and his face beamed with light. He was standing in the wide doorway that led into the drawing-room. On sight of him, Natasha's doubting heart became certain and she was reminded of her resolve: seeing him at home with his wife was going to help her to quash her dangerous feelings. Unaware of Isabel's recent trauma, Sebastian grinned freely and welcomed Natasha with open arms, as he came over and took the lilies from her.

"Oh Natasha, clever you, Itzy just loves lilies!" he declared, enthusiastically.

'You could have fooled me!' was the thought that sprang to Natasha's mind, however, she kept it to herself. It appeared Sebastian was suffering from no moral dilemmas this evening, for his mood was more joyous than ever.

"Give me your coat." he commanded.

Natasha did so and then, nervously, she peered past him to glance into the grand drawing-room, to see if she could find Isabel. She saw many gorgeous, glamorous, gregarious guests, but no Isabel. Sebastian leant down to kiss her, lingeringly, on each cheek and then whispered, daringly, into her ear, "I love you."

With these three words Natasha blushed and her troubled heart leapt to the heavens! How swiftly did his declaration shed the suffocating shame that had crept up on her like poison ivy. Sebastian called over one of the staff, and then handed him Natasha's coat, along with the bunch of lilies. He gestured to the beautiful flowers.

"Put these in water, and then place them in my bedroom, please." he requested.

Natasha flinched, for she knew his instruction was sure to upset Isabel later. Never before had a bunch of lilies inflicted such deep wounds! Oblivious, Sebastian took Natasha's arm and led her to the back of the drawing-room, where there was a table that served as the bar, behind which stood two cocktail waiters, smartly dressed in fitted black waistcoats, white shirts and black bow-ties. Their faces were handsome, calm and serene as, expertly, they mixed exotic cocktails, on demand.

"What can I get for you, Natasha?" Sebastian inquired before adding enthusiastically, "These chaps can make any cocktail you desire. The only limitation is your imagination! Such fun, what?"

Natasha nodded, then managed a smile even though she had no fondness for cocktails.

"So, tell me: what do you want?" he persisted.

"Just champagne, please."

Sebastian seemed disappointed yet, synchronous to her request, a pretty young waitress appeared carrying a large round, polished, silver tray filled with flutes full of bubbling champagne. Natasha and Sebastian grinned knowingly and, as the girl floated past, Sebastian took two glasses from her. Even though the novelty of the cocktail waiters had not yet worn off, such a coincidence was irresistible. He handed one to Natasha, and then continued to play the host.

"Thank you so much for coming. It means a lot to me."

Sebastian then stared into her eyes as they drank, before he suggested, with great enthusiasm, "Come with me, Natasha. I have so many people I want you to meet!"

He took her by the hand to drag her across the room towards a group of three attractive women, who were clustered in front of the fireplace. Their faces were lit orange from beneath by a roaring fire. As Sebastian and Natasha approached, the women became increasingly animated and their heads inclined towards each others' as they shared secret whisperings. Ravenous eyes devoured Natasha's every detail, while eager grins illuminated the girls' fetching faces more effectively than the fire. Natasha felt consumed by the intensity of their interest. Sebastian was about to introduce her, but before he had the chance, the shortest of the girls interjected:

"The Miss Natasha Flynn, I presume?"

"The very same." Sebastian confirmed, delighted, before adding, "Isn't she fantastic?"

Natasha cringed, for it was most disconcerting to be discussed so. The girl who had just spoken, held eye contact with her and retorted:

"Give us a chance Sebastian. We've not even been properly introduced yet!"

Sebastian grinned, sheepishly, before making the formal introduction:

"Miss Juliette Sebire, please may I present, Miss Natasha Flynn."

Juliette was pretty, in a St. Trinian's style. She had long, thick, ash blonde hair, sharp, inquisitive blue eyes and a suggestive smile that made her face light up like a star. Happily, Juliette took Natasha's hand and shook it, firmly, while scanning her face, as if to get the measure of her. Sebastian then went on to introduce Natasha to a less animated, but astonishingly beautiful, statuesque blonde lady called Camilla Fairweather, before introducing her to the rather prim, toffee-nosed, but pretty brunette Gabriella Aubrey. They were all perfectly polite, but they made Natasha feel like some kind of strange specimen presented for their approval. Once Natasha had executed her, "How do you do?"s, Juliette continued to dominate.

"Well Natasha, I have to say I feel I know you intimately, already, for our dear friend Sebastian simply cannot stop talking about you!" she said, before adding wryly, "May I be so bold as to inquire precisely what you have done to him?"

Thankfully, it seemed this question was not designed to elicit a response, for the woman just erupted into hysterical laughter. Now Sebastian was embarrassed, and he admonished Juliette with a stern eye, to encourage her to collect herself, which she soon did. The lady's acquiescence was not to last, however, for the incorrigible Juliette soon continued to goad:

"Have you met the birthday girl yet? I think she was even more curious to meet you than we. Mind you, Sebastian has tired her so very much with talk of you, I'm surprised she let you in at all!"

Here, Juliette lost all self-restraint and all of them burst into laughter more cackling than before, even Gabriella was covering her mouth to stifle giggles. It appeared Juliette had pushed Sebastian too far for, even in this light, there was a rose tint beneath his tanned complexion. Indeed, he looked uncharacteristically cross. Sensitive to Sebastian's shift in spirits, the beautiful, light-green-eyed Camilla stepped forward and placed her hand on Natasha's lower arm.

"Natasha, please, you must ignore Juliette's rudeness. She has known Sebastian since she was twelve and she seems never to tire of teasing him, mercilessly. I am certain that Isabel is as thrilled to have you here as we." she consoled, sympathetically.

Sebastian then started, when a large male hand slapped him, heavily, on the back and the sound of base chuckling cascaded all around them. Everyone turned to fix on the man who had just struck Sebastian. There, to Sebastian's left, stood a richly tanned, broadly smiling gentleman in his

early-forties, whose presence was drastically disproportionate to his size. His hair was chocolate brown, very
thick and loosely curled, the locks of which bounced luxuriously over his stiff, crisp, white collar. He had comically
expressive large brown eyes, the irises of which were im-
bued with a warm apricot-colour. He had a closely-
trimmed dark brown beard that framed his plump-lipped
mouth, the strong redness of which only served to make his
large teeth look exceptionally white, so much so, that they
matched the sparkling glint that traversed his incorrigibly
roving eyes. His blatant lustful attentions were not exclusive to Natasha, for the man's famished, fast-moving
glances fed shamelessly on all of the females encircling
Sebastian. Sebastian just raised an eyebrow, with a touch
of disdain, as he looked down at this new arrival.

"Why, Sebastian old boy, are you going to introduce me
to your gorgeous new friend?" the grinning stranger
boomed.

As he asked this question, the man did not look at
Sebastian but, instead, he intensified his concentration on
Natasha. She looked back at him, in bashful bemusement,
for his slightly bulging eyes were wandering, relentlessly,
all over her body, only to be punctuated with several ap-
proving wide-eyed glances at her face. Sebastian stiffened,
and then adopted a smile that seemed to require some effort, as he turned to address the man in question:

"Why, why, why, if it isn't Miles Monroe. So you managed to find your way back from Bolivia? And there was I
thinking we'd lost you to the allures of high altitude lakes
forever."

"I suspect you had hoped so Sebastian, but I'm afraid
not. Allures satisfyingly explored, the traveller returns to
seek novel adventures."

Miles continued to hold his hand on Sebastian's back
but his eyes were still fixed on Natasha. Despite his somewhat frosty reception, Miles could not have looked more
relaxed. He continued to pat Sebastian on the back, like
some loyal hunting dog, while he took a deep slug from the

crushed-ice-filled raspberry cocktail he held in his hand. Having finished almost all of his drink, Miles then repeated his request, with a steeliness that undercut his rich, reverberating voice, "Your new friend, Sebastian?"

Resigned before Miles' extreme determination, Sebastian introduced them, "Natasha Flynn, Miles Monroe."

This curt introduction was Miles' starting gun for, immediately, he refrained from patting Sebastian and lunged forward to take Natasha's hand in his before, flamboyantly, bending down to kiss the back of it three times. Still lingering, with head bowed and his lips barely parted from it, Miles raised his curled lashes to stare into Natasha's eyes as he announced, in tones so bass they were worthy of a pantomime villain, "The pleasure is all mine Miss Flynn. The pleasure is all mine."

Miles held this pose for dramatic effect before, finally, he kissed Natasha's hand, once more, for good measure. He executed this last kiss torturously slowly and, shockingly, for a brief snapshot of time the stranger's tongue became fleetingly involved. Then, suddenly, Miles was erect and grinning at Natasha, more dirtily than a pirate, while the whites of his eyes flashed, expectantly. The back of Natasha's hand was still wet from his oral attention. Feeling repulsed, she discreetly wiped the saliva remnants on the side of her dress. Now he was standing so close to her, Natasha was able to determine that Miles was about six-foot one, for in her heels his eye-level was uncomfortably aligned with her own. Miles exuded distilled, animalistic lust and he seemed to possess a rare and mischievous inner confidence. Such a character appeared far more suited to a place like Bolivia than to a banker's wife's birthday party in Chelsea. What is more, had Miles Monroe still been there, our heroine would have felt safer here!

Indeed, Natasha was actually slightly afraid of Miles and, as he edged farther and farther towards her, her level of discomfort increased. She began to take tiny steps back, in order to escape from this intrusive character. Her shuffling retreat offered no reprieve, however, for every time she edged back, Miles simply moved farther forward, licentiously eyeing her physique all the while. The man's lewdness was so extreme that, for the first time, Natasha would have been grateful for the refuge of a hijab.

Miles' effective and aggressive body blocking had managed to remove Sebastian from the scene entirely. Natasha could not even see him, by this point, and it was becoming increasingly clear that she would have to fend for herself at this party. It was also fast becoming apparent that the perils here, rivalled those of the trading floor. Inevitably, Miles soon had Natasha pinned-up against the drawing-room wall, yet still he moved closer. Natasha was trapped and Miles was looking ever so pleased with himself having successfully engineered it so. He then noticed that her glass was empty and, smiling encouragingly, he took it, before replacing it with another, effortlessly lifted from a passing silver tray. Natasha was reluctant to concede that the frequency with which such champagne-filled trays circulated this party, tragically detracted from the apparently remarkable champagne-coincidence earlier with Sebastian. Miles was so close to Natasha now, that she could feel his thick humid breath against her face. She was trying to plot her escape when, suddenly, this forward man began to recite one of her favourite poems, suggestively:

"Let us go then, you and I,
When the evening is spread out against the sky
Like a patient etherized upon a table;
Let us go, through certain half-deserted streets
The muttering..."

Soothed by the familiar lyricism, Natasha began to recite the poem with him and, surprised, Miles paused his recital to listen to hers:

"...retreats
Of restless nights in one-night cheap hotels
And sawdust restaurants with oyster-shells:"

242

As Miles listened to Natasha, his face lit up and he stepped back, as if to see her with new eyes. Then, with impassioned voice, he joined her, and the pair recited some more verse from 'The Love Song of J. Alfred Prufrock', in unison:

"Streets that follow like a tedious argument
Of insidious intent
To lead you to an overwhelming question...
Oh, do not ask "What is it?"
Let us go and make our visit.
In the room the women come and go
Talking of Michelangelo."

By this stage the two of them were laughing hard, before Natasha interjected:

"This could go on all night, I know much of T. S. Elliot's poetry off by heart."

"As do I my dear, as do I, shall we continue?"

"I don't think so, besides I'm far more interested in talking to you now than I was before!"

Miles roared with laughter at her boldness, and then he barked in a parody of outrage:

"Darling, did you just say you weren't interested in talking to me before?"

"Absolutely! From the way you were behaving, I thought you were a lecherous old creep and talking was the last thing on your mind!" Natasha was greeted by more of Miles' raucous laughter, before she added, pensively, "In fact, I was on the verge of plotting my escape!"

"Guilty as charged my dear, guilty as charged, but please do not run away, I think the fun is only just beginning..."

"I sometimes wonder if parties are ever really any fun at all." Natasha said, as Miles looked at her quizzically and, for the first time, seemed to be genuinely interested in what she might have to say. She frowned slightly, and then continued, "I've already had my 'formulated, sprawling on a pin' moment from Sebastian's female friends..."

"Oh yes, I saw that... Sebastian's beautiful harem, prone to great jealousies, I'm afraid. Hardly surprising, given his track record..."

Natasha did not like the sound of that, but she was damned if she was going to display her vulnerability by asking Miles to elaborate. Instead, she just continued.

"And then you come along to force me to be 'pinned and wriggling on the wall,'" for Natasha's back was still jammed up against one, and then, with mock indignation, she demanded, in raised voice, "Mr. Monroe, a little space please?"

Miles looked abashed, then took a little step back.

"Oh my dear, please forgive me, sometimes I just can't help myself. But of course, it's all your fault, you have absolutely no business being so delectable! What's a red-blooded male to do?"

"Behave?" Natasha suggested, sternly.

To which Miles roared with even more boisterous laughter, before spluttering:

"Why my dear, that's even less fun than fucking parties!" He paused, for a moment, before adding hopefully, "Fucking at parties however..?"

Natasha bristled with the audacity of this man and then wagged her index finger in his face, strictly.

"Enough!" she commanded.

Miles turned the corners of his mouth down, dropped his head sulkily, and slumped his shoulders. It seemed Elliot's lyricism, and our heroine's scolding, had managed to contain the man's carnal lust; for now. Natasha was just beginning to appreciate her newly found personal space when, in an instant, the vacuum left by Miles Monroe was soon filled by none other than Bruno Monmouth.

Her ex-Lover, appeared from nowhere, to insert himself in between her and Miles, as he rested his arm, proprietarily, on the wall above her head. His body leant even more closely into hers than Miles' had done, and Natasha could see that Miles was less than happy with this turn of events. In fact, she had not seen Bruno for almost two weeks and, as he stood so close to her, it was obvious that they still had chemistry. Bruno then boomed in his plummy voice:

"My God Natasha, you're looking bloody gorgeous tonight." Before he turned to Miles and added in a confidential aside, "I'll have you know, Natasha and I were passionate lovers not so very long ago."

Miles just rolled his eyes at Natasha and muttered, huskily, under his breath:

"Hmm, passionate sounds promising..."

Then he flicked his tongue at her, provocatively. Natasha blushed. By now, Bruno's eloquent eyes were on fire with interest, and he stared searingly into hers. Clearly, Bruno felt he had adequately justified his intrusion and he turned his back on Miles, entirely, to focus all of his attention on Natasha. She did not know what was going on tonight, and she wondered if the waiters had been adding Spanish Fly to the colourful cocktails, for all the men here seemed to be randier than rabbits. Bruno's arm was still resting above her head, and now his crotch was so close that it was almost touching hers. He stared earnestly into her face with his lips provocatively near, as he questioned:

"So Natasha, tell me, how have you really been?" Nodding his head gravely as he did so, in an attempt to encourage an honest response.

"Very well thank you Bruno, how have you been?" she replied, meekly.

"Missing you hot stuff, bloody well missing you." He burst into bombastic laughter until he pulled himself together and readjusted his expression to one of grave seriousness, once again, before adding, "That's the truth."

Then Bruno held her gaze, penetratingly, for some time, as he continued to nod his head. His face was still less than an inch away. Natasha was trapped, yet again, and she feared that Sebastian was watching them when, suddenly, a man's hand thwacked Bruno on his muscular back. With palpable relief Natasha looked up to discover Sebastian. He continued to slap his cousin on his back, with apparent affection, but so hard that it almost approached violence, as if he was finding a disguised physical outlet for his suppressed jealousy. Bruno pulled away from Natasha, immediately, to greet his cousin warmly and he engaged in some hearty back-slapping with equal force. Natasha looked at Sebastian, enquiringly, for he was grinning a little too manically for her comfort. It seemed that witnessing the seductive manoeuvres of Miles and Bruno had all been too much for him. Quite how the two of them were to break the frenzied scene seemed to defeat them, until a woman's arm slid onto Sebastian's back, and then her other one onto Bruno's, before she pushed herself, assertively, in between the pair of them. Natasha stiffened when she saw that the woman who stood before her was Isabel.

Immediately, both Sebastian and Bruno were sobered, and their mutual back-pounding fast aborted. Sebastian's manic grin had been wiped from his face and he now adopted a steely countenance. Even Bruno seemed strangely contained. Sebastian looked to Isabel, as if seeking instruction, as his eyes darted in between her and Natasha, nervously. The voice Sebastian now opened with was that international, expressionless one, he adopted when trading or in the morning meetings: "Isabel, please allow me to introduce you to Natasha Flynn, the new girl who is working with us at the moment. I think I mentioned her to you."

Natasha looked at this small, blonde, impeccably groomed woman, apprehensively. She was on the verge of offering Isabel her hand but, when she noticed her stony expression, she feared that Isabel had no intention of engaging in such an act with a girl whom, clearly, she found to be tastelessly presumptuous for being there at all. In fact, Isabel made no action to greet Natasha, instead, she just stared daggers at her, while both of her arms remained stubbornly encircling the backs of these two big men, like a lioness owning its recent kill. All her facial expression communicated was 'Mine: back off.' While, with a fixed smile, her emotionless, determined eyes bored into Natasha's until, finally, she gave one curt nod in stern acknowledgement.

The woman standing before her, was an entirely different Isabel from the threatened, speechless one Natasha had encountered, off guard, at the front door. This version of Sebastian's wife was utterly composed, calculating, and drawing up the psychological battle lines necessary, in order to defend her human property. Feeling acutely uncomfortable, due to the awkward, prolonged silence, Natasha ventured, quietly, "Hello Isabel. I believe we met, briefly, at the front door."

To prompt Sebastian to turn to Natasha, with a most surprised expression.

"That's right." Isabel confirmed, in a voice devoid of warmth or welcome.

The women said nothing more. Then Sebastian and Bruno started to talk, with excessive animation, to fill in the gaps made by the females' silence. The foursome stood like this, for several minutes, with the men babbling, and the ladies eyeing each other up, before Isabel, at last, patted Bruno, and then Sebastian, decisively, on their backs, before moving away to join the throng of her crowded birthday party.

Natasha stayed less than an hour more, but continued to marvel at the fact that the 'married couple' spent hardly any time together and, when they did, she could detect no warmth but, instead, Sebastian's stature seemed to fracture and he became unrecognizable to her. Throughout the night Isabel followed his every move, fearfully, as she scrutinized the women with whom he spent too much time and, if necessary, went over to reclaim him, just as she had done earlier with Natasha.

Natasha had seen enough. She wanted to go home. It was gone midnight, and she had to be up at six. She did not wish to say goodbye to anyone, not even to Sebastian, for she felt too morose. Discreetly, she made her way to the front door, where one of the staff went to get her coat.

While she waited, at the foot of the stairs, Miles Monroe, suddenly, popped up in front of her, more startling than a jack-in-the-box.

Natasha's coat arrived, and the man who had retrieved it held it up for her to put on. Having done so, she smiled fondly at Miles and, as she was about to walk past him, she said, sweetly, "Good night Miles, it was surprisingly wonderful to meet you."

At which point, he stretched out his arms, and placed his hands flat on each wall of the corridor, to effectively block her exit and declared, categorically:

"Natasha, I will not allow you to leave until you have, at least, given me your 'phone number. I simply refuse." Then he shook his head, from side to side, to make his locks swing around his face with the drama of a flamenco dancer's skirt, as he added petulantly, "No, no, no, no, no!"

Too tired to resist, Natasha conceded and delved into her handbag to retrieve a business card, which she then handed him. Miles took it, smiled mischievously, and then bowed before reluctantly allowing her to pass. As she did so, he kissed her card, adoringly, then uttered under his breath in the filthiest voice imaginable:

"Until the next time Na-tash-a."

She opened the front door, before glancing behind her to catch his eye. He was still staring after her and, to her shame, Natasha was unable to suppress a wry smirk at this extraordinary character's performance. She then turned to walk out into the night, closing the door, softly, behind her.

Chapter Eighteen - Crossing the line

I drank from his flaming cup
and lost my mind
Now, like a moth, I am circling
Around his sun.

Rumi

The next morning Natasha was sitting at her desk trying to concentrate on the bank's daily market commentary publication. As was increasingly the case, she was feeling distracted. The only thing that sustained her was the mantra, 'Only one more day, only one more day, only one more day...' for she had only one more day of exposure to Sebastian, before she would have two weeks reprieve, from him, and the trading floor, to study for, then sit, her Financial Services Authority (F.S.A.) exams.

Natasha was desperate for some space. Last night's endeavour to quash her obsessive love for Sebastian had backfired entirely, for now her heart seemed even more fixed on its fateful course than before. Witnessing the complete lack of trust, and spiritual connection, between Sebastian and his wife, firsthand, had only made matters worse. Rather than continuing to feel horrendously guilty about loving a married man, now Natasha was actually fearful for Sebastian's welfare, having discovered that he was locked in a union based on fear, control and grasping. It was as if, now more than ever, she was careering unchecked into his arms.

The image of Sebastian standing next to Isabel, kept infecting our heroine's mind. Forget the inner glow she so delighted in witnessing, when standing next to his wife, Sebastian's energy field could not compete with that of a three-day-old corpse. Indeed, his face became, instantly, more ashen than his wife's had done at the front door, when confronted with Natasha for the first time, to such an extent that not only did he become a stranger to her, it was as if he became a stranger to himself. Witnessing such diabolical energy-depletion had made Natasha's mission clearer than ever: she must rescue Sebastian from his marriage! Yes, yes, yes, Natasha had a divine PURPOSE, beyond the making oodles of money via the sale of complex financial instruments! Oh, how obvious it all seemed now, Natasha must save Sebastian from the worst of fates: soul death. It was all down to her, for only she knew and understood the REAL HIM! He needed her help, urgently, before he was to be lost forever. Natasha was determined to fight this battle to the death! With each forceful gush of conviction, little shots of adrenaline spurted into our heroine's pulsating, caffeine-rich blood, to stimulate her heart and mind in preparation for her noble quest. Natasha was all-powerful. She was infused with the torrent of LOVE that pulses through all creation, to flush out the poverty of self: NATASHA HAD BECOME TRUTH!

As the wildly bubbling brook of Natasha's consciousness eddied through her head, eagerly embracing each jagged rock of captivating conviction along the way, in her silent soul depth, she feared she would be sucked under, and drowned in the whirlpool of her obsessive passion. Indeed, who was she to judge another's marriage? Oh, and how self-serving to deduce that the marriage of the man with whom you are in love, is a sham? Even if she was right, what then? Why should Natasha see fit to cast herself in the role of saviour? Sebastian's saviour no less: an attractive, intelligent, successful man with a wife and two children. Oh, what delusions of grandeur had so overcome our heroine that she, a twenty-three-year-old girl with nothing, designed to 'rescue' a man a decade older than herself, who had everything?

Round and round and round her mind whizzed, whirring like a gaudy spinning top that, for all its eye-catching amusement, served no useful purpose. Yet Natasha's mental manic whirring was not amusing. It was torturous: 'Stop it! Stop it! stop it!!' her inner voice begged. 'Forget rescuing the married bloke, focus on saving yourself!' Then, suddenly, the nauseating spinning of her thoughts ground to an abrupt halt, the moment Natasha's mind managed to leap from its bubbling brook of mental agitation to grasp, gratefully, the only hanging vine in reach: avoidance. Yes, she may have to see Sebastian every day at work, but she did not have to go out for lunch and drinks with him. Natasha must determine never to spend any more time alone with him. Just as the cement of her prudent resolve was about to set, the urgent orange light of Bloomberg's message function demanded her immediate attention, for the name that flashed on screen was, 'Butler'. So powerful was its call that Natasha's recent resolve, instantly, was supplanted, and the indelible imprint of 'Butler' cemented instead! In a swift heartbeat, for how frantically did her heart race now, Natasha had accessed Sebastian's message to read:

'Lunch?'

And before she had even recalled the wisdom of her 'avoidance' strategy, she had typed in, and sent, her reply:

'Done.'

She was even denied the leisure to regret so doing for, in a thrice, Sebastian had commanded:

'12 our flash fish & chippy. Be there!'

For a miniature moment, having resolved to forsake time alone with her Love forever, and now, to be due to meet him for lunch in less than four and a half hours' time, well, the oscillation of her emotions were simply too violent to contain. Natasha was off, free floating in heaven at the mere prospect! Abruptly, she was knocked off course, to land with a thump on the threadbare carpet, as soon as she heard Freddie's gruff voice bellow:

"Oy! Natasha, line eight, Miles Monroe."

In an instant, our heroine's serene smile of celestial anticipation, was twisted into a grin of sheer devilment, for Sebastian and heaven had just been usurped by Miles Monroe and the temptations of hell. Oh, how ashamed was she that Miles' lavish attention and obscene lewdness thrilled her so? Natasha thwacked the button on her dealer board to click into line eight. As she picked up the handset

251

she gave a sidelong glance, to find her Love sitting at his desk staring at her; observant. Guiltily, she averted her eyes, to stare down at her empty dealer pad, as she said, with detachment:

"Miles. Hi. What can I do for you?"

A deep, throaty chuckle reverberated down the line before Miles managed to stifle it, and reply:

"Why Natasha, I'm so much more interested in what I can do to you!"

Then his laughter spluttered for a protracted period of time, as he no doubt envisaged several despicable sexual acts. It was only seven-forty in the morning and simply far too early for the shenanigans of Miles Monroe.

"You're up bright and early Miles. I thought such discipline was reserved for investment bankers and contract cleaners." Natasha remarked, wryly.

"Oh darling, you are funny! I will have you know, I'm actually on my way to bed!"

"I should have guessed as much."

"Natasha my love, I have not stopped thinking about you since the moment we met. The way your eyes screw up when you smile is mesmeric. You simply must allow me to take your delectable self out for dinner. What about next Tuesday? Please just say 'purrrrfect'."

Natasha was silent, debating whether it was wise to increase the intrigue in her life any further. She had only just recovered from the whole Bruno affair. Then she consoled herself, at least Miles wasn't related to Sebastian and, as she did so, he encouraged with sweet optimism:

"Please?"

"OK Miles, OK, I relent, just for you. Tuesday suits me 'purrrrfectly'."

Miles virtually squealed with glee before, finally, composing himself.

"Natasha, I will pick you up at eight. Your address?"

Natasha supplied it, and he thanked her before saying goodbye. She then pressed the black button on the dealer board to cut off the call, while suppressing a smirk as she contemplated this new chapter in her life. Then she remembered the epic she was living through, and glanced behind her. Sebastian stared at her with hollow eyes. Suddenly, the thought of Miles Monroe did not seem so amusing. Natasha spent the next four hours and twenty-five minutes making calls and tracking down and dazzling corporate treasurers, in order to fix up introductory meetings with them, once she was qualified. By eleven-fifty she had seven new appointments set, umpteen calls answered and many messages taken. This job was easy. Love was not.

When Natasha arrived at the intimate 'fish and chippy' at twelve o'clock, Sebastian was already seated. He had taken the table that they had sat at before. He looked handsome, regal and relaxed. Impatient to join him, Natasha passed her coat to the young hostess at reception and made her way over. On sight of her, Sebastian stood up and brushed the front of his suit jacket down. A waiter pulled out a chair for Natasha and they sat down together. They grinned at each other and, immediately, started to beam brightly with the simple joy of being together. However, today, Natasha detected a hint of conceit in Sebastian's eye that seemed to make him a touch remote.

"I've already ordered for us. I'm famished." he informed her, straight away.

"Would you be kind enough to inform me what I will be having for lunch?"

Instead of answering her, Sebastian put his hands together, rested his elbows on the table and then lurched forward until his face was within an inch of hers.

"Only time, will tell." he whispered, cryptically.

"Not Sebastian?"

"Only time, will tell." he repeated, while his face remained temptingly close.

Recalling the limited menu, Natasha thought it safe to allow time to do so. She moved her face, imperceptibly, closer to his, until their lips almost brushed, as she replied, under her breath:

"OK Sebastian, I trust you."

Sebastian took this slug of obligation like a man. He held his position and the intensity of his stare. With souls locked and lips so close, all Natasha yearned to do was wrap her hands around the nape of his elegant neck, close her eyes and kiss him. Sebastian did something different. Serenely, he closed his eyes then, delicately, leant his forehead against hers. Natasha closed her eyes as well and, with her forehead resting on his and her concentration acute, time stopped and the common world was distilled into the matterless expanse of truth: BLISS. In this little restaurant in the City, Natasha could not have been happier for, as far as highs go, bizarrely, this forehead-on-forehead action had just set the precedent and, surely, such indulgence was safer than most? Or was it?

A tentative cough from a perplexed, plate-carrying waiter then penetrated their soulful communion and, reluctantly, they pulled apart and then opened their eyes, as if to a new world. The bemused waiter, hastily, put down the food then scurried away. Sebastian and Natasha were too dizzy to experience embarrassment; instead, they caught each other's eye and laughed, still high from their togetherness. Natasha then looked down at the golden food: battered fish and chips, haddock she presumed, just like last time. Sebastian had the same. Eagerly the pair tucked in. Having chewed and swallowed several mouthfuls, Sebastian shone the spell of his full attention upon Natasha.

"So, when are you going to have dinner with him then?" he inquired, with laconic inquisitiveness.

Natasha was jarred by Sebastian's reference to Miles Monroe, for to whom else could he be referring? She dipped her head and played dumb.

"Dinner with whom?"

"Natasha?" he encouraged, gravely, utterly unperturbed.

She soon worked out that further resistance was pointless and she replied, matter-of-factly:

"He's taking me out for dinner on Tuesday night." Before adding, "Besides, Sebastian, how did you know he'd asked me out at all?"

"My darling one, in certain social circles, London becomes a very small place indeed. Miles and I have heavily overlapping circles. In fact, within half an hour of your getting off the 'phone with him, even Isabel knew he was taking you out. She was rather put out about it, actually."

Strangely, Sebastian smiled, indulgently, before he added, with nonchalance, "Of course Miles is highly entertaining, Natasha, but please be warned: he's more of a tart than you are."

Self-servingly, Natasha quickly attributed Sebastian's gibe to jealousy. She said nothing and continued to eat her tasty lunch. Having taken a few more mouthfuls of his own, Sebastian commented in an off-hand manner:

"It's quite ironic really, Isabel has always fancied Miles and now he's all over you like a rash. A rash it appears you're quite happy to scratch..." Sebastian then ate some more, before continuing, "Miles reminds me of sand: we all love the idea of it but, in truth, the bloody stuff gets into everything, especially the places you least want it." He looked pensive, for a moment, before he exclaimed with jovial exasperation, "Circumcision was invented by desert dwellers for Christ's Sake. I think that says it all!"

Natasha could not help but laugh, and she began to appreciate the degree to which Miles irritated Sebastian. She strove to reassure him.

"Sebastian, I can't speak for Isabel but, as far as I am concerned, you have nothing to fear from Miles Monroe. I think he is a tremendous character, but I don't fancy him; besides, I'm in love with you."

Sebastian seemed unconvinced but, clearly, he had had enough of the subject. Miles Monroe was brushed away as vigorously as a mother dusts dry sand off a toddler's tiny toes. He shrugged before suggesting with enthusiasm:

"Natasha, tonight I want to take you out for dinner. I'm a member of a charming private members' club in Mayfair: exquisite food, fabulous wine list, roaring fires, unpretentious. Will you join me?"

All Natasha seemed to do these days was eat, yet how

could she resist a dinner invitation from Sebastian?

"Oh Sebastian, I would love to." she replied, overjoyed.

This time Natasha did not enquire after Isabel's where-abouts at the time of their allotted rendezvous. Having met her, she would rather not know. She would have Sebastian all to herself and, increasingly, that was all she cared about.

When Natasha left work that evening, she saw that Sebastian was gripped in an unpleasant conversation on the telephone, as he paced up and down the corridor in be-tween the back-to-back trading and sales desks. His brow was deeply furrowed, and he looked terribly downcast as he rubbed his forehead, as if to massage away a headache. His voice was soft, but stubborn and determined. Natasha was concerned and wondered if she should wait to see if everything was OK. She hovered by his desk, for a mo-ment, reluctant to leave him in distress. Sebastian shot a look at her and the clouds of disturb parted from his brow.

"I'll pick you up at seven-thirty." he mouthed, before he looked, solemnly, back down at the floor to re-engage in his telephone conversation.

Reassured, Natasha made for the door.

"Oy, Natasha, if you don't pass your exams don't bother coming back!" Freddie screamed after her.

She caught his cheeky ice-blue eyes and smiled wryly at him. She hoped Freddie was joking, but suspected that he was not. Sebastian then darted another look in her direction and, covering the mouthpiece of the telephone with his free hand, he shouted with Freddie, in chorus:

"No pressure!"

Natasha just grinned at the pair of them, and then flounced off the trading floor, with her nose stuck up in the air, defiantly. As soon as she got home and began to get ready for the night ahead, she realized just how different she felt. Her heart was light and her soul joyful. In short, she felt liberated. Only last night, Natasha had been so guilt-ridden as she battled, mercilessly, with her conscience about going to Isabel's party, at all. Indeed, for two-months now, she had fought bitterly against her feelings for Sebastian. She had even dated Bruno in an earnest attempt to fall for him, and prevent herself from embarking on an adulterous affair. Oh, how she had struggled against her impossibly passionate feelings! Then, with dread-laced excitement, the proverbial penny dropped and, suddenly, Natasha realized that her liberation was born of abandoning that struggle. Possibly for the first time, she became resigned to the fact that she was just a young girl in love, and there was absolutely nothing she could do about it.

So eager was Natasha to see Sebastian that evening, that by seven twenty-five she was already standing on her front doorstep waiting for him. She looked radiant in her restlessness as she paced up and down, distractedly, on the wide, stone, top step of her house. Tonight, she cut an extraordinarily dramatic figure. She was wearing a full-length, charcoal-grey, military style, tailored ladies coat with light grey-white fluffy fur collar and cuffs. It flattered her neat waist and made her look even taller than usual. Indeed, she would have looked most at home on an Anna Karenina film set, braving the driving snow. All Natasha lacked was an audience and he was on his way. Beneath her coat she was wearing an elegant, Chanel, black A-line dress that stopped several inches above her knee. The dress was by far the most expensive item of clothing she had ever owned. It sported a neat little white V-neck collar, which started at the top of a narrow split that delved down her chest, only to be arrested at the precise point at which her cleavage began. The mixture of simple elegance, spiced with such a discreet, but tantalizing, tease was captivating. She was shod in her black satin Jimmy Choo sling-back heels, and she held an exquisite, faux-diamond clasped, matching clutch bag. The most beautiful thing about our heroine tonight, however, was the incandescence that radiated from her face in anticipation of imminent timeless-time with Sebastian.

Suddenly, Natasha's whole body stiffened and her heart felt fit to burst, for in the distance she could make out the distinctive grumbling purr of a shockingly powerful engine, as it roared towards her. Surely that must be him? The car's distant growling fluctuations seemed furiously curtailed, as it, sporadically, spat out threats of its potential force, in frustration at being so confined to narrow, traffic-filled, city streets. Natasha was shot through with extreme excitement, and she felt herself resonate with the engine's juddering shudders, as if she too were poised, and ready to ROAR!

Oh, how ludicrously thrilling was this love? The mechanical racket continued to increase until, finally, Natasha spied the low nose of a black sports car poking around the corner of her garden square. In the split of an eardrum, a shiny, black Aston Martin had screeched to a halt outside her home. Even in its idling state, the degree to which the scrumptious sound of the car dominated this residential square, could match that of a Red-Arrows aerial display slicing through the sky over some English summer's country festival. With lips slightly parted, Natasha stood stock still on the top step as she stared down at the car. It must be Sebastian, but she had never seen this car before and its tinted windows withheld the driver's identity. Then, suddenly, the front window rolled down, to reveal her Love's smiling face. Then Sebastian cried, over the engine's competing noise, "Hello you."

Natasha swept down the steps as Sebastian's tall figure emerged from the humming car. Her lips were on his, and his arms wrapped around her, in a heartbeat: fused. Finally disengaging, Natasha stepped back.

"Hello, you." she replied.

Then she began to admire the new car at closer quarters.

"Bloody beautiful car!" she soon exclaimed.

Sebastian just smiled, sheepishly, and shrugged, as if a touch embarrassed by his flagrant employment of such a flashy prop.

"I thought it would be a bit of fun... if it doesn't kill me that is!"

Natasha huffed at his flabbergasting flippancy.

"Scarily, my thought process regarding you was not dissimilar!" Sebastian added, with a humorous look of horror.

Natasha giggled, shamelessly, for she did not doubt it. Sebastian offered her his arm, then escorted her around the car and opened her door for her. Once inside, Natasha was blessed to experience that wonderful olfactory pleasure, of the delicious smell of brand-new leather and, in no time, Sebastian was sitting by her side and they were zipping off to Mayfair. With each lurch of acceleration, Natasha giggled with adrenaline-induced glee. Oh, how shallow felt she to be so delighted by the power of a car yet, though her mind now value-judged her brain's triggers, her brain just continued to respond happily to the effect of them. Was it Natasha's fault that she was never more thrilled than when flooded with adrenaline? Flash cars may be superficial, but they were undeniably good fun. In her amusement, it took Natasha a while to realize that Sebastian was not himself. Though he concentrated, fiercely, on his driving, he seemed uncomfortably preoccupied.

"Is something the matter Sebastian?" Natasha coaxed, wishing him to be just as jolly as she.

He shot a glance at her open, hopeful face before, quickly, turning his attention back to the road.

"You mean other than the cruel fact that I am completely in love with a woman who is not my wife?"

Natasha's heart sank for she had only just allowed herself to love Sebastian unhindered, and she replied, with subdued curtness, "Yes, other than that."

"Forgive me Natasha. I'll snap out of it. It's just been a difficult few hours that's all."

She retorted, unfairly, "What choosing the colour of the car?" And Sebastian shot her a sharp look of reproach.

"No Natasha, not choosing the colour of the car and, for your information, I bought it last week."

There was silence, for a few moments. At last, she responded, softly, "I'm sorry Sebastian. What's the matter?"

Sebastian gave a despondent sigh, before stretching his neck on one side, then the other, in an attempt to loosen the tight knots that had gathered there.

"I was supposed to go to the British Bankers Association Conference tonight, and listen to my wife give a keynote speech. She has not taken the fact that I will not be attending well." he confessed, with shame.

Natasha smarted. Of course he should be there. It was natural for Isabel to expect his support.

"You should go, Sebastian. Just drop me home."

He turned to look at her, helplessly.

She insisted, "Really, just take me home. I understand."

"Natasha, I knew about this speech weeks ago. I knew about this speech when I asked you out for dinner earlier today. The truth is, I don't want to go there. I just want to be here, with you. Oh Natasha, what have you done to me?" She shook her head, for she had no adequate explanation for their extreme reaction to each other. Reflective he continued, "Of course I should have gone, but it seems I have voted with my feet. I am here with you, the only place in the world I want to be. I have argued with, and upset my wife and I don't even care."

"Well Mr. Butler, if that is the case, then why are you in a grump?"

"I'm in a grump, Miss Flynn, because it appears you command control over me! How do you expect a lifelong control freak to react in such a situation?"

"Grumpily?" Natasha laughed.

"No more." Sebastian declared, with determination.

Just then the formidable car screeched to a halt outside his club in the narrow Mayfair street. Two short, bald, thickset, middle-aged bouncers stood, with their hands locked in front of them, either side of a gigantic, but discreet, panelled doorway. There was a black, gold-tasselled awning above it. The bouncers were wearing black-tie and they looked so similar they may well have been brothers. One of them walked around to open Natasha's door for her, while the other opened Sebastian's.

"Good evening Mr. Butler." he muttered, civilly.

Sebastian just nodded, then handed him the car keys before the man, immediately, crouched into the Aston to valet park it. The remaining bouncer held the club's front door open for them to enter. Having exchanged pleasantries with a beautiful blonde hostess, with whom Sebastian seemed to be on familiar terms, he signed them in before leading Natasha down a wide, high-ceilinged corridor that had a geometric-patterned black and white marble floor. Soon enough, the couple stepped into the bar, the atmosphere of which was more that of a friend's country house, than a Mayfair private members' club. The maitre d' whisked over to Sebastian the moment he saw him. He was smiling, amiably, and dressed in black trousers and a blazer the colour of red wine. He had thick rubbery skin that was nearly as shiny as his short, black, slicked-back hair. He greeted Sebastian, obsequiously, before leading them over to the best table in the house, in front of an enormous fireplace with a delicately carved oak mantel. A roaring golden, orange fire burned beneath in hot welcome.

Sebastian and Natasha sat down at a forty-five degree angle to one another on low, dark brown, button-backed, leather armchairs. The maitre d' then handed Sebastian a black, gold-tasselled wine menu before making himself scarce. Huffing, Sebastian soon discarded it on the sidetable before leaning forward to take Natasha's hand.

"Natasha, every one of my waking moments you invade my mind." he confessed, in confusion.

There was something unrestrained and feverish about Sebastian now, as if some breakthrough had occurred. His resistance, like Natasha's, seemed to have fled. His eyes bored into hers, and they seemed to pour a torrent of urgent, gushing, love-energy into her soul. Their hands were inseparably intertwined, continually fondling each other's, as they flipped between light toying, then firm, intense grasping, while their fingers played like a pack of jostling, newborn puppies. Natasha sighed, deeply, before responding, helplessly:

"Oh Sebastian, don't blame me, I can't begin to describe how scrambled my brain becomes every minute I'm not with you, and then..." she flung out her upturned hands to emphatically express her exasperation, before continuing, "and then, just as I'm about to voluntarily section myself into the Hampstead Royal Free psychiatric ward, you arrive and, suddenly, I feel more sane than I have ever felt." Natasha paused, for some time, as she stared into the flickering flames before she caught Sebastian's eye to concede, humourously, "Which, come to think of it, is not much to boast about..."

The mercurial Sebastian smirked for he understood, all too well, the precariousness of personality to which Natasha alluded. Staring at her with eccentric intensity, suddenly, he exclaimed, "Drinks!"

And, as if the maitre d', instinctively, knew Sebastian had been about to say it, he sprung up by his side to take his order. A chilled bottle of Krug soon arrived, in a silver ice bucket, and the strange urgency between this couple, this evening, was so compelling that they sipped their way through the bottle of divine, golden bubbly in less than twenty-minutes. When Sebastian smacked his lips, with satisfaction, having drained the final sip from his champagne flute, he focused his attention even more exclusively onto Natasha, as he confided under his breath:

"Natasha, I don't want dinner." Intrigued, she arched her eyebrow, before Sebastian leaned farther forward to declare, quietly, into her straining ear, "I want you."

Natasha froze. It seemed the moment that had always seemed so inevitable, had just arrived. Sebastian was less than a centimetre away and she could feel his warm breath against her cheek. Her eyes were wide and she stared into space, as she began to absorb the magnitude of what he had just said. Sebastian then suggested, softly.

"Fuck supper, let's go back to yours. Now."

Without one more word, the pair stood up, as if in slow motion. Sebastian took Natasha by her hand and led her out of the bar, down the long corridor and towards the grand front entrance. As they floated past the hostess, he glanced over his shoulder to inform her:

"We won't be dining with you this evening, after all,

please just charge the bar bill to my account."

By the time they had stepped out onto the pavement, Sebastian's new toy was waiting to greet them with its vibrating growl. Not surprisingly, considering the car's power, Sebastian's skill and their intention, they were scooting around the corner into Pembridge Square, in a flash, and the Aston Martin was parked, adeptly, directly outside Natasha's home. Sebastian and Natasha got out and climbed the stone steps to her front door, hand in hand. She then let them in, before they made their way up to her little bedsit in serendipitous silence.

Once inside, Sebastian gently removed Natasha's coat and hung it over the back of the tiny sofa, while Natasha placed her handbag beside it as she, delicately, kicked off her beautiful satin shoes. Once Sebastian had removed his jacket he turned around to face her. His sparkling, bright green eyes met hers and the sharpness of his look of profound longing, pierced Natasha's soul. Her throat constricted with emotion, at the excruciating spiritual presence of this long-averted moment. The pair hesitated, lost in their exploration of each other's spirits before Sebastian, at last, stepped forward to take Natasha into his arms and draw her close to him. With a sigh of eternal gratitude, she fell into his strength and wrapped her arms, tightly, around his body. Oh, how long had our protagonists resisted this? Oh, how long had they yearned just for this? Beyond ecstasy, Natasha nuzzled her cheek into Sebastian's upper chest, closed her eyes, held him tightly and, in a star-burst of bliss, she was HOME.

Gorging on the extreme glory of their togetherness, like blind newborn kittens to their mother's teat, our lovers' lips, instinctively, sought each other's out and they began to kiss. Union: two souls mingled, two minds merged, curtains of blinding white light, envelop. The enraptured couple, imperceptibly, edged towards the bed until Natasha felt her calf press against its hard base. Still locked together, they dropped upon it like a felled tree. Sebastian was on top of her, and his weight crushed down on her, deliciously, as they kissed and kissed and kissed some more. Finally, a joyous, breathless Sebastian broke away to prop himself up, on flexing arms, above Natasha's smitten face. His expression was dopey, as if drunk with awe. Longingly, Sebastian delved into the black mesmerizing depths of Natasha's soul.

"I love you." he uttered, with grave import.

To hear his words echoed back to him, fervently, in canorous female tones, "I love you, I love you, I love you…" Natasha's yearning made her whole body convulse with longing, for she knew what was to come.

"Sebastian, have you ever done this before?" she questioned, with trepidation, as her wide guileless eyes stared deeply into his.

"Never."

She narrowed her eyes.

"All of those gorgeous 'intimate' friends Sebastian, never once?" she pressed.

He just smiled at her, indulgently. His mouth was partially open and his upper lip curled in a sanguine smirk to show his top teeth, glinting. Sebastian shook his head.

"Never." he repeated, definitively, before elaborating, with calm assurance, "Twelve years of marriage, and I have never had sex with a woman other than my wife."

Natasha was overwhelmed by the enormity of what was about to occur, and she quizzed, in sheer bewilderment.

"Why me?"

Sebastian paused, for a long time, as if in deep thought.

"Because you're strong." he, finally, articulated.

He then leant down, to place his soft lips onto hers, once again. As they kissed, caressed, merged and moaned, ecstatic teardrops of unbearable happiness began to well up behind Natasha's closed eyelids, only to escape, and gradually trickle down her temples to then seep into her thick, titian hair. Simply, the sheer bliss of this fateful coupling was so profound, it pierced the membrane of ecstasy itself to touch Natasha's soul with unspeakable sorrow. Extremes, after all, forever meet their antithesis in the closed circle of human emotion, only ever to be truly experienced in tandem. As Natasha relinquished her soul-self to HIM, she hovered on the brink of exaltation and agony, as tears continued to trickle from closed eyes.

As he continued to make her dizzy with his exquisite kisses, Sebastian edged his hands behind Natasha's back and slowly began to unzip her dress. Compliantly, she used the strength of her back to sit up, so he could unzip it completely, while her mouth was still fused to his. She raised her arms and, for a moment, they disengaged their intoxicating connection so Sebastian could pull the dress carefully over her head. Immediately, their eyes closed, once again, and their mouths fixed on each other's, as Sebastian let the garment drop to the floor.

Natasha was hungry to feel his soft flesh against hers and, with the calm ritual of a geisha, she began to unbutton his thick cotton shirt, very slowly, all the way down his chest, before easing it over, and then off, his broad shoulders to then drop it to the floor. Still kissing him, ardently, she started to undo his belt, then his trouser button and, finally, his fly. Never before had she felt so serene and calm. There was no need for an urgent lustful rush to intercourse. Simply, they wished to be naked and intertwined; flesh upon flesh, to forever encircle and explore the essence of the other. As she pushed Sebastian's trousers and boxer shorts over his bottom and down his thighs, he undid her bra and removed it, before undoing her black suspender belt and then beginning to slide it, slowly, along with her knickers and stockings, down her trembling white legs.

At last, they were laid bare, impossibly soft skin on soft skin, currents of electric sensitivity coursed all over them and aroused genitals fixed snug to each other's. Finally, there were no barriers left to surmount. With ecstatic shock, Sebastian slid his large penis inside the wet silky warmth of our heroine. They were joined. He, clutched tightly by her. She, filled with the firm girth and length of him. Everything that had been before, had been wrong. This was right. Oh, the sheer euphoric surprise of this inevitable, longed for, penetration. Sebastian supported the weight of his upper body on his flexing arms and he stared, intently, into Natasha's open eyes as he continued to insert himself, more and more deeply, into her, while hungrily watching the effect of his so doing. Bewitched, Natasha stared back at him as she locked herself, ever more tightly, around him; never wanting to let go. Captivated by what they saw beyond each other's pupils, our Lovers registered their mutual joy at this defining moment. The line had been crossed. There was no turning back. Sebastian closed his eyes and fell upon her. He began to kiss her, and she him; souls and flesh united. Their loving hearts became more expansive than outer space, combined consciousness acquired King Solomon's wisdom, while each and every one of their bodily cells ignited: incandescent. Intimately conjoined thus, Sebastian and Natasha were as vital as a star.

Resonating souls vibrated in elevated rhapsody, and the depths of eternal, profound gratitude were plunged. They became one, blissfully to traverse the deserts of time, and fleetingly comprehend the truth of infinity; just like the moment their eyes had first met. In the darkness, their enraptured souls soared, while ecstatic bodies explored the delights to be found in one another. This night, this entwined, adulterous pair dwelt in LOVE, for hours, and the shabby tragedy of intercourse without, was shamefully exposed. The nature of their reality had shifted. Neither of them would ever be the same again.

Chapter Nineteen - An object of pity

It's not me that's glorified in the acts of worship.
It's the worshipers!

Rumi

Natasha opened her eyes with a start. Bright October sunlight burst through the gap between the blind and the skylight's frame above her bed. Without a thought, she rejoiced to be greeted by rays of sunshine, following the recent working week of waking to the ethereal, pre-dawn sky found at six o'clock in the morning. Then her heart skipped, joyously, when flashes of delightful, bliss-promoting recollections cascaded into her mind, just like the cheerful sunlight into her bedsit. Ah, Sebastian! Last night with HIM Natasha had frolicked in LOVE, boundaries had dissolved and UNION been attained! The vivid memory of their recent communion made Natasha's soul shimmer, and her body tingle with sheer delight. Never before had it been like that. Making love with Sebastian, compared to Natasha's previous sexual encounters, was what Michelangelo's Sistine Chapel frescoes were to Pop Art: worlds apart.

Had she dreamt it? No, she had not for, today, everything felt different. Natasha was madly in love: pure HEAVEN. Then, with panic, she recalled that she was not going to be on the trading floor for the next two weeks, while she studied for her F.S.A. exams. Her heart began to race. How was she to survive without him? More to the point, how was she supposed to pass her exams in such a state of blissful confusion? Freddie had already warned her about the consequences of failing: do not bother coming back! But what did she care? Natasha was in love and nothing else mattered!

She listened to her heart pound violently in her chest, and she frowned as she realized that this had become its habit of late. Maybe she should join a gym to give it biological cause to behave so? She must calm down before she had a heart attack and, just like that, Natasha decided she would go for a nice, long walk through the park. The wonders of fresh air, exercise and Nature would work their usual magic and, hopefully, rein-in her racing mind and heart to a less life-threatening pace.

Then, suddenly, she remembered she was due to meet her best friend, Katarina, for lunch at one o'clock. Her eyes darted over to her alarm clock: it was eleven a.m. Perfect, she had plenty of time to get ready, then walk across Kensington Gardens and down through South Kensington, to meet up for lunch in Hollywood Road. Katarina had just returned from a three-month spell on Block Island. She had been working there in a very trendy art gallery, owned by one of her father's old friends whom he knew from his time at INSEAD. Oh, Natasha could not wait to hear all Katarina's news, not to mention inform her of her own awesome developments. It felt like so long since she had seen Katarina that she had almost forgotten what she looked like. In fact, Natasha was so excited by the prospect that, for a second, she almost forgot about Sebastian!

With her plan formulated for the day, Natasha sat up in bed and gave an extravagant starfish yawn, to be greeted by disconcerting bone clicking as her skeleton rattled itself into alignment. From the sound of that, she really must join a gym! Feeling more awake, Natasha blinked, several times, before focusing on the scene around her. Her Chanel dress lay rumpled in a black heap on the floor by her bed, next to her knickers, while her suspenders and stockings lay twisted, in a snake-like roll, beside them. Her striking grey coat was still neatly laid upon the sofa, exactly where Sebastian had left it.

Oh, what a night! She wrapped her arms around herself as she smiled, ecstatically, in recollection. Her Love had left just before two o'clock this morning, so she must have slept for nine hours flat. It was no wonder that she felt groggy. She decided she needed a coffee urgently and, inspired, she leapt out of bed and sauntered over to the tiny kitchenette to make up a cafetière. While she waited for the kettle to boil, she wandered over to the window, which had not had a curtain since she moved in. It made no difference for she usually got up, and went to bed, in the dark; besides, its stirrup-shape was charmingly pretty to look at, especially when it framed the glorious colours of the remaining autumnal leaves, which stubbornly clung to the bouncing branches of the enormous trees outside; as it did now. In fact, unless she was sitting inside the window, all Natasha could ever see from the bedsit itself was sky and treetops. Right now, she craved to see more, so she turned to place the heels of her hands onto the window-ledge, did a little jump, and then pulled herself up, before shifting her bottom all the way over to the window pane, to rest her head against the wall of the alcove, as she brought her knees up to her chin. Hugging her legs, tightly, she gave a sigh of appreciation, as she looked out over the beautiful garden square. It was simply a magnificent October day, and the garden was drenched in rich golden sunshine and bursting with jolly birdsong. The leaves quivered, violently, or fell from the tress to be blown around, erratically, by the boisterous breeze. Oh, how Natasha loved it up here. At this elevation she felt as carefree as a one of the chirping birds. Then, suddenly, she heard the kettle click from across the room, as its button popped-up to boast its boiling. She was just about to get down when the intercom sounded. Natasha almost fell off the window-ledge, with surprise, for who on earth could it be? Intrigued, she dashed over to answer it.

"Hello?"

To her astonishment the voice that replied was Sebastian's, "Hello you. It's me. Let me in."

Her eyes widened, with excitement and fright commingled. Sebastian, here, right now! Oh, the shock of being so unprepared! Oh, but the joy to have her Love here, right now! Her pulse started to pound in her ears.

"Sebastian! Come up." she squealed.

She let him in, and her mind began to race overtime as she tried to work out what to do first. For once, she was grateful for the three-flights of stairs that led up to her bed-sit. Having ordered her priorities, Natasha dashed to the wardrobe and opened the door to check her face in the mirror. She was relieved that she had been too delightfully pre-occupied last night to remove her make-up, for she still had enough traces left on to improve her 'first thing in the morning' appearance. Next, she rushed over to her chest of drawers, grabbed her hairbrush and quickly dragged it through her hair, before rushing to the kitchen sink and fumbling for her toothbrush and toothpaste, which she kept there to save her from having to go down to the shared bathroom all the time. Frantically, she cleaned her teeth, using so much toothpaste, in her hurry, that it stung her mouth. By the time Sebastian was tapping at her door, she was dabbing her lips on the tea towel. Quickly, she bolted over to open it. She was slightly flushed when she set eyes on him. He looked so relaxed and refreshed, as he cocked his head to one side, while swinging a bulging, Marks and Spencer carrier bag backwards and forwards.

"I've brought you breakfast." he announced, while smiling, sheepishly.

Immediately, Natasha's self-consciousness fled. She just beamed and pulled him into her tiny bedsit.

"Sorry I'm in such a state, I just woke up." she apologised, still a touch flustered. Then she added, wickedly, through a broad smirk, "Some bloke kept me up far too late last night."

"Lucky bloke." Sebastian chuckled.

"No. Lucky me." Natasha corrected, before teasing, "He only just left, in fact..."

Sebastian glared at her, most unamused.

"Ha ha ha." he added, in staccato.

He then strolled in and placed the plastic bag onto the sofa. Natasha slipped her arms around his waist and tugged him towards her, before resting the palms of her hands against his chest, as she reached up on tiptoes to kiss him on his tempting mouth. The minute her lips touched his, that divine, dizzy-making sensation enveloped her: FLY-

ING! The sensation was so intense, Natasha felt as if she was going to faint. She pulled away; intoxicated. When she lifted her hands from his chest, she was mortified to discover a small tear had appeared on the left side of his shirt. Horrified, her startled eyes stared into his. Sebastian looked down to assess the damage but fast resigned himself to it. Shrugging, he went on to comment, with soft exasperation:

"Not content with ripping the fabric of my life apart, my Love?"

Natasha covered her mouth, in genuine contrition, for she felt terrible to have ruined such a fine shirt.

"I promise Sebastian, I barely touched it. It just came apart in my hands."

"Comme moi, ma chérie, comme moi."

She giggled, guiltily, for the shirt and for her effect on him. He just pulled her farther into his hips, and she arched her back so she could look up into his captivating face.

"I'm so sorry, Sebastian."

"Oh Natasha, believe me, it's not the shirt I'm worried about. I woke up today and I just had to see you. The drive to be with you was insurmountable. After I'd wolfed down breakfast with the family, I announced that I was going for a walk, just like that." He was grinning, as if liberated, then he shook his head and explained, "Natasha, you don't understand. I don't go for walks… well not unless I'm in the country and carrying a gun!"

"Wasn't Isabel suspicious? Late home last night and then exhibiting unrecognizable behaviour this morning?"

"Probably, but I was out of the door too quickly to give a sound judgement call on that. Then again, maybe she will think that I have just matured into the type of man who likes to go off for walks by himself. In which case, the precedent is set, and it will be a lot easier for me to see you outside of work, in future." Natasha smiled sadly, feeling less amused and more guilt-ridden. He went on.

"Anyway, off I went, bought you breakfast on the way here, then crossed the park. It only took me forty-five minutes. So, my Love, do you think you deserve it?"

"Now you ask, Sebastian, I'm not sure if I deserve it but, be warned, I could certainly get used to it."

He smiled, adoringly, before letting her go, to delve into the Marks and Spencer bag, which he had brought with him. Enthusiastically, he started to unpack the contents and lay the items out onto the sofa: eggs, smoked salmon, granary bread, a lemon, a bottle of freshly squeezed orange juice and the Saturday Financial Times.

"Voila!" he declared, triumphantly.

Natasha came over to cuddle him, from behind.

"Thank you Sebastian, for breakfast, but mostly for coming to see me."

He looked over his shoulder at her and smirked. Then he turned to face her and take her in his arms, however, his brow darkened and he seemed, increasingly, preoccupied.

"I'll have to buy a new shirt of course." he mused, pensively, before adding, "Persuading your wife that you have acquired a taste for early morning strolls, is one thing, returning from one with a ripped shirt, is quite another."

"Won't returning from one wearing a different shirt be even worse?"

"No, not as long as I can buy something similar and get rid of this one, I don't think she'll notice..."

Natasha nodded in solemn agreement. Having drifted into a brief discussion concerning the logistics of deceit, she had lost her appetite. Looking earnestly up at him, she suggested, "Why don't I come with you? I'll have a quick shower, get ready and we can go together. I'll even help you choose the shirt."

"What about breakfast?" he exclaimed in dismay.

"Don't worry, I promise to eat it later. Besides, it's such a stunning day I want to get outside. I've already missed most of the morning."

A touch disappointed that she was not going to eat the breakfast that he had brought for her, but nevertheless happy for her company, Sebastian relented.

"OK. We can even go for a walk if you like?"

"Why not? You might even enjoy it!"

Natasha gave him a final squeeze, before she released him to go and wash. Sebastian then sat down, and made himself comfortable on the sofa before picking up the F.T.

Twenty-five minutes later they were strolling, arm in arm, in the fresh, blustery breeze, snuggly wrapped in winter coats as the butter-yellow sunshine hit their backs to warm them further. They crossed the square, as the whisking wind blew their hair all over the place, soon to turn into Moscow Road then take a right into Palace Court. It took no time for the glorious green spaces of Kensington Gardens to open up before them. They took the curved path that brought them to the wide, sandy pathway that led down to High Street Kensington. The beautiful Royal Park was brimming with life, populated with brisk pram-pushing mummies, disgruntled daddies, dashing children, whizzing cyclists and slaloming roller-bladers. Our couple drifted through the diverse commotion, oblivious, for their attention was exclusively captivated by each other.

When they hit the Saturday-packed High Street Kensington, a new shirt was soon bought, astonishingly similar to the one Sebastian had arrived in and, certainly, Isabel would never notice the difference. He changed and the damaged one was dumped, discreetly, in a big iron, black dustbin outside Kensington High Street tube station. As they ambled through the crowded high street, hand in hand, they simply yearned for a place to be alone. Instinctively, they turned down Wrights Lane, took a right and soon happen upon Iverna Court. They drew to a halt outside the small, Portland stone, Armenian Church that supported a delightful, open belfry. The square was so silent and peaceful, filled only with their happiness and, delighted, they held one another, in a clinch, as they nestled up against the iron railings while they kissed, cuddled and nuzzled, dreading the cruel moment when they would be forced to part.

Eventually, Sebastian disengaged, for the time had come for him to return home. In a flash, his feverish lips were back on Natasha's to linger, for one more moment, in exquisite, spiritually turbo-charging intimacy, as their souls ruthlessly plundered bliss. Finally, a dishevelled Sebastian pulled away, with determination. Natasha was left awestruck. The tips of her fingers gently touching her tingling lips, while her ravenous eyes watched him as, reluctantly, he strolled off. Then, on the spur of the moment, Sebastian glanced over his shoulder and assured, prophetically:

"It won't be long Natasha, I promise."

Natasha could not move, she just continued to stare after him, until he turned left into Iverna Gardens and finally disappeared from view. He was gone. She was alone. It hurt. Then, with panic, she remembered Katarina. She shot a glance at her watch. It was already twelve-forty. She just had time to get to the restaurant, but she had to be quick. With a spring in her stride and her heart bursting with joy, Natasha waltzed through the pretty gold, yellow and brown leaf littered backstreets of Kensington, and then into South Kensington, on her way to meet her dear friend for lunch.

When Natasha approached the Italian restaurant she saw Katarina immediately, sitting at a little table next to the full-frontage window. Her friend looked tanned, slim, blonde and gorgeous and she was sporting gigantic, jet-black sunglasses, alluringly, that managed to make her long, thick hair look even more golden. A wave of excitement surged from the tips of Natasha's toes to the top of her head, for she had not realized quite how much she had missed her friend, until now. She floated into the restaurant, handed her coat to the hostess, and then rushed over to a gleeful Katarina, who had stood up to greet her. In no time, the girls were hugging, squealing and air kissing three times 'moi, moi-ing' all the while, before Natasha kicked-off an overexcited verbal torrent of exchange.

"Oh Kat, you look amazing! So slender, so tanned, so healthy, dare I say it, so blonde!"

"What about you? You must have lost more than half a stone! Your cheek-bones are positively jutting out to be admired and your skin is simply glowing!" Before adding, in afterthought, "If I thought banking could do that for a girl's complexion, I might have given it a shot myself."

"Trust me Kat, it's got nothing to do with banking..."

Immediately, Katarina looked intrigued. Natasha pulled her chair out, its legs scraping harshly across the wooden floor as she did so, and then she sat down.

"Either you've just had sex or you're in love. Tell me, which is it?" Katarina was quick to question.

"Oh Kat, can't it be both?"

Katarina lurched forward, with the ferocity of a Rottweiler, and spluttered, with urgency:

"Oh, you lucky cow! Who is he? Oh Natasha, tell me who he is?"

"Oh Kat, I'm certain I'll be boring you on the subject for weeks to come. You are the one who has been away to far-flung places. First you must tell me all your news. How was Block Island? Did you meet any decent men? Most importantly, did you have fun?"

"Don't you dare Natasha Flynn. Don't you dare try and change the subject. Clearly, you are madly in love. I am not. Your news trumps mine. I insist that you tell me all about him; immediately!"

Secretly delighted at having been given the green light to fill the little restaurant with talk of Sebastian, Natasha smiled, serenely, before taking a deep breath and embarking on precisely that. Kat's eyes burnt with intense interest as she leaned farther forward, hungry for every morsel of information.

"Oh Kat, I'm so hopelessly in love."

Just declaring it seemed to sate Natasha, entirely, and she went all-quiet as she contemplated her state. Natasha may have been delirious but Katarina was becoming, increasingly, infuriated and she began to scold Natasha as only a best friend can.

"How dare you madam! Three-months I have not seen you, or had one bit of news from you, and now, and now, you meet me for lunch, announce you're in love, then expect me to sit and look at that ridiculous doe-eyed expression, without the slightest bit of information about the man who is the cause of it! What on earth has befallen

275

my erstwhile cynical best friend? Tell me, who is he?"

"Oh, I'm sorry Kat. I'm just so in love." Natasha apologised, as she laughed at her friend's heartfelt fury.

"You already told me that much..."

It was becoming increasingly obvious that Katarina was losing her patience. A chastised Natasha decided to put her out of her misery.

"Once again I'm sorry, it appears being in love has disabled my mind to make me a very dull companion."

"You said it!" Katarina grunted, impatiently.

The waitress arrived and Katarina ordered two glasses of prosecco "to start with" before she continued, "Maybe a glass of bubbly will loosen your tongue! Natasha, please at least tell me his name?" Natasha smiled in acquiescence, as Katarina added cheekily, "Oh, and of course: how old he is, what he looks like, what he does for a living and how you met him?"

Natasha took a deep breath before she embarked on satisfying Katarina's curiosity.

"His name is Sebastian Butler, he is thirty-five years old, six-foot four with dark hair, green eyes and he is as successful as he is handsome. Oh yes, and he has a brilliant sense of humour."

Katarina was as transfixed by the description of Sebastian, as was Natasha by the man.

"Oh Natasha, how wonderful. He sounds too good to be true! Tell me what does he do? How did you meet him?"

Natasha was more than overjoyed at how well her thrilling news was being received.

"Well he's an investment banker and I met him at work only a few days after I started. He works on the Debt Floor like me, but he's on the trading side. The minute we saw each other we were hooked and, as soon as we started to talk, we completely clicked. We got on so well, in fact, that we ended up having lunch together that very same day! The long and the short of it is, I'm now working directly for him. We sit less than five feet apart, everyday. Can you believe it? Oh Kat, it was magical! We fell in love the minute we saw each other. I know it sounds corny, but it was literally that lightning bolt legend: love at first sight."

Katarina looked wonderstruck.

"Oh Natasha, I never thought such things actually happened, not to us at least. How thoroughly inspiring..." she mused, breathlessly.

"Oh Kat, it's true. Love at first sight does exist! It may be madness, but it's not a myth."

"So it would seem..." Katarina answered, quietly, while lost in her own reflections.

"Well, that was well over two months ago now." Natasha gushed on, still full of excitement.

Katarina's ears pricked at the chance of a gibe.

"My God, Natasha, a long term relationship no less." she interjected, sarcastically, before bursting into giggles.

"Ha, Ha, not." Natasha responded, as she shot her friend a stern warning look.

"Oh, I'm only teasing. Please, tell me everything."

"Kat, we slept together for the first time last night. It was simply celestial." Katarina's eyes were as round as buttons, so thrilled was she with such juicy information. Inspired, Natasha leaned forward to explain, "Oh, but Kat, we didn't just have sex, we made love. I visited places and experienced emotions I never knew even existed. Oh Kat, he's the one, I just know it."

The glasses of prosecco arrived, as if in time to toast Natasha's knowing, and she raised hers while she looked her friend in the eye with genuine warmth.

"Welcome home Kat... I've missed you."

They drank. Katarina then placed her glass onto the table, pensively, and gave a tranquil smile. All of her boisterous bossiness was banished for, as she looked at Natasha's ecstatic expression, she became convinced that her friend's new love was true. Katarina's face had been transformed and an iridescent light infused her arresting, deep-set, lime-green eyes. It was clear she was overjoyed to hear Natasha's tale of love, for such stories give hope to each and every lonely one of us. It is always heart-warming when a sequence of events, springs from the world's callous chaos, to provide a cherished glimpse of God's grand design, for these flashes of divinity fortify our indispensable companions, faltering Faith and fearful Hope, to help each of us on our muddled way. Approaching joyous, Katarina leaned forward and placed her warm hand, affectionately, onto Natasha's and gave it a firm a squeeze.

"Natasha, I'm so happy for you." Then she let go, slumped back into her chair and looked slightly dazed and confused by it all. Wondrously, she pointed at the top of her arm and announced, "Look, you've made all the hairs on my forearms stand up!"

"It's a sign! It's a sign! Sebastian and I belong together!" Our heroine exclaimed, with exaggerated fervour, but though she said it in jest, in her heart she meant it.

"Oh, stop it Natasha... be serious for a minute, I'm having a moment."

"I am being serious!" Natasha objected.

"Oh, do be quiet! But I have to admit it all sounds rather amazing. In fact, your tale sent a chill down my spine, and that doesn't happen often I can tell you. No, really, it sounds extraordinary."

Katarina's epiphany, however, did not last as long as her prosecco. Gradually, her face began to darken, her serene smile started to fade, and her expression shifted to one of concentration, as the gears of her brain began to re-engage. Several seconds passed, while Natasha watched the effects of Katarina's grey matter at work, with interest, for, soon enough, her tanned forehead began to furrow, and she raised her eyebrow as her wondering intensified.

Finally, the stubborn question that had formulated in her mind, popped out of her mouth, "Seriously though, why did it take you guys so long to have sex?" before Katarina smirked, "Your uncharacteristic self-control astounds me."

"Thanks a lot!" Natasha barked, before fast correcting, "Anyway, we didn't have sex, we made love."

Natasha then reached for her glass and took a deep gulp of her drink. When she put it back down, her eyes began to dart around the restaurant, fitfully, for she was trying to look anywhere else but at her friend. She was hot and irritable and she could feel the tangible intensity of Katarina's eyes boring into her, willing her to provide an answer.

"Seriously, Natasha, why so long?" Katarina repeated, increasingly intrigued.

Knowing Katarina was not going to let this drop, reluctantly, Natasha decided to get it over with. She looked, challengingly, into Katarina's attentive face before delivering the final, but most pertinent, piece of information in a terribly quiet voice.

"He's married..." In a flash, the pupils of Katarina's pretty eyes contracted to pinpoints. Feeling gutted, Natasha then added, pathetically, "with two children."

Katarina's face began to contort with pity and an interminable silence followed, as both girls absorbed the reality of the unadorned facts of Natasha's predicament.

"Oh, Natasha…" Katarina, finally, muttered tragically.

Now Natasha had said it all out loud, it did not seem in the least bit fun to talk about. Now the full facts had spilled across this coarse little lunch table, Natasha felt bereft. The naked truth of her position began to coat her like an oil slick, and the wings of joy on which she had soared, so recently, became stickier and stickier until their accumulated weight sent her into nauseating freefall. Indeed, Natasha was teetering on the verge of tears. She started to wring her hands, distractedly, as she shook her head from side to side, while her eyes darted all over the restaurant, in an attempt to frustrate her tears from forming and spilling down her hot cheeks. Why the hell was she so emotional? She had been, enthusiastically, celebrating her passion, only moments ago, and now she was on the verge of a breakdown. What a fool she was, to be so excited about sharing her love with a friend, when so doing, only highlighted the precariousness of her position. Now she had told the full facts to someone who cared for her, the devastating truth crashed in around her. The sublime love that she had so blissfully experienced last night, and then again this morning, had no foundation in real life and with that savage exposure, Natasha's hopes and dreams were smashed to smithereens. A perplexed Natasha peered into Katarina's face, her pupils still darting from left to right, as if searching her friend's eyes for some solution. All Natasha could find was compassion. Realizing how fragile Natasha was, Katarina reached across the table, took her hand and squeezed it, once again.

"Oh, Natasha, what are you going to do?"

"Love him?" she ventured, wishfully, as her eyes glistened with hopeful optimism.

Yet Natasha knew in her heart that she had just become an object of extreme pity, and she could not bear it. She wanted to shout out in desperation, 'It isn't like it sounds! This is different!' but the very expressions made her feel even more doleful than she did already. Instead, Natasha reached for her glass and downed the rest of her drink. She then caught the eye of the passing waitress and indicted that she would like two more of the same. Surely, in the circumstances, Katarina would join her in another? Appreciating just how close to tears Natasha was, Katarina came to her rescue and changed the subject.

"Let's just order and get it out of the way, so we can talk properly?" Natasha nodded. She had managed not to breakdown after all. Smiling encouragingly, Katarina continued to distract her, "Besides I have all my news to tell you." Then her face became anxious, as she considered it, before she added, apologetically, "Well, what there is to tell..."

Natasha was grateful for Katarina's tact and she realized, with regret, that she must have looked just as vulnerable as she had felt. For the rest of this long lunch, the girls munched on warm bread dipped in delicious Tuscan virgin olive oil, scoffed divine spaghetti vongole and drank glass upon glass of innocuous prosecco, until everything made them giggle and they discussed how, really, they ought to have ordered a bottle (or was it two?) in the first place.

Natasha did not speak of Sebastian again. Instead, Katarina entertained her with hilarious stories of her time on Block Island. The island seemed to be full of gorgeous young men, however, the ones that Katarina had encountered, frustratingly, all seemed to be gay. She had come across heterosexual men too, but sadly they were older and much less gorgeous although, inevitably, they had been phenomenally rich and, most usually, perpetually lecherous. In short, Katarina had not found love on that Atlantic isle, indeed, she had not even had sex, for the men she lusted after, were too busy lusting after each other, while the ones that lusted after her, had only made her stomach churn. Regretfully, Katarina had also discovered that the art world was one that she had struggled to take seriously for three months, and she certainly could not entertain taking it seriously for a lifetime. No, she had missed London and her quick-witted friends and she was back, for good, to get a proper job; she hoped.

It was past five o'clock when Natasha, finally, stumbled into her bedsit. She had walked, or rather zigzagged, all the way back home from the restaurant. Once through the door, she had made a wavy beeline to her bed, crashed on top of it and, still soaked full of bubbles and the tingling legacy of heartfelt laughter with a friend, she had fallen fast asleep.

*****

SNORING... SNORING... SNORING... MORE SNORING... BLACK... BLACK... BLACK... ALL BLACKNESS... Consciousness had emerged enough to observe that, but it had not yet recovered memory. Something had aroused it. How did it get here? Where is here? What's all that noise? What was that irritating, jarring, persistent, reverberating sound in space? It was very loud. It was very annoying. It was not going away. It was getting louder. That horrid noise produced a deep want in consciousness for it to stop. Stop! Stop! STOP! WILL it to

STOP. WILL it to STOP. WILL IT TO STOP NOW!

It was not bloody stopping...

Memory, jarringly recalled by fury, at last, made realization strike, to rouse Natasha from deep sleep. Immediately, her inner voice was driven to rant:

'That bloody noise, is my doorbell. I live alone. It won't bloody stop until I answer it... Who the fuck is that?'

Natasha was awake but very peevish. With great reluctance, and irritability, she lurched out of bed with the intention of answering the intercom, in order to put a stop to that awful sound. Her eyes were still screwed up as she scrabbled in the darkness, whacking the palm of her hand along the front of her wardrobe doors, as she guided herself towards the hand set. She fumbled around, impatiently, until she found it and then picked it up.

"Who is it?" Natasha snapped, crossly.

There was a long pause.

"Natasha? Is that you?" a disbelieving voice questioned.

Suddenly, realization enveloped and Love's angel waved his magic wand to make Natasha's dark disgruntlement, instantaneously, metamorphose into joyous, sparkling light. The frown clinching her brow vanished and, in a heartbeat, her resentment waltzed into wonder.

"Sebastian?"

"Natasha, I didn't recognize your voice."

"Thankfully." she answered, before adding, with embarrassment, "You woke me up."

"Really?" Sebastian replied, more than a little puzzled.

"Just come up."

Natasha buzzed him in before, once again, she found her herself bent over her kitchen sink as she brushed her teeth in an urgent hurry. Once she had finished, she dashed to the front door, opened it and stepped onto the landing to peer down the stairwell. The moment she saw the top of Sebastian's head, he lifted his face to lock eyes with her.

As soon as he turned the final corner to ascend the last half-staircase, Natasha could see just how dressed up he was. He wore a white shirt, a black bow-tie, black trousers and a deep purple, velvet smoking jacket. Now Natasha could see his shoes, she noticed their flamboyance. They were also deep purple velvet and in a quasi slipper design, with an elaborate gold emblem embroidered across the front. Sebastian's hair was slicked-back, rather dramatically, and his face freshly-shaven.

He would have looked most at home at some secret, decadent party in Transylvania held on a full moon. Now he stood before her, his smile was one of exquisite contentment. Arriving so unexpectedly, and dressed so, Natasha half-expected him to perform some trick.

"I did promise you it wouldn't be long." he just muttered, nonchalantly, before he put his arms around her and added, while staring into her captivated eyes, "Frankly my darling, nearly eight hours was quite long enough."

They both burst into thrilled laughter, until Natasha managed to contain her delight for long enough to speak.

"Sebastian you're incorrigible!"

His soft lips were pressed on hers, in a flash, and for the second time that day, he made her giddy with his kisses. So blissful was the effect that Natasha could have stayed like that forever. With enforced self-control, Sebastian stopped and pulled back.

"My darling one, you smell of stale alcohol and taste of toothpaste..." he scolded, gently, still collecting her in his arms before adding, through languid laughter, "Charming."

Natasha slapped him, lightly, on his shoulder.

"You caught me." she confessed. He looked into her joyous face with aroused curiosity. She continued, "I had a long lunch with my girlfriend, we had too much prosecco and then, when I finally got home, I fell fast asleep."

"Fell asleep or passed out?"

His comment elicited a sharper slap on his shoulder.

"At least I brushed my teeth for you." she added coyly, while fluttering her eyelashes.

He smirked, held her ever more tightly, and then pushed her into the little bedsit. Once inside, he let go.

"I have a little present for you." he announced, with unconcealed excitement. Sebastian then reached into his velvet jacket pocket to pull out an engraved, solid silver pillbox. Natasha was intrigued. Taking his time, he unscrewed the lid, carefully, to reveal that is was packed to the brim with snow-white powder.

"Cocaine?" she questioned, in astonishment.

"Maybe..."

He then screwed the lid back on, before he made his way to her bedside table, where something had caught his eye. He picked up a round silver make-up mirror, and then began to rub the surface with the sleeve of his jacket as he sat down on the bed. Once he had finished, Sebastian took a close look and, satisfied with his inspection, he placed the mirror flat on his lap. He then looked up at Natasha and, smiling broadly, he reopened the pillbox, carefully, to tip a small mound of powder onto the mirror, before he closed it and put it safely away.

He took his black leather wallet from his inside pocket and removed a platinum credit card. Then he placed his wallet, next to him, on the bed. Natasha was still standing staring at him, lost in her observation of this ritual. Her eyes were wide with fascination, and her lips slightly parted. She became increasingly mesmerized, as she watched Sebastian crush and crunch all of the tiny unwanted lumps in the cocaine, with his credit card, before he began to chop the powder up, meticulously, first horizontally many times, and then vertically for the same. At last, Sebastian seemed to be content with the consistency of the drug, and he began to separate the mound into four different little piles, before rearranging each of them into four, evenly distributed, long, skinny lines. Once the lines were all neatly laid out, Sebastian picked up his wallet and took out a single fifty-pound note from the thick, pink wedge of them, with which it was stuffed. He then rolled it up tightly and, grinning a little crazily, he handed it to Natasha.

"Please, after you." he encouraged.

Tentatively, Natasha took the note gently between her thumb and forefinger. She had not done cocaine since university and she was not sure she wanted to do it now. Her aristocratic ex-boyfriend had had quite a habit and ample funds to indulge it, but Natasha, sorely, recalled how depressed, not to say suicidal, she would feel after a big session. She soon learnt that her brain chemistry was simply too fragile to recover easily from this drug, but Sebastian was looking so pleased with himself for coming to share it with her, and she did not wish to disappoint him. She remembered his being upset enough about her not eating the breakfast he had brought for her and, besides, she could not deny that she loved the high she got from the stuff, when she indulged, for as long as it lasted. Surely, a little bit would not do her too much harm...

Slowly, Natasha began to wind her thick chestnut hair into a heavy roll, with her left hand, before carefully placing it down the centre of her back. Ready to go, she knelt down in front of Sebastian. Brimming with excitement, he watched her every move like a starving dog. She lifted her face to search his, in order to gauge his mood. This evening Sebastian's usually eloquent eyes were inscrutable. Gaining no comfort, Natasha looked down again and put the end of the rolled note to her right nostril, bent her head over the mirror, and lined up the bottom of the note with the end of her selected line. She then blocked her left nostril, with her left forefinger, before quickly snorting the cocaine.

Natasha's body, suddenly, straightened while she continued to sniff, aggressively, to ensure that none of the precious stuff got away. Instantly, she was shot through with a rush more powerful than Sebastian's new car. Her whole head was tingling and electric rushes coursed down her spine and up the back of her head to her crown. Only beginning to appreciate the strength of this drug, Natasha, immediately, craved another line. Checking her hair was still secure so it would not to fall down and mess up the lines, she bent over again and snorted a second one: SMACK! Natasha's brain was working so fast now, it felt paralysed. WOOOOOSH! Natasha straightened up, for a second time, and continued to sniff aggressively.

Sebastian was laughing while he observed her, clinically, as she was so thoroughly swept away. Smiling, inanely, from the hit, she managed to get to her feet before passing him the note. Quickly, he snorted the two remaining lines, one for each nostril, to make his eyes startled and wide as he savoured the intense force of his hit. Natasha stared at the miniscule bloodshot veins at the edges of the whites of his eyes, before Sebastian began to blink, repeatedly, as he stretched his face with an enormous yawn. When he had finished, he appeared even more fiercely alert than usual. He then put the mirror down on the bed, got up, leant over to pick up his wallet, and put it back into his pocket before turning to grab Natasha, firmly, around her waist. They were both far too high to connect with each other, as they had done when he had arrived. Natasha just wanted to go out and dance. She also wanted to talk and talk and talk but she could not even begin to formulate a sentence. Instead, she clutched Sebastian, in silence, still dumbstruck from these first remarkably strong rushes. He looked down at her with unfamiliar eyes. Her mind was functioning enough to register that these eyes recalled the swirly ones that had transfixed her so, the first time they had spoken. Then Sebastian gave a surprise announcement:

"Well my Love, I have to go now." Natasha was flabbergasted. He had only just arrived. He could not leave her flying this high, all on her own. Noticing her disquiet, he explained with even more intensely swirling eyes:

"I have some blasted party to go to in Belgravia. Isabel is waiting for me." He then smiled sadly, "I don't want to leave you my darling one, really I don't, but I must."

Sebastian then squeezed an unresponsive Natasha, before he pecked her on the lips and let her go. He took three long, deliberate, strides towards the door, turned to look at her, regretfully, one more time, and then left.

Natasha was flummoxed. HE had arrived from nowhere. HE had given her two lines of remarkably strong cocaine. HE had left her none. Then HE had gone. Natasha's confused head dropped in despair and her eyes scanned the room, in panic, as she searched for something to fix on. Finally, they landed on the pink, now loosely rolled, fifty-pound note that Sebastian had discarded on the bed, next to her mirror, which was still smudged with traces of powder.

Seeking solace, Natasha took a step towards it, stuck her index finger into her mouth, licked it, and then used it to wipe the front of the mirror to collect all of the traces of cocaine, before rubbing it across the top of her gums. Instantly, they became more numb than her heart felt now. God, this stuff was pure, even if Sebastian was not.

Chapter Twenty - I have a surprise for you

The telephone was ringing in the darkness. Natasha had almost fallen asleep, for God knows she needed an early night. Reluctantly, she stretched over to answer it.

"Hello?" she mumbled, weakly.

"It's me."

It was HIM! Immediately, Natasha propped herself up and, though she felt she should have been cross with him after last night, all that happened was her heart skipped a beat and she sighed, adoringly, "Hello you."

It was past ten o'clock at night and, despite the fact that she was talking to her Love, now she was upright, Natasha realized just how much her head ached and her organs hurt. After Sebastian had left her, high as a kite, yesterday evening, stuck in her bedsit all alone, she had had to go out, or she was certain she would have gone crazy. Luckily, she had managed to persuade her old university friend Justin to go clubbing with her. He only lived around the corner and he was always up for partying, or 'raving' as he preferred to call it. She had managed to get them both on the guest list for the Cross and, as ever, Jazzy's D.J.-ing had been superb. When the effect of the cocaine began to flag, She had started on vodka and red-bull and, between too many of those, Justin, memories of Sebastian, and the brilliant music, she had danced, demonically, until well past four o'clock this morning.

Two bottles of prosecco at lunch-time, and then a couple of lines of coke with Sebastian, followed by all of that booze, throughout the night, had given Natasha's constitution a real battering. All day long she had felt as if she was bruised internally. Sebastian was just the tonic she needed. Even the sound of his voice sent shivers up her spine, dissipated her fatigue and set her mind, heart and soul ablaze.

"Hello you." Sebastian echoed.

Listening intently to nothing, they managed to feed to their fill, simply by being utterly attentive to each other's presence. In the mute silence, a strange and powerful blissfulness enshrouded Natasha and her depleted batteries became mysteriously charged. After a long time, she broke their silent communion.

"What time is it?"

"Oh, I don't know. Time I saw you, no?"

She giggled, contentedly, for what an absurd suggestion at this time on a Sunday night. Then Natasha remembered that she was not happy with him.

"Don't ever do that again!" she scolded.

"Do what?"

"Show up here, get me all excited and Sebastianed then bloody well piss-off!"

He chuckled.

"Oh, I'm sorry. I couldn't help it. I just had to see you, but I couldn't stay, that's all." He paused, as they basked in their zone of disembodied togetherness, once again, before he added in apology, "Anyway you'll be pleased to hear that the party was crap. Isabel hogged the cocaine, the guests were beyond boring and, on top of that, I had to get up at the crack of dawn to go up to Yorkshire for a shoot." Chuckling some more, he added, "Oh, and my shooting was worse than the party!"

Natasha giggled, and then darted:

"Serves you right!" before adding, triumphantly, "Well, I went out with my gorgeous friend Justin and I danced until dawn; well, almost." Natasha could sense Sebastian's grin distorting with discomfort before she felt obliged to mollify him, "We went to the Cross, which was a grave mistake because all I could think about was you." He chuckled, with relief, before she explained, "I was pining for you, so badly, that I had to drink vodka all night long until I couldn't think of anything at all!"

Now they were laughing, in unison.

"How am I going to last without having you on the floor for the next two weeks? It seems I'm incapable of lasting even for a few hours." Sebastian mused, sadly.

"You will just have to; carpet burns don't suit me!" Natasha could not help but quip, before she giggled at her silly joke. Sebastian did not. He just added, distractedly:

"That reminds me, I have a surprise for you!"

"Haven't I had enough surprises this weekend?"

"It's not for this weekend, it's for tomorrow night."

"What?" Natasha inquired, curious.

"I want you to come to my house, tomorrow evening. You'll see then."

"If I show up at your house on Monday night, it will be your wife who gets the surprise."

"Don't be catty, my dear. Tomorrow afternoon Isabel leaves for Singapore, on business. Tomorrow night, I want you to come to my house and discover what the surprise is. Will you come? Will you come tomorrow?"

There was a long pause.

"Sebastian, you know I will." she replied, helplessly.

"Eight o'clock then."

The love-struck couple lingered on the line, not wanting their togetherness to end.

"Good night, my darling one." Sebastian managed to say, at last, with great tenderness.

"Good night, my Love." Natasha whispered back, in tones softer than velvet.

Then with a click, he was gone. For a long time she clutched the receiver, longingly, to her breast, as if Sebastian's energy essence still radiated from it. Eventually, she hung up, lay back down on her soft pillow, pulled her duvet snuggly around herself and closed her eyes, suddenly eager to dream of what tomorrow might bring.

Chapter Twenty-one - Spirit's rally cry

Lover, tell the night
that your day
will never end in its arms.
The religion of Love
is a sea without a shore
where lovers drown
without a sigh,
without a cry.

Rumi

At eight o'clock the next evening, Natasha found herself standing outside Sebastian's tall Chelsea terraced house, for the second time in less than a week. Once again, she was dressed up to the nines, terrifyingly nervous and tottering in high heels. How could so much have happened in so little time? Only five days ago, standing in this very spot, she had harboured sincere hopes that seeing Sebastian with his wife would cure her of her captivating obsession. Yet, the very next night, she had spent hours making love to him, only to find herself even more fiercely consumed by Sebastian than before. Then now, on a Monday night, she was waiting outside his marital home, planning to spend the evening with him while his wife was away on a business-trip. When Natasha thought about it, it all sounded so sordid, yet could she stop herself from reaching for the doorbell? Not a chance. Almost as soon as she had rung it, the glossy blue front door swung opened. He must have been waiting for her.

The moment their eyes met, they glowed; clearly entranced by each other. Immediately, Natasha's nerves were nullified. So suddenly content was she, that she did not even register how shockingly overdressed she was, for Sebastian was barefoot and wearing jeans and a simple white cotton shirt that he had not even bothered to tuck in. Natasha was so used to seeing him in a suit that the surprise of seeing him dressed so casually just snatched her breath away, for how young and handsome he looked attired like some beach bum. Though his presence never failed to sweep Natasha off her feet, tonight this vision of him did so even more effectively than his cocaine had done in her bedsit. Natasha simply stood stock-still and stared at him, agape.

For several minutes, Sebastian studied her as, languorously, he rested his head against the side of his front door. He then began to smile, shyly, as if abashed by his obvious fascination with her. They both began to chuckle for, as was usual, Cheshire Cat grins spread across their faces, in duplicate. He laughed, nervously.

"Natasha, is this not getting a little ridiculous, not to say predictable?" She was too captivated to answer. He continued with a touch of desperation, "When is this going to wear off, I ask you?"

"Not imminently by the look of it, so may I please come in?" she replied, with serenity.

In one sweeping gesture, Sebastian ushered Natasha into his home. This time there was no reluctance nor trepidation, just heady anticipation. Sebastian closed the front door and, in one easy stride, he was standing next to her. He took her coat, then strolled to the end of the corridor to hang it up in the cloakroom. When he returned, he reached for her hand and led her downstairs to the basement. Natasha had not been down here before, and she eyed this more domestic scene with interest. She found herself in the dining-room, where a large, oval, mahogany, gilt-inlaid table dominated, surrounded by eight mahogany dining chairs, the seats of which were upholstered in racing-green velvet. Two place settings had been laid out at the far end. Was this a clue to her surprise? Natasha's eye was then caught by the pretty little faces that peered out of numerous, shining silver frames, placed on top of the mantelpiece on the far wall. All the photographs were black and white. In fact, they were so slick and stylized that Natasha was convinced a professional photographer must have taken them. Without exception, the subjects were of the same two gorgeous, blonde, though slightly serious looking, young children, either together or as individual portraits. Natasha's heart contracted with sadness for she knew they must be Sebastian's daughters. It felt more than inappropriate to be here, with him, while their little faces looked on, impassively. Fast averting her gaze from the evidence that her Love's commitments lay elsewhere, Natasha scanned the room for more pictures, eager to read the stories that photographs so indiscreetly tell. She found none. There was not a single photograph of Isabel, or Sebastian for that matter, in the entire room. Sebastian pulled Natasha along, until she stepped into the kitchen that led off the dining-room. She listened to the low hum of the fan oven as her eyes squinted to adjust to the brighter lighting. She could smell cooking and she sniffed, inquiringly, to see what it might be. Fish perhaps? Sebastian was still beaming, but his exuberance was peppered with bemusement as he gestured towards the cooker.

"Surprise! I'm cooking you dinner." he announced then waited, in silence, for Natasha to respond. From the way he was fidgeting, it was as if he was prickling with pride. She looked at him, quizzically, not quite understanding what he expected from her. Clearly, becoming a touch exasperated by her slowness, he explained simply, "Natasha, I do not cook." Again he waited for a reaction. Once again, Natasha looked at him, still clueless. Impatient, he elaborated, "Don't you understand Natasha? I have not turned on an oven for over ten years. I have not attempted to cook since I was at university. Natasha, I barely knew what our kitchen looked like until this evening!" Natasha started to laugh for, finally, she understood how exceptional this gesture was for him. Strangely, her first thought was 'how very different he is from his cousin.' Inspired by her giggles he elaborated, "Don't you get it? I have this overwhelming desire to cook for you. I desperately wanted to cook dinner for you! Natasha, now I know I'm in love, there's no doubt about it!"

Sebastian then collapsed into disbelieving laughter, for

it appeared the greatest surprise this evening had been his, about himself. Natasha smiled, indulgently, overjoyed by his declarations and beyond touched by his sentiments.

"So what's for dinner?"

"Wild sea bass, spinach and new potatoes!"

"Delicious!"

"I hope so... ten years remember." Sebastian qualified, apprehensively.

Then they both burst into guilty giggles, for who in the world deserves to be so stupefied by love? Having recovered himself, he took a bottle of chilled, vintage Krug from the fridge. It was so cold that the black glass was coated with a layer of white condensate and, when he put it down on the granite worktop, you could see the watery mark left by his handprint.

"Champagne my dear?" he inquired, casually, while taking two cut-crystal champagne flutes from an overhead cupboard. Then, in answer to his own question, he sing-songed, "I think so."

Sebastian picked up the bottle, again, which now had cloudy wisps of steam condensate gently licking its wet coldness, and he opened it up with a practised dexterity of wrist to elicit an expensive sounding pop. Carefully, he poured each of them a glass, before passing one to Natasha, and then he raised his own.

"To love." he toasted, with wild abandon.

They both took thirsty sips of the truly excellent champagne, the fine bubbles of which tantalized Natasha's tongue so much so that she heard herself groan, involuntarily, with appreciation. Sebastian, on the other hand, put his glass down, stared seriously at the flagstone floor, and then slapped his hands, decisively, against his thighs while he tried to remember everything he still had to do. In a spontaneous flurry of activity, he placed a jade green Morano glass bowl, full of gigantic bright red strawberries, onto a silver tray with a large, dark, wooden peppershaker and an ice bucket, which contained the open bottle of Krug. He picked up the tray, and then explained:

"I have to confess, it took me so long to figure out how the bloody oven works, that the food won't be ready for ages. Let's go upstairs."

Obediently, she followed him, champagne flute in hand, all the way up to the formal drawing-room on the ground floor. The room looked so big and empty without all of those people from Itzy's party filling it. Once Sebastian had put the tray down, on the sturdy coffee table in front of the cream and burgundy striped sofa, she raised her glass.

"I think it's my turn to toast: to my favourite man, my favourite fruit, and my favourite drink. Thank you so much, Sebastian; for everything."

Natasha then took one of the enormous strawberries and, just as it was on its way to her salivating mouth, Sebastian intercepted, and took her, gently, by the wrist.

"Natasha, dip it in the champagne first, then add a touch of pepper, trust me, doing so brings out the true essence of the flavour." he advised, knowingly.

Natasha looked at him sceptically. Champagne and strawberries certainly, but pepper too? However, she did as suggested, only to find herself nodding with sincere approval, as she finished her exquisitely flavoured mouthful.

"Gosh Sebastian, you're quite right, what a perfect combination!" Natasha declared, enthusiastically, before cooing, "A little like us, no?"

His eyes sparkled, devilishly, as he looked from under raised brows and corrected:

"My darling one, you don't just bring out my essence, you make me more than I ever was before…" Then, looking comically aghast, he exclaimed, "I've started taking walks and cooking for Christ's sake! Believe me, I hardly recognize myself!"

Yet again, they found themselves giggling like little children, until the telephone began to ring to make Sebastian start and, instantly, they were silenced. Natasha turned to stare, disapprovingly, at the thing that had so interrupted them. It was sitting, innocently, on a fitted cupboard set in one of the alcoves either side of the fireplace. Impervious, the 'phone continued to ring, persistently. Sebastian and Natasha looked at each other, with sheer dread. It was Isabel. They just knew it was Isabel. Eventually, Sebastian spoke, softly, as if seeking permission, "I'd better take it, Natasha. She'll just call back later, if I don't."

She nodded, acquiescent. Then our heroine turned and walked to the back of the house, where the French windows had been left slightly ajar. The heavy silk curtains, periodically, shifted whenever the evening's chill breeze blew into the airy room. Natasha opened the windows wider, to discover a Victorian wrought iron waist-high window guard in place, to prevent anyone from stepping, or falling, out. It was perfect for leaning on and, as Natasha did so, she hoped it was as sturdy as it looked. Leaning out into the walled-garden like some lonesome Juliette, Natasha looked up into the night sky as she struggled to forget the conversation that was going on next door. Now she was alone, her breathing seemed to be embarrassingly loud. Natasha took another sip of her champagne before folding-in her lips and pressing them hard, in between her teeth, as she so often did when she felt tense or uncertain.

It was chilly standing there in an evening dress. The fresh night air was vivifying and, slowly, she became aware of the world beyond Sebastian. The stone paved garden, on which she looked out, was prettily lit by external wall lights. Natasha began to admire the rose bushes that bordered it, as she listened to the low buzz of distant traffic from the Fulham Road. More distinctly, she could hear the leaves shuffling and rustling every time a gust of wind disturbed them. The sound was ominous and soothing, all at once. Regrettably, as much as she tried not to, Natasha could hear Sebastian's meticulously annunciated voice in the background. He was speaking in the subtle tones of that 'international' accent so commonly produced by the best schools in Switzerland, and frequently adopted by con men, for its capacity to convey pedigree and invoke trust. If God were ever to talk to her, Natasha imagined it would be in such a voice, for was there ever one more unassumingly authoritative? She had noticed that Sebastian was prone to adopting such a cadence when he was dealing and, in so doing, he appeared even more important and considered; and then Natasha thought, how odd for him to be talking like that now, considering he was speaking to his wife. Then she remembered he had done exactly the same thing at the party, when Isabel had come over to them. Did he always talk to her like that, or only when he was nervous? If he were attempting to hide his jitters then Isabel would be sure to notice and become suspicious. Now Natasha felt anxious for Sebastian. How she did not wish to but, unfortunately, she could not avoid catching snippets of the conversation.

"No, that's not possible... I'm afraid they're already asleep..." 'Good God! The children were asleep upstairs!' Natasha concluded with horror, "...tomorrow then... yes very well... that won't be a problem, I'll take care of it... OK Friday... Good night. Take care Itzy, good night."

When Natasha heard the receiver click, she let out an involuntary gasp of relief and, only then did she realize just how on edge she must have felt. Heavy-hearted, she began to wonder how she had ended up leaning out of a window, getting cold, as she waited for a man to get off the 'phone to his wife, so she could spend the evening with him, in the basement, while his young children slept upstairs.

In short, as fantastic as Sebastian made her feel, such circumstances filled her with repugnance. This was not a future Natasha had ever envisaged for herself. She jumped when she felt his warm hands slip around her hips. She straightened and leant back into the warmth and protection of him. Sebastian then put both of his arms around her upper shoulders, just below her neck, and he clasped her there. He then brought his lips to her ear, and said softly, in his true voice, "Let's eat."

His closeness nudged her back to happiness. She consoled herself that a 'change of scene' would help her snap out of the morose mood that had descended upon her. Then Sebastian released her and she followed him back downstairs. As soon as Natasha approached the dining-room, she remembered the photographs and started to feel miserable again: adultery was not for the faint-hearted.

Sebastian topped up Natasha's glass and told her to sit down and relax, before he disappeared into the kitchen. Just like his cousin, he would not hear of her helping him. She did as she was told, deliberately taking the chair facing the kitchen so that her back was to the pictures that so disturbed her. Taking deep breaths and trying not to think about what was behind her, Natasha sipped her exquisite drink and, once again, she found herself waiting for Sebastian as she stared into the garden, just this time from a different level. How much larger it looked from this perspective, and how much smaller the sky, for the blackened brick garden walls were so high, and Natasha's position so low, that she had to strain to see it at all.

With all of the loud, chaotic, stainless steel clattering coming from the kitchen, her attention happily returned to Sebastian. As she listened to his antics, it began to sink in just how far outside his comfort zone he had ventured to impress her. She took another sip of her superb drink and, all of a sudden, she began to feel so much better, for her heart was now pounding merrily as it engaged in its favourite pursuit: loving HIM. She took another little sip, for how well this fine champagne went down, and then she began to wonder, idly, how the first meal Sebastian had cooked in a decade might turn out. Diligently, she took sip upon sip of her bloody delicious champagne and, with each one, her reservations were increasingly anaesthetized and her frame of mind incrementally improved. In fact, by the time she had finished her second glass, she was feeling perfectly jolly and rather hungry. Synchronous to her tummy rumbling, Sebastian appeared.

"Ta-dah! Dinner is served."

He held two steaming plates in the air like trophies. He looked preposterously pleased with himself. He put them down on the place-mats, and then spun on his heels to go straight back into the kitchen. Soon, he reappeared with a second opened bottle of Krug. He refilled their flutes. He then clapped his hands with glee and sat down opposite Natasha. Sebastian looked more than relieved, and he began to laugh, nervously. Indeed, the habitually poised man of high-finance had almost broken out into a sweat. He looked rather bewildered by the whole experience, before he managed to conclude, flippantly, "God does our chef deserve a pay rise! I thought trading was supposed to be stressful!"

Natasha laughed fondly, before she looked down at her plate to see what he had managed to produce. It was a length of sea bass, meticulously filleted, with not a bone in sight. The spinach had been sautéed and looked perfectly presentable, if a touch stalky. As for the new potatoes, they were drenched in butter, with a speckling of chopped parsley on top. In fact, on first sight, the meal looked a remarkable accomplishment, considering. Natasha was impressed. Then, suddenly, an irked Sebastian clenched his fists in the air and exclaimed:

"Damn, I forgot!"

Sebastian leapt up, shot back into the kitchen and re-emerged with an oversized box of matches. He lit the candles on the dinning-table, before turning the main dining-room lights out. The dinner was cooked and the scene was set. Then he sat down, again, and emitted more of a puff than a sigh, a little like a mildly disgruntled magic dragon. It was most obvious that he was relieved that it was all over. He raised his glass:

"To staff!"

Then they both doubled up with guilty laughter: Sebastian for being so spoilt, and Natasha for her collusion. When they had recovered, Natasha and Sebastian tucked in. The meal was simple but turned out to be very tasty. Natasha was relieved to discover a couple of bones in her fillet, for this fact made HIM just a little bit more human. Sebastian, however, was looking unusually pensive. He swallowed his mouthful and then expostulated:

"Just think about it though, Natasha: all of that stress

and effort for what? One meal, a rather good meal if I may say so myself, a messy kitchen and a load of dirty dishes."

Of course Natasha understood his point, however, she was feeling playful and teased, with mock disappointment:

"I thought you did it all for me?"

Sebastian darted a reproachful eye at her.

"Seriously, though, give me a Trading Desk any day of the week. It's less stressful, less messy and a damn sight more profitable." he exclaimed, with conviction.

"So I take it this is a one off?" Natasha pursued.

"Comme toi, ma chérie, comme toi." Sebastian replied, in flattering tones.

Natasha grinned as she absorbed the compliment, besides she preferred eating out. Sebastian's candle-lit dinner was as delicious as it was intimate. Any outside observer would have been touched by this pretender to domestic bliss. Fiery eyes were alight and restless hands continually caressed while our clandestine lovers delighted in good food, fine booze and each other. All the while, Sebastian's children slumbered on at the top of this tall house, oblivious to the fact that the foundations of their security were being threatened by the subsidence of illicit love that was exploring itself in the basement. Finally, the meal was finished and the second bottle of champagne on its way to the same fate. Sebastian took Natasha's hand and then he said, earnestly:

"Natasha, I want to show you something very special." Before standing up and instructing, "Come with me."

She rose, to find herself a little unsteady on her feet. Slowly, she made her way around the table to join Sebastian, then he led her up the stairs to the ground floor, before leading her up the next flight of stairs, then the next, then the next, then the next, to the very top of the high house. She was almost out of breath by the time Sebastian came to a halt outside a light mauve panelled door that stood half-open. Sebastian turned around to look, excitedly, into Natasha's face and he brought his forefinger to his puckered lips, as he mouthed, "Shhh", allowing a rush of breath to escape as he did so. Still holding her hand, he tiptoed towards the door, placed his hand on its edge and peered around to take a look. Having done so he emerged with a beatific smile on his face, then he stepped back and gestured for Natasha to take a peak too. She popped her head around the door to find a small bedroom with a bunk bed in it. Underneath shambolic, puffy white, duvet covers that were prettily embroidered with pink ponies and butterflies, she spied two little blonde heads poking out. Natasha could not see the face of the larger child on the top bunk, for she could only catch a tuft of yellow hair protruding from the top of the duvet, however, she could see, clearly, the angelic, peaceful face of the little girl fast asleep on the bottom bunk. She must only have been three or four years of age. Natasha took a long look at that sleeping child and she marvelled at the innocent trustfulness of her expression. The conviction that Natasha had so longed to feel at Isabel's party, suddenly, welled up violently inside her to puncture her heart with this message, at this moment: stop loving a man whose place is with his wife and children. Natasha fought back hot tears at the simple truth of it.

Eventually, she became aware that Sebastian was tugging her hand, gently, from behind. Masochistically, she could not tear her eyes away from the youngest child's little face. Finally, his persistence managed to rescue her and she backed, slowly, out of the room and onto the little landing. In surreal silence they began, carefully, to tiptoe back down the stairs. It was not until they had climbed down three-flights of stairs that Sebastian abandoned his tiptoeing and started to walk normally. He brought Natasha to the only large white door on the first floor landing. He reached forwards to turn the ceramic porcelain doorknob and he opened it, before leading Natasha into the room and closing the door quietly behind them. Still dazed from the flesh and blood sight of his children, Natasha looked around to find herself presented with the marital bedroom. A giant, carved-walnut, four-poster, king size bed stood in front of her, complete with tan, gold and wine patterned tapestry canopy and curtains. The enormous structure dominated the grand room, more imposing than a mausoleum, and the only competing interest was a pair of French windows, to the left, which overlooked the treeless Chelsea street outside. Sebastian began to pull Natasha towards the formidable bed. Horrified, she stopped dead in her tracks.

"No." she exclaimed.

Sebastian turned to look at her with surprise.

"What's the matter?" he questioned, before adding, "The children can't hear a thing from up there, besides they sleep very soundly."

"No." Natasha insisted, before she spelt it out, "Please, not in your wife's bed."

Sebastian pouted and looked down at his feet. After a moment, he raised his head and looked at her with fierce eyes as he said, categorically:

"It's my bed too, you know."

"No." she repeated, adamantly, while shaking her head.

Natasha then let go of his hand, turned her back on him and left the room. With head and heart low, she returned to the living room where she slumped, defeated, onto the sofa. Natasha could hear Sebastian's naked footsteps following close behind. Suddenly, she felt emotionally exhausted and a little drunk. She stared at the remaining strawberries in the fine glass bowl that sat next to the peppershaker in front of her. The sight made her sigh sadly and, as she did so, she felt Sebastian's warm hands grasp each of her shoulders, before squeezing them reassuringly. For once, his comfort did not help, for tonight Natasha had faced the true extent to which Sebastian's life was inextricably intertwined with another woman. What is more, she had, momentarily, comprehended the true magnitude of a parent's immense responsibility to an innocent, dependant, and adorable child.

Natasha's own father had said goodbye once; long ago. He had struggled to suppress his tears as he made his choked farewells before walking out of the house, his frame held in an uncharacteristic stoop while his big hand covered his agonized face. Soon enough, all the little Natasha could see was his back, as she watched his distant figure climb into a white removal van. Her father then gave a single wave to his two tiny daughters who were standing, frozen to the spot, in the front porch of their house as they stared out at him, with traumatized eyes. Mute, they watched him grip the steering-wheel and start the van, before hearing the chug of the engine. Then daddy drove away from the family home, with all of his personal belongings, never to return. At the time, the little girls did not understand the significance of what was occurring but, in their guts they knew, it was as terrible as terrible could be.

The Flynn children did not see daddy again for many empty years, filled only with the loneliness, stress and screams of an unsupported single mother. When the young girls eventually did see 'daddy', years later, it was too late. The core abandonment, betrayal and the deep emotional damage had been done for, long ago, their hearts had had to close to their own father, in order to survive the infernal longing for his love, presence and protection. A lump lodged in Natasha's throat at the vivid memory of it... and to think she had been less than three years old when that had happened. Younger than the littlest of Sebastian's sleeping children upstairs; the one whom she could not stop staring at. Yes, Natasha knew firsthand the cost of a natural parent's unnatural absence. She would not wish to inflict that deep sorrow, pain and confusion on her worst enemy; let alone a child. As certain as she was that Sebastian was hers, she was doubly certain that he belonged with those two little girls upstairs. Morose, she tilted her head backwards to stare into Sebastian's upside down face as he smiled down at her with sympathetic eyes. They studied each other's expressions, in this unfamiliar pose, for a while, and then he said, sincerely:

"You know Natasha we don't have to do anything. Just being with you is enough."

Natasha continued to admire Sebastian's face from this novel position, her chestnut hair falling down the back of the striped sofa and her topsy-turvy mouth now open in a soft smile, to reveal a flash of her white teeth. Relieved Natasha was smiling again, Sebastian dared jocularity and declared, extravagantly, "In fact, we never have to sleep together again, and my feelings for you will not diminish."

"Steady on Sebastian..." Natasha cautioned, for thankfully she was feeling much less wretched now.

He chuckled, then gave her a twisted smile.

"Seriously Natasha, you must know by now, what I feel for you has nothing to do with sex."

Natasha knew that to be true, yet she could not help but jest, "Speak for yourself!"

Sebastian squeezed her shoulders, a little too tightly, in admonishment. Natasha just flashed a fiery glance at him, while he continued to stare down at this inverse version of her face. He released his grip, impulsively, and then left the room. In his absence, Natasha stared blankly into the primal, crimson, yellow and bright orange flames of the fire in front of her. It was not long before she heard the sound of his naked feet peeling off the oiled wooden floorboards. He seemed very relaxed and strolled over to her, carrying two fresh flutes of champagne. He sat down, snuggly, next to her, passed her hers, and then raised his.

"To this."

Natasha smiled, meekly, and took a long sip before resting her head, affectionately, on his shoulder. Sebastian laid his on top of hers. They sat there and stared into the mesmerizing fire for an unfathomable length of time. The longer they sat cheek by jowl, the more their hearts became warmed by their proximity, and the louder the call of their souls. The vibrations of the trillions and trillions of atoms that formed them began to resonate, as the rally cry for Spirit's completion urged their coupling. Essence craved like essence; a deep longing to revisit that miraculous, time-defying, ecstatic space accessed in union, manifested and burgeoned with each tick of the solid gold clock above the fireplace. Their souls' calls were amoral and relentless, birthed by vigorous, fearless, insatiable, spirit appetites, to exert an insurmountable compulsion towards satisfaction. Here there were no photographs of Sebastian's children. Here there was no marital bed. Here there was just one another, sitting on a sofa, feeling the heat of the fire and each other's pure spirit longing. The drug that is love slowly tranquilized all misgivings (along with two bottles of bloody good champagne) and the inexorable drive to conjoin was on the ascendant, as if as natural and inevitable as dawn. Without a word, Sebastian took Natasha's glass from her and placed it on the table with his own. He shifted his position to bring his face close to hers. Immediately, eyes were transfixed. Mesmerized, they stared into each other's souls, uncomprehendingly. Never before had they been so dictated to by such a tyrannical force as this inescapable pull to copulate. This inverse gender yearning, him to penetrate, her to clamp inside, took imperceptible steps towards satisfaction for the drive to join their physical energy fields was unstoppable. Will-less Natasha cocked her head to the side and tilted her chin upwards to bring her lips to his. When her lips felt the joy of his against them, a whimper escaped from our heroine and she shut her eyes in eager surrender. As Sebastian kissed her, her heart took flight with the tragic bliss of it. They kissed tenderly and repeatedly until the pressure and the passion began to mount, exponentially. Sebastian sat back in the sofa, kissing her all the while before he pulled her onto his lap. As he kissed her, poetically, her arms wrapped around his majestic shoulders, slowly he began to undo his jeans then he pushed them down in order to release his erect penis. Natasha gasped with the intimacy of this togetherness. Sebastian began to massage Natasha's thighs. She was wearing black suspenders, so the probing fingertip flesh on soft thigh flesh sensation, was immediate. He did not bother to remove her knickers he just assertively pushed them to one side, before inserting an inquisitive finger up inside her hot, moist, welcoming readiness.

All the foreplay Natasha needed had already occurred by virtue of sitting next to him. Now she just longed to hold him deep inside her most precious place. Satisfied she was ready for him, Sebastian shifted her hips so she was directly above him, before he used his hand to line his erect manhood up directly beneath her pussy. Natasha dropped her hand to spread her labia apart with her fingers then, with a breathless sigh, she plunged down onto his divine wide girthed member, until her buttocks slapped against his lap and his turgid throbbing penis was deeply inside her, and filling her all up to nudge her cervix. She did not move, she just clamped him ever more tightly between her strong, tight, muscular internal walls. He was inside her. She took ownership. Their bodies were in a writhing clinch and their lips and tongues incessantly active, as if part of a single slippery organ. Et voila: bodies, minds and souls fused to cruise in passionate, perpetual ecstasy!

After an indeterminable time of being just so, Natasha began to use her internal vaginal muscles to squeeze his virility tightly, over and over again, simply to accolade the bliss of having him inside her. Yet again, teardrops engendered underneath closed eyelids, for the beauty of this celestial intimacy, was simply too devastating. Soon enough, salty fluid leaked out of eyes, to roll over cheekbones then run down ecstatic, celestial features and glisten in random rivulets on flushed, flame-lit skin. The boundaries of devouring lips, exploring tongues, nuzzling noses and contact seeking flesh dissolved in soul merging. As their bodies were ravished, their unified consciousness transcended common reality. Instantaneously, overwhelmingly incandescent, they were back in that state for which they so yearned with their 'selves' relinquished and spirit essence liberated from earthly bondage to dwell in original source: pure LOVE. For rare amoureux such as these, there is no orgasmic destination towards which they must pound, grunt and rub. When entwined so, each is eternally poised as ONE on the pinnacle of climactic perfection, for every moment attains and retains the pitch of perpetual orgasm. Simply, they had become LOVE itself: c'est fini.

Sebastian and Natasha spent many hours in each other's

arms this night, forever loathsome to return to the state, reality was, without the other. The elaborate gold clock, nestling on the white marble mantelpiece chimed twice, hauntingly. Natasha registered the late hour. She must go home. She had to get up in four hours time. Disorientated, she lifted her head from Sebastian's chest. Only then did she become aware that they were both stark naked. She groaned, softly, so melancholy was she to have to move; yet she must. Natasha just looked into Sebastian's beautiful face, with adoration, his eyelashes were still glistening from earlier tears. She was captivated all over again and could barely pull herself away from the universal secrets that lurked in his eyes; but she must. Sebastian understood. She wrenched herself off his gorgeous body that for so many hours had become part of her very self. For the first time, she felt cold. She located, and then picked up, her crumpled clothes, which were strewn across the floor. She then sat down close to him and steadily began to dress, in sleepy silence. Soon enough Sebastian did the same.

As soon as they were ready, the pair of them, arm in arm, stepped out into the cold, dimly-lit residential street. Sebastian was only wearing his shirt and his body soon began to shiver in the chill temperature of the small hours of the morning. Clamping Natasha's arm, more tightly, he hunched his shoulders against the elements as he led Natasha towards the Fulham Road at a gallop. She almost tripped trying to keep up with him, for her shoes were not designed for such a pace. When they hit the Fulham Road, the brighter street lighting greeted them jauntily and two expectant faces stared down the empty road, optimistically. Sebastian's teeth started to chatter, noisily, through a fixed, stoic smile. He felt foolish for venturing out on an October night, wearing nothing more than a shirt. Natasha giggled at his plight, before she took pity on him and began to cuddle him, as she attempted to wrap the flaps of her coat around his body. He was too big for that solution, so she resorted to rubbing his back, up and down, vigorously, as she continued to try to warm him. They felt like naïve chil-

dren caught unprepared, and they both began to laugh, almost hysterically.

Suddenly, Sebastian's face became solemn, for he had
just spotted that familiar yellow light of a London winter's
night that reads, 'TAXI'. The time was approaching for
them to part. Sebastian hailed the cab and, obediently, it
screeched to a halt in front of them. He stepped forward
into the street to open the heavy door for Natasha. She was
about to get in when, suddenly, Sebastian pulled her towards him and gave her the sweetest of loitering kisses, as
he cupped her soft cheek gently with his hand, while slipping a twenty-pound note into her pocket. Reluctantly,
Natasha got into the cab and slumped back into the worn
leather seat. When the taxi trundled off, its passenger remained rapturously enveloped in the after-glow of HIM, all
of her juddering way home. When she got out, she was still
in a heavenly daze and, unquestioningly, she handed the
driver Sebastian's money, not caring to calculate, nor collect, the change. It was a happy man who waited, patiently,
for Natasha to let herself into her home that night.

When Natasha stepped into her bedsit, she was still
blissed-out, but knackered. She walked towards her bed,
undressing on the way, letting everything, from her coat to
her knickers, fall to the floor, for she did not have the energy to do more. Naked now, she simply collapsed onto the
bed, with a bounce. Gratefully, she burrowed underneath
her duvet cover to rest her weary head on the cool pillow.
Natasha then flashed a look at her watch. It was two thirty-
eight a.m. She had to get up in three and a half hours time.
No problem, for how charged was she with all this spiritual
fire and, just as Natasha was smugly contemplating her
blessed, super-energized state, she fell fast asleep.

Chapter Twenty-two - A little house

Natasha had spent a second morning being bored beyond death in one of the bank's many lecture rooms. A specialist training company had come in to instruct the graduates on the F.S.A.'s rules and regulations for a week and a half, in preparation for their important exams next Thursday. It had soon become apparent that the course was not demanding, but just required a lot of tedious rote learning, if such method deserved the title of 'learning' at all. Natasha had been so tired, and the subject matter so dull, that it had taken immense concentration merely to stay awake, let alone retain any of the pedantically detailed information. Her only solace was, that for the days spent studying, she would have a defined hour and a half lunch-break without fail. In short, Natasha could be certain of getting at least one full hour's daylight a day. This thrilled her beyond belief for natural daylight was a commodity she was beginning to prize even more highly than coffee. It seemed that 'scarcity, increased value' resultant, proved as intractable off the trading floor, as on it.

Natasha was on such a break now, and she was strolling towards Exchange Square to buy a sandwich. She winced at the loudness of her high heels' screeching, each time they clicked on the highly polished, grey and pinky-rust tessellated stone slabs. Her reaction was no doubt exacerbated by her hangover. Once she was, embarrassingly, aware of the racket, she slowly became conscious of all the other women's heels' click-screeching, as well, and she breathed a sigh of relief as she merged, anonymously, with the collective before Natasha began to ponder the peculiarity of this strange, chaotic, female percussion.

Once she had mounted the steep, slate-grey stone steps to reach the high plateau of Exchange Square she gasped for, whenever Natasha arrived in this special place, her breath was simply snatched away by the intense, vital energy that never failed to invigorate her. Wind, light and cascading blue-white water hitting rock, conspired to create a most stimulating tonic. Immediately, she hunched her shoulders and gripped her coat tightly around herself, as its collar began to flap, repeatedly, in her face for the force of the wind, suddenly, had become very fierce. Natasha had just stepped into a powerful wind tunnel. It gushed, unobstructed, from under the bowels of the steel-stilted, black glass and concrete constructed office building at the top of the square, which somehow managed to collect, then concentrate it, before the gust blew, violently, across the stage of leaf-fluttering ornamental silver birch trees, down the terrace of giant steps, to then whoosh over the closely-trimmed patch of green lawn and then, finally, rush into the giant, yawning arches of Liverpool Street Station's light-bathed eaves, buoying several stray pigeons on the way.

Indeed, the wind was even more energetic than the multitudes of hurrying office workers whom it battered, snatching impudently at clothes, forcing ties to perform erratic dances or creating havoc with hair, as it blasted on its interfering course. Now, our heroine need not just contending with coat-grasping, collar flapping, and high heel clicking, she was also being veritably whipped across the face by strands of her own hair. Vanity aside, it hurt! Natasha took a deep breath of the boisterous air and braced herself against its power, as she clutched her coat ever more tightly to persevere, with head down, across the square. Through the corner of her eye, in between hair obscuring moments, Natasha saw lunch-munching men, sitting on the massive stone steps that overlooked the green, directly in front of the station's wide-toothed roof. Their jacket, or coat-clad backs were rounded like swans' necks. Their elbows rested on their knees while their hands gripped fat, ingredient-spilling sandwiches. Intermittently, they would lunge forward to take greedy bites, before focusing on chewing fast, displaying rippling jaw muscles as they did so, while their lips oscillated in varying degrees of protrusion. These blokes all looked rather glum, and very fidgety, with heads jerking around, brows furrowed and eyes keen, as their minds fretted about possible malicious market movements that might occur during this brief, stomach-filling, thirst-quenching, head-clearing absence from their multiple trading-screens.

Others, more sanguine, perhaps with successful positions closed out and profits banked, already held beers in front of bulging bellies with their top shirt buttons undone and ties askew. These groups of drinking men, loitered around the outdoor metal bar stools and the high, round tables that rose out of the rust-pink patterned, stone slabs in front of the small glass bar at the bottom of the bright, busy waterfall. These men had secured snug shelter from the violent wind, for they were shielded by the high stepped watery back of the post modern waterfall. In the bright, thin October sunlight the beer (and high blood pressure no doubt) drew ruddy faces, self-satisfied smiles and sudden outbursts of coarse, cackling laughter.

Walking past the top of the waterfall, Natasha stared down at the jumping sea of sparkling, white, dancing diamonds of light that bounced off the running water, as it surged down the steps before flooding the length of cobblestones to crash around the incidental, light grey, jagged rocks that littered its flow. The frenetically active fast flowing water spewed so much blinding light and playful splashing sound that it bedazzled her. Natasha's eye then came to rest, as usual, on the magnificent, shiny, chocolate brown, bronze Fat Lady statue, so luxuriously cast by the 'curved bounty of flesh' adoring Botero. Never before, however, did it come to rest so satisfyingly as today for leaning casually against the base of it was Sebastian, with his arms and ankles crossed as he watched Natasha, patiently. From his expression, it was obvious that he had seen her long before she had him, for he stared at her with indulgent, captivated eyes. Natasha's face lit up and her mouth broke into a broad, sparkling smile. Her thumping heart lurched towards him and a happy Sebastian peeled himself away from the statue's base before ambling, idly, towards her. When they met, they just beamed.

"I had a feeling you'd come here." Sebastian uttered,

while his green eyes glinted and his long lashes fluttered in self-congratulation.

Though Natasha was awestruck, strangely, seeing Sebastian here, like this, seemed the most natural thing in the world and she exclaimed:

"Clever you!" Before noticing, "You don't look half as tired as I feel."

He gave a semi-smile, but seemed happily preoccupied.

"Well, my darling one, I'm very sorry if I kept you up too late."

In an instant, Natasha's hand was on his forearm.

"Oh Sebastian, please don't apologise. It was more than magical..."

He stared at her, lost in love and clearly forgetting himself, for this was a most public place and their body language could not have been more indiscreet. He began to laugh, helplessly, for really how ridiculous was all of it. At last his chuckles subsided.

"Well, my Love, I'm glad my instinct was correct for there is something I want you to see. Will you come with me?" he requested, matter-of-factly.

Natasha just grinned and linked his arm.

"What do you think?" she questioned, rhetorically.

Without another word, Sebastian led her across the square's terrace, up the black steps and underneath the stilted office building, where they continued to be bashed ferociously by the wind, before they dropped down the steps on the other side and took a left to escape the fierce wind-tunnel's force, at last. Arm in arm they walked on in sunny, peaceful silence. The day, suddenly, seemed so much brighter, and their hearts lighter, now that they were together again.

Sebastian cut off from the main thoroughfare and began to pursue, unfamiliar, narrow, cobblestoned alleyways, twisting and turning, all the while. Natasha was itching with curiosity and struggling to imagine where he might be taking her. She was so enchanted by this strange surprise, however, that she held her tongue in order to silently discover where he might lead her. They ambled on down a cobbled alleyway that turned into a pedestrianized, empty, tarmac road before, finally, coming to a small, pretty, yellow cobble-stoned square. He came to a halt outside a glossy, black front door that had an exceptionally shiny brass doorknob and letterbox. Sebastian turned to stare at Natasha with wide, excited eyes, inexplicably triumphant.

They were standing in a suntrap, for the strength of the delicate autumn sunshine intensified significantly here. The area was completely sheltered, while the cheerful cobble-stones chucked up the heat that they had been absorbing all morning, to make the soles of Natasha's feet comfortingly warm. Several large, terracotta pots sat outside the small, Georgian, blackened-brick house and they spewed bright red, pink, white, and orange assorted, fragile flowers, which fell luxuriously over their brims as if to flirt with the bees. Natasha stared, questioningly, at Sebastian. He said nothing, instead, he took out a brand-new set of brass door keys from his trouser pocket, then jangled them in front of her face with palpable excitement. Next he stepped forward and inserted one into the door lock and turned it, to elicit a click. Gently, he pushed the panelled door open, before stepping back to allow Natasha to go in first. Hesitantly, she ducked under the arch of his arm, then crossed the threshold. Sebastian followed, before closing the door softly behind them.

It was so quiet inside. Sebastian had brought her to a silent, bright, private space, hidden away in the midst of the hectic, City of London. Quizzically, Natasha began to look around and take in her surroundings to find herself in a charming, miniature house. The place, obviously, had been recently refurbished with ivory painted, pristinely plastered walls and solid oak wood floorboards that still smelt of the forest. There were two large Georgian sash-windows that overlooked the sunny courtyard while, to her left, she found a spanking new, fully fitted, open plan kitchen with a wooden galleried area above. To her right, was the open plan living area with an exceptionally high ceiling that rose

313

all the way up to the exposed wooden-beamed eaves. The room was simply furnished, with empty, gloss white bookshelves, a cream sofa with matching armchair, a coffee table and an ultra modern flat screen television with a DVD player beneath, all set flat into the wall.

Next to the kitchen a narrow, wooden, spiral staircase led up to the galleried area lodged above the kitchen. This was the direction in which Sebastian motioned. Natasha went over to the staircase and began to climb, while he followed close behind. The only sound in the little house was their breathing. When she reached the top of the staircase, she discovered a bedroom with a king size double bed, fully made up, taking up almost all of the space. At the foot of the bed was a gigantic, round, wooden paned window, which allowed the sunlight to flood into the room to strike the pristine, white cotton, bed cover with splashes of golden yellow. Natasha turned to look at Sebastian. He was stooped over, for the ceiling height up here was not sufficient for him to stand upright. Clearly impatient with such diminished posture, he sat down on the puffy bed cover then patted the place next to him twice, in quick succession, to indicate that Natasha should sit also. Once she had done so, she stared at him for an explanation.

"Natasha, I have found this place for you!" Sebastian announced, gleefully.

"Sebastian, what are you talking about?"

He sighed, tenderly, and then he shook his head a few times before he explained, "My darling one, you cannot continue to live in a minute bedsit where you're reduced to sharing a lavatory and shower with two others. I won't have it! I've found this place for you and I want you to move in, as soon as you can."

Sebastian was smiling, broadly, his eyes alight and his face shining with excitement. Clearly, he was thrilled with his proposition and certain Natasha would be too, as soon as she grasped exactly what was on offer. He looked at her, with determination. She just stared at her feet, with narrowed eyes, for she seemed to be having some trouble processing his simple, and surely rather attractive, offer. Natasha felt confused and unsure how to react, however, what she did know was that she felt most uncomfortable. Playing for time, she quickly grasped at the most practical of objections and said:

"Sebastian, I couldn't possibly afford a place like this, on a graduate's starting salary, and besides, I like it where I live."

He laughed out loud.

"Natasha my Love, I don't expect you to pay for it, this would be my present to you." he patronized before shrugging and mitigating his generosity, "A friend of mine owns it, he's given me a very good deal, so really it's my treat. Indeed, if you move in here, you'll save money, for you won't have rent to pay." Now it was Natasha who was shaking her head, for she was in a state straddling disbelief and outright objection. Sebastian remained unperturbed, "Oh Natasha, just think about it, you have to confess it's a charming little house and it is less than ten-minutes from the office. Our very own little home, we could come back here at lunch-times, after work even."

Slowly, the full implications of the arrangement Sebastian was suggesting sank in. Once again, Natasha found herself staring at her feet so she could communicate, unhindered, with her heart and extract her true response from there. As she waited, patiently, for her inner voice to speak, Sebastian's enthusiastic proselytizing continued.

"Please say you'll take it? Please allow me to do this little thing for you, for us?"

Natasha looked up at his hopeful face as it willed her agreement, but she knew she could not accept his offer. She did not know if it was pride or self-preservation that spurred her decision but, either way, she had come to one.

"I can't accept this Sebastian, but thank you." she replied, with sadness, for how she hated to disappoint the man she loved.

It appeared Sebastian was unprepared for this response. The fire in his eyes was snuffed out and, suddenly, he looked hurt. Finally, he was courageous enough to venture:

"Why ever not?" before adding, "I want to do this for you, why won't you allow me to?"

Natasha tried to make him understand.

"Think about it Sebastian, all of my friends live in West London. My social life is in West London. You live in West London! Come to think of it, I don't know anyone who actually lives in the City. No matter how charming this place is, I'd be lonely, and feel completely cut-off if I lived here."

"But Natasha, I'll be here with you, this house will be for us."

All of the pitfalls of such a set-up, suddenly, become painfully apparent. Indeed, he cannot have really considered her at all! Natasha felt emboldened.

"Sure Sebastian, you'll be here with me for a few lunch-times and a few nights after work, but every weekend, every holiday and most evenings, you'll be participating in your real life in West London. I, on the other hand, will be here all alone with nothing but my memory of you for company. I feel enslaved enough already. For me, such an arrangement would be a recipe for disaster."

Sebastian was listening, but very reluctant to allow his inspirational idea to be aborted. He sought to convince her.

"Natasha, it won't be like that, let's face it, I always want to be with you anyway, this will just make it easier for both of us."

"No Sebastian, it will make it easier for you. If I were to live here, I would be completely 'on tap' and utterly de-pendent on you to pay the rent. Then not only my professional life, but also my domestic existence, would rely entirely on you. Plus, I would be miles away from my friends. For me to give up my home, albeit a humble one, and move in here, would be tantamount to courting insan-ity." Natasha was laughing now at the preposterousness of Sebastian's well-intentioned suggestion, before she took his hand and added, conciliatorily, through her smile, "Sebastian, you make me feel quite mad enough as it is!"

It was clear, Natasha was adamant. Finally, Sebastian seemed to accept that she was beyond persuasion. He even managed to laugh, lightly, as he questioned, with comically raised brows, "I take it the answer is no then?"

Natasha just smiled, kindly.

"I love a perceptive man!"

He shrugged off this rebuff, grabbed Natasha's hand and leapt up, only to hit his head on the white ceiling with a loud bang.

"Ouch!" he exclaimed. Then he hunched over to rub the spot he had just struck, as he added, sulkily, "Well, the ceilings are too bloody low anyway..."

Natasha gave a carefree laugh, before she slowly got to her feet. She then took his hand and suggested, encouragingly, "Come on, let's go for lunch, I'm starving!"

The pair soon left and strolled the short distance to Sebastian's favourite Indian restaurant on Brick Lane. The subject of the charming little house, and the less charming 'arrangement', was never mentioned again. Over their feast of chicken tikka massala, sag baggie, pweshari naans and Cobra beer, Natasha happened to mention her imminent dinner date with Miles Monroe.

"You think I could have forgotten about that?" Sebastian replied, sullenly, before taking another mouthful of food. He chewed pensively and then, having swallowed, he instructed, ominously:

"Natasha, for Christ's sake, don't have sex with Miles."

Natasha sat bolt upright with indignation, for she was most disconcerted to have received such an instruction from him. How could Sebastian possibly conceive of her wanting to do such a thing, in the circumstances? She felt wounded. Instinctively, she wanted to strike out at him, both for his audacity and for such gross, insulting presumption. Reacting, she leaned over the table and challenged him.

"I bet you're still sleeping with your wife, Sebastian." A comment he chose, irritatingly, not to deny nor confirm as he stared at her, impassively. Frustrated by his reticence,

Natasha added with perverse logic, "Surely it would only balance our romantic equation, if I were to sleep with someone else too?"

Sebastian flinched minutely. His expression hardened, as dark and frosty as the cold, brown bottle of Cobra beer. He then retorted, petulantly, "If that's how you feel Natasha, why did you not continue to date Bruno as I encouraged?"

Natasha was cross that he had not jumped in to rescue them from diligently digging this restrictive, accusatory trench. Stubbornly, she cut deeper into the familiar, murky ditch of emotional detachment.

"Because Bruno is an entirely different animal, from Miles Monroe. If I were to have sex with Miles, I would feel no betrayal towards him by loving you. Firstly, he is not your cousin, and secondly, he is not a man to expect, nor deliver, fidelity."

He was studying Natasha's face, fascinated by the unfamiliar coldness of her familiar eyes. She topped up her beer and took a long sip before she began to reminisce, dreamily.

"What were your words Sebastian? 'Because you're strong'?" The moment she had said the phrase she was, abruptly, transported her back to her bed and that moment of first penetration. It seemed blasphemous to revisit that space with even the concept of Miles Monroe for company. She flinched before suggesting, expressionlessly:

"Maybe, I think Miles is strong enough to play such a rebalancing role?"

Sebastian stared at her icily. He took a deep draught of his beer while Natasha's gaze fixed on his Adam's apple to watch it move, rhythmically, up and down. Staring at his neck, watching the simple honesty of this motion, reminded her of the intense intimacy of his body with hers. Suddenly, she wanted to stop all this foolish emotional posturing. She just wanted to collapse forward and kiss the base of his beautiful neck and taste him on her tongue. She wanted to curl up on that sunny bed, back in that little house, and nuzzle her cheek into that inviting hollow just above his collarbone. Natasha did not want to discuss having sex with Miles Monroe. All Natasha wanted to do was love Sebastian. Oh, how confusing this lunch-time was becoming! And oh, how hard it was to traverse such a treacherous emotional continent with a shocking hangover. At this moment, Natasha did not feel 'strong' at all. She just felt like crying. What is more, Sebastian was still sleeping with his wife. She knew it! Sad and exhausted, she stared into his disdainful eyes as she mouthed, apologetically, "I'm sorry Sebastian. I didn't mean a word of it."

Immediately, the impenetrable barrier Sebastian had so recently erected, shattered. He reached across the table and grasped her hand with relief. Natasha took comfort from his touch as she confided, somberly:

"It's just maybe, I'm not as strong as you think?" There, she had said it. Softening, Natasha looked at him and tried to explain, "It's just that the feelings you arouse in me are so frightening, I take refuge in tangled emotional web weaving just to try and numb myself."

In short, it was her vulnerability that had prompted Natasha's silly statements, for the thought of Sebastian sleeping with Isabel mutilated her heart. Now he could understand what drove her perverse comments, he could forgive them. All love once again, he sighed, forlornly.

"Good God Natasha, you even manage to possess me with the ugly monster Jealousy... and I, you, it appears. It's a foe with which I am unfamiliar."

Natasha squeezed his hand.

"I'm sorry for being so ghastly..." she muttered, quietly.

Sebastian shook his head in defeat.

"What we do to one another..."

Natasha huffed, softly, before catching sight of her watch. It was already two o'clock.

"Make me bloody late for a start!" she answered shrilly, before insisting with urgency, "Sebastian, I have to go!"

He grinned with amusement, then called for the bill. He soon paid and they left. All was forgiven. Natasha and

Sebastian's love had shyly re-emerged with a new awareness: each of them had received a small warning, and a
little house had been forgotten, all during the course of a
clandestine City-lunch between lovers.

Chapter Twenty-three - Inimitable seduction

Natasha was oddly nervous. She was also very tired following such a late night with Sebastian and, after lunch with him today, the last thing she felt like doing was going out with Miles Monroe. She was afraid she did not have sufficient energy reserves to deal with his forceful advances. As soon as the doorbell sounded, the twittering doubts taking fidgety roost in her head, were scattered in panicked flight. It was too late for second thoughts now. Miles had just arrived. The minute she answered the intercom, Natasha's tummy was beset by butterflies.

"Hello?"

Immediately, bass, filthy laughter rolled into her ear, to make its drum vibrate so wildly that it started to tickle. Indeed, Miles Monroe's laugh seemed to flood into, then fill, her entire bedsit.

"Hello trouble..." he articulated, with devilish relish.

There was something about the way he said it, that made Natasha feel foolish to have agreed to go out on a date with him in the first place.

"Speak for yourself." she retorted, defensively.

To be bombarded with more laughter, so forceful that her eardrum's ticklishness turned to wincing. In fact, Miles Monroe's sonorous energy was so powerful, it was as if he was already standing in her bedsit, flesh and scorching hot-blood, before her. Even the intercom's plastic handset had started to hum, as if to imitate the original sound of the Universe: AUMMMMMMM. Well, as effectively as cheap cream plastic is able. Following an interminably long time, Miles' canorous voice finally spoke.

"Well my dear, aren't you going to invite me in?"

Natasha freaked out! The thought of Miles coming up to her bedsit, made her unusually active adrenal gland surpass itself with its secretions. Natasha's eyes darted around the little space, frantically. It was so dominated by the double bed that allowing Miles Monroe to enter, felt like a virtual invitation to intercourse! The man had invaded her personal space enough in public. She could not imagine what he might be capable of in this private setting.

"NO!" Natasha blurted, terrified by the very prospect, only to shock herself further, with the hysteria of her negative yelp. Pausing, for a moment, to collect herself she added with borrowed nonchalance, "That would be asking for trouble. I'll be right down."

Natasha then left her bedsit to face her fate, picking up her handbag and coat on the way before, precariously, tottering down the three-flights of stairs. The cavorting pace of her heartbeat pounding in her ears puzzled her and, for a second time, she wondered why Miles Monroe frightened her so? Even more puzzling: why had she agreed to go out with him, in the first place? That same question was still ricocheting around her head when her pale, manicured hand reached for the latch on the front door to open it. Cautiously, she peered around to rediscover that most unusual, but strangely charismatic man from Isabel's party.

Miles was standing on the top step with his broad chest puffed out. His posture was bolt upright and his arms clamped straight down by his sides. He looked like some young army cadet. He was flashing an enormous, dazzling smile, while the sparks of light glinting in his big brown eyes seemed to dance with sheer devilment. On first sight, he reminded her of a mature opera singer playing the part of an audacious rake standing to arrogant attention, confident that he would soon catch the eye of his new amour. Natasha was beside herself with delight when Miles, as if reading her thoughts, abruptly gave a perfect salute!

Miles had made her laugh, already. Feeling a little more relaxed, Natasha stepped out to join him. He was chuckling, contagiously, as if the whole scene was just a game to him. Then he held his arms wide open in welcome, as if expecting Natasha to fall straight into them. Instead, our nervous heroine just gave Miles the once over. His smile was just as smutty as she remembered. In fact, it was so broad that it made his chocolate brown eyes squint, cheekily, but not quite enough to conceal the softness that permeated them. Familiar smile and warm eyes aside, something was very different. In a flash, Natasha had pinpointed it: Miles had shaved off his beard and, in so doing, he had exposed an exceptionally handsome face. In fact, now he could quite easily have passed for the gorgeous Fabio's older, naughtier, prodigal brother: the one with oodles of reckless, self-destructive and experience gobbling charm. Oh, what a thoroughly dangerous combination!

Miles was still grinning at her, but now he took a couple of steps back down the outdoor steps, in order to check Natasha out, shamelessly. In her sobriety, her shyness was more acute and she began to blush. Miles leaned back, slightly, and crossed his arms while he took his time to study her carefully. Satisfied, he threw his arms wide open.

"Why Natasha, just as beautiful as I remember!" he bellowed, then he tipped his head to one side, rubbed his large hands together and fixed his gaze on Natasha's face before his eyes widened, with interest, as he exclaimed, "Oh, what sweet blush my dear! How it suits your colouring and conjures thoughts of virginity ripe for plucking..."

Natasha's pink blush, shot strawberry red with reference to it! What is more, she knew she looked knackered, and so she began to suspect that Miles was as free with his lavish compliments, as he was with his smutty laughter and roaming hands. Our heroine willed her red-fruit-flushed cheeks to return to freckly cream and declared:

"Miles you are more of a drama queen than I, and if it's virginity plucking you're after, I'm afraid you've come to the wrong house!"

Miles dropped his chin to fix her with a pitiful hangdog stare. It was effective for, within seconds, he had managed to extract a genuine compliment.

"Besides Miles, it is you who looks gorgeous this evening, not I." Clearly tickled pink, Miles gave a dazzling smile while Natasha added, definitively, with a nod, "In actual fact Miles, you really are rather handsome, so much better without the beard Mr. Monroe."

He beamed, bashfully, back at her then bowed so low in

thanks that the tips of his luscious locks brushed the top of the stone step in front of him. Miles held this position, for a moment, before abruptly flinging back his head to stand to attention again. Then with a neat click of his heels he said, possibly his first sincere sentence so far:

"Thank you, Miss Flynn."

He soon leapt up to the top step, once again, executed a precise about-turn and cocked his right arm to offer it to Natasha. Warming to him by the minute, she slipped hers into his and he escorted her down the steps and to his car.

Miles was wearing a dark camel linen suit, the jacket of which was casually undone, more appropriate for the tropics than a cold October night in London. His only concession to the truth of the climate he currently inhabited was the snug, cashmere, moss green polo-neck jumper he wore beneath it. When Natasha looked down to navigate the steps, she noticed that Miles betrayed his rebellious streak for, despite the chill, he was not wearing any socks. The skin of the tops of his honey-brown, no doubt rather freezing, feet peeped out between the bottom of his trousers and his dark brown, tasselled, suede Todd loafers.

Just as at the party, it seemed Miles Monroe was ill suited, literally and metaphorically, to London. Indeed, Natasha imagined his element to be one of the sun-drenched, dusty outposts of the planet, that always prove such powerful draws for characters whom are either too individual, criminal or flamboyant to exist, comfortably, within the ordered, efficient confines of the inescapably consequential, Western world. Miles Monroe exuded the persona of a well-heeled, utterly unflappable, world-weary traveller who has already experienced most of what life has to offer, however, he appeared ever hopeful that Surprise might be gracious enough to reintroduce herself, if he were sufficiently chivalrous to entice that natural companion of the young back into his fascinating orbit.

When they reached the bottom of the steps, Miles enveloped Natasha's waist with both hands before she had even registered the intimacy of his gesture. Firmly held thus Miles, assertively, directed her to the passenger door of his remarkable car, in the manner in which a top designer might manhandle one of his many models: more as an incidental prop to his creativity than as a separate individual. Natasha found such treatment unusual, yet strangely comforting. The car was a bright yellow, souped-up mini, with more sparkling chrome protrusions than Natasha could count, let alone believe to be strictly necessary for the art of motoring.

It was parked directly in front of her house, and Miles leant down to open the passenger door for her, then walked around to get in and sink into the driver's seat. Miles was a big man and now he was inside the little vehicle, it seemed as full as a fairground's dodgem car. His square knees were jammed up against the dashboard, while his hair touched the roof where it, inconveniently, collected static electricity, as if the man did not have enough already; hair and energy both! Miles soon slipped the key into the ignition to spark a loud clapping noise, much like a go-kart. His powerful hands gripped almost the entire steering-wheel, before he turned to catch Natasha's alert eye and give her a splendid grin. Disturbingly, Natasha could feel her excitement rising and she commented, "Cool car!"

Miles tipped his head towards her and batted his long eyelashes, as flirtatiously as a six-year-old boy wanting mummy to buy him an ice cream on a hot sunny day. He then confided, naughtily, while his strangely fragrant, humid breath billowed over her cheek:

"Darling, the greatest thing about the littlest car, is that it facilitates easy access to my female prey." Before he, quickly, covered his mouth in mock horror, "Whoops! Did I say prey? Of course I meant 'companion' my dear. What must you think me?"

He then revved the engine, aggressively, and the little car buzzed off to take them on a nocturnal adventure, its busy, surprisingly powerful engine sounding like a giant wasp on steroids. As they whizzed down the Bayswater Road, Miles shot a glance at her, and smiled, most innocently, as if to establish that he was, in truth, rather harmless before he questioned, cheekily:

"Now, Natasha, who was it who said, with such authority, 'size doesn't matter'?"

"Surely, it must have been a small man who made such a comment." Natasha fired.

Miles' laughter roared so much, in this small car, that Natasha's innards began to vibrate to produce the most invasive sensation imaginable. Talk about penetration! Anyway, she was starting to enjoy herself, for having spent so many long days over the last several weeks working with a bunch of investment bankers, fixated on making money and more seduced by power than pleasure, Miles was a most refreshing tonic. Come to think of it, even his car was so much more charming than the staple of exorbitantly expensive sports cars preferred by the City crew. Natasha had almost come to believe that the only car a man cared to drive, was a Porsche, Ferrari or an Aston Martin.

The more Natasha thought about it, the more different Miles was from the other men whom she had been meeting recently. Her male colleagues pounded the financial market treadmill, to finance the acquisition of trophies, in order to impress their peers and pull pretty women. Miles, on the other hand, dispensed with the obvious trappings of wealth, did not seem to give a hoot for others' opinion of him but instead, invariably, performed captivatingly in order to amuse himself, and pull pretty women. Miles' method seemed a lot more fun, and a damn sight cheaper.

"I guess a man needs a big personality to drive a small car, Miles." Natasha mused, provocatively, through a smirk.

"No darling." he declared, confidently, "He just needs a gigantic cock."

Natasha's eyes sprang open, so shocked was she by his brazenness, yet she could not prevent herself from giving a moan of amusement as she shifted, uncomfortably, in her seat as she added, primly, "More information than I require thank you Miles Monroe!"

Miles stared at her, seductively, for a moment, before snatching his attention back to the road.

"I've always believed it serves in one's best interests to divulge pertinent information promptly." he asserted. "Would madam appreciate precise dimensions?"

"Enough!" she cried.

"Clearly my dear, I was referring to the car! What do you take me for?"

Natasha just shook her head in resignation. Miles may drive a less 'obvious' car than City boys, but his intentions were the most naked she had encountered to date, and that was saying something, for was there ever a City boy who could be described as subtle? As if to concur with Natasha's silent observation, Miles' hand was suddenly on, then massaging, her right knee while he continued to speed down the Bayswater Road as they approached Marble Arch. At this very moment, Natasha was experiencing firsthand, the advantages detailed with regard to a small car. Natasha just found herself wondering which girl had been here last, and how had she dealt with this man's blatant advances?

Determinedly, she collected Miles' warm hand, with both of hers, to return it to his lap, for good. Well that is what she had hoped. Miles, however, had other ideas for he continued to repeat this manoeuvre, many times, on the short drive to the outskirts of Covent Garden, as did Natasha her adamant response. Though she suspected she ought to have been cross, or even outraged, by Miles' tenacious groping, with each repetition of said actions, Miles' and Natasha's resolve to reverse them was strengthened to the point at which a physical tussle broke out, which would have been far more suited to a bawdy pantomime scene, than to any sincere attempt at seduction.

Miles proved to be, simply, incorrigible yet he had succeeded in making Natasha laugh her heart out. By the time he had parked in an alley-way behind St. Martin's Lane, her cheeks were aching from all her giggling. Then perhaps that had been Miles' true design all along for, all clever men know, laughter is the most powerful aphrodisiac. If his clownishness was really so calculated, then Miles was even more dangerous than Natasha had feared...

In no time, Miles was leading her down an extremely narrow alley, as his hand grasped her slim waist to pull her snugly into him. After no more than ten metres, he stopped outside an inconspicuous, blood-red door. It was set in a dark-brown brick Georgian terraced wall that had no ground floor windows. Miles wrapped his knuckles loudly on it, four times, "Rat, tat, tat, tat." He then looked down to make his chocolate-coloured curls cascade over his face while he waited. In a heartbeat, a tiny hatch, set in the upper part of the door, burst open to expose a large, ice-blue eye, dramatically underscored with thick black eye-liner and surrounded by mascara-laden false eyelashes. The piercing blue eye peeped out, inquisitively, to discover by whom it had been summoned while blinking, repeatedly, as if affronted to have been so disturbed. The diminutive size of the hatch, afforded a view of less than a quarter of the rest of the smooth, tanned face to which the bright-eye belonged. The eye soon narrowed to reveal fine creases beneath, as if the face that owned it had just broken into a broad smile, on sight of Miles.

"MILESY!" a perfectly annunciated, foreign accent squealed with excitement.

The little hatch then slammed shut. Several noisy latches were then fumbled with, before the blood-red door was flung open to reveal a rather beautiful, slight man of indiscernible age, for he was wearing far too much make-up to work it out. He was almost Miles' height, but only half his width. The man had short, jet-black, slicked-back hair accentuating a very high forehead, and his classical bone structure played host to a perfect nose. He held his ruby red lips in a provocative pout, as he stood before them with an extremely precise, posed posture. He wore black fitted trousers to reveal a trim waistline into which he had tucked his emerald green silk shirt. His sparkling silver shirt-buttons were undone all the way down to his waist, to display his lithe chest that was so toned, yet non bulky, that he must have once been a gymnast, acrobat or dancer. For several minutes, he stared, expressionlessly, at the pair of them from his android-like, blue eyes, in silence, as if to provide them with sufficient opportunity to admire him before, suddenly, he erupted into bubbling, breathy, verbosity, "Oh Miles, Miles, Miles, Miles, Miles..." He then grabbed Miles by the arm, and tugged him into his establishment as he continued to gush, "Oh Miles, how we've missed you. I was terrified that you'd abandoned us forever! Why, why, why, why, why did you desert us for so long?" The man rested his hand on his heart, and looked into the near distance, for a moment, as if in mourning before, recklessly, flinging both of his arms into the air, along with the need for an answer, it would appear, for he just continued with his hands now held neatly together in front of him, "No matter. My prayers have been answered. You have returned." Then he gave a ballet dancer's bow, as he uttered, "Welcome, welcome, welcome!"

Miles had silently endured his friend's rather dramatic performance while sporting a long-suffering, but affectionate grin until, finally, he spoke.

"Arturo... please forgive me. You are so right of course. I know it's been far too long, but if it's any consolation, I've been to Bolivia and back since I saw you last." Miles then turned his attention to Natasha and declared, triumphantly, "Anyway, look what I've brought you!"

Arturo shone his penetrating stare onto Natasha and tilted his head like a curious, yet slightly suspicious, peacock. Miles went on to formally introduce them.

"Arturo Mancini, please allow me to present Miss Natasha Flynn?"

Arturo's chilling eyes studied Natasha's face as meticulously and critically as a woman's. He soon gave a curt nod of his head, and then his deadpan expression became more human, for his sulky pout transformed into a conspiratorial smile. He then leant forward to touch her on the arm, and he said, with genuine warmth:

329

"Miss Flynn, any friend of Miles Monroe, is a dear friend of mine. Welcome, welcome."

They were in. Arturo took, and then quickly hung up, Natasha's coat, before escorting them up a flight of steep, narrow, wonky wooden stairs, the central band of which was covered with a thin carpet, the colour of the front door, which was, quaintly, fixed down with old-fashioned brass stair-rods. Every footstep made the stairs creak and Natasha ran her hands along the plastered walls, to steady herself, as they climbed four demi-flights of stairs, passing empty, intimate, dining-rooms on each floor and half-landing, on the way. Arturo then walked to the back of one of these little rooms and extended his arm, gracefully, to indicate a table in an alcove next to a big sash-window. The low table was formally set with a starched white table-cloth and full glass and silverware, while either side there were two miniature double sofas, upholstered in pitch-black velvet.

"Arturo, my favourite table, thank you." Miles exclaimed, with gratitude.

Arturo just dropped his head and closed his eyelids, modestly, before suddenly looking up with startling eyes, which were now wide enough to flash the whites of them.

"Champagne?" he questioned, enticingly.

And that is precisely what Natasha ended up drinking all night; yet again. Arturo never gave them a menu, instead, he described each delicacy and gastronomic triumph the kitchen could produce, in a detail as precise as his diction. Miles' trust in him was absolute for, once every dish had been painstakingly described, Miles directed Arturo to serve them exactly what he believed to be the most exquisite of the selection that evening, and not once did he confer with Natasha, as to her preference. Arturo then turned to leave.

"No red meat for me please." Natasha, quickly, instructed after him, in a timid voice, utterly unconfident that this dramatic character had paid her any heed.

Trusting in providence, Natasha just began to look

around the room while she waited for her drink. The uneven walls were the colour of red wine, the woodwork satin-white, while the drapes, mirrors and picture frames were all antique gold. There were a couple of large oil paintings squeezed onto the limited wall space, and both were of a young female brunette. The biggest of them dominated the wall in front of her, and depicted the rear view of a reclining, classical nude peering, coquettishly, over her shoulder to catch the viewer's eye, as she immodestly flashed the fullness of her ivory, pink-blushed, peach-shaped bottom, before the plunging curve of her hips cut into her waist, to then soar up her shapely back, to give the overall impression of an appealing, racy roller-coaster of Rubenesque female form. The second portrait, to Natasha's half-left, was of a beautiful, prim, young girl in full Sunday best. She wore a yellow satin, cream-lace frilled dress and she looked most demure with pensive, downcast but captivating, eyes. Natasha was thrilled the moment she realized that the same girl, but with two very different presentations, was portrayed in each painting. Intrigued, she studied them further, to find the artistry to be so fine that every time she looked away from either picture, her eye was, continually, drawn back in a manner as persistent, pleasurable and inexhaustible as Miles' groping. Quality art aside, the ambience of the establishment was that of an up-market brothel. That being said, once the food started to arrive, it soon became apparent that such a categorization did the place a horrible disservice for, first and foremost, it turned out that she had, in fact, been brought to a most accomplished restaurant.

Fortunately, providence delivered, for Arturo had indeed heeded Natasha's request, and she dined royally on lobster bisque, followed by monkfish medallions with scallop sauce, while Miles switched to red wine and enjoyed mackerel pâté on golden toast, followed by beef Wellington with roast potatoes and winter vegetables. The combination of fine drink, divine food and a luxurious baroque setting, proved a veritable sensory paradise for punters conspiring to serve most of their sensual appetites. By the end of the second course, and well into the second bottle of champagne, Miles was sitting jam next to Natasha on the miniature sofa (even more snugly than he had done in his car) from which position he entertained, seduced and titillated the inebriated girl, for hours to come.

More fatally, he kept making her laugh, with tales of far-flung lands and the remarkable antics, infidelities, betrayals and cruelties of kings and tribal heads, of islands and countries of which our heroine had never even heard. The common denominator was always thus: Miles was simply adored everywhere he went, and all men of influence and fortune wished to bestow upon him their daughters and their lands. Already, he claimed to be the proud owner of a small South Pacific isle that, recently, had been gifted to him by its King, following a three-day feast. The King had found Miles to be a most scintillating raconteur but, more specifically, he had been astounded by Miles' phenomenal sexual stamina and imposing genitalia when observed, in action, during the orgiastic sex-acts performed in between the innumerable courses served at the Feast of Fertility.

"Of course," Miles added, insouciantly, "one can never rely on clean title in such cases for, my dear, an island is as easily taken away, as it is given."

Indeed, Miles was keen to take Natasha there, while he was still the pronounced owner. She was just beginning to warm to the idea, when he informed her that on his island the natives considered it an insult, of the greatest magnitude and worthy of the harshest punishment, if one were to deny sexual intercourse to anyone of them who requested the pleasure of it! He was most eager to stress that he had never encountered such a jolly tribe in all his life! Natasha remained unconvinced and was swift to decline his kind offer, before she commented, archly:

"Is flying to an island in the South Pacific not a rather expensive, and time consuming, way to get laid Miles?"

To make him laugh so much so that he clutched his

sides, and his ribcage juddered. Miles then recovered enough to assure her, with great confidence:

"Oh darling, I don't need to go for the sex, I choose to go for the massages. They last for many hours and are simply the best in the world. Besides, I can get as much sex as I want, with as many women as I want, just as easily right here in London my dear…"

Natasha did not doubt him. With every burst of laughter, with each tug of fascination, with every glimpse of the warmth of this intelligent man's heart, and with each glass of remarkably good champagne, Natasha found herself allowing Miles greater and greater liberties, in relation to his appreciation, not to say worship, of her stockinged-legs.

His strong, agile hands were forever following the lines of them and, with each and every touch, a bolt of electricity enlivened her whole body to quivering pitch. His focused attention was more relentless than that of a trader at his screens. Miles' hands moved so fast, and with such inspired variety, that Natasha was confused as to precisely when he crossed the 'no-go' line. Besides, she felt so extraordinarily relaxed in this charming environment and she was really rather tipsy by now, so she was not inclined to take offence.

Indeed, no man had ever made Natasha feel so irresistible. Miles' adoring hands were forever in multi-paced motion, lingering, for a moment on her knee before, enticingly, sweeping up her thigh then, suddenly, to stop dead in their tracks as soon as they were about to reach the place to which they had not been invited, only to be snatched away, dramatically. Immediately, Miles would give an impassioned groan of astonishment at his capacity for self-control, and so draw delighted, tinkling giggles from the sozzled object of his affections.

It was as if Miles played the artist besotted by our heroine's perceived beauty yet, rather than expressing his appreciation with brush-strokes, he did so with his hypnotizing, sensitive, intuitive touch as he, humbly, sought increasing intimacy with this long-legged sliver of God's creation. He became ever more breathlessly inspired with each stroke of her, while Natasha became more and more tempted, intoxicated and bewitched by him. With each subsequent caress, Miles would dare to explore farther and farther up Natasha's thigh, and for longer and longer periods. So anesthetized by alcohol and stimulated by Miles' tireless attention was the young Natasha that, by the time the coffee arrived, she had allowed him liberties for which other men would have been arrested.

In short, he was now familiar with Natasha's lingerie and, more shockingly, for brief snapshots of time, the forbidden places it was designed to conceal.

When the sumptuous meal was over and Miles' salacious exploration of Natasha finally complete, it was past twelve-thirty. Our heroine's extreme exhaustion from her late night, compounded by so much tantalizing mental and physical stimulation, forced the fatigue that had been lurking beneath her fascination all evening, to pounce. Even in the fogginess of her mind, Natasha knew she was knackered and that she had to get up at six. What is more, her brain had to function effectively soon after seven. She needed to go to sleep. Sweetly, she asked the increasingly adorable Miles to take her home. He was crestfallen and begged her to come dancing with him at his private members' club just around the corner, but Natasha, categorically, refused. It was only Tuesday after all, and following last night with Sebastian, she did not have the stamina to stay up until the small hours again. Disappointed, yet chivalrous, Miles drove the befuddled creature back home, making her laugh and molesting her legs all the way, as if for consolation. After such a fabulous evening, surely it was the least she could allow him?

When Natasha finally turned to say good night, Miles' eyes requested more intimacy with her mouth, but now Natasha's heart just yearned for Sebastian. She could not allow this to go any further than it already had. With resolve, she clutched her handbag to her chest and leant forward to give him a chaste kiss on each of his smooth, brown cheeks. So struck by his exotic musky scent was she that, when she did so, she was shamefully tempted to linger instead, however, she pulled back to find herself looking directly into his big brown eyes. There was no devilment or merriment in them now. Distressingly, all Natasha could detect was an eternal yearning for love, affection and tenderness. Impulsively, she flung her arms around the solid bulk of him to give him the biggest, warmest hug she knew how. At last, she broke her clench and slowly climbed the stone steps to her front door. Once Natasha had unlocked it, she turned to look over her shoulder to catch her date's observant eye, as she whispered, sincerely:

"Thank you so much for a wonderful evening, Miles. I had fun. Good night."

Then she stepped into the safety of her house, while a strangely melancholy Miles Monroe disappeared into the black, silky silence of the night.

<u>Chapter Twenty-four</u> - Losing it

*When my soul soared
to that blessed sphere
I was free of the tyranny
of 'why?' and 'how?'
At last
the thousand veils lifted
and I could behold
the hidden secret.*

Rumi

Natasha and Maria burst out of the revolving rear doors of U.C.B. and into the dull, daylight of a blustery, late October day in the heart of Broadgate Circus. They had just left the bank's lecture rooms following a third morning studying for their impending F.S.A. exams. The course was beyond boring, but our heroine was thankful to be reunited with the European graduates, for they had come to London to study for, and sit, the qualifying papers. Natasha was particularly thrilled to see Maria again, oh, and of course Emmanuel, for she had almost forgotten how bloody beautiful he was to look at. Maria and Natasha kept finding themselves giggling in each other's company, which was no mean feat considering the subject matter with which they were forced to grapple.

As for Emmanuel, well they remained firm flirt friends and the chemistry that had swept them away that night in Switzerland, provided a welcome titillation to help counteract the tedium of rote learning F.S.A. rules and regulations. Natasha was curious to observe that the mere recollection of orgasms managed to invigorate. Indeed, what a pleasure it was to admire his gorgeous face every day. She had missed him. Of course it was mildly torturous not being able to touch something she was so bloody attracted to but, not surprisingly, they had never really recovered from the condom conundrum. Not to forget the inconvenient truth that he was already engaged to someone else. Yet despite all that, Natasha and Emmanuel still found themselves sitting next to each other at every opportunity. They still flirted, outrageously, together. Their eyes still flashed a little too brightly when in conversation, and they still found themselves laughing, too loudly, at each other's jokes.

After so many weeks working with a load of grumpy traders and stressed salesmen, Natasha was relieved to feel genuine camaraderie with her fellow graduates. When she thought about it, she did not feel any on the trading floor, as everyone was so obviously out for themselves. The fact that Freddie was only too happy to remind her, and often, that she was just 'a cost to be carried' did not help. What a brutal environment it was, where everyone's worth was defined by directly correlating it to the money they made for the bottom line! She was, increasingly, impatient to become qualified so that she could start to contribute and stop being considered an expensive burden, for how disproportionately wearing it was to be perceived as such, daily, by so many. At times, she could almost see the resentment smouldering, scorchingly, in her colleagues' eyes and, with the thought of it, Natasha was inspired to adopt Maria's tactile ways prompting her, impulsively, to link arms with her warm-hearted Spanish friend as they crossed Broadgate Circus.

The rest of the smart graduate group of nascent professionals was spilling out around them and, just as the girls were deciding where to go to eat, Natasha felt someone touch her on the shoulder. She spun around to discover Emmanuel, breathless and grinning at her. Encouragingly, he suggested that the girls join Klaus and him for lunch. Natasha spotted Klaus out of the corner of her eye, lagging behind, but walking in their direction. For a moment, Natasha just stared at Emmanuel's handsome, vibrant face, which exuded such fresh optimism. She fixed on his remarkable turquoise eyes, which reflected so much daylight that they bedazzled her and, for a moment, she was lost for words. In the ensuing silence, the intimacy of their mute connection seemed dangerously obvious.

Embarrassed, Natasha blushed and, as soon as Maria caught her eye, she quickly attempted to blink away her discomposure. The moment she looked back at Emmanuel, she saw that his mouth had curled up into a smile of dolphin cuteness and his eyes twinkled, most smugly. Clearly, he found it amusing that his presence had such a noticeable effect on her pale complexion. Natasha glared at him, infuriated by his burgeoning conceit and, as soon as she did so, he was quick to swipe the smile from his face. Questioningly, Natasha then looked into Maria's eyes and she silently urged her to agree to Emmanuel's tempting proposition. Being the sport she was, Maria gave a taciturn nod of consent to her still pink-faced friend. By now, Klaus had joined them and he gave a single nod of acknowledgement to each. Maria threw Klaus a flirtatious sidelong glance.

"Hi Klaus." she purred, seductively, through a demure smile that flashed her large white teeth.

Natasha looked at Maria with new eyes.

"Hi there." she said to Klaus absent-mindedly, while absorbing the ramifications of Maria's apparent interest in him. Well, at least Klaus was single, or so Natasha supposed, for he had not mentioned Kate since Switzerland. At last, Natasha turned back to Emmanuel and replied, casually, "Why not?"

Knowing full well 'why not' all along! Maria then jabbed Natasha in the ribs with her sharp elbow, as she giggled, playfully, and flicked her voluminous brown hair in an impressive curl-cascading sweep. Indeed, Maria had repeated the rib-jab action since Monday, every time she had noticed Emmanuel flirting with Natasha. Natasha suspected that an unsightly bruise was bound to be developing.

Now they were all in accordance, Emmanuel's smile broadened to reveal his sparkling teeth set against his hazelnut tan. This vision looked so pristine and perfect that, combined with his brimming enthusiasm, Emmanuel bore more of a resemblance to a 1950's poster boy advertising toothpaste, than to a modern day investment banker. Indeed, he was so thrilled that his face lit up and his captivating turquoise eyes, suddenly, appeared more tranquil than his native reef-sheltered Caribbean waters. His eyes then drifted down Natasha's face to fix on her, slightly parted, lips and, for a moment, the smooth-talking, unflappable, sophisticated Emmanuel was as lost for words as she had been, only moments before. The group lurched into an awkward silence before Klaus saw fit to fill it.

"So ladies, where would you like us to take you?" Natasha paid him no heed for now she was staring at Emmanuel's kissable mouth. With insistency Klaus spoke again, "Come on girls, what do you fancy?"

As Emmanuel stared at Natasha and as Natasha stared at Emmanuel, all she could think was 'You!' Then suddenly, his gaze was drawn away to fix on something behind her, with a wary curiosity. Intrigued, she turned to discover what had so distracted him. When she saw at whom he was staring, her heart leapt into her mouth and her lustful longings for Emmanuel were obliterated, for there stood a stormy-faced Sebastian. His tall, broad, impeccably attired, imposing physical presence towered above them. The absolute force of the power, wealth and importance he exuded seemed to strike them dumb. All eyes now rested on him in puzzled wonder. With the sheer, shock sight of Sebastian, Emmanuel's extreme beauty and delectable charm was made impotent. Now, Natasha was not just lost for words, she was blissfully lost in ubiquity.

"Please forgive my sudden intrusion, but I'm afraid I need a private word with Miss Flynn, regarding a pressing matter." Sebastian explained with condescending politeness, for the words he used belied the willful manner in which they were spoken. He then smiled and added more amenably, "I'm confident that everything can be cleared up quickly and she will be able to rejoin you, in no time."

Sebastian then shot Emmanuel a fierce look, laden with warning, as he grasped Natasha, proprietorially, by her upper right arm and led her away. Emmanuel was panicked by her enforced departure. Quickly, he took the decision for their dining destination upon himself and shouted after her, assertively, in his delicious accent:

"Hey, Natasha, we'll be at the little sushi bar in the Circle. See you there!"

Blissfully lost in ubiquity aside, Natasha was pricked by flattery, for Emmanuel must have remembered that sushi was her favourite. When she turned to give him an acquiescent nod, she found all of them staring, with strange fascination, after her and the tall man who had taken her away. When Natasha then looked back at Sebastian, he appeared to be very restless. It was as if he was uncomfortable in his own skin, for he kept twitching his limbs, then re-adjusting his shoulders, or stretching out his neck on one side, then the other. Knowing Natasha's eyes were on him, Sebastian darted a censorious look at her.

"If Mr. bloody Bright-Eyes looks at you like that again, I'll fucking fire him!" he muttered under his breath, with jocular vindictiveness.

"Oh Sebastian, you wouldn't!"

He just stared at her with sulky admonishment.

"Come to think of it, if I see you looking at Mr. bloody Bright-Eyes like that again, I'll fucking fire you too!" he then added, in afterthought.

Natasha giggled with glee and then teased:

"My, my, Sebastian, it appears Jealousy, so long a stranger, has recently become close companion..."

"Oh do shut up." he grumbled, affectionately.

Then he flashed his green eyes at her in a fast move, intense enough to act as warning, yet long enough for Natasha to detect his coyness. She just smiled back at him, serenely, for she loved him and the fact that he cared who looked at her, and how.

As they continued to walk, in silence, Natasha began to readjust to the elevated state of consciousness that she experienced when next to him. As she acclimatized to his presence, her thoughts jostled busily in her head and she was becoming increasingly familiar with their course, at such times, viz. 'I know this place. This is where I belong.' Then slowly the noise of thought would recede, entirely, and her heart would start to pump to splitting with a rapturous epiphany, 'This state is more familiar to me than life itself. How I remember it all now: the joy, the love, the laughter, the sheer invincibility. The Source.' Natasha then paused in rhapsody, almost unaware of Sebastian until, suddenly, a stubborn phrase composed itself to flash, garishly, across her consciousness like a surreptitiously planted internet pop-up, 'What an idiot you are to have squandered so much time in misery. How stupid of you, not to have resided HERE before now.' Natasha would be left, momentarily, dumbfounded, for surely that was a jolly good point! Thankfully, however, it took no time for Natasha's Sebastian-induced enlightenment to re-elevate her back to a plateau of certitude thus allowing her to rejoice, 'Well, I am HERE now, and HERE is all there is, and HERE is all there ever was. HERE is where I belong: Home,' before the wisdom of her knowing would, fearlessly, expand to envelop the cosmos, 'HERE is where all manifestations came from, HERE is where all will return and, thank God, HERE is heavenly!' Then, just like each and every time before, when alone for long enough with HIM, thought ceased entirely to herald the arrival of sheer spiritual BLISS!

By now Natasha and Sebastian had left Broadgate Circle, and the curious eyes of her friends, behind. They had passed one of the entrances to Liverpool Street Station, with the imposing rusted sheets of steel outside that compose Richard Serra's sculpture: Fulcrum. They had descended the outdoor steps and then crossed Liverpool Street, before diagonally cutting a right into Finsbury Circus. They then walked through the wrought iron double gates, which led into the elliptical green park found at the heart of it. Impulsively, Sebastian turned around to face her and confessed, in a quiet, but urgent, voice:

"Natasha, I need to see you tonight."

The excitement generated by his statement snapped Natasha from her celestial reverie. Her heart pounded and her tummy transformed into a veritable butterfly garden. Sebastian soon continued, anxiously, "Because of you, mademoiselle, I did not have a wink of sleep last night and I have not been able to do a jot of work all morning. Having fought my discomforting distraction to no avail, I've reluctantly conceded that my only hope of accomplishing anything today, is if I can return to the trading floor, certain that I will have you all to myself this evening."

Natasha's laughter pealed from her, as cheerful as village bell-ringing announcing the impending marriage of a local lad and lass, where the Bell Master is the father of the bride to be.

"Can I see you tonight Natasha? Please?" Sebastian cajoled, insistent.

"I see. The matter was indeed most pressing."

Sebastian stopped dead in his tracks and stared at her in exasperation as he questioned, "Natasha, yes or no?"

Natasha was, suddenly, overwhelmed by an urge to collapse into the warm strength of him and kiss him to death. Fortunately, for the pair of them, she resisted such reckless, not to say criminal, impulse and instead she looked into his wondrous eyes that never ceased to transport her.

"Do you doubt it?" she answered.

Sebastian relief was palpable. The strain in his features drained away, brightness shone from his face and his twitching and fidgeting ceased. Natasha's breast swelled as she realized the urgency of his need for her. She was overjoyed, for not only did he love her, but tonight she would spend time, alone, with him. Peaceful now, Sebastian looked straight ahead and continued to walk, but at a slower pace. In the enveloping calm, strolling side by side, Natasha felt a second urge but, in this instance, it was safe to indulge it; or so she thought, "You know Sebastian, last night, nothing actually happened..."

Sebastian fell into an uneasy silence. Natasha strained her ears, waiting for him to say something. Nothing. All Natasha could hear was the tapping of her heels on tarmac and shrill chirping. Now she had become aware of the birdsong, she noticed the boisterous culprits producing it. Indeed, the little green park was packed with an astonishing quantity of starlings. They were everywhere. Their tiny black, fawn-specked, yellow-beaked heads were jerking around, as their shiny eyes relentlessly searched for signs of danger. They reminded her of the watchful, anxious men on the Debt Floor. How stressful to be always so on guard. Natasha felt exhausted just watching them: birds and traders both. She studied the tweeting things as they dug, destructively, for worms in the sodden brown earth. Then, suddenly, they took fright and, in an instant, they swooped up as one, to perform a spectacular, synchronized, spiralling and snaking display, hypnotically choreographed by chaos. The murmuration of black dots was moving like a single, ever mutating, feathered behemoth, back then forth, thinning then thickening in concentration, soaring up to twirl, only then to plunge back down, before rising high again, all across the cloudy canvas of the autumnal sky. As awe-inspiring as the display was, Sebastian remained stubbornly unresponsive. Natasha looked at him, once again, to find that he was frowning with his lips forced into a thoughtful pout. His silence spurred her to clarify her earlier statement.

"With Miles, last night, nothing happened..."

There was an excruciating pause and the renewed arrival of tension in Sebastian's shoulders.

"I wouldn't call it nothing, precisely, Natasha... but I know you didn't have sex with him if that's what you mean. Even if you wanted to..." he said, finally.

Sebastian glanced sideways at her, with raised eyebrows, as if to observe the effect of his knowing. Immediately, Natasha fell into an unspeakable panic. Involuntarily, all of the scenes from the previous' evening started to flood, vigorously, into her brain constructing a sorry roller deck of incrimination. She felt nauseating discomfort, for she knew Sebastian had free access to this disturbing flow of images. The more Natasha tried to stop

343

her reconjuring of these mental pictures, the more resolute
they became, just like when one is told not to think of
something, it brings to mind the very thing one should not
be thinking about.

As the unsavoury storyboard of 'Miles and Natasha's
Night Out' was mentally laid out between them, frame by
frame, Natasha found herself wince, repeatedly. Miles'
hands, relentlessly, touching her legs on the drive. His tantalizing caresses in the restaurant. His repeated attempts to
breach the boundary set by her hemline. Then, most
shamefully of all, his rare successes at so doing to snatch a
fleeting chance to forage in her underwear, before being
beaten back into chuckling, wet-fingered retreat. Then,
Miles grinning at her, with devilment, as he slowly licked
his fingers while his large brown eyes fixed her with a las-
civious, yet apologetic, stare. Natasha groaned with the
memory of it. Oh, the acute embarrassment of it all. Why
ever had she allowed him such liberties? Why ever had she
brought it up? What a foolish girl to think the whole excursion so innocent, for now, looking through Sebastian's
eyes, she felt like some stupid shallow slut. Then Natasha
remembered that it was Sebastian who had encouraged her
to sleep with his cousin, after all, and she began to wonder.
Maybe it was not the crude scenes that afflicted him most?
Maybe it was the fact that her heart expanded each time
she caught sight of Miles' tenderness? Or maybe it was
because, in every scene, the only constant was her thrilled
laughter? Or could it be due to the fact Miles made her feel
like the most beautiful woman in the world? Or just maybe,
it was their fledgeling friendship that threatened Sebastian
far more than any of their slapstick sexual bravado, and her
titillation from it?"

But hell, what was the point of quibbling over particu-
lars when the full revealing cartoon strip of last night's
antics sat suspended across our lovers' psychic space? Natasha's face was now burning like a winter's fire, stoked by
humiliation and shame. Sebastian, on the other hand, was
ashen and staring at his feet. His brow was fixed in concen-

tration, as if he was struggling to block their telepathic connection. Oh, the horror, the horror, how did he manage to invade her mind so? Could he really know everything that had happened? Then she recalled that the very same thing had happened with Bruno. On one specific occasion, Sebastian may as well have been in the same room, if not the same bloody bed as they. Why was she surprised now? Yet still, she could not understand how Sebastian always knew everything about her, without the telling of it. No wonder he was so disturbed today, for last night must have been sheer hell for him. Ashamed, Natasha gave a heartfelt apology, "I'm sorry Sebastian."

For several paces he did not speak.

"Don't be sorry Natasha. I have no rights over you, I have nothing to offer, or expect from you... I just love you." He said, finally.

Natasha listened to sentiments that she felt should make her heart rejoice, yet she just felt wretched. 'I have nothing to offer you?' That unadorned phrase echoed in her head, more searing with each repetition. Natasha stifled tears and her tummy flipped, for she must have left it behind when she ratcheted down a notch into the dense bog of self-pity with a squelch. 'I have nothing to offer you.' Absorbing the truth of that simple fact, left Natasha to question, helplessly, 'Why am I here, fixated on a man who has "nothing to offer" me? Did growing up without a dad programme me to expect nothing? Am I emotionally wired to exist on the periphery of male affection? Is that the reason I'm so fixated on chasing after "nothing", for that is all I have ever known?' Our heroine's conjecture seemed to have struck a nerve, for she bit her lip in confusion and tears sprang up in her perplexed eyes.

Sebastian's emotions were running high too, for he began to describe his plight in desperate tones, his voice becoming indiscreetly louder with every word, "The thought of you with another man torments me. Last night, I felt physically sick, I was so ravaged by jealousy! Natasha, I couldn't sleep all night, nor concentrate all morning."

Natasha struggled to fight back her hot tears.

"Forgive me, Sebastian, I don't know what came over me. You're the one I love. Last night with Miles, they were just harmless games that got out of hand."

Natasha looked away and she shook her head from side to side, despondently, while trying to fathom her confusing behaviour and tumultuous emotions. Now her tear-filled eyes were darting all over, before she grasped at an explanation, "I think it happened because I'm trying to desensitize myself. I love you, but you're married to someone else. If I don't manage to curb my feelings for you, somehow, how am I going to survive them? My entire happiness hinges on the next time I'm due to see you. It's hellish. Miles just helped to fill the yawning gap that erupts inside of me when you're not there."

Finally, a couple of tears leaked from Natasha's eyes and Sebastian watched them roll down her cheek, with dispassion. Embarrassed, Natasha quickly wiped them away with the back of her fluffy coat cuffs. Snivelling, she tried to make light of her emotion.

"In the circumstances Sebastian, I think the very least you could do is allow me my harmless flirtations with the Miles of this world, without making such a damn fuss about it." She grumbled, then darted a look at him to discover that she had managed to coax a faint smirk. Relieved she repeated, "All the same, I'm sorry to have upset you."

Sebastian stopped, suddenly, and spun to face Natasha, with a wild look in his eye, and suggested, petulantly:

"Don't be sorry Natasha, just stop doing it!"

He then laughed before shrugging his shoulders as if to comment on the simplicity of such a solution, before he began to walk on in silence.

He loved her. She loved him. They would be together tonight, and that was all that mattered. Sebastian and Natasha's impromptu meeting had come to an end, for they had walked all the way around the little park, and now they were presented with the gates through which they had entered. As soon as Broadgate was in sight, Sebastian specified the details of their evening's rendezvous, in a cadence of instruction, not inquiry:

"The car park, five-thirty."

"I'll be there." Natasha assured.

He smiled at her, briefly, before walking away. Natasha's gaze followed his back, as her heart poured an ocean of love after him, for as long as she could see him. Only once he was out of sight, did Natasha make her way to the sushi bar to join her friends. Now she was so full of Sebastian, she did not even feel like flirting with Emmanuel, or eating for that matter.

When Natasha entered the small bar, her friends had been true to their word, for they were there waiting for her. They were sipping on dark brown, steaming bowls of miso soup and, compulsively, sucking off the orange spice, and the little green beans out of, stacks of edamame. One big bowl, at the centre of their table, was half-filled with it, while another contained a growing pile of discarded bean sheaves. They all stared at her, as if they had been itching for this moment. She just smiled at them, before hanging up her coat on the rack by the door. Having picked her way through the crowded restaurant she sat down on the hard, beech bench, next to Emmanuel. The noise was deafening and the table so cramped that her arm and upper thigh could not avoid brushing his. Natasha's expression was one of bovine bliss, and seemed to agitate their suspicions further. No one said a word, but Natasha knew that the question which hovered on their spiced lips was this, 'Who was that man, and what were you doing with him?' Or, if she were to interpret their unspoken inquiry with less generosity, the question would have been a more direct, 'Are you fucking that bloke?' Then Natasha reminded herself that Europeans seemed more sophisticated, regarding such matters, than the English, and she feared she could be doing them a disservice by phrasing it so.

It was clear however, that some explanation was urgently required from her, especially by Emmanuel, for his 'bright-eyes' stared into hers with demanding expectation.

Impatient, he opted for a more tangible means of encouragement than facial expression alone, and he picked up the cream, glazed jug of sake and began to pour Natasha a cup. He continued to stare, fiercely, at her as he did so, and for a touch too long because when he finally paid attention to the task in hand, he only just managed to avoid spilling the strong rice spirit. Emmanuel grunted sulkily at his uncharacteristic incompetence, before he looked back at her with his determination to elicit an explanation, stubbornly intact.

Natasha just avoided his eyes and looked down, to find her little cup full to the brim; the sake's meniscus clinging to its slippery circumference with sheer molecular force. In fact, it was too full to pick up without making the mess Emmanuel had so narrowly avoided. Instead, she just carefully drew the thing towards her, then leant down to its level, to take a long sweet sip of her drink. She then sat upright to relish the peculiarly comforting feeling of the warm alcohol sliding down her throat, then her gullet to finally slip into her stomach. Maria was the one bold enough to say what everyone else was thinking and she inquired, insistently, in her strong Spanish accent, "So?"

Maria then raised an eyebrow and spread her hands open in front of her, as if waiting to catch Natasha's racy revelations. Natasha, on the other hand, just batted her eyelashes, innocently, picked up the laminated menu card and surveyed it, while taking another sip of sake, before looking back at the expectant Maria.

"So what?" she questioned, to elicit a jarring 'BANG' as Emmanuel's heavy brown fist smashed down onto the table, to make Natasha, the shiny black bowls, and the little sake cups jump. What a passionate reaction from a man engaged to be married to someone else! Startled, Natasha just stared at him and repeated with indignation:

"So what?" As if she was genuinely confused by their inference and mounting fury. Natasha's reticence forced Maria to snap.

"Natasha, we are not so curious as to your sushi order!"

Realizing she had overreacted, Maria then sighed as she

cast her gaze around the crowded restaurant, to notice that the clientele had begun to show an intrusive interest in the emotive conversation happening at their table. Wishing to diffuse the situation, she looked at Natasha, again, shrugged her shoulders and then spelt it out.

"Drink some more of your sake Natasha, and then tell us the whole deal with the tall guy. Is he your boyfriend? Are you two together? Are you madly in love?"

Klaus and Emmanuel were studying Natasha's face, in order to gauge her reaction to this direct line of inquiry. Natasha fast concluded that offence was her best, if only, line of defence.

"Don't be ridiculous, he's my boss." she blurted, before drinking the rest of her sake, down in one, and then adding as an aside, "Besides, he's married."

Natasha's eyes then flitted across the animated faces in the restaurant, all, except for the open-mouthed ones at her table. The intelligent, beautiful Emmanuel was crestfallen and he stared straight ahead as if in slow shock before, despondently, he reached for, then downed, his sake. He soon refilled his cup and downed that too. Only then did this man of impeccable (lapsed) manners refill Natasha's, this time, however, he paid full attention to the task in hand, and none to Natasha, as he muttered to himself, in a disapproving growl while shaking his head:

"Natasha is fucking her boss."

At which point Natasha realized that she had been in no danger of doing Europeans a disservice! Emmanuel then looked her straight in the eye, his expression filled with grave disappointment.

"Already." he then added, disdainfully.

The corners of Emmanuel's mouth were pressed down, dejectedly, and his beautiful eyes looked beyond sad as he clinked his little cup, roughly, with Natasha's before downing his third. Natasha looked to Maria, and then Klaus, but she could tell from their demystified expressions, that they had drawn the same conclusion. Emmanuel still looked disproportionately miserable, and his successive intake of sake had turned his smooth, tanned cheeks the colour of desert rose. Natasha spent the rest of the lunch denying the truth, picking at sushi, admiring Emmanuel and drinking sake. Emmanuel spent the rest of the lunch contemplating the truth, munching lots of sushi, sulking with Natasha and downing sake. Maria spent the rest of the lunch giving Natasha disappointed looks, for not confiding in her, interspersed with lots of flirtatious ones to Klaus, in an effort to cheer herself up. Klaus, on the other hand, was the only one who seemed not to care what Natasha was, or was not, doing with the man who had accosted her earlier and what a blessing that was, for it was he who kept the conversation, and the drink, flowing.

Thanks to the sake, it proved to be a wasted afternoon as far as instruction went for all four of them and, thanks to the sake, it was a tipsy Natasha who met Sebastian at the end of it. When Sebastian arrived to meet the addled girl outside the car park, later that day, he looked tired and agitated. Thankfully, it was an unfamiliar car park attendant and Natasha was to be spared the knowing looks and congratulatory smiles from the usual, conclusion jumping chap. Instead, she just kept finding herself silent and smiling, so mutely delighted was she to be spending unexpected time with Sebastian.

Sebastian, however, seemed possessed by a demonic urgency. He gave Natasha a tight smile, and he was very fidgety as they waited for the attendant to bring his car around. It was his new car that nosed its way up the spiralling ramp, spluttering its excess power, to echo its growl throughout the underground car park. As soon the car pulled up in front of them, Sebastian opened Natasha's door for her and then, in a flash, he was in the driver's seat with his foot on the accelerator. The fearsomely powerful engine churned out a vibrating, guttural roar as they sped up the concrete ramp, so quickly that Natasha's guts lurched backwards and took some time to reposition themselves. The sensation was even more dizzy-making than sake! Sebastian's extreme urgency and concentration were unrelenting, and he cut through the thick London traffic with the unforgiving speed, certainty and aggression of a siren-spewing ambulance. Oh, how the car displayed its engineering excellence with each and every one of Sebastian's demanding manoeuvres. His mood was so intense, and the car so powerful, that the combination proved to be most adrenaline-promoting, so much so, that by the time Sebastian had roared to a halt outside Natasha's home, she felt stone cold sober. He parked the car, turned the engine off and then said, intently:

"Upstairs now, I need to hold you."

Natasha sensed his longing and, unquestioningly, she followed his instructions. As soon as they were inside the little bedsit, she turned to shut the door. When she looked back, in the semi-darkness, she found that Sebastian was already getting undressed. His expensive shoes had been kicked off, and lay higgledy-piggledy on the fake marble linoleum floor of her miniscule kitchenette. His midnight blue suit jacket was already draped over the cream sofa, and he was now looking down as he fiddled with the gold buckle on his belt.

It was late October and already dark outside. Meager, yellow street lamplight filtered in through the windows, while a much brighter illumination flooded underneath the gap at the bottom of the front door, to spread across the carpet like a luminous, semi-circular stain, the colour of English mustard. It was this cheerful light that lit Natasha from below, like an inverse demi-halo. She was still wearing her coat as she stood, transfixed, watching Sebastian undress. He stared back at her, his eyes more alive than electricity and his expression still one of distilled concentration. It was as if he was still driving too fast down busy roads, slicing through ambling London traffic. The intensity of his stare cut through Natasha, and she felt her stomach flip and her knees weaken with her want for him. It was not a lustful surge she experienced, but an overwhelming longing. She craved to hold him too, and now.

"Natasha, take off your clothes. Come to bed. I want to

hold you naked next to me: no boundaries."

She nodded in understanding. She turned her back on him, undid the suede belt tie on her coat and then took it off. As she did so, she eased off one of her shoes with the heel of her foot, before repeating the process with the other. Shorter now that she was in stocking feet, Natasha reached up to hook her coat on the peg next to the front door. There was a serene leisure in her movements, almost ceremony, for she knew where she was going, and that place was timeless. There was no need to hurry, now that he was here.

Shirtless, Sebastian was sitting on the end of the bed wearing only his royal blue, boxer shorts while in the process of removing his knee-length, navy blue, finely ribbed, silk socks. When Natasha approached him, he looked up at her with an expression as ecstatically content as that of Buddha. Natasha just stared deeply into his eyes, as she began to undo the wool covered buttons on her fitted, deep magenta jacket before taking it off, completely, and allowing it to drop to the floor.

Our lovers continued to stare at each other, spellbound by the eternal presence that they beheld beyond each other's glistening pupils. Their spiritual energy began to leak and conjoin, to create a single tranquil reservoir of essential love. Sebastian's socks now rested in silk balls at the end of the bed, and Natasha had begun to unbutton her cream silk shirt. The lock of their eyes was never breached and, by the time Natasha stood wearing only her white lace bra and knickers, Sebastian was lying naked on the bed and holding the duvet cover open for her in puffy welcome. Natasha reached behind her back to unhook her bra then, delicately, she picked the straps from her shoulders to remove it, exposing her small, apple-shaped breasts, from the zenith of which protruded neat, rose-tinted, erect nipples. Undistracted by carnal beauty, Sebastian's eyes still locked with hers, as she let her bra fall, silently, to the floor. It landed on top of the little pile of clothes that had materialized to her right. At last, Natasha leaned forward to pull down her knickers, before pushing them aside with her impeccably manicured toes. Naked and exposed, Natasha stood in front of him in the other-worldly semi-darkness.

Sebastian patted the cotton bed sheet by his side, and Natasha obediently crawled towards, and then snuggled up close next to him. He covered them both with the duvet and, like a pair of indistinguishable, wriggling snakes in a tight wicker basket, they wrapped themselves, inextricably, around the warm, silky, softness of each other, mouth on mouth, tongue to tongue, flesh against flesh, mind fused with mind. Their souls resonating, to expand as dramatically as oil splashed on still water, while their writhing bodies melded in perpetual, intoxicating motion. This night, our lovers spent many glorious, private hours, rapturously replenishing mind, body and spirit in euphoria.

CY BLACK

<u>Chapter Twenty-five</u> - Soul Flight

I am no longer just one drop,
I have become the entire Sea.
I speak the language of the heart
where every particle of me,
united, shouts in ecstasy.

Rumi

There was a quick burst of scrunching, as the match-stick's head was scratched down the matchbox's mustard-coloured, strike strip. The phosphorus, obediently, caught light to summon a startled yellow flame, which flared up and jumped about with its potential. Oh, how its eye-catching gyrations boasted its destructive power, having already burnt the red match-head, charcoal black at birth. Natasha cupped the erratic flame with her hand, to protect it from darting draughts, before lighting one of the cream candles, which stood in the blue and white pottery candle-sticks on her mantelpiece. The match was burning shorter and shorter, and she only just managed to light the second candle, before her thumb and forefinger felt the scorching heat of the flame. Natasha blew it out, with urgency, and then discarded the brittle match corpse on the white shelf, to leave a charcoal smudge.

The simple mantelpiece sat above the original fireplace, which had been, sacrilegiously, boxed in, to render the whole thing rather pointless. Natasha took a step back to check the sorry scene, watching the little yellow flames jump up and down, energetically, either side of it, to cast shifting shadows across her cream walls. Her eye then came to rest on the dozen red roses, which stood in a tear-drop-shaped glass vase in the middle of the mantelpiece. She had bought them for herself on Thursday, as she so often did, for fresh flowers never failed to lift her spirits. In the candlelight, the roses looked a deep port red; a shade almost too profound for flowers, unless painted in oil and hanging in some gilded frame in a grand art gallery; or so

354

Natasha supposed. The roses were at their fullest bloom, the petals expanding generously to offer up the height of their gorgeousness to any observer. They were probably less than a day away, from starting to shed their petals, one by one, over several days, like slow-falling confetti, as they would begin to die their measured death.

These roses would never look more beautiful than on this night. Momentarily, Natasha was simply overwhelmed by their ephemeral, Fibonacci structured beauty. Then, to her distaste, she noticed that the water, in which the flowers stood, had become cloudy. That would not do. Not tonight. She went over to pick the vase up, heavy with its liquid cargo, before putting it down next to the kitchen sink. Natasha then took out the roses, one by one, and pulled off any leaves that had become dark green and soggy with decay, before placing the stems, gently, on the draining board. She was careful not to prick herself yet, despite her caution, when she took out the last rose, to pull off a particularly mushy leaf, a hidden thorn managed to catch her middle finger, and a tiny dash of scarlet blood oozed from the break in her skin. Natasha tut-tutted, for it was surprisingly painful. Once she had placed the offending rose on top of the others, she sucked her sore finger. When she took it out and inspected it, all that remained was a tiny red mark, like a pinprick.

Getting straight back to work, she poured the dirty water down the sink, before refilling the vase with fresh. Then she put the flowers back, and placed the vase on top of the mantelpiece, once again. Holding her hands together in front of her, as if in prayer, Natasha took a step back to admire her handywork: perfect and not a petal lost.

She then went to get two champagne flutes, from the little overhead kitchen cupboard, before taking a bottle of chilled Bollinger from the fridge. Natasha soon ripped off the foil and untwisted the wire, before grasping the cork, firmly, in one hand, while swivelling the bottle around with the other, in order to open it with a forlorn pop, for the pop of a champagne cork demands an audience of more than one, if it is to sound cheerful. Having poured herself a glass, Natasha put the bottle back into the fridge, before going to put on a C.D. She knew she was in the mood for classical music, but she was not sure what. As she surveyed her small but eclectic collection, Natasha knew to what she wanted to listen, the minute she spotted it. Of course: Turandot. How fitting: Puccini, Pavarotti and petals! Thrilled with her inspired choice, she became even more excited when she realized just how appropriate it was, for the aria she wished to play was 'Nessun Dorma'. Translation? 'None shall sleep,' and surely that was to be her lot, this night.

It was already approaching midnight, and Natasha had another hour to wait before Sebastian was due to arrive. Indeed, at this very moment, he was driving through the night on his way to her. Rapturous at the mere prospect of his imminent arrival, Natasha put on the C.D. and forwarded it to 'Nessun Dorma'. Oh, how happy was she! Despite the fact that they had spent hours intimately entwined with each other only yesterday evening, when Sebastian had, finally, began to dress himself, in order to set off for his weekend off-site management conference, he had declared that he simply could not bear the idea of not seeing her again until Monday. Indeed, the more he considered it, the more panicked he had become. Natasha remembered, fondly, how his brow had furrowed, in stern concentration, as he had tried to work out a way to dispel his acute discomfort. When he began to do up the buttons on his shirt, his forehead started to clear, more swiftly than the cloudy water had done down the sink, only moments ago, for an inspired idea had presented itself. By the time Sebastian had finished buckling his belt, he was beaming with pride, for he had managed to persuade himself that it would be a brilliant solution if he were to sneak out of his off-site management conference on Saturday night, and drive to Natasha's to spend the small hours with her.

In fact, he calculated confidently that, if he managed to escape unobserved from the hotel by eleven, he should be with Natasha by one o'clock, for there was sure to be no traffic at that time. Of course, he would have to drive back for the scheduled management breakfast-meeting at eight o'clock on the Sunday morning. Once Sebastian had put on his jacket, and straightened his shoulders and tie, he was decided. He would spend Saturday night with Natasha, and then get up at five-thirty on Sunday morning to head straight back for his meeting.

'No problem.' he had grinned. 'In fact that's hardly any earlier than on a normal working day!'

Natasha had reminded him, gently, that on 'a normal working day' he would actually have had some sleep between the hours of eleven at night and six in the morning.

Sebastian had just scolded her, saying that he would be here for 'a good four-and-a-half hours and, surely, she would allow him some sleep during that time!'

Natasha found herself smiling, serenely, as she remembered it. So, that was how it had come to pass that Natasha was drinking at home, alone, late on a Saturday night, waiting for her Love to arrive. As the time approached, increasingly, her soul fluttered with delicious anticipation until she could barely contain herself. The strings and voice of 'Nessun Dorma' had begun. The escalating music blared out, bravely, from the shuddering speakers, pouring Pavarotti's impossible passion into the tiny bedsit, transforming it into a space worthy of the highest drama.

Natasha closed her eyes, tilted her chin towards the heavens and, with bated breath, she caught each, then yearned for the next, excruciatingly elevated pitch. One minute her chest would be swelling with gratitude, the next collapsing with humility, to be so blessed with such exceptional sound. Each instrumental note, and each tone of voice, seemed even more exquisite than the last, and tingles began to course though Natasha's body, building as exponentially as the intensity of the music. Rushes shot down her spine and flared up at the base of our heroine's brain and across her face; not dissimilar to cocaine she thought, briefly, before realizing that the joy that filled her now, was a joy of spirit that no intoxicant could ever simulate, for taking them just affronted soul, to make it flee and be spared the alien, chemically unbalancing, biological mastery. Natasha was standing in front of her stereo, her eyes still closed and her hand touching the centre of her chest, as she listened to the impossibly passionate undulations of Pavarotti's pure tear-engendering tenor. Her body rocked to and fro, and her soul soared. At last, the drama of the final drum roll reverberated through the barrel of Natasha's chest, even more penetrating than Miles' laugh. The aria was over. Natasha's chin dropped, melodramatically, to her chest, as she stood motionless to savour the emotional roller-coaster that she had just ridden. Being of an addictive nature, however, her 'savouring' did not last as long as it might and, in no time, she lurched forward to press the stereo's double arrowed 'back' button, so she could listen to it all over again, and again, and again...

By the time Natasha was at last sated, she had listened to 'Nessun Dorma' more than half-a-dozen times. Having done so, two things occurred to her: one, her neighbours would not be getting any sleep tonight either, if she was not to be more considerate, and two, her champagne must be warm by now. She turned the stereo down, started the C.D. from the beginning, and then put her full glass into the fridge to re-chill, before pouring herself a fresh one. Breathing out a satisfied sigh, Natasha then sat down on the sofa, for all of this waiting was really rather tiring. She checked the clock. It was twelve thirty-five. Sebastian should be here in twenty-five minutes. A thought she found even more exhilarating than 'Nessun Dorma'. She took a long sip of her drink, closed her eyes, and then rested her head back on the sofa while she listened to the music, to be transported into the operatic arena where passions are so powerful that they burst the breasts of the one's they possess, hearts are broken, and bright red blood is spilt.

Natasha was so engrossed in the music, that when the buzzer sounded it made her start. Immediately, she snapped to attention and sat bolt upright. HE was here! She looked at her watch. It was only twelve forty-five. He must have made even better time than he had imagined, or he had managed to get away earlier than planned. She dashed over to pick up the intercom, as butterflies stormed her tummy.

"It's me." Sebastian said, quietly.

"Hello me. Come up." Natasha replied, as her face broke into a brilliant smile.

She buzzed him in, opened the front door, and then leaned, eagerly, over the banister, with one foot in the air as she stared down the stairwell, straining to catch sight of his face. The music was still playing in the background. Calaf had fallen in love with the cruel Turandot, and Liu was in the middle of pleading with him not to risk his life in pursuit of her. At last, Natasha could see Sebastian's face peering up at her and, immediately, their eyes locked. The moment she set eyes on him, she could tell there was something different about him tonight. He was not feverish, nor was he in conquering mode. Instead, he looked resigned, yet managed to exude a contentment of spirit, so seldom attained by mere mortals. Indeed, he almost lolled up the stairs for, as content as he appeared, clearly, he was exhausted. Compassion swelled in Natasha's heart, seeing her Love so fatigued, and all on her account. She wanted to take him by the hand and put him to bed, where she could stroke his brow, and kiss him all over, while he slept to regain his vitality.

When Sebastian, finally, reached the top of the stairs, he smiled at her, crookedly, and his glistening green eyes seemed to glint with sparks of other-worldly illumination. He came to a halt directly in front of her, and dropped a small Louis Vitton overnight bag onto the floor, to give an expensive-leather sounding thud. Natasha was alight with delight, and she flung her arms around his neck and kissed him, repeatedly, on his delectable mouth.

"I love you, I love you, I love you, I love you..."

Neither of them counted the number of times Natasha whispered this truth between kisses but, certainly, it made her obsessive playing of 'Nessun Dorma' look restrained.

Finally, our love-struck heroine paused for breath, and they embraced, tightly, forehead blissfully resting against forehead until Sebastian muttered, matter-of-factly:

"One hour and forty-three minutes."

Natasha beamed and began to chuckle, for how fast must he have driven, so set was he on seeing her.

"Well done baby." she congratulated.

Then she kissed him, gently, all over his soft, but slightly prickly face. Finally, Natasha released him, and then bent down to pick up his bag. She took him by the hand and led him over to the bed, where Sebastian sat down with relief. She put the bag down, before turning her attention back to him, to help him ease off his jacket. Having done so, she hung it up next to the front door, which she then closed, at last, to seal our lovers into a little world of opera, candlelight and kisses.

When Natasha turned to face Sebastian, she found him tugging, roughly, at his tie-knot. He was having difficulty, for his chin was pointing upwards, as he strained his neck in the opposite direction from that in which he pulled. He was struggling, and seemed desperate to be rid of the thing.

"I can't believe I drove all this way, wearing a fucking tie..." Sebastian commented, with exasperation. Then he laughed, helplessly, and explained, "I was in such a hurry to get here, and so worried about being seen creeping out, that I didn't even think to change." He shook his head, in disbelief, as he muttered, "Visiting Swiss fucking management, expecting fucking suits on a Saturday. Can you believe it?"

Sebastian laughed, lightly, at his venting before, unceremoniously, flinging his horribly expensive silk tie to the floor, and then leaning down to unlace his shoes. Natasha picked it up, unknotted it, stroked its silkiness flat between her fingers, and then hung it up neatly with his jacket, before fetching him the full flute of champagne from the fridge, and then topping up her own. By the time she was placing the glasses onto the bedside table, Sebastian was naked and sitting up in bed smiling, happily; all vexation fled. In the candlelight, our lovers drew shadowy figures. The music was still playing, and Natasha sat down next to him, smiling with impossible joy to have him here at last. It was twelve fifty-five and she had him all to herself for more than four hours. Bursting with bliss, she passed him his glass. Sebastian just locked her gaze, and then took her by the wrist to direct her hand back to the bedside table, to put it down. He then leaned forward, with resolve, clasped Natasha by the nape of her neck and pulled her face to his. He stared into her eyes then began to kiss her, slowly, with the tenderness and awareness of an angel. His kisses made Natasha's head lighter than fluffy falling snow, and she sighed with pure longing.

When he released her, she hung in suspension, hankering after his kisses, more desperately than she had for the next exquisite note from Turandot. Sebastian still held her head between his hands, a little back from his face, so he could stare into her pupils with primordial yearning. Drunk with pleasure, and with jolts of joy coursing through her veins, Natasha stared at him with sheer enchantment. She could see herself reflected in the large, watery, blackness of his pupils, which were dilated to capacity with love. Natasha's pale, constant face stared back at her, with the reflection of the distant candle flame appearing to adorn her hair with a pretty, yellow, star-shaped flower, like some Polynesian bride. Sebastian and Natasha were locked now, as they stared beyond their own reflections, deep, deep, deep into the entrancing infinity found within the other's soul, as the frequencies of their spirits combined to resonate with God. Sebastian's face was serious. There were no crooked smiles, nor rants regarding ties. There was just eternal want. Exhaustion, like poverty and terminal illness, had distilled intent. He had no excess energy to spare and whirr around to agitate, froth-up and confuse the deep waters of the mind. Like the sorting of wheat from chaff, the weight of Sebastian's want had settled, unencumbered, at the bottom of his heart, and he expressed it:

"I don't want champagne Natasha. I want you."

A sentiment so simple, so true, so perfect, it was painful. Tears sprang to Natasha's eyes. Her felicity so acute it made her weep. She too, took his noble head between her hands, forever stroking and caressing his soft cool cheeks, then his warm neck as she pulled him ever closer to her. Holding each other so, and still staring into each other's eyes, they kissed again and again and again, with excruciating intimacy. The biological, brain electricity of their minds had reacted, more spectacular than a sparkler touched by flame: scorched. The fires had started.

Sebastian's body tensed with the ferocity of a wildcat, and Natasha mirrored his force with feline precision. Like power locked with like, entangled in the pursuit of love. Clenching each other's head now, they kissed, and kissed and kissed as if to kill. Hair was tangled, flesh caressed and breathing became a crescendo of gasping pants, as tongues delved, fitfully, deeper and deeper, as if to feast on the entrails of the other. Pulses accelerated to racing, eardrums pounded with hot thumping lifeblood, propelled by frantic heartbeats, while beads of glistening sweat began to break, bestowing appetizing salts on satin flesh, to be licked, to be tasted, to be consumed, more compelling than popcorn yet so much more delicious. Sebastian's manhood was as hard, and robust, as tyre rubber and it stirred powerfully beneath the cool cotton covers. Excited, Natasha pushed the duvet from him, to expose the pulsing boldness that coursed beneath. Murmuring sounds of worship, Sebastian tousled through Natasha's thick chestnut waves of hair, the roots of which were already slightly wet behind her neck, with the sweat of her increasing arousal. He gripped her firmly there, to make her head tilt upwards, even more, as he continued to kiss her, insatiably, while relentlessly nudging her body closer and closer towards his, trying to pull her on top of him, still kissing her, ever more forcefully, up and down the side of her neck, as if to bruise the whiteness of her soft, delicate skin with the red-brown-blue marks of love. Sebastian's strong wet tongue, forever licking at the sweet salt that tempted all the way, then teasing her ear lobe with fast flicks, then slow sucks, before finally returning with his now salt-tasting mouth, to drink more deeply from the pleasures to be found in the full, red prettiness of hers.

One of his kisses would last for a dozen, then a dozen would be dispensed in the space of one; the tempo ever altered to interest, to surprise, to entrance. Now his free hand clasped the small of her waist and, with increasing urgency, he shunted her slap against his hard torso. Natasha was drunk with desire, and she rubbed herself against him, light-headed with love, as her hand took his penis and she began to touch and adore it, the infinite variety of her fondling driving Sebastian to distraction, to make him moan wildly with pleasure. His fierce arousal had enlivened him and fearless abandon possessed him. He grasped her buxom bottom and brought her ever closer. He ripped up her dress before plunging his hand down into her knickers to touch her. Oh, how thankfully accessible was she tonight, for Natasha had worn stockings, especially. In a rush of passion, Sebastian penetrated her with his finger, and began to play there, expertly, to prepare her for, and enhance, her forthcoming pleasure.

Natasha knew she was ready. She had always been ready for him. Now Sebastian knew it too. He continued to stroke, plunge and touch her there, her clitoris as hard as a tiny walnut, silkily lubricated with her copious juices. Sebastian slid his agile fingers up and down, up and down, up and down, before he pressed hard on it, as he wiggled his finger around, wildly, as if suffering an electric shock. Then, daringly, he plunged inside her, again, to collect and generate more of her sweet cum, before starting all over again, and again, and again. The pleasure was impossible, almost torturous. Through their kisses, Sebastian moaned and Natasha gasped and yelped, continually. Natasha was panting, almost hyperventilating. She could wait no longer. This zenith of love, and craving of soul, demanded fulfilment. She began to pull off her knickers, Sebastian helping. Finally, she hooked them over her heels, and she was set free. Her pulse was pounding. Her quivering mouth and dancing tongue never left his, as she climbed on top of him. How she throbbed and burned with the need for him to be inside her. Kneeling astride him, Natasha's hand delved down to her own sex, touching the sweet viscous wetness of her vagina to part its engorged lips, while he continued to play inside her. Her eardrums were crowded with the pounding of her own heartbeat, as her speakers spewed the operatic chants of the hungry crowd, baying for the Prince of Persia's blood. Natasha kneeled up high, raising herself, and then she shuffled forward on her knees, until her aching pussy was directly above his hardness. Spreading herself farther apart, as the bloodthirsty rabble cheered wildly for execution, Natasha took his eager erectness firmly in one hand, and then she lined him up below her before, with a powerful thrust of hips, she dropped farther and farther down his thick shaft, sliding, ecstatically, onto him. At last, pelvic bone clashed with pelvic bone. Calmer, now she was filled with HIM, she wrapped her long legs around him, gripping him tightly around his bottom, as she clasped his back with her elegant arms and her vagina clamped itself around his turgid penis, proprietorially. Sitting on, and wrapped around, Sebastian like that, with the length and the throbbing girth of his extreme excitement, conspiring with gravity's downward drag, Natasha was penetrated to capacity. The top of him touched her cervix, but not to hurting. Natasha was as full as she had ever been. They were together. They were joined. They were ONE. Locked together, like this, Sebastian with his strength, and with her collaboration, rocked her up and down, repeatedly, as they continually moaned, ecstatically, and forever caressed, kissed, licked, nibbled and loved; delirious.

Then it happened.

SOUL FLIGHT.

The transporting beauty of kisses, the enticing taste of salt and sex, the warmth of human caresses, the exquisite rewards and spurts of strokes and touch. All mechanics of cock and cunt, OBLITERATED.

SOUL FLIGHT.

A disembodied Natasha drifts in the black Void of space: floating, sublime, timeless, matterless; space-time continuum breached. Just Super Consciousness left: back to the beginning, back to the 'Word'. Awestruck, without eyes, Consciousness watched the colourful trail-blaze of 'Natasha's' legacy human emotions as it accelerates away, to abandon them. All Consciousness did was observe, impartially, the spectrum of colours splashed on the infinite blackness of Void, discrete, but joined, clumps of light: red, orange, yellow, green, blue, indigo, violet. A discarded light-artist's palette of, unbalanced in quantity, but equally vivid, hues.

The splinter of Super Consciousness that the erstwhile 'Natasha' had become, was omniscient, omnipresent and omnipotent. It knew the multi-coloured light splurges that it observed, to be light-energy representations, of every feeling and emotion to which our heroine's heart had ever clung. It also knew that there was no possession of such, just processing of. This was just the pictorial, visible-light energy vibration of 'Natasha's' sorry heart's flux of suffering, confusion, pain and imbalance. Consciousness also knew, though it was just 'Word' (well a stream of them, in fact) in 'Void', that it was moving with extreme velocity: very quickly and away from Earth. If all light travels at the same speed (186,282 miles per second) and Consciousness was leaving enormous clumps of it behind, then how bloody fast was Consciousness travelling, and where?

Impassively, staring at the colourful-swirls of the erstwhile 'Natasha's' unprocessed human-energy reduction, Consciousness, suddenly, flipped into panic. Consciousness knew, instinctively, 'Natasha's' work was not yet done. It must return to reinhabit that abandoned, sentient vessel. The nano-second Consciousness willed return, instantaneously, (swirls of rainbow-colours of light subsumed on the way) Natasha was back in her bedroom with arms, legs and self wrapped around HIM. Natasha's startled eyes were wide open, and her ears splitting with the extreme shock of her own scream as she climaxed:

AAAHHHHHHHHH!!!

Well, that was certainly worth coming back for!

When the paralysing heights of the waves of orgasm had swept over our lovers, they found themselves wet with sweat from head to toe. Natasha's most intimate body part continued to convulse in violent spasms around Sebastian's cock, as she shuddered with the intense aftershocks of her mind-blowing experience. Still engulfed in, a now softer, ecstasy, Natasha closed her eyes as they collapsed into each other's arms embracing, tightly, in a sweat-sealed clinch. She rested her head in the hollow between his shoulder and his neck, her mouth open, slightly, so that her tongue could taste the salt of him. Both were overwhelmed and whimpering with exhaustion. With a warm flush, the milky, glistening fluid of their love began to dribble from Natasha's cunt, to make wet and warm the crevices of crotch. They stayed clamped in each other's arms for hours. Their sighs of longing lingering to mingle into one breath, their loving hearts pouring away, into a reservoir of one love, and their yearning spirits spiralling high to find a place called Peace.

When Natasha was at last ready to let go, she opened her eyes to the darkness of her room. The candles had burnt down to stumps, the bubbles in the champagne had waned and the opera was finished. The only light that remained was the meagre green neon glow coming from her alarm clock. It was three thirty-six a.m. Sebastian had to wake up in less than two hours time.

Chapter Twenty-six - A cry for help

In love, ask for madness
A life abandoned and a mind lost
Ask for dangerous adventures
In deserts filled with blood and fire.

Rumi

It was Friday evening, and Sebastian and Natasha had spent every lunch-time and evening together since last Saturday. Well, every evening until he had to go home to his wife and family. A deadline that proved to be most malleable, for each night he seemed to be leaving Natasha with greater and greater reluctance, at a later and later hour. Certainly, he had not seen his children all week but, then of course, that was usual. Our lovers had, feverishly, snatched every moment possible that they could spend together, breathlessly dashing off to secret get-togethers for lunch in discreet City restaurants, to then escape the City, entirely, after work and ensconce themselves in salubrious, deserted bars or, instead, in Natasha's home for hours and hours.

Their meetings had been easier to pull off this week for, still, Natasha had been spending much of her time in the bank's lecture rooms with the other graduates so, thankfully, their inseparableness had gone unobserved by the boys on the trading floor. Of course, Maria and Emmanuel raised their eyebrows, every time Natasha was so eager to disappear alone at lunch-time, or after work. They remembered how keen she had been in Switzerland to hang out and have drinks with them. In fact, their newfound, initially fun, friend was turning out to be rather a bore.

Natasha could sense their sullen disappointment with her. Maria had even stopped jabbing her in the ribs but, then again, Emmanuel had stopped showering his bright turquoise-eyed attention on her. Instead, now when the gorgeous Frenchman was caught contemplating Natasha, he was usually to be found pouting rather sullenly.

Well not to worry, for Natasha was too in love with

367

Sebastian to dwell on Emmanuel any more. Besides, her European friends had already drawn their own (accurate) conclusions about where she disappeared to twice a day. In any case, their silent disapproval could not interfere with her career, for Natasha knew she would never work, directly, with any of them as they were destined to trot off to different departments across different geographical locations, now that the F.S.A. exams were over. It was true that a couple of the English graduates would end up on the Debt Floor, but she had not bonded with them in the same way, so they cared not where she went nor with whom. No, she was safe, for now, to discreetly pursue her passion, and her all consuming passion was HIM.

Since that remarkable Saturday night's soul flight, when apart from Sebastian, Natasha was in considerable torment. All day long, when not with him, she suffered an unpleasant low-level nausea, and a restlessness of spirit that was so excruciating it made her fidget and squirm, as if she had any hope of escaping the gruesome gnawing at her innards. So distracted was she, that she genuinely struggled to memorize all of the information necessary for her exams, sorely aggravated by the fact that the knowledge she must acquire was dryer and more condensed than vacuum packed, powdered milk past its sell-by date. Thankfully, despite the lunacy of love, Natasha did manage to pass for, only today, had she received the good news. At least Freddie would condescend to allow her back onto the trading floor, but, then of course, now that she was fully qualified, the real pressure had only just begun.

Well, not yet at least, for tonight Sebastian had taken her out to dinner, to celebrate. They were at his private members club in Mayfair, once again, but this time they had managed to make it as far as the intimate basement dining-room. It was only seven o'clock and the lighting was low-level, predominantly provided by small copper oil lamps at the centre of each table. The advantage of dining so early was the fact that there were no other diners present, as was so often the case when with Sebastian. It was as if the luxurious facilities of London existed to serve our Lovers alone. Sebastian was studying his menu card, while Natasha cast her gaze around the plush room, with interest, as she greedily sipped her Cristal champagne. Well, they were celebrating, after all. Indeed, Natasha was looking forward to sampling the food from this rather interesting menu. She had already decided upon the lavender and lime scallops, in a champagne reduction, for how delicious did that sound? She took another sip of her exquisite drink, before she broke into a smirk, as she recalled the happy reason why they had not managed to eat here the last time. Natasha then realized that the visit had occurred only two weeks ago! She could not believe it. Surely that could not be the case, for absolutely everything had changed. Now it felt as if their psychic fields had merged entirely for, increasingly, their thoughts indiscriminately spilled into each other's minds. When close together, that familiar gravitational pull that sought to join them physically, seemed to be getting more and more powerful. When they embraced to commune, the motion of time constantly played its tricks, as if when together they stepped outside of it. It was only when their combined Super Consciousness returned to awareness of the external world, that they realized just how long they had been absent. Indeed, the Universe itself seemed to have begun to share its miraculous secrets with her. This was a brand-new and brilliantly blissful reality! Except, of course, for the times when they were not together. Then it was sheer hell on earth.

If Natasha's extreme love had sorely compromised her concentration, for the last two weeks, this evening Sebastian's symptoms appeared even more acute. Still, he had not chosen what he wanted to eat and, though they were supposed to be celebrating, Sebastian was looking befuddled and had not touched his champagne. Indeed, he seemed to be very ill at ease. He was possessed with that demonic look, he sometimes got, as if he were in perplexed shock to discover that he was him, living the life in which he found himself. For all of her happiness, Natasha eyed him with concern, as she reminded herself how much harder everything must be for him. She knew how she felt now that he was in her life and, being single, she was free to dwell on the ecstasy he induced in her, all day, and all night. Sebastian, on the other hand, had to return to his wife and family, following every single one of their encounters, to act as if nothing utterly extraordinary had just happened.

Natasha's breast swelled with empathy for the man she loved and, suddenly, feeling sorry for him, she reached across the table to take his hand and gave it a reassuring squeeze. Though Natasha's action had been intended to comfort, her gentle touch of kindness prompted a desperately doleful sigh and then, out of the blue, Sebastian's eyes sprang fat tears, which he managed not to shed, as he began to confess his unspeakable wretchedness.

"Natasha... my whole life is a lie." before he slumped forward to bury his head in his hands.

Natasha sat bolt upright with alertness. She leaned ever closer towards him, as she took his hands in hers. She squeezed both of them, firmly, to coax eye contact. Tentatively, he looked up, and she stared into his traumatized soul. She gripped his hands, ever more tightly, silently encouraging him to continue. He did so with abject dejection.

"Oh Natasha, all I want in this world is to be with you. If I weren't married already, I would have married you by now for, having met you, it is as if I can't survive without you. I've been a walking corpse going through the motions of my life for years, and then along you came, to wake me up to a nightmare..."

Sebastian's breathing was hoarse, as he struggled to maintain his self-control. Impulsively, he extracted his hands from hers, and sat back in his chair to exclaim:

"I can't stand all the lies, Natasha. I can't stand all the lies. I have to face Itzy every night. I have to look her in the eyes and pretend everything is OK..." A face could not look more forlorn than Sebastian's did, as he continued, "Living like this is ripping me apart. I can't carry on like this Natasha. I just can't do it any more..."

Sebastian was shaking his head from side to side, as if unable to believe the predicament he described was his own. With his head still shaking, he gave a reflective shrug and held his hands wide open as he explained:

"Isabel is a beautiful person, really she is. I am so very fond of her. Ever since university she has been my rock. I don't know how I would have survived without her, really I don't, but Natasha, I never really loved her, not like this..." Sebastian motioned between them, as was his habit, to ensure she was in no doubt. He then began to shake his head again, but this time more violently, "I never believed this was even possible." He then grabbed Natasha by the hand and, frowning, he muttered hopelessly, "Natasha, the apparently golden life I am living, is one big fat lie."

A tear finally escaped and swiftly ran its course down Sebastian's chiselled cheek. In an instant, he snatched his hand away, to mop up the embarrassing evidence. Crying out for help, his bright-eyes christened with the product of this truth, Sebastian looked at Natasha, imploringly, and begged, "Natasha... tell me what to do. Please... Natasha, tell me what to do?"

Sebastian's face was as open and spellbinding as a double rainbow, as he stared into Natasha's eyes, with great expectation. He had exposed the extent of his emotional vulnerability and, patiently, he waited for his Love to instruct him on the solution. The imponderable weight of Sebastian's request slowly sliced through Natasha's guts, and its lethal sharpness came to settle, excruciatingly, at the pit of her being. It was Natasha's turn to be in shock. She slumped back into her chair with a thud. She was dumbfounded. Still, Sebastian looked, urgently, at her, with glistening, hopeful eyes.

Suddenly, Natasha felt sick. She knew this was her moment. She knew that Fate now teased her, mercilessly, with this 'opportunity'. Natasha could get what she wanted. Natasha could get HIM. This was her chance and, if she were to take it, she must take it now. If she played it well, she knew she could extract him, gingerly, from his marriage. She could have HIM all for herself. The gates of heaven stood open before her and beaconed enticingly.

Sebastian still stared at her, lost, confused and utterly vulnerable. The man she celebrated more than the living do dawn, the man she craved more than a beached, spluttering fish craves water, the man she loved more than life itself, this was her chance to have him. With soft feminine wiles, with lowered, fluttering lashes, with suggestive, convincing whispers, with cuddles as soothing as swaddling, and kisses sweeter than syrup, ah yes, with the full arsenal of self-interested female persuasion at her disposal, Natasha knew she could get him.

Images of little blonde fluffy heads, poking out of pristine, white, pink patterned, cotton duvets came to haunt her. Natasha's heart sank in her breast and she, suddenly, felt emptier than outer space, for as much as she wanted HIM, she could not take him on these terms. To cajole a floundering man from his children, was a thing Natasha could never do. The sharp barbs of Sebastian's request tore, painfully, at the soft, deep purple, pumping muscle of her sunken heart, and its agony reminded Natasha from where she must source her reply.

A great grief flushed over our heroine, for she knew she could do no other thing than, passively, allow such opportunity to flow right past her. What is more, she feared that Sebastian may well be washed away forever, by her so doing. With this apocalyptic realization, Natasha's eyes sprang the hottest, wettest tears they had ever shed, for how she dreaded that her resolve not to extract Sebastian, for herself, at this moment, would invite the most horrendous calamity imaginable: the loss of HIM.

Yet as much as she wanted him, in the stillness of her soul, Natasha knew how cursed would be the woman prepared to strike such enticing bargain with the spiteful gods. With tears streaming down her face, a miserable Natasha finally found the strength to yelp reply.

"Oh Sebastian, how can you ask such a thing of me?"

Aware of the sorry sight that she must make, she reached for her napkin and began to dab her face. With trembling, blood engorged lips she cried, "How can I tell you what to do?" Then Natasha buried her face into the napkin, in an attempt to muffle her grief stricken moans. Following an interminable time, her breath became more regular and, slowly, she managed to collect herself. She stared, hopelessly, into space as she began to flirt with this rejected future, "Even if I did, even if I did, how could I live with myself? If I used my influence to deprive your children of their father, how could I live with myself?" Another pathetic sob escaped from the wretched girl as she questioned, passionately, "And you, how could you bear to be with a woman who could do such a thing?"

Sebastian stared at her, his eyes as black as coal. He looked more desolate than an abandoned Alberta tar sands exploitation site. His expression screamed a single question: why had she not rescued him from his terrible predicament? Oh, how Natasha had to make him understand. In a voice laced with desperation she sought to explain.

"Sebastian, this is the hardest decision of your life. You will never make another choice that has such profound consequences. You cannot ask someone else to assume responsibility for it. Indeed, you must never allow someone else to do so."

With fresh tears spilling, Natasha's mind raced, violently, to justify her position. Besides, if she did what he wished, they were sure to be doomed anyway. It would only postpone the inevitable pain. Vehemently, Natasha continued to elaborate.

"And what if, what if I were to tell you what to do? What if I told you, 'You must leave Isabel now, for not doing so is just cruel and dishonest?'"

Natasha heard the frustrated rage in her voice as she spoke. Oh, how furious was she with him for dangling this temptation in front of her, like Eden's enticing apple before Eve. How dare he, when surely he knew her character forbade her to pluck it? Yet still, she could barely believe that she was not sinking her brilliant teeth into such delicious, crunchy flesh, to relish its forbidden flavours, at this very moment. Confused, Natasha continued to career down Sebastian's proffered path, determined to prove its course would lead only to devastation and despair.

"What if I demanded that you call Itzy up, at this very moment? Make you tell her you've been in love with me for three months and in my bed for the last two weeks. Make you tell Itzy that you're leaving her because you have to be with me." Exhausted, Natasha slumped back into her chair, as she asked with haunting softness, "What then Sebastian? What then?"

Sebastian's head had dropped into his hands, with his fingers spread across his brow, as if to cradle his torment. His eyes were screwed shut, tightly, in a vain attempt to block Natasha out. He had sought help not punishment. He was too emotionally worn out to cope with this tirade. Natasha's vision though, was too blurred by her tears to heed his agony, and her mind too consumed with hurtling down its terrible trajectory: "What then?"

Natasha's tears had stopped flowing, at last, though her face was still washed and glistening with their mascara-blackened wetness. Her voice had become so fragile now, that it was not far beyond breath, and her question hung between them with macabre wondering.

Slowly Natasha's brow began to clear with sweet serenity and her bright, wondrous eyes opened wide with tentative hope. She began to emit a surreal light as she, momentarily, dared to dream of their unhindered togetherness. The light that shone from her became brighter and brighter, as she became, increasingly, captivated by her happy imaginings. Her voice was soft and sonorous as she began to paint Sebastian the picture of their blissful beginning, "We run off into the glorious, peach-red richness of the sunset, gambolling hand in hand. We spend every waking hour intoxicated with each other's kisses, buoyed beyond belief by the beauty we find in each other's being, having set up house, like all of the other carefree lovers on the planet."

Then, as Natasha searched Sebastian's eyes, that had now opened to her, her face became disfigured with her pain for, she knew, it was only a matter of time before the canvas of that beatific picture, would be torn to shreds by the writhing suffering of abandoned wife and children, unable to contain their cries of torment.

Sebastian still held his head in his hands, his eyes peering at her from between the lattice of his fingers, more penetrating than darts. His face was dark as night and his unfathomable pupils seemed to plunge despair. He listened, transfixed, while she started to deconstruct their imagined domestic bliss. With every word she spoke, the light in her face began to dim, until it became dark enough to match his.

"Yet, it wouldn't be that simple for us would it Sebastian? That would just be the blissful beginning, a brief interlude before the savage realization dawned: our happiness was built on the gruesome foundation of the suffering of your infant flesh and blood."

Sebastian winced with each word she spoke. He screwed his eyes shut, tightly, again, and he began to massage his troubled brow to try to squeeze away its pain. Natasha continued, more to herself than to the tormented Sebastian, so determined was she to vindicate her decision, not to get him this way.

"First comes Isabel's denial, then her fury, then her grief. Worse still, all the tears and sorrow of your children. Then the guilt Sebastian, so much guilt. How could we ever live happily with so much bloody guilt?" She paused as she considered, impassively, "And how long would it take Sebastian, how long would it take before you began to blame me for being the cause of all the emotional carnage in your erstwhile family?"

Sebastian was slumped over now. His head resting, heavily, on one hand, while the other arm lay, lifelessly, across the table. His eyes were still closed. Natasha continued with a tragic shrug as she questioned, flatly:

"What do your little daughters care for your 'true' Love? One minute you were there, and you were theirs. The next, you were gone, and you were not. That's all a child knows. Then their little hearts begin to crack, as they wildly search the vast, abyss left by your absence; all on their own."

Natasha's voice began to singsong with sickly-sweetness as she mimicked the mutterings of miniature, emotionally muddled minds:

"Daddy did not love us enough to stay. There must be something wrong with us. What's wrong with us? Why are all those other daughters with live-at-home daddies, so much more lovable than we?"

She broke off, closed her eyes and her hand shot flat across her mouth, to muffle the unearthly wheezing noise of her mounting hysteria, before she grabbed the napkin from her lap and buried her grief-stricken face into it. Natasha's chest was juddering, violently, as a torrential surge of legacy grief swelled up inside her, and threatened to torrent forth: for she had only just recognized these sentiments to be the very ones that had haunted her for the interminable expanse of her childhood. Unhinged and gasping, she struggled to control her breathing. She sucked in the air, with raspy breaths, trying to force each lungful deeper and deeper, in an attempt to regain her self-composure. Overwrought, with trembling hands and quivering lips, Natasha tried to clear up the mess across her face, as she dabbed away the mascara-stained tears that continued to streak down her reddened cheeks, methodically. Soon enough, the napkin was sodden with wet blackness, before Natasha found the self-control to continue, in tones flatter than putrid cider.

"And believe me, Sebastian, your little girls would spend the rest of their lives, wondering why they were not quite lovable enough for daddy to stay."

While our heroine had been losing her self-possession, Sebastian had managed to reconstruct his; with a new awareness. For the first time, he had reached out to Natasha for help, and she had not given it. He looked her in the eye now, solemn, but square.

"I cannot tell you what to do Sebastian." she said, definitively. "You must be strong and find your own way. The man who is capable of that, is a man I can love forever."

Sebastian and Natasha stared, long and hard, at one another in acknowledgement. There was no easy way forward from here, for either of them.

Then, with the immediacy of a lightning bolt, a nervous waiter sprang up next to them and, just as with lightning, there was a time-lag between the seeing and the hearing of the thing, for he just hovered there, awkwardly, uncertain where to look, or what to say. The poor chap must have witnessed the whole sorry spectacle from the sidelines, waiting for a suitable moment to approach these embarrassingly emotional customers. He was a handsome youth, though a little too slight ever to become an impressive male. It took no time for him to begin to irritate the pair of them, as he grinned, inanely, at the melancholy Sebastian. The waiter deliberately avoided eye contact with Natasha, and she assumed he did not wish to humiliate her by staring at her tear-streaked complexion. Touched, the fragile girl felt a rush of gratitude for his sensitivity. At last, he was bold enough to inquire after Sebastian's order, to then hold a fixed smile. Sebastian shot him a look, colder than an aristocratic mother's heart, and stated, "Just the bill."

The waiter was crestfallen. Not only were they still the only people in the place, but after all of that lurking in the background he had had to contend with, and now this? Clearly, he found our lovers' behaviour to be beyond galling, for he almost twitched with irritation, before giving a curt flick of his head and spinning on his heels to strut away. When Natasha noticed his wince, she concluded that it had not been his delicacy that had prompted him to turn from her, but merely his sexual preference! Oh, when would the silly girl ever learn to stop attributing sensitivities to people whom simply did not possess them?

In a flash, he was back to pass a small black leather folder to Sebastian, with the bill inside. Sebastian did not bother to check it. He just pressed a black credit card onto the white tablecloth. Still sporting a pout, the waiter disappeared with the card, only to return, quickly, with a machine. The bill was paid and Sebastian and Natasha stood to leave, with hearts and limbs as heavy as a defeated boxer's who'd just fought too many bloody rounds. He put his arm around her shoulder.

"Let's go back to your place. No more talking." Sebastian suggested, softly.

She gave a single nod as her guts, spontaneously, convulsed. Our lovers left, leaving behind an opportunity for togetherness, a half-filled bottle of exceptional champagne, a sulky waiter, and a mascara-stained napkin perched on the edge of an almost untouched table. It seemed that Sebastian and Natasha were destined never to dine in this rather charming establishment, for each attempt to date had been sabotaged by lust, or trauma.

Chapter Twenty-seven - This has to stop

Do not leave me,
hide in my heart like a secret,
wind around my head like a turban
"I come and go as I please,"
you say, "swift as a heartbeat."
You can tease me as much as you like
but never leave me.

Rumi

Natasha put all her weight behind her shoulder to push open the heavy glass door that led onto the Debt Floor. She was so tired and bleary-eyed that she could not stop blinking, while her eyes still felt sore and dehydrated from her sleepless, and tearful, nights over the weekend. As she walked towards her desk, she was puzzled to hear loud, slow, rhythmical clapping. Indeed, until noticing this sound, Natasha realized that she had not been cognizant of her surroundings at all. She deduced she must have been on autopilot for her entire commute to work. In fact, she even was surprised to discover that she held a pink F.T. in her hand. Intrigued as to the source of the clapping, Natasha quickly looked in the direction it was coming from. She was most perplexed to discover Freddie standing at his desk, with his penetrating blue eyes set on her, while he continued to clap, robustly, with his large dry hands. He looked preposterously pleased, and he was grinning from chubby cheek to chubby cheek like a chipmunk. She stared at him, questioningly, and cocked her head to one side, to prompt Freddie to growl a compliment:

"Well done my girl, good on ya." Natasha continued to look quizzical and, impatiently, Freddie clarified, "You passed girl, you passed." before he mumbled in explanation, "Seb told us."

Finally, the apparently slow-witted Natasha understood, and she gave him a thankful smile. Having stopped clapping, Freddie stuck his elbows out and hooked his thumbs

379

into his belt keepers, to assume a posture that only drew attention to the fact that the front of his trousers buckled beneath the strain of supporting his beer belly, for it protruded from his stockiness with stubborn pertness. Freddie's shoulders then jiggled up and down as he chuckled, avariciously:

"You can start making the Desk some fuckin' cash na, Na-ta-sha, 'bout bloody time!" Freddie chuckled some more, so tickled was he with the prospect. Freddie's cheeks then puffed out like an ugly, deep sea fish, as he emptied his lungs of breath, in a gust of great force, before his brow contorted in concentration as he began to calculate, "Wos i' bin then girl, wos i' bin? Free munfs?"

Natasha then titled her head to the other side as she, once again, tried to work out what he was talking about, before she managed to decipher the meaning of his Essex tongue.

"That's about right Freddie, coming up to three months."

"Na le' me tell ya how long it's bin girl, too bloody long tha's wo'…"

Followed by more chuckling, shoulder jiggling and tummy juddering. Natasha grinned back at him, happily, for she knew he meant well.

"Thank you Freddie, I appreciate it." she said, before doubt began to creep across her face, and she added, "I think…"

He laughed, raucously, and then smirked at her in challenge, as he growled:

"Gizzus a trade by the end of next week Tasha, go on, I dare ya."

"I'll do my best." Natasha ventured, doubtfully.

At last, Freddie had finished with his bit of Monday morning fun and, promptly, he turned his back on her.

"Mornin' meetin' in ten." he mumbled, almost to himself. Then he sat down and began to scan his screens as, feverishly, he scrawled down some numerical notes.

Freddie chaired the meeting that morning, for Sebastian

was nowhere to be seen. The very first thing he did was to embrace Natasha as a fully qualified member of the team for, as soon as she had passed her F.S.A. exams, Sebastian had offered her a permanent position on the Desk, which she had, already, accepted. Freddie's enthusiasm was infectious, and Natasha started to feel thoroughly proud of herself. Her cosy feeling of appreciation and worth did not last long, however, for Freddie was quick to announce Natasha's expected contribution to the bottom line: one-and-a-half million dollars worth of sales credits. The consequent pumping of Natasha's heart was not much reduced, when Freddie explained that he did not expect a lot from her this side of Christmas.

"We all know 're-lation-ships' take a li'ul time... but given tha', one-and-a-half bucks is wo' we expect Miss Flynn to produce in her first year, cu' off next Christmas. Go for it Na-tash-a and good luck." Then he chuckled, "Better lucky than clever girl, better lucky than clever!"

Once he was done, Freddie bestowed a genuinely well-meaning grin on Natasha and, for the first time since arriving on the Desk, the other traders and sales people in Sebastian's team actually seemed to take note of her. Their unfamiliar attention was intense. Natasha could almost detect their grey matter ticking furiously, as they computed the probability of her achieving her sales target. It was safe to say, Natasha was struggling to do the same.

Following the meeting, Natasha spent the rest of the morning working through dormant client lists as she continued to assemble likely prospects to actively cover, now that she was primed and qualified to get on with the job for which she had been hired. She did not set eyes on Sebastian all morning until, at eleven fifty-two a.m. out of nowhere, the Bloomberg started to flash 'Butler' in bright orange at the top right hand corner of the screen. Instantaneously, Natasha accessed the message to read:

'Lunch 12 Pezzoli's'

In a flash, she swivelled around in her chair, making her hair swirl out, luxuriously, before swinging back to whip her in the face, only to find that Sebastian was not at his desk. He must be somewhere else in the bank with access to a Bloomberg terminal. In a heartbeat, she had typed and sent her reply: 'Done.'

It was, already, eleven fifty-three and she had to run. Natasha dug her handbag out from under her desk, and then slinked down the corridor, between the backs of the salesmen's and traders' chairs, hoping against hope to leave unobserved: not a chance.

"Done your first trade then 'av ya?" Freddie grumbled, disapprovingly, as she passed behind him.

Natasha ignored him and, with the urgency of fleeing rats scurrying across vibrating Underground tube tracks, she scampered off, guiltily, to get her coat and go and meet Sebastian. Unfortunately, she was not quick enough to be spared a further guttural grunt of disgust from Sebastian's loyal Head Trader.

When a panting Natasha burst in through the revolving doors of the large Italian basement restaurant, her eyes, miraculously, fixed directly on HIM. He was sitting facing the door, halfway down the room, in the middle of the several rows of tables, which were all covered in striking red and white checked tablecloths. The whole scene conjured visions of first aid boxes in Natasha's mind. It would not take long for our, sporadically clairvoyant, heroine to discover why that might have been the case. With eyes perpetually locked with his, wordlessly Natasha handed her coat to the hostess as she glided towards him. By the time the breathless girl had arrived at the table, an attentive waiter was beaming at her, and holding out a chair.

As soon as Natasha sat down, she could sense that something was horribly wrong, for Sebastian did not smile. His face had an unhealthy grey pallor, and his eyes were jet-black hollows. Instantly, evil foreboding flushed into her system to make Natasha feel nauseous. Even though he reached to clasp both of her hands, and his knees were firmly pressed up against hers under the table, she was becoming increasingly panic-stricken. Her mind started to scan for an excuse to explain her discomfort. She must be feeling sick because she was exhausted, for she had hardly slept all weekend. Feeling restless, Natasha tried to take her hand from his, to get one of the packets of bread sticks from the vase at the centre of the table, but Sebastian only tightened his grip. Only when she gave up on that idea, did he relax. His eyes bored into hers with intent and Natasha was, spontaneously, swept away by their inevitable conjoining. She was just beginning to recover herself when, in the voice of a conspiring child, Sebastian blurted out, disturbingly, as he glared at her with bloodshot eyes that bulged like a pair of golf-balls:

"Wouldn't it be terrible if Isabel died."

"Sebastian, how can you say such a thing?" Natasha gasped, horrified.

He just narrowed his eyes, as they continued to bore into her soul, to make it shudder.

"Don't judge me Natasha, just look at the state I'm in." Intrepidly, Sebastian let go of her hands to hold his up in front of her, in the manner of a zombie. Both of them were shaking, shockingly. Natasha's mouth fell open at this alarming phenomenon to prompt Sebastian to jest sardonically, "And, no, I don't have an appalling hangover, or the initial symptoms of some catastrophic sickness of the central nervous system." Still staring, at his own trembling, with strange fascination, he declared with dread, "Look Natasha, this is what you've reduced me to." Then he pushed his hands closer to her and repeated, with alarm, "Natasha, what are you doing to me?" before he snatched them away, to drop his long arms down by his sides and shake them out in an effort to stem the trembling.

Sebastian then lifted his chin, to suck in a deep draught of air through his nostrils, as ferociously as he had snorted cocaine in her bedsit. His eyes then began to rove restlessly around the room, for it was fast filling up with the deafening noise and gaudy bustle of a typical City lunch-time, in a highly popular restaurant haunt. More and more dark-suited businessmen began to pull up chairs around the cheery, checked tablecloths to soon pack the restaurant to capacity.

"Is it safe to be here? Won't someone see us?" Natasha inquired, warily.

Sebastian cast his eyes up to heaven and then gasped, despondently, "I don't even care any more, Natasha. I don't even care."

Natasha was increasingly concerned by his behaviour, and she clasped her hands together in front of her as she stared into his distressed eyes and probed, gently:

"Baby, what are we going to do?"

Sebastian glared at her with chronic desperation. His whole upper body was shivering now and even his teeth (imperceptible to all but her) were chattering, minutely. Lost for words, Natasha took a packet of bread sticks, ripped it open, and then offered him one, before she began, compulsively, to munch her own. As soon as she had finished the first, she started to gnaw on the next, her mind as active as her jaws. Sebastian's bread stick just broke in his hand and he discarded the fragments and crusty crumbs on the tablecloth, before flicking the mound of debris to the floor. Then he gripped the table's edge, to steady his shaking, as he spoke:

"Natasha, I cannot carry on like this. I am as close to breaking-point as I want to get." he said, with gravitas. Then his eyes dived into her core as he declared with grisly resolve, "This has to stop, Natasha. As much as I love you, this has to stop. I must fight this love to the death."

Natasha stopped munching, immediately. Her mouth became as dry as desert sands. Her throat became so constricted by terror that she could barely breathe. Sebastian's announcement had simply garrotted her. She reached for the thick-bottomed glass tumbler of still water, in front of her, and took a long gulp, before putting it back down and meeting his dark determined eyes.

Thoughts tumbled through her mind, as she tried to persuade herself that this could not be the new TRUTH. Sebastian could not really mean what he was saying for, if he did, the consequences were far too atrocious even to be comprehensible to her. Her brain sped on. 'Sebastian is not himself. All he needs is some sleep. Once he has slept properly, he will think more clearly. I should have given him more guidance on Friday night. I did not realize he was this vulnerable. He needed my help, and I did not give it. Once he is well rested, everything will go back to normal. Everything will be all-right. It has to be. Today he is just frightened. I must humour him, play along.'

Natasha did not speak, for she did not trust the voice that would come out of her mouth. She took deep breaths, repeatedly, and then reached for the water, again, to gulp the rest of it down. Finally, in a voice that was more hoarse than she would have liked, Natasha replied, as calmly as she was able, "I understand Sebastian. You have to do, what you have to do."

Sebastian looked wrecked, but he managed to give a grateful nod, as he replied:

"Thank you Natasha, thank you."

Eventually, they ordered food and she forced herself to eat, a feat made far easier by the fact that her arrabiatta was beyond good. They hardly spoke for the rest of the lunch yet, even after what Sebastian had said, they could not stop themselves from staring wondrously at each other. As was usual, they kept discovering that their hands were entwined, while their knees never once lost contact. The longer Natasha was with him, the less scared she felt. She convinced herself, nothing had really changed. Sebastian had said something awful and dramatic, so he could feel like he had some control. He would not really follow through. He was just terribly tired today. Certainly, after a good night's sleep, all would be well. As they returned to the office together, with full tummies, but traumatized hearts, Sebastian surprised Natasha, once again, when he grabbed her hand. Suddenly, he whisked her into a deserted doorway and fell upon her to embrace her, fervidly, with a force so ferocious it crushed her ribs, while he covered her yearning mouth with kisses, desperate enough to split her lips. Natasha's guts dropped hellward to splatter into the unquenchable fires that raged there, the moment she was slaughtered with this knowing: Sebastian was saying good-bye. Unbearably bereft, a lump the size of a loaf of bread wedged in her throat to choke her. Overwhelmed by raging emotions, Natasha started to whimper, as she resisted his kisses, to instead burrow her pain-contorted face into the soft wool of his navy blue jacket, as she let out a heart-rending sob. Sebastian clutched Natasha ever more tightly as he gave an imponderable groan of torment and im-mersed his face in her silken hair. They clamped each other so, for a long time, as if to fortify themselves in preparation for the agonizing separation that Sebastian had, so recently, decreed. Held like this, Natasha was the happiest, and the most miserable, she ever had been. The train track of time that eternally trundles across the landscape of human expe-rience, had been momentarily hijacked. Natasha was no more, for she had become absorbed in the timeless ubiquity that is all matter and mental states, from heaven to hell, simultaneously, conspiring to create ultimate, omniscient, spiritual bliss.

After much time spent snatching this undeserved feast in the state of enlightenment, anguish-ridden, Sebastian peeled himself away, to promote such acute pain in our heroine that it was as if she had just been brutally flayed. He gave her a final, briefest brush of a kiss on her lips, be-fore he hid his tear-streaked face behind his arm, as dramatically as if he had just drawn an imaginary black, purple satin lined, cloak around himself. Then the desper-ately distressed man vanished.

Natasha stood alone in the doorway's obscurity with appalled eyes staring into space, while her fingers touched her lips, where only seconds ago Sebastian had been fused. Now he was gone, Natasha clutched her stomach as if in pain. She felt like some invisible, steel-toe-capped Doc. Martin boot-wearing wastrel had just kicked her in the guts. Then, suddenly, in one swift lurch, Natasha spun around and threw up, right in front of the black gloss door behind her. She continued to retch violently, again and again, until her tummy was finally empty, only to leave her dry retching, painfully, for some time to come.

At last, Natasha was finished, and she spat out as much of the putrid tasting saliva as she could, then straightened up, in a daze, and wiped away the remaining strands from her mouth with the back of her trembling hand. She stared down, morosely, at the creamy pink, semi-digested mess she had made on the black-tiled doorway floor, before wiping her mouth, once again, as she forced herself to swallow the acidic gunk that, stubbornly, lurked around her tonsils. Natasha kept swallowing, determined to dilute the revolting taste with fresh saliva, as she looked down to check her watch. It was past two o'clock. How could it possibly be that late, for they had left the restaurant at ten-minutes past one? Our lovers' embrace must have distorted the perception of the passing of time, yet again. Natasha had to get back to work; and fast.

She stepped out of the foul smelling doorway. She drew deep draughts of the sharp air, then fumbled, shakily, in her handbag to take out her powder compact. Natasha flicked its black, plastic cover open to peer, intently, at herself in the tiny, powder-smeared mirror on the inside of it. She looked a wreck. She searched some more in her handbag until, thankfully, she managed to dig out an old tissue. She licked it to make it slightly damp, before she began to wipe away all the black mascara that was smudged around her eyes. She then patted her nose and cheeks with the powder puff, hoping to disguise the pink blotchiness of her skin, before at last applying some lipstick. She pressed her full lips together, firmly, and then slid them over each other to distribute the pretty pigment, evenly. Today, the unpleasant taste of lipstick was a relief, for it managed to usurp an even more revolting one.

Natasha checked herself again in the smeary mirror to find that she looked, marginally, less of a wreck. Decisively, she snapped the compact shut and put it back in her bag. When she did so, she spotted a forgotten packet of chewing gum, with great relief. Immediately, she squeezed out two little, white, candy-coated slugs of gum and then popped them into her mouth. Never had chewing gum tasted so sweet. She felt better already. Sebastian would not really do what he said he was going to. Everything would work out. She was certain.

She pulled her shoulders back and puffed out her chest, to adopt a posture of borrowed confidence, as she braced herself to face Freddie's wrath, along with the collective, derisory glances from the rest of the team. Simply, Natasha was not senior enough to get away with yet another long lunch, without incurring unwelcome comment. Feeling the panic rising inside her, the shaky Natasha aped defiance and held her head high, for she knew if she betrayed any glimmer of guilt on her return, she would only incur more vitriolic attack. She then dashed back to the office, as fast as she could, and away from the unsightly, stinking pool of lumpy vomit she had left behind in an empty doorway.

Chapter Twenty-eight - Miles to the rescue

Seek love, seek love
for it is the gem of your essence.
Seek the One, seek the One
for He is yours for eternity.
But forbid yourself to call Him yours
for what is yours is only
the sorrow
and the longing.

Rumi

Natasha was leaning over a glass-topped coffee table, with her right nostril fixed over the end of a rolled up twenty-pound note. She held it, carefully, in her right hand between her thumb and forefinger, while blocking her other nostril, by pressing her left index finger, firmly, against the fine bridge of her neat nose. She was perfectly poised to snort, for the bottom of the purple note hovered, only a millimetre or so, above a thin line of white powder. Then, in one fell swoop, sniffing as hard as she could all the way, she whipped along the length of it before, immediately, lining up to snort the second one up her other nostril. Having finished, and still sniffing manically, Natasha inspected the glass to find two minuscule, lightly smudged traces of coke that had escaped her suction. She licked her index finger, and then ran it across to collect the stray stuff, before rubbing it along the top of her gums and, instantly, they became as numb as her heart. She nodded twice and smiled.

"Nice." she commented, with approval, before passing Miles the rolled note.

The stuff was bloody strong. Natasha's mind became a collision of dazzling white, and shooting tingles rushed up the back of her head, to then swipe across her face, before the intense sensation kept repeating over and over again. Despite the strength of the stuff, when the delicate membrane inside her nose began to itch, reluctantly, Natasha

389

concluded that quality coke had been cut with some caustic substance. Sadly, Miles' gear was not as pure as Sebastian's had been. Immediately, Natasha thought 'Fuck!' for she had just brought to mind the very person whom she was trying, so desperately hard, to forget.

Natasha then squeezed the end of her nose between her thumb and forefinger to try and ease its itchiness, for she did not wish to be distracted from her high. Soon enough, she was swept away by drug-induced rapture and a soft smile of gratitude spread across her face. The rushes continued to intensify and, increasingly, she was transported from the cruel torment with which she had been afflicted, ever since that fateful lunch with Sebastian on Monday, almost two weeks ago.

Oh, she knew she would feel worse tomorrow but she could not care less, for she was too relieved to be spared her intolerable torment right now. Still sniffing, repeatedly, so determined was she that none of the powder stuck up her nose could escape, she flung her head back to rest its crown against the hard wall, while she became overwhelmed by more and more powerful shots of tingles that made it feel like the hairs on her head were standing on end. Waves of pleasure and invincibility swept through her, and the consequent chemical exhilaration made her pant. Her heart was now working as hard as if she had just done a forty-minute run around Hyde Park, while her brain was firing even more endorphins, than if that had been the case. Yet of course, in this instance, her high had been achieved without any effort; only sinister costs - actual, physical and spiritual. But what did Natasha care? She was simply grinning with glee, for the cocaine had worked its full magic, to whisk her away to Euphoria and far from Misery.

Thus our heroine, at last, gained toxic relief following two weeks of HELL for, to Natasha's horror, Sebastian had followed through with his announced intention. She had barely seen him on the trading floor since that fateful lunch and, when she had, he had deliberately avoided eye contact. In fact, he had hardly spoken a single word to her, let alone taken her out for lunch, driven her home, or gone out to dinner with her. Ever since Sebastian had scarpered to leave Natasha, all alone, in a dark doorway to puke, they had had no material contact. Oh, but thank God - well Miles, in fact - for Natasha's unbearable anguish was now blown, or rather 'snorted,' to oblivion. The events of the past two weeks drifted through her wired mind but, at least now, she was not afflicted with the accompanying torment. For the entire time, she had been nothing but a hollow, human form, mechanically going through the motions of a life she took no pleasure in living. All she had done was immerse her shattered self into work. She had not left the office during the day, except to grab a sandwich, or a sushi box for lunch, instead, she had spent up to eleven-hours a day on the telephone, locating, charming and setting up meetings with prospective clients. Then, at night, how grateful had she been for the exhaustion that tipped her straight into a black, dreamless sleep, to switch her off like a light, until the alarm clock blared at six a.m. to wake her, so she could start all over again.

As the effect of the drug took its predictable course, Natasha's confidence, entitlement, aggression and arrogance, began to soar to influence the content of her mental rambling recollections, 'Everyone noticed how hard I was working, why, I even managed to impress Freddie with that trade today, hell I impressed myself! He got his bloody trade from me inside two weeks. Fucking astonishing result!' Our heroine's smile had flipped into one of sneering self-satisfaction, while her mind continued on its self-congratulating meanderings, 'My first trade, I fucking did it! What a fucking STAR! Just a crappy three-month, fifteen-buck E.C.P. trade, I know, but hell, that's what they told me to sell, and I bloody well sold it... and all in spite of HIM. Only a three hundred and fifty dollar sales credit though... not much at all... so what's that then?'

Natasha screwed up her face, as she concentrated on working out the maths. A simple sum that seemed unduly challenging having just snorted two lines of coke until, at last, she got it: 'One million four hundred and ninety-nine thousand, six-hundred and fifty bucks to go… EASY!' Natasha then smiled as she remembered the entire Desk standing up to applaud her first ever trade. 'Yeah, I bloody well impressed them, I know I did. Now they know I'm not there just to get coffee, answer the 'phones and fuck the boss… No, now I'm qualified, I'm there to make 'shed loads' of money and I'll do it too. Fuck HIM, he's just an old, weak, married, bastard.' And with that definitive definition of Sebastian, Natasha turned her attention to Miles. She watched him with increasing interest and smiled, indulgently, while he made his way through the next two lines of coke, laid out on the glass table in front of her. Then she began to contemplate the man.

'Ah Miles, sweet Miles to the rescue… All those calls, all those, 'not tonights'. He never bloody well gave up though… and then today… God, when I saw Sebastian leave the office for the weekend, again, just like that, at five o'clock on the fucking dot, without a single word. He just walked out of the door, not even a glance in my direction. Then I knew for sure, he was following through with what he told me he would do. Sebastian was doing exactly what I thought he never could…'

Natasha frowned and, for a fraction of a moment, she looked beyond abject. Her face screwed up, and she bit hard into her lip, and then began to chew it, before she stopped herself. She just pressed her lips together, firmly, between her teeth and shut her eyes as if in mortal pain. She had to get a grip. She could not dwell on this. With a determination that her sanity depended upon, Natasha channelled her mind to contemplate different subject-matter and, slowly, her countenance began to brighten, like the sun breaking through a blanket of blue-black, sinister clouds following a freak storm.

'Then Matt… when Matt grunted, "Miles Monroe, line three", just after Sebastian had left, well, it was as if he had thrown me a rope while I was drowning. Fate, I guess. There was no bloody way I could have been alone tonight.

Miles' perseverance had paid off. Finally, the bloke got the 'yes' he was after; and thank fuck for that.'

Natasha was feeling increasingly well disposed towards Miles tonight. She found herself staring fondly at the top of his silky, brown, lock-laden head as he finished his second line. When he was done, he threw his head up and grinned, dementedly, at her. She gave a huff of laughter, and then cheekily extracted the note from his hand, before quickly snorting one of the last two remaining lines. Having finished the full snort/sniff/gum-rub ritual, Natasha handed the note back to Miles, encouragingly, so he could take the last one. He was quick to caution:

"Steady on Natasha, I have no interest in taking a surprise trip to the Chelsea and Westminster A. & E. department, this evening, thank you." Before accepting the note, anyway, and snorting the last line.

When Miles was finished, he sniffed, and then repeatedly took deep breaths, to help rock the substance around his system, as he got to his feet. He strolled over to his stereo and began to peruse his frighteningly extensive CD collection. The grand period room in which they were sitting, had been painted deep burnt terracotta, ceiling included, and the stucco cornicing, dado and picture rails had been painted pewter. The stereo and CD area that now captivated Miles' attention, had been seamlessly incorporated into his bookshelves, which ran the entire length of one of the large walls, all the way up, to stop just short of the picture rail.

The unusual, but imposing, room must have had a ceiling height of five-metres with a width of almost eight. The two discrete areas that the CDs occupied, must have been two-metres square each. Here, the shelves were the width of an upright CD, with the depth exactly matching those of the same, and they were jam-packed full. These purpose built spaces were set inside thick gilt frames, to give the effect of two simplistic cubist works of art, rather than just dull, unattractive, storage facilities.

When Natasha began to look around the room, with increasing interest, she noticed several paintings of similar magnitude each displayed in like frames. To her ignorant eye, she suspected them to be early twentieth century, so the apparent 'cubist CD paintings' were particularly apt. She then spotted a charming old-fashioned set of mahogany library stairs, which had rectangles of green leather with gold patterned boarders decorating the steps. There was a carved, spindly handrail on one side, and the steps ran on thin brass rails, all the way along the wall of shelves to prettily provide Miles with full access to his book and music collection.

Natasha thought the room, and its contents, to be exceptional and she concluded with satisfaction: though Miles may well be a tart, he was clearly a tart of exquisite taste. She was making her pleasing observations while seated on Miles' low, soft, velvet sofa the colour of taupe. It was so ridiculously deep, that her feet did not touch the floor, but instead stuck out straight in front of her, which made her feel peculiarly childlike. The sofa was strewn with brightly patterned tapestry cushions, the velvet backs of which were even softer than the sofa. Natasha picked one up and jammed it in between the hard wall and her head, as she continued to experience rush after rush, though slightly less intensely than earlier. Still, the effect of the drug was so strong that she felt conversation eluded her. Instead, Natasha just stared at Miles, as she continued to marvel at the size and presentation of his music collection. Finally, she did manage to assemble two words, in the correct order, to construct a short question, the answer to which she was genuinely interested in, for she could not help but compare these impressive 'pictures' with the pathetic C.D. rack she had back at her bedsit.

"How many?"

Immediately, Miles turned to look at her.

"C.D.s?" he inquired, with brows raised.

She nodded and smiled at him, for how she appreciated an intelligent man.

"Six thousand two hundred and forty-four, to be precise." he replied, proudly, before he turned his attention back to them, and extracted one from the display, to leave a solitary, dark slit, to make Natasha wonder, out loud:

"So what happens when you get new ones?"

"Well, some just get lost along the way, so there's a natural attrition rate or, I dispose of the ones of which I tire, gifts to friends usually…" he replied, absent-mindedly, while carefully placing his chosen C.D. into the stereo.

Then, just as Miles pressed the 'play' button, Natasha began to do just that.

"Just like women then Miles?" she teased, coyly.

To which he smiled bashfully, to himself, as if he had just been caught doing something rather naughty, which he sort of had. Slowly, he turned to meet Natasha's challenging eyes and, while passionate, South American music began to pour into the elegant space, Miles started to prance towards her, as he conceded, provocatively:

"Yes, I suppose so. Natasha, just like women."

Then Miles sat down next to her. She was surprised to find herself giggling, hysterically, for she had decided that Miles was almost as much fun as his coke! They had both just come from dinner. Miles had taken her to a rustic, but rather expensive, Italian restaurant that was conveniently located around the corner. Having got through two divine bottles of Uccellanda, it had not been difficult for Miles to persuade Natasha to come back to his house for a couple of lines of cocaine.

So here they were, and Natasha was still giggling. He then poured her a large glass of white wine, not Uccellanda perhaps, but decent white nonetheless. Natasha though, had another idea. The rushes were wearing off and she wanted more drugs. She caught Miles' eye, then put her warm hand, affectionately, on his knee, cocked her head to one side and looked at him imploringly, much like an optimistic dog begging for scraps at the table. Miles understood her meaning, instantly, and he boomed with laughter so powerful, that it really ought to have shifted one piece of light furniture; the library stairs on runners at the very least! Then he exclaimed, with exasperation:

"Natasha you're insatiable!" Before denying her, "No, no, no, no, no. Not yet…"

Natasha intensified her 'imploring' expression and began to whimper for added effect; predictably, having been denied it, she wanted it all the more. Miles laughed again, and then slapped her on the knee for persisting to make such a nuisance of herself. He then reclined along the bed-like sofa, propping himself up on his elbow, with his head resting on his hand as he stretched his legs out and kicked off his loafers. Tonight, Miles was wearing socks, burnt orange silk socks to be precise; one of Natasha's favourite colours. Once he was stretched out like an ancient Roman, waiting to be hand fed grapes, Miles continued.

"Now, now Natasha, I think I need to distract you from your excessive cravings."

Impatient, for Natasha did not want to be distracted, she wanted more cocaine, she huffed crossly and folded her arms in front of her to sulk, with her bottom lip pushed out into an exaggerated pout. Miles leaned forward to collect her glass of wine then, graciously, he handed it to her.

"Backgammon?" he suggested, encouragingly, with mischievous eyes.

Natasha noticeably perked up, for it was a game she loved. It was also a game at which she was rather good.

"Done!" she replied, and then she took a long sip of her cold drink, while Miles added the condition.

"For every game you win, you will be rewarded with a line. For every game you lose, you will suffer a penalty…"

Natasha took another sip of her drink, while staring at the glints of light that sparkled from Miles' inspired, big brown eyes.

"Penalty?" she enquired, with cautious interest. Only to extract his filthiest laugh to date, before she insisted, "What sort of penalty exactly, Miles?"

He stretched his arms up into the air, with fists clenched.

"Some despicable act of my choosing Natasha, that's

what!" he articulated, with relish.

Then he flicked his hair, as flirtatiously as a prostitute, before resting his head back on his hand, as he added, adamantly, "Those are my non-negotiable terms!"

Natasha looked straight ahead and thought about it. As her mind ticked over, she continued to drink the wine, which was in fact rather good. She wanted more cocaine. She wanted to forget, and she was, in fact, very good at backgammon. In a bizarre way, she also trusted Miles.

"No suffering of vulnerable creatures, including me?" she checked.

Miles' eyes fired up.

"No, suffering. Promise." he confirmed, in a bass growl, to elicit an eager nod, and an animated grin, from Natasha, as she exclaimed:

"Terms agreed!"

Suddenly, she was happier and more excited than she had been for ages. Miles then leant forward and pulled out a beautiful, chocolate brown and burnt cream, handcrafted backgammon set from under the sofa. He placed it between them, unlatched it, then opened it up and the pair of them, immediately, began to set up the counters, with a swiftness dictated by the drug of which they were full. The game was quickly ready to play, and Miles acted as the master of ceremonies, "Let the games begin!"

And with that, Miles and Natasha each threw one of their heavy dice, to clatter across the hard board until coming to informative rest. Miles got a '3', and Natasha a '5'. Natasha had the first go and she went on to win the first three games. Natasha was rewarded with a line of cocaine after each victory, as promised, not to mention the couple of glasses of wine she drank while she played. It took her less than an hour to do this and, by the end of it, she was feeling as high as prime, London property, price inflation and as smug as someone who owns a slice of it. That was until the fourth game, when the bubble well and truly burst! So convincing was her defeat in the fourth game, that Natasha began to wonder if Miles had strategically allowed her to win the first three. She may have believed herself to be jolly good at backgammon, but she began to suspect Miles was irritatingly brilliant. She had played on until the bitter end and when Miles took his final chocolate brown counter off the board, Natasha had only just begun to remove her cream ones. She stared down dolefully at her thirteen remaining counters, all lined up, in five neat redundant points.

Not only was Natasha feeling a touch humiliated, she was beginning to wonder what, exactly, qualified as a despicable act. As she did so, she regretted not being more specific regarding the terms of engagement, before she had agreed to engage! Fortunately, however, by now Natasha had had so much to drink, and so much up her nose, that her capacity to feel, or think, anything was significantly diminished. Certainly, that must have been why she had lost in the first place! A relatively compos mentis Miles, on the other hand, remained reclined on the sofa with a grin as wide as the Milky Way. He was staring at Natasha, predatorily, as he uttered, in a voice so deep that it made the barrel of her chest vibrate:

"Despicable act please?"

Natasha just batted her eyelashes at him with the most innocence she could muster.

"Elaborate?" she inquired, quietly.

"A blow-job will do to start with darling..."

"Miles, please!" Natasha objected, profusely. "Losing one silly little game of backgammon can hardly command such an exacting penalty!"

Miles gaze remained steady as he studied the panicked, shrill-voiced Natasha.

"So Natasha, how many games do you now think you need to lose, before you begin to honour a watered down version of our agreement?" he patronized.

Natasha's racing mind then began to think about three things, concurrently: 1) the possibility of more lines of Charlie, 2) the truth that she did actually rather fancy Miles and when he had asked her to perform oral sex, just now, she had become dangerously excited and 3) Miles may well have just got lucky on the last game, which looped back to number one: more coke! The swift culmination of these various considerations was a self-righteously spluttered: "Well I'd say three, at the very least."

"Three it is then Natasha... one down, two to go." Miles replied, long-sufferingly.

Then they set up another game, in silence. Natasha won the next two games, and Miles continued to stick to his side of the initial agreement, even though Natasha had not, and even though there was very little cocaine left. It was not long, however, before the same pattern emerged, just compressed this time around. Natasha's winning streak was fast halted and Miles won the next two games with ease. This fact led her, reluctantly, to suspect that Miles had allowed her to win the last two games, deliberately, no doubt hoping that more lines of cocaine would make her more malleable.

Miles said nothing. He just smirked, sat up on the sofa, leaned forward, cut the last of the cocaine into two little white powder piles, chopped up each, crunching any hard rocks to fine powder, before he made two long, neat lines out of them. Still grinning, he handed Natasha the note. Natasha snorted one of them, then handed the note back, and Miles, promptly, finished off the last. Natasha was, by now, convinced that her suspicion had been correct and she finished her wine, in a single gulp, before putting her glass down, gently, on the table.

It was almost one o'clock in the morning and, at last, Natasha was completely addled. When Miles had finished his line, he dropped the rolled note onto the table and took Natasha's hand in his, then placed it, firmly, on his erect cock. No longer really knowing, or caring, what she did, a fatalistic Natasha stared down at the burgeoning bulge in his pants, and she began to rub it while, using her other hand, she began, slowly, to unbuckle his chunky belt and unzip the fly of his thick, cotton, dark blue trousers. Natasha then, inquisitively, tucked her warm, slightly perspiring, hand inside his fly and squeezed it into the slit at the front of his boxer shorts, which cheerfully matched his socks, both in material and colour. Natasha then wrapped her hand around, and pulled out, Miles' wide girthed, pulsing penis.

An ecstatic, dashingly handsome Miles was sitting on the sofa's edge watching her with awe. His hands were placed palm-side down, either side of him, and both of his feet were planted on the floor with his knees wide apart. Natasha just slipped her bottom off the sofa, and dropped down to stand on her knees. She then shuffled along until she was positioned in between his legs, directly in front of his member. Natasha met his astonished, ravenous eyes and she smiled, mischievously, at him. Suddenly, she was feeling exceptionally excited and her mind was intrigued to discover how play-acting the 'hooker' would make her feel. She caught herself strangely relishing this moment, backgammon aside, for she was on the cusp of performing a sexual favour in exchange for drugs. Did prostitution ever get more classic than that?

Immersing herself fully in her new role, which she had to admit made her feel a lot sexier than the one of 'investment banker', slowly, she leaned down and carefully placed her full lips on the supremely soft tip of Miles' penis, where she began to kiss him, gently and all over. Her hand then crept up, to cup the base of his cock, firmly, and she began to move it up and down, pulling the loose penile skin up and down his shaft as she did so, while exerting gradually increasing pressure. Miles gasped with extreme arousal. He then began to gather up her hair, in order to see the action of her mouth on his penis, clearly. Natasha continued to wank him off, while she began, relentlessly, to stimulate the top of his penis with her tongue, ever playful and ever varied. Miles' gasps had become groans and Natasha was becoming increasingly aroused. Oh, how she loved the soft smoothness of him inside her mouth. She then started to lick the helmet of his penis like a Popsicle, paying particular attention to the ridge of it. Her actions were tantalizing Miles to distraction. She would then, suddenly, begin to suck the top if it hard, before playing with it, again, with her tongue.

The noises Miles was making now, could have woken the dead and Natasha was becoming, ever more, seduced by her power over him. She was feeling exceptionally horny and she pushed her head down and slid his engorged penis into her warm wet mouth, as far as the top of her throat, before she took it even more deeply to push past her gagging reflex. She then began to move her head up and down, up and down, while her moist mouth continually sucked his thick shaft as she did so. Natasha was taking him so deeply into her mouth that the actions of her ever-active tongue were constricted, now that the cavity it lived in was so full of his pumping flesh. Up and down, up and down, up and down, up down, faster and faster.

Miles now held her head firmly in his hands and he began to force her motion faster and faster, deeper and deeper. He was fucking her face, while regulating her rhythm to the height of his satisfaction. Natasha's eyes were tightly shut, her mouth was wet and her gagging reflex had surrendered to such force, completely. She had given herself over to Miles' sexual will and she began to moan along with him, while his pleasure appeared so intense it seemed to border on agony. Up and down, up and down, up and down she went until, suddenly, she would resist and stop the motion to administer all of her active attention on the tip of his penis instead, kissing, licking and sucking it, only then to plunge down on him again, and again and again.

Miles was crying out, as if in pain, and he seemed precipitously close to climax. Suddenly, he pulled Natasha off him and he pulled her head up to his mouth and he began to kiss her, feverishly. As he kissed her, he forced her down into a lying position on the sofa. Miles then climbed on top of her and his significant, solid weight bore down on her. Miles' unnaturally strong tongue invaded her mouth and his firm lips almost bruised hers with the force of his kissing. He then broke away and ravished her, all the way down the neck, while he massaged her breasts with great pressure.

Suddenly, his long tongue was licking inside her ear, as if to tickle her very brain. The cocaine had heightened Natasha tactile senses, and she began to feel overwhelmed by the forceful, relentless, stimulation. She was panting breathlessly, as was he, and she could feel the pulsing of her blood in her genitals, for lust and longing had been aroused there. As physically aroused as her body felt, now Miles was on top of her, with his head so close to hers, with his mouth and his hands all over her, and his hard cock burrowing into her body, suddenly, everything felt too intimate, too close, too invasive. This 'game' Natasha had thought she was playing, had just got terribly out of hand. She was no longer in control. Miles was on a mission and fast working towards fucking her brains out.

Then the newly terrified Natasha had a panic attack so powerful, that no ingested amount of drink or drugs could subdue it. She felt nauseatingly claustrophobic, her heart was palpitating wildly, she was breaking out into a clammy sweat and simply she had to get away. The man who was crushing down on her now, was not Sebastian. Everything was so different. Everything felt so raw, so animalistic, so soulless: so wrong. She wanted Sebastian. She did not want this. What on earth had she been thinking?

Miles continued to kiss and caress her with primordial force. His hands moved farther and farther down her body, down her long thighs, massaging them as he did so. In an instant, he stuck one roughly up her skirt and, immediately, slipped it inside her knickers. Natasha tensed up with fright. As he pushed his strong agile finger up inside her and began to tease her clitoris with his thumb, Natasha began to push him away. This was not right. She wanted to make love. She did not want to fuck. Natasha wanted to make love to HIM. The very thought made her heart swell with the missing of HIM. Her throat constricted and silent, hot, fat tears started to stream down her piteous face.

Immediately, Miles' attentions were abated. He was utterly confused. The girl who had willingly administered the best blow-job he had ever had in his life, had just seized-up and become completely unresponsive; more tense than a racehorse. He could still feel the sweet, viscous wetness inside her, and the hardness of her clitoris, but she was now, determinedly, trying to push him away, with clenched fists. Her face was screwed up now, and she was struggling to get away from his invasive kisses. What the hell was going on?

Reluctantly, Miles stopped doing what he wanted to, and promptly withdrew his hand from Natasha's vagina and his tongue from her mouth. He propped himself up on his elbows, while holding her firmly by the shoulders. He strained in the dim light to see her expression and was more than shocked when he saw her distressed, frightened eyes. When he spied the rivulets of tears that flowed from them, to cascade down her temples, Miles gasped, appalled, and then asked, with bafflement:

"Natasha, what on earth is the matter?"

When Natasha sensed the force of Miles' genuine concern, Natasha's barriers of self-preservation spontaneously splintered like rotten wood. All of the despair, suffering and confusion that had been locked inside her for the last two weeks, welled up to flood out in a wretched cry. Quickly, Miles pulled himself off her entirely, but still lay next to her. He took her in his arms and gave her a giant, warm hug. His kindness only made matters worse, and Natasha broke into unrestrained sobbing, muffling the excessiveness of her grief, by burying her face into the cushion of his right pectoral muscle to contend with the fluff of his lime green, cashmere, crew neck jumper as it tickled her nose. Miles just held the pathetic, snivelling, clearly slightly psychotic, creature in his arms, cradling her lovingly as he cooed soothingly into her ear, all the while.

"Shhh, shhh, shhh... don't cry Natasha, please don't cry. Shhh, shhh, shhh, come on Natasha stop crying now... Shhh... it's all OK Natasha... Shhh now..."

403

Miles held Natasha close like this, gently soothing her, for a very long time. Long enough for Natasha's whimpering to cease, at last. Long enough, for her inexhaustible reservoir of tears, finally, to stop flowing. Long enough, even, for her, eventually, to pass out. It seemed that no amount of chemical stimulant was strong enough to overcome Natasha's physical and emotional exhaustion, for by three forty-three a.m. she was, at last, curled up and fast asleep on Miles' sofa still cradled, lovingly, in his arms.

* * * * *

It was the blue-grey-white, early November light that filtered in through three gigantic sash-windows, which woke Natasha up at eight fifty-one on Saturday morning. She found herself covered by a thick, yellow, brown and green tartan woollen blanket, and her head resting, comfortably, on one of the tapestry cushions, with the soft velvet side to her cheek. She felt terrible and looked worse.

Immediately, Natasha lifted her hand to her temple, and tried to massage away the pain that packed her delicate head, like shards of shattered glass. Her eyes were just beginning to adjust to the daylight, when she heard the large, grey, panelled door to the room, suddenly, being kicked open, before Miles appeared from behind it carrying a big silver tray. Steam was rising from the plates and mugs that sat on it. An appetizing smell of cooked eggs and something much stronger, with a unique, delectable aroma, filled her abused nostrils to comfort her and, in an instant, the thought 'truffles' came to mind.

Miles put the heavy tray down on the coffee table in front of her, but she could not see what was on it, for he sat down on the edge of the sofa in between her and the tray. He soon revealed two large pink ball-shaped pills in the palm of his hand, then he passed her a glass of water.

"What are they?" Natasha asked, with piqued interest.

To which Miles laughed, humorously.

"Good God Natasha, after last night, no more drugs for

you, possibly ever again, and certainly not for breakfast."

"So what are the pink pills?"

"One-thousand milligram doses of ibuprofen. You need good friends with access to hospital supplies to get these, I can tell you. I can also tell you, take both!"

"But Ibuprofen is a drug Miles..." she teased.

"Natasha, just do what good girls are supposed to, for a change. Shut up and swallow!" he retorted.

Natasha smirked broadly and, feeling mortified by her behaviour last night, she obediently popped one of the pills into her mouth, took a big sip of water then swallowed it down in a gulp, before doing the same with the next. Well, that should take care of her headache, at least. Smiling at the bedraggled Natasha with affectionate satisfaction, Miles then passed her a silver knife and fork, wrapped neatly in a white linen napkin before standing up.

"I trust, espresso, freshly squeezed orange juice and poached eggs on granary toast with tartufo bianco d'Alba shavings, is to your liking Mademoiselle?"

Natasha nodded eagerly, for how she craved the first two, while her Italian extended as far as being able to translate 'white truffles', and how she loved them almost as much as the language.

"Tartufo fresh off a plane from Turin, only yesterday, may I add." Miles then informed her, proudly.

Natasha was now paying attention for, clearly, Miles had spoilt her. She then sat up, properly, on the sofa as she groaned, slightly, from the effort of so doing, for all of her organs felt tender and sore this morning. Modestly, she tugged at the hem of her, now rather crumpled, black scoop-necked dress, so that it almost reached her knees. She then tucked her tangled hair, as neatly as she could, behind her ears before grinning at Miles, with genuine glee, as he smiled at her and passed her her plate.

Natasha placed the cushion, which she had slept on, onto her lap and then rested the breakfast plate on top of it, before, enthusiastically, helping herself to some poached egg and toast, making sure she got some truffle shavings too. As she began to eat the scrumptious breakfast, its flavour could not have contrasted more agreeably with the taste she had in her mouth when she had woken, only moments ago. As soon as she had finished chewing, Natasha applauded: "Superb Miles! Utterly superb."

Then she finished off Miles' delicious breakfast, faster than she had his cocaine. Once that was done, she started to celebrate the strength and quality of the coffee and the sweetness of the fresh orange juice. What a guest-house! By the time she had consumed all of the refreshments, her headache had vanished in an ibuprofen haze, her tummy was full of quality food, and her heart was replenished by Miles' bonhomie. In fact, Natasha stayed with Miles all day Saturday, staving off the time when she would have to face being alone. What is more, she thoroughly enjoyed his company and they ended up going out for a very late lunch with a crowd of eight of his friends at a cosy basement restaurant behind Holland Park Avenue, where Natasha drank too many of the best Bloody Mary's she had ever had. When the long, lingering, laughter-strewn lunch was done, Natasha knew it was time to go home and Miles, kindly, drove her the short distance back to her bedsit. When they said goodbye at the bottom of the steps, she found that she was most reluctant to release him, following the big bear-hug he had given her.

"Miles, I can't begin to tell you how grateful I am, for everything. Thank you for being such a good friend to me." Natasha said, sincerely, as she still clung on to him, tightly.

Miles took Natasha's head in between his hands and forced her to look into his compassionate eyes.

"Natasha, please don't feel too bloody grateful or you'll make me feel guilty." he answered, with light exasperation.

Then he paused, for a moment, as he inspected her face, and then confessed with naked candour:

"You must know by now, the only reason I'm so jolly nice to you, is because I fancy you rotten? I don't want to be your friend Natasha, I want to have endless sex with you. Preferably when you're not blubbering."

Natasha looked down at nothing and her energy field contracted, for a moment, before she met Miles' eyes, once again, and said, thoughtfully:

"But we didn't have sex Miles, and you have been nice to me."

Miles gave a helpless shrug, and then he let her go. She spun on her heels and fled up the stone steps to her front door. As soon as she had turned the lock, she glanced behind her. He was still standing at the foot of the steps, looking most pensive, with his broad tanned hand held high in adieu. Natasha gave him a big smile, softer than his cashmere jumper, before she retreated, slowly, into the big, old villa, alone.

<u>Chapter Twenty-nine</u> - **Best Friends**

*In the kitchen of love
only the beautiful are killed.
Death does not frighten a true lover
for those not dying for love
are already corpses.*

Rumi

"Come up." Natasha invited down the intercom, before buzzing Katrina in.

Then she finished putting in her second pretty, clotted-cream-coloured pearl earring, which dropped from a sparkling diamond cluster, set in white gold. Her face was ghostly white and she wore a fitted cashmere, black polo-neck jumper, figure hugging trousers and silk black socks. Not surprisingly, since that catastrophic lunch with Sebastian, everything she had worn had been black, and tonight was no exception. Even after all of those Bloody Marys, earlier, Natasha still felt as if she were in mourning. By the time Katarina gave a quiet knock on her door, she had just finished brushing her long, shiny hair and was ready. Dumping the brush on her chest of drawers, she went to let her friend in.

As soon as Natasha opened the door, Katarina was urgently seeking eye contact, for her face had adopted that 'tell me what's the matter' look, with her eyebrows raised, curiously, and bottom her lip stuck out, as if to express, pictorially, her sympathy for her friend's current emotional condition. Clearly, Katarina had picked up that all was not well, earlier, when she called Natasha. Our heroine just gave a tired smile and, not wishing to discuss her distress so quickly, she looked away before giving Katarina a brusque kiss, on each of her frozen cheeks, in welcome. Natasha took the bottle Katarina offered her.

"Keep your coat on." she instructed.

Katarina smiled then patted her thighs with her magenta mitten-clad hands. Natasha got a bottle of champagne from the fridge, took a glass out of the cupboard, and then poured Katarina some champagne, before topping up her own. Her friend just watched her with concern, as she removed her gloves and stuffed them into her grey duffle-coat pockets. Finally, Natasha looked Katarina square in the eye, as she passed her the glass and raised her own.

"To bright lights, crackles and multiple - not gang - bangs!" Natasha forced, in jovial toast.

As soon as she had said it, her hand leapt up to cover her mouth, and her eyes sprang open, so shocked was she by her coarseness. What a ridiculous thing to have said! Katarina's eyes widened too, but she was sensitive enough to let it pass with nothing but a questioning glare. They clinked glasses and drank. Then Natasha let out a desolate sigh, while she stared down, dejectedly, at the bland carpet. Now Katarina had arrived, Natasha knew it was only a matter of time before she would get around to sharing her woes; even the thought of so doing made her tearful. Determined not to collapse into misery, quite so quickly, Natasha sought solace in pragmatism, for clearly humour had failed. She checked her watch. It was six fifty-five.

"We should get outside soon. The display starts at seven and we don't want to miss the beginning." Natasha suggested encouragingly, doing her best to present an enthusiastic face.

Katarina nodded. Natasha got her suede coat from the hook by the front door, put it on and did up her belt, as she walked towards the window and inquired, matter-of-factly:

"Do you have gloves?"

Katarina frowned in disbelief for, surely, her scatty friend must have noticed the bright ones she had been wearing, on arrival. She scoffed then delved into her pockets to lift them out and show Natasha. Our heroine, however, was too preoccupied to react. Instead, she just nodded, absent-mindedly, and checked:

"Do you want to borrow a hat?"

For it was so much easier to immerse herself in practicalities, rather than tackle her tumultuous emotions.

"Why not?" Katarina indulged, shaking her head, softly.

Natasha extracted two hats, and a pair of gloves for herself, from the colourful piles of wool and cashmere in the bottom of her chest of drawers. Then, as soon as the girls were all wrapped up, Natasha felt marginally more cheerful. Whether this was due to the giant bobble on top of her baby blue hat, or from the effect of the champagne she had already drunk, she did not know or care, she was just relieved that she was not fighting back tears.

Natasha then placed the bottles onto the window-ledge, along with a family packet of Doritos, before turning around, placing her hands onto it, then giving a little jump to pull herself up. Once she was sitting in the window's alcove, she opened the window then clambered out onto the flat part of the roof directly in front. As soon as she was outside, in the freezing November night air, she gave a little shiver and her warm breath started to form billowing, milk-white, cumulus clouds in the darkness. Katarina was about to negotiate the same manoeuvres.

"Wait, I forgot the blanket, can you bring it? It's on my bed." Natasha requested, quickly, in afterthought.

Katarina then grabbed the bright red and black tartan rug before joining her friend on the roof, to huddle up next to her, with the warm blanket wrapped around their legs. It felt disproportionately exciting to be outside, snug and supplied. The girls found themselves enlivened and grinning, as they started to guzzle their champagne and tuck into the Doritos.

Maybe it was the height, and the sense of danger, that made them feel quite so exhilarated but, whatever it was, Natasha was relieved to find that sitting among the tree-tops, staring out, hopefully, into the mustard glow of Notting Hill's night sky, while waiting for fireworks to start, made her feel more cheerful and carefree than she had felt, for a very long time. Our hostess may well have been in better shape, but her reticence was taking its toll on her guest. After just a few minutes silence, Katarina began to fidget before, finally, she gave a little cough and inquired, gently, "So Natasha, what's up?"

Natasha squirmed and hugged her knees more tightly.

"After the show Kat, I'll tell you everything after the show..." she replied, evasively.

Katarina looked at her friend with concern then licked her lips once.

"I'm just worried about you Natasha. You're not your usual self. In fact, when I spoke to you on the 'phone earlier you sounded really weird..." She then fixed Natasha with a preposterously serious stare and continued, "and then when you suggested we spend Guy Fawkes on your roof, I felt duty bound to call the Samaritans. They're on their way as we speak."

Natasha shot Katarina a look, and the mischievous glint she caught in her friend's eye managed to coax a smile. She then nudged Katarina in the ribs.

"Oh goodie, a party, we'd better save some champagne..." she jested, sardonically.

Looking a little less troubled, Katarina raised her eyebrows and inquired:

"So not quite as bad as I feared then Natasha?"

"Worse." she uttered under her breath, faster than a firecracker. Instantly, a fat lump was engendered in Natasha's throat, before she added dismissively, "Not now Kat, not now. I'll tell you after the fireworks. I promise." She then added with abandon, "Enough, let's just watch explosive, bright lights, freeze to death and get pissed in peace."

Katrina acquiesced with a mute nod and then, as if on cue, an incredibly loud bang made Natasha jump, fortunately not too violently, considering the precariousness of her position. The girls craned their necks to their far right, to watch the multitudes of electric white, red, orange, green, purple and blue sparkling stars of brilliant light that illuminated the night sky in the distance. Natasha nodded, sagely.

"Ladbroke Square, I reckon..."

Grateful for the distraction, Natasha devoured the visual spectacle of flashing, shooting, spiralling, diving, multi-coloured lights of the private square's firework display, against the darkness, combined with the aural experience of bangs, fizzes, cracks, spits, splutters and whistles. By the time the last whizz of the display had finally petered out, twenty-minutes later, the girls had eaten all of the Doritos, finished the first, and start on the second, bottle of booze and Natasha had managed to develop a stiff crick in her neck. When the frozen girls looked at each other's red noses and crimson cheeks, they both knew exactly what the other was thinking, but Natasha was first to say it.

"Inside?"

"Now!" Katarina yelped in reply.

Immediately, the pair scrambled through the window, scraping knees and taking the debris of their modest feast on their way. The bedsit was cold now and Natasha quickly closed the big window, before turning the heating up full blast. They kept their coats on, while Natasha topped up their glasses before sitting down next to Katarina on the little sofa. There were no more excuses. Katarina stared, expectantly, at her friend, while Natasha tried to work out how she could begin without falling to pieces.

"Oh, Kat... I don't know where to start..."

Katarina looked at her, sympathetically.

"Anywhere Natasha, just begin." she advised.

Natasha gave a couple of sniffs, as the pain welled up inside her, and she confessed, in a gush:

"He's avoiding me Katarina. I mean total, and utter, shut down."

"Go on."

Warm teardrops began to roll down Natasha's cold face and, swiftly, she brushed them away.

"He did warn me." she continued. "He told me he was going to do it the Monday before last. 'I'm going to fight this love to the death' he said. He was very melodramatic, but Kat, I really didn't think he would go through with it..."

Tears threatened to flow again, and Natasha placed her fingers flat against her trembling lips, as she stared fiercely at the floor, trying to summon the strength not to break-down, while agonizing feelings ruptured inside her. Katarina put her hand affectionately on Natasha's knee and squeezed. When our heroine, at last, mustered sufficient self-composure, she re-engaged eye contact. Katarina nod-ded, encouragingly. Natasha just gave a fatalistic huff.

"I didn't realize it was my death to which he was refer-ring…" she then uttered, caustically.

Katarina smiled, sadly, and squeezed her knee, again.

"I've never seen you like this Natasha. It's frightening. This man has got so far under your skin that I barely rec-ognize you."

"Forget 'under my skin' Katarina, he's performed a coup d'état in my head. I've never felt as crazy as I do now. No one's ever made me feel so miserable or, not so long ago, so ecstatic." Natasha was wringing her hands, fretfully, before she looked straight into Katarina's eyes.

"It gets worse…" she warned, eerily.

"What do you mean?"

"Last night..." Katarina's interest was hotter than the fireworks. She leaned in close, hankering after the next revelation. Shame drove Natasha to qualify what she had done, before she detailed it, "You have to understand Kat, I've been bereft for almost two weeks. It was as if I were losing my mind. He was hardly on the trading floor at all and, when he was, he wouldn't even look at me. It was a living hell. I felt as if my guts were packed with shards of glass. Even though we've not spoken a word since that lunch, his presence has been in my head the whole time. It's so hard to articulate how mentally and emotionally in-capacitating such a weird, uncontrollable and powerful phenomenon is."

"Natasha, what are you trying to tell me exactly?"

"Last night... I had dinner with Miles Monroe."

Katarina's aquamarine eyes were shimmering with heightened interest as they blinked at her. Natasha clued her friend up with the back-story:

"You remember, I told you about Miles before. He is

413

the guy that I met at Sebastian's wife's birthday party..."

Katarina recalled the name, and Natasha's description of the man. She nodded, and then questioned:

"So?"

"Oh Katarina, I can't believe what I ended up doing... It's so humiliating."

Katarina was becoming impatient.

"Oh Natasha, for pity's sake spit it out?"

Natasha's face grimaced and she took a gulp of her drink, as she stared at the floor and summoned the courage to confess. Finally, she blurted, indelicately:

"I gave Miles a blow-job."

Natasha then threw her head into her hands, and continued to stare down, morosely, at her feet. Katarina was so flabbergasted, she was speechless. What on earth was happening to her friend?

"It all got so out of hand Kat. We almost had sex then, 'in flagrante delicto', I had a total breakdown and we didn't." Natasha then mumbled, sheepishly, before sitting up properly to brave eye contact, once again. Shrugging helplessly, she reflected on the previous evenings' surprising turn of events and added, "In the circumstances, Miles was sweet, really. It would never have happened if I hadn't had all that coke..."

"Cocaine?" Katarina spluttered, "Since when, are you taking cocaine?"

Katarina's expression was dumbfounded, as if unable to process this string of shocking revelations. Natasha just took a contemplative sip of her drink, in silence. Suddenly, the telephone began to ring. The shrill sound sliced clear through Natasha, while Katarina seemed oblivious, for she was now just shaking her head slowly, from side to side, as if hypnotized by a sedate tennis rally. Natasha got to her feet and went to answer the 'phone.

"Hello?"

As soon as she heard chuckling, a tender smile spread across Natasha's face. The change in her demeanor pulled Katarina out of her dull daze. Natasha felt her friend's attention on her, while she listened to an appealing, sonorous suggestion, becoming increasingly comforted, as she heard more, until she spoke to the caller, "That would have been lovely, but I can't I'm afraid, I've got a girlfriend with me." Natasha replied, softly. She continued to listen to the voice that seemed to cheer her until, at last, she seemed persuaded and spoke again, "Are you quite sure? Really? Oh, in which case, OK, I think we'd be delighted. What time? Perfect, OK, see you then."

Natasha hung up. She appeared a touch bewildered.

"Talk of the devil..." she muttered, to herself, under her breath. Then Katarina questioned:

"Natasha, don't tell me that was this man Miles?"

"The very same."

"I don't believe you!"

"Well, I suggest you do, because he's picking us up in forty-five minutes to take us out for dinner."

"I can't go out to dinner Natasha, I'm wearing jeans and a duffle-coat for Christ's sake!" Calmly, Natasha just looked at her friend, with one eyebrow arched in challenge, but Katarina dug her heels in, and insisted, "Listen to me, I'm not going anywhere dressed like this!"

But our heroine wasn't listening, she was already rifling through her wardrobe and stroking her hand down the materials that fell, lifelessly, from jam-packed hangers, as she briskly slipped it in between each garment, to create enough space to eye them, critically, and in quick succession. Soon enough, Natasha had plucked out two simple, fitted, black dresses that would be perfect for the evening. She then draped them across her bed, took her coat off and pointed to one of them.

"You can wear that, it should just fit..." she suggested to Katarina, thoughtfully, before with a flick of her wrist she pointed at the other, to declare, "and I shall wear this one."

Katarina stood and went over to the dress in question, to take a closer look, while Natasha returned to the wardrobe, articulating her intention as she went, "Now for shoes..." then, after a few moments rummaging through the designer

shoeboxes in the bottom, she lined up two exquisite pairs
of black high heels, in front of Katarina, like pricey sacri-
fices, before adding, "We're the same size, so you choose?
I even have matching handbags, for each pair, so you really
don't have any excuse not to come now."

From the look of increasing scintillation on her friend's
face, Natasha could tell Katarina was intrigued to meet
Miles Monroe, following such salacious revelations and,
now she had something to wear, she was certain she would
come out with them. Natasha proved to be correct for Katarina had allowed her duffle-coat to drop to the floor and,
already, she was stripping off to try on the suggested outfit.
Natasha was quick to follow her lead and, as soon as the
girls had changed, they started on their make-up. Only then
did Natasha begin to share Miles' plan for the evening,
pausing only to apply her red lipstick.

"Miles said he was going to take us to that wonderful
restaurant I told you about, then afterwards he wants to
take us to some private members club on Jermyn Street."

And, as if the saying of the name had summoned the
man, Natasha's doorbell sounded. As soon as Katarina
heard Miles' forceful laughter resonate out of the intercom,
she raised her eyebrows in mild alarm.

"We'll be right down." Natasha, quickly, informed him.

When the pair checked their efforts in the full-length
mirror, it was evident that the goodies in Natasha's cos-
metic bag had magically transformed a couple of attractive
girls by day, into a pair of devastating beauties by night.
Miles would be thrilled!

It was only a matter of minutes, before Katarina was
squashed into the back of Miles' little car and his hands
were exploring Natasha's elegant legs, once again, as he
whisked them off to the West End. And so it was, that on
this cold November night, Katarina got to experience, firsthand, the marvellousness of Arturo's eyes, his superlative
service and the deliciousness of the cuisine served in his
remarkable establishment. Katarina was also a reluctant
witness to Miles' lewd groping of Natasha's squirming

body, to be at times graced with a titillating dash of his fondling for herself, whenever he felt inspired enough to pepper his persistent adoration of Natasha with a touch of variety. Once the magnificent feast was finished and Miles had paid, the iridescent, exultant, handsome, Mr. Monroe escorted these tall, slim, long-haired, bright-eyed females to his private members' club behind Piccadilly, where he was encircled by them all night long, like beautiful, captivated butterflies dancing around a bright bulb. Miles regularly refuelled his young charges with golden bubbly booze, or with the contents of white, tight, square paper-wraps, which he kept discreetly pressing into Natasha's sweaty palm. Predictably enough, once the white powder was neatly lined up on top of the flat porcelain lavatory cistern in the club loos, Katarina was not nearly so judgemental regarding the consumption of the stuff, as she had been back in Natasha's bedsit, only hours before. Indeed, by the end of the dance-packed night, the delicate pink lining of Katarina's nose was just as itchy as theirs, her pupils just as dilated, and her conversation just as fast and futile.

Booze, drugs, music, sexual titillation, laughter and company, once again, helped Natasha forget her new romantic reality, with which she was so, fundamentally, ill-equipped to cope.

<u>Chapter Thirty</u> - Can't stay away

The sun is love. The lover,
a speck circling the sun.
A Spring wind moves to dance
any branch that isn't dead.

Rumi

Natasha pushed against the heavy glass revolving door of U.C.B. to get out of the building. As soon as the cold fresh air hit her face, and her heels hit the pavement, she gave a deep sigh of relief, following another eleven-hour day of stress in the stuffy office. As was becoming her habit, Natasha had only left her desk for the fifteen minutes, or so, it took to pick up some lunch. On days such as these, it was even a relief to stand up for, with so many hours of sitting at a desk, Natasha felt as stiff as an old corpse and, following last weekend, about as lively.

In fact, after the toxic substance overload Miles had so generously, or perhaps self-servingly, provided (for she clearly remembered Katarina sticking her tongue down his throat by the end of Saturday night) Natasha had felt chronically below par ever since. She had felt perpetually exhausted, and her mood swings had been most extreme. The fact that Sebastian had not shown his face in work for the last three days, had only exacerbated her physical and mental malaise.

Natasha sniffed, morosely, when she thought about how tearful, dull and listless she felt. This was most unfortunate, because following her breakthrough with her first trade last week, the pressure to perform was increasing by the hour. She had continued to slog her guts out, resolutely keeping her head down, as she doggedly employed the method of that old sales axiom 'smile and dial', in the belief that it was only a matter of time before so doing would reap tangible rewards. So far this week, though, it had not. Besides, Natasha had always suspected that sparkling results sprang from inspiration, not from hard graft, which of course was

418

a rather convenient belief to hold, if one suffered from a lazy streak, such as she.

Fortunately, every time our heroine was tempted to give up, Freddie's no nonsense voice would ring in her ears with his oft repeated bastardization of Thomas Jefferson's profound quote, 'The harder I work the luckier I ge',' which he would relish every time he had closed-out a particularly profitable trade while, Shylock-like, rubbing his big hands together with glee.

Spookily, Natasha seemed utterly unable to shake this stubborn, vivid image and, following years of sore experience, she had learned that one ignores such persistent hints from the Universe at one's peril. In short, Natasha continued to pursue her 'dogged dialling' method and refused to become so easily disheartened. Unfortunately, as Natasha made her way in the dark to Liverpool Street Station, alone, to catch the tube home, alone, to go back to her bedsit, alone, that was precisely how she felt. Worse, she was on the verge of being swept away by the swirling, vortex rotation of self-pity, to be inexorably sucked down the dirty, stray-hair-strand strewn plug-hole of DESPAIR when, suddenly, with shocking rigid bolt, Natasha was set ABLAZE!

In an instant, her heart was enlivened to leave her brilliantly buzzing from head to toe! YES, YES, YES, she had just clapped eyes on HIM! There he stood before her, the breadth of him obstructing her path. Well, at least one knotty conundrum had been solved. All of Natasha's recent, lacklustre symptoms, were not due her physical toxicity, but merely to lack of exposure to HIM, for now that HE was here, they had not only vanished but inversed! As dazzling as a sunbeam in blackness, Sebastian transfixed her.

"Natasha, I can't do this any more. I have to see you." he announced, dramatically, as he stared, penetratingly, into her eyes. Then he eyed her, prophetically, before taking her by the arm and muttering, "Come on let's go."

Sebastian then escorted the flabbergasted girl off to the

long, chugging taxi rank in front of their gigantic office building. It was undulating vertically, like a shiny black caterpillar, covered in the yellow and red splodges, cast by the headlights and brake lights. The growling black beast was forever losing its head, every time the front taxi pulled away to feast on fares, and continually regrowing its tail, each time a replacement taxi trundled up to join the back of the line. Effortlessly, he waltzed the dazed and bedazzled Natasha to the lead taxi.

"West." Sebastian instructed, as soon as they were sitting in the back of it.

Natasha was flushed and panting with excitement. To her surprise, she found her hand already entwined with his, nestling contentedly on the seat in between them, and warming the cold black leather beneath. Tentatively, for still Natasha could not believe this was true, she turned to meet his gaze. In an instant, they were connected and her pounding heart rejoiced with impossible happiness.

So overwhelmed was she by this sudden, unexpected drift into his, so recently absent, orbit, she could have wept tears of pleasure, pain and relief, on that very spot, but Sebastian gave her no time for such frivolities. His eyes were alight and he lunged towards her to engulf her whole being in his embrace. His mouth was on hers, in an instant, and he smothered her with hot kisses, more passionate than a condemned man's pleas of innocence.

Sebastian kissed and kissed and kissed and kissed her. He extracted his soul-fill, gobbling her all up with his mouth, as he collected her in his strong arms. Interlaced and gorging in the back of a black cab, Sebastian urgently compensated for so many days without such sweet sustenance. Whimpering, and tearful, Natasha clutched the solid bulk of him, and her heart erupted with the force of this impossible pleasure. Natasha was simply delirious to be so unexpectedly feasting on his divine energy, once again. Flying in blissfulness they conjoined.

Time stopped, souls soared and the heavens split open to cascade their exquisite secrets upon them. Secrets classified to all, but those who dare to dabble in the trials, traumas and tribulations of unconditional love.

TWO SOULS ONE.

ONE SOUL ALL.

ALL IS ONE. ONE IS ALL. ALL IS NONE.

REPLENISHED. RESPLENDENT. NIRVANA.

Well, that was until Nirvana was curtly interrupted by a catarrhal cough, and the gruff growls of the taxi driver whose spluttering axed our lovers back to being. Once again, Time's motion jerked forward, to resume its relentless, merciless march:

Tick-tock, tick-tock, tick-tock, tick-tock...

And the taxi chugged along...

Tick-tock, tick-tock, tick-tock, tick-tock...

And their heartbeats pounded on:

b-boom, b-boom, b-boom, b-boom...

The person, who had just interrupted BLISS, went on to present a precise question, expecting specific reply:

"'West' sir? You said 'west' sir. Where 'west' do you mean then, sir?"

As disgruntled as a toddler, interrupted from his afternoon nap, a sleepy Sebastian, reluctantly, opened his eyes. His brow furrowed into a frown, for thought was required. Natasha watched him, wonder-struck as he acclimatized to his reawakening. Cautiously, his curiosity for this material world was reignited. He mustered the will to pull away from the soft, seductive pillow of LOVE. Natasha straightened up too, yet still she clasped Sebastian's hand, firmly. He leant forward and rested his right elbow on his bony knee, as he prepared to respond to this call, from this world. He opened his mouth, but the only sound that came out was a breathless laugh, for he had no idea where they were going. He had only had one thought in his mind from the minute he had set eyes on Natasha, and that was to hold her. Bashful, to be caught so unprepared, he shot a sidelong glance at the giggling Natasha. How delighted was she to have so bedazzled and bedevilled HIM!

"Where are we going?" he inquired of her, helplessly, to

elicit a further gush of giggles.

"Sebastian, what do you mean, 'where are we going?' It was you who commandeered me! It was you who said 'West' with such conviction. Where do you want to go?"

"To heaven. NOW."

"Isn't that where we've just been?"

"More!" Sebastian demanded, wildly.

"Looks like my place then." she suggested, cheekily.

"Take us to Pembridge Square please, number twenty-six." he instructed, in a heartbeat.

He then sighed, deeply, and he leaned back in his seat, while their hands started to frolic together, like lion cubs testing their strength. Slowly, Sebastian's brow began to darken, and he set his mouth into an unhappy pout. Only now did he remember quite how upset he was with Natasha. Sebastian tightened his grip on her hand and then began to squeeze it to the point of pain. For a moment, his sweet mouth became so twisted it looked strangely cruel. Natasha was startled.

"Ouch!" she squealed, as she attempted to snatch her hand away, but he held it too tightly. Confused, she questioned, "Why are you hurting me?"

Sebastian just stared down at her hand. Gradually, in his own time, he began to release his grip before he started to toy idly with it, as he stroked it, in silent apology, luxuriating in the length of her delicate fingers as he did so. Natasha watched him with suspicious fascination, as she tried to fathom what was happening.

"Oh Natasha, Natasha, Natasha." he sighed wearily, at last. Then shaking his head, despondently, he entreated, "Why did you have to hurt me?"

Then he shot her a look laced with accusation. She was confused. Why was he so upset with her, when it was he who had shut her out? Sebastian then let go of her hand and leaned over to grip the nape of her neck before, with his thumb and forefinger, he dispassionately traced the plump contours of her lips as he stared down at them.

"Those beautiful lips... why did you have to pollute

them?" Sebastian probed, and his pertinent question hung, menacingly, in the taxi's stale air.

Instantly, a single tear began to swell in the corner of Natasha's eye, and, soon enough, it was so full that the reflective, salty liquid began to roll down her flushed cheek. No more fathoming necessary. Natasha knew exactly to what Sebastian referred. She knew he knew, and he knew, she knew he knew. Looking beyond the surface of her shining eyes, directly into her bruised heart, Sebastian pinched Natasha's bottom lip, gently, and continued, "That sweet, sweet mouth... desecrated by Miles Monroe."

Natasha was so overcome with hurt and self-disgust, it was as if her bruised heart had just been minced. Her face became scorched by the heat of the blush that had just risen. She was on the verge of breaking into a panicked sweat. Her mind raced, ineptly, trying to contrive a string of words that could concoct her salvation. But how could she begin? How could she attempt to express an emotional turmoil beyond words? How could anyone understand the dark and desperate depths to which she had wandered, all alone, to prompt such profligate behaviour?

Petulantly, Natasha brushed Sebastian's hand away from her mouth. Shell-shocked, she stared blankly at the grubby, slate grey rubber floor of the taxi and inquired, meekly, "How do you know?"

But as soon as she had the courage to look into his familiar eyes, she knew the folly of her question. Sebastian knew everything about her. He knew everything he wished to know, and was forced to know everything he would rather not. Shamefully, she looked back down at the floor before mumbling weakly:

"You abandoned me Sebastian. I went to hell." Then she snivelled and her voice became more urgent, "I thought I'd never hold you again. I thought it was over. I was beyond desperate. Miles kept calling. He kept reaching out to me. He offered me comfort..." She tailed off helpless, before, suddenly, becoming inspired and re-seeking eye contact as she spluttered with fervour, "If you know about that, you must also know that I couldn't sleep with him. When it came down to it, I couldn't be with another man!" Then finally, she concluded with bewilderment, "Even I have no real understanding of what happened, or why."

Sebastian had relaxed. He did not look angry any more. The corners of his mouth had subtly upturned, just like a porpoise. He grunted with resignation and then commented, cryptically, "Well it bloody well worked didn't it."

"Worked?" Natasha questioned, perplexed.

Sebastian began to laugh, lightly.

"That blow-job drove me so bloody mad I could no longer be without you." He then chuckled in sick afterthought, "Maybe I should send Miles some flowers? Surely I owe him that much for bringing me to my senses?"

His warped suggestion was met with Natasha's scowl, though a hint of a smile shadowed the natural curve of her offending lips. With a face as sombre as an executioner's, Sebastian finally relented.

"I love you Natasha Flynn, as much as I try my hardest not to, it seems that most inconvenient fact is inescapable."

Sebastian held Natasha's head, firmly, between his hands and he kissed her parted mouth, tenderly, in forgiveness. Having so sealed his message of import, he requested humbly:

"Please, don't ever do that again?"

Natasha agreed with a tiny nod.

"Likewise?" she implored, hopefully.

Sebastian stared back at her, with profound connection, encircling her in his comforting arms, while she nuzzled into his broad chest, and clutched him more tightly than the drowning do driftwood.

Chapter Thirty-one - Once and for all

Those beautiful words we said to one another
are hidden in the secret heart of heaven.
One day, like the rain, they will pour
our love story all over the world.

Rumi

Sebastian and Natasha's excessive passion heated up the rest of the bitterly cold, bare branched, soggy month of November, as it recklessly veered towards fever pitch. Simply, the pair became inseparable. Our heroine was completely intoxicated by her exponentially increasing infatuation with Sebastian, while HE, inexorably, encircled Natasha like a disorientated moth mistaking flame for moonlight. Friends and colleagues no longer recognized either of them. The erstwhile enthusiastic, dedicated, analytical Natasha had acquired the far-away look of a girl apparently no longer in command of her faculties, while the once collected, calm and ruthlessly calculating politician of high finance, had developed an inane grin, accompanied by an unfamiliar gazelle's spring in his long stride.

Fortunately, Natasha's new found state of sheer invincibility infected all aspects of her life, for how effortlessly and regularly she was printing coveted sales-tickets now. What is more, she was thrilled to observe that the size of her increasing trades was happily ballooning too. Was all that 'smile and dial' hard graft finally paying dividends? Or was it simply that residing in a permanent state of ecstasy, extracted the most positive energy the Universe had to offer and, on a trading floor, how else could that manifest but by making bucket loads of money? Either way, by November's close, our heroine's social standing amongst her peers had been elevated as much as her heart.

Even in her love-induced haze, Natasha's pretty brow was prone to wrinkle into a light frown, whenever she, momentarily, dwelt on the direct alignment of her perceived worth, with her success at generating profits. In spite of such lackadaisical reservations, the excessive accompanying accolade did not fail to turbo charge her, already love-inflated, self-confidence to dangerously titanic proportions. It seemed everything for Natasha was on the up and up, except, of course, for the quantity and quality of her sleep but, what did that matter, for when one is higher than a satellite sleep becomes strangely dispensable. Good health, blissful romance and the promise of lots and lots of cash. What could possibly go wrong?

In the whirring beat of a bright hummingbird's wing, December careered into being. Finally, the punishing slog of the financiers' year was interspersed with a carousal of client and colleague entertainment. Marathon lunches became commonplace, where traders, sales people and clients would, eventually, stagger out of revoltingly expensive, central London restaurants into cold, dark, damp nights. Their breath would reek of pungent fumes, which odorously betrayed the copious quantities of champagne, wine and ancient ports that had been, greedily, thrown back, for sometimes more than six hours on the trot, while their shouts, curses and hacking laughter would audibly do the very same.

The inevitably male dominated, dishevelled, smart-suited, skew-whiff-tie-wearing, expensively-shod gang, would then meander across the dark pavement, while strong arms lolled around each others' shoulders, as much for support as for displays of sloppy, alcohol-induced affection. Suddenly, a man would be curiously inspired to act, and he would, clumsily, hail a black taxi with an overly extended arm, as his hand flapped limply around in the air, with befuddled impatience. Such action would inevitably be accompanied by a pitiful lurch forward, followed by a steadying backward stagger. Then a reluctant cabbie would then screech to a halt, having fast weighed the vomit versus massive-tip equation; clearly in marginal favour of the latter. Next, a second man would be emboldened to attempt the same, with equally undulating physical posture, and then a third, and slowly the shuffling, raucous, drunken crowd would split into packs of four or five. These groups would hail, and then fall into more taxis, to squeeze hip to hip onto squeaky leather seats, while laughing too loudly and jostling too boisterously before, at last, becoming settled. The taxis would then pull away, lurch forward, stop, start, lurch again, lean left, and then right, then left again, as they expertly negotiated the tight corners of the narrow City streets on their way to the next destination.

The occupants would become, increasingly, mute while nausea would begin to take hold, over most of them, as all of the liquor they had drunk sloshed around in their tummies, hampering honest attempts to digest too much rich food, guzzled at lunch-time, to leave it sitting, heavily, in the pit of their extended stomachs, all afternoon. Then suddenly, the first taxi would pull up outside some pre-agreed, insalubrious, smoky night haunt. The cabbie would breathe a heavy sigh of relief, for no one had thrown up, this time. Soon enough, more chugging cabs would pull up behind, to complete the erstwhile fragmented convoy, with each driver equally eager to discharge their drunken load. Steal door handles would be fumbled with before, eventually, being yanked up to emit an encouraging click, and then heavy doors shoved open, to let a blast of cold night air gush in to help sober up the occupants.

The time to get out had arrived. Huffs and puffs of effort would be heard, and wobbly limbs called upon to perform, as a confetti of screwed up banknotes would be chucked through the little gap that had, suddenly, appeared in the scratched, plastic window behind the driver; for only now did he deign to slide it open to take payment. Slowly, one by one, the mumbling hunched over passengers would step out, tentatively, onto the pavement, most distrustful of the reliability of their legs. As they piled out, the competing men's monetary largesse would be accompanied by the muttering of condescending slurs in multiple:

"Go o' kee' ze shange..."

"Yeah, yeah you do jus' tha'...jus' you kee' i'"

"Thas for you ma'e, thas yours..."

The seasoned cabbie ignores the comments and collects the screwed up paper balls before, carefully, flattening the notes out into the palm of his dry hand: three brown, one purple. Fifty quid for a twenty-three pound fare. He nods in satisfaction. Drunk City blokes, he just loves 'em when they don't spew. Risk, reward, ain't that what they call it? He took the risk, now he's counting the reward. Bloody deserves i' 'n' all!

The men are outside some club now, with much effort they straighten up, as they try to look important and more sober than they are. They approach the doormen with serious, big-hitter looks before names are given and booking arrangements referenced. Even before they have managed to focus, if such an ambition were ever a realistic aspiration following such a lunch, the bankers find themselves in the darkness of the strip-club. A new surge of energy lifts the flagging group, as the promise of female flesh dawns. The vibrations of the thumping music penetrates and judders internal organs and splits wincing eardrums, while the bright flashing multi-coloured lights startle eyes to attention. It is dark, humid and hot inside; like a woman. Thick, tailored, navy blue, black, caramel and fawn coats are taken off, one by one, and off-handedly dumped into the frail arms of a heavily made-up hostess. The pile develops into a metre-high cloth mound of multi-colours, over which the poor girl pokes her chin, in an attempt to contain it, before she whisks off, to get rid of such cumbersome bulk.

Liberated, the straggling, unsteady crew is carefully escorted to one of the large, low round tables, in order to comfortably, and expensively, continue with their self-destructive self-indulgence while a purple-suspender-wearing, topless young blonde dances, provocatively, in the centre of their table. Such a sight is more than enough to reinvigorate the men and elicit enthusiastic, animalistic cheers and loud cries for Methuselahs of Cristal! The music is louder here. Gruff catcalls add to the din, while young men, and old, are increasingly worked up by younger women. Semi-naked girls of every hue strut on tables, brandishing enormous breasts that they continually caress (their own or some others') or provocatively tweak at erect nipples (their own or some others') as they lick glossy, red lips (their own or some others') before, frantically, darting wet, pink tongues in and out like starving frogs. Silver poles enjoy intense attention as long, tanned, oiled legs wrap around them, or rhythmically ride up and down, before backs are arched and the girls, suddenly, twirl and swirl around them, so shiny, long, black, brown, auburn and blonde hair dusts tables and floors in thick varied fans. Hips are ground and gyrated while bottoms and bosoms, hypnotically, undulate to the music, always stuck out as far as each girl's spine will allow.

All this erotic performance, to encourage patrons to part with cash. For the price of a purple or pink crinkled banknote, a punter secures the privilege of increased physical and visual intimacy with the girls, as his sweaty, lecherous hand stuffs the note into a tight, sparkly, g-string, momentarily, to enjoy the excruciating pleasure of the transient touch of a pretty, big-breasted, young girl's bare skin; and all in the name of Client Entertainment!

For even comatose bankers never forget, great client entertainment generates gigantic tickets, and gigantic tickets produce mammoth profits, and mammoth profits procure behemoth bonuses! And everyone must know the City's Christmas carol, or for some, their Easter hymn:

"BIG BONUSES, BIG BONUSES,
BIG BONUSES ALL THE WAY,
OH WHAT FUN WE NEED TO HAVE,
WITH OUR CLIENTS EVERYDAY! HEY!"

"BIG BONUSES, BIG BONUSES,
BIG BONUSES ALL THE WAY,
OH WHAT FUN WE NEED TO HAVE
WITH OUR CLIENTS EVERYDAY! HEY!"

And so, after an exhausting carousel of 'Client Entertainment', 'it' was upon them. 'It' being Miss Flynn's first ever Debt Division Christmas Party. Well to qualify, it may go by the name of 'Christmas Party' but it was usually held pre-mid December, for the closer one got to Christmas, the fewer bosses and employees left in London to attend. Top management would soon flee, with families, to luxurious snow-covered Alpine chalets, to ski in exclusive resorts and heli-ski inaccessible terrain, or perhaps fly to hotter climes to bask in Caribbean, Mauritian or Martiniquean sunshine, to lounge on boats, swim in enticing, turquoise waters, or stroll the softness of white sands under the cool shade of giant, gnarled palm trees.

Natasha was soon to learn that the antics at the Debt Division Christmas party, made the shenanigans in the topless nightclubs of London look innocent. If sexual relations occurred at the latter, at least the girls got paid for it. What is more, they were spared the humiliation of arriving at work the next day, to find themselves ignored by the man who was so attentive, and keen to get inside all of their orifices, the night before.

Indeed, the U.C.B. Christmas party was a more sinister affair all together. Cocktails and champagne flowed, limitlessly, and the atmosphere of camaraderie gave the girls present a false sense of security. This was the event to celebrate a successful year with the people with whom you had worked, intensely, (to which spouses were uninvited) yet the men attending were just as predatory and lecherous as they were when in strip joints, however, here the prey was not 'professional' but usually, junior, naïve, hopeful female 'colleagues'.

As the music played, alcohol flowed and time passed, in the darkness, many girls started to lose their inhibitions and, with such a small pool of females to source from, many of the men lowered their standards. The consequences of such, invited the most extraordinary and unexpected sexual encounters that, tragically for the women involved, were all too often quickly forgotten, or worse, electronically discussed and dissected for months to come. Needless to say, it was most rare for a pretty young girl from the 'back office' to procure herself a handsome, rich husband from the 'front', but all too common for a not so handsome bloke from the 'front office' to get to carnally, and undeservedly, enjoy the favours of a hopeful young lady from the 'back'. The only certainties were shocking hangovers and blushing faces the following morning. To quote a popular trading floor joke:

"A dog is for life, not just for Christmas. Remember that at the office party!"

Thankfully, Natasha was protected from such a sorry dynamic, for she was in LOVE! She knew with whom she would be leaving, and she had eyes for no other. Sebastian and Natasha stayed long enough for Sebastian to deliver his speech and, just long enough, not to raise too many curious eyebrows at a suspiciously early departure.

Pretending to be having fun when they were not at liberty to touch one another was torturous. Sebastian had alleviated the discomfort of this anticipated charade, somewhat, by bringing along some Charlie, neatly piled up in his round silver Burberry pillbox. With all of the booze and intermittent, but regular, trips to the lavatory, suddenly, one a.m. was approaching. Finally, Sebastian decided that they had done sufficient duty, and they could now slip off. Indeed, by now, everyone was so drunk that he even deemed it safe to leave together. Well they both lived in West London, after all. If they were grilled, they could say they were just sharing a taxi home, which is in fact exactly what they were doing.

When they were, at last, back in Natasha's bedsit, they were both a bit drunk, sky-high on coke and strangely emotional. Miraculously, Sebastian managed to perform admirably and, yet again, our lovers hungrily partook of profound spiritual and physical pleasures, for many hours, as they cruised the inexhaustible ecstasies they never failed to find in one another. It seemed even multiple-chemical intoxication was incapable of dulling the light that shone from them when entwined for, if one were to observe the curtainless, stirrup-shaped window in the top right hand corner, of number twenty-six Pembridge Square, one would have detected an ethereal glow flooding from it, and out into the starless night. By four-sixteen a.m. Sebastian and Natasha were, at last, fast asleep, lying naked in each other's arms.

It was Natasha who stirred first. That strange internal clock that ticks within us all, somehow, managed to prompt her from deep sleep. Her eyeballs began to move rapidly, from side to side, under closed lids, and she became convinced that she must get up soon for, surely, morning was approaching. In an instant, she willed herself awake and, immediately, her heartbeat quickened. Her eyes then darted over to the green neon digits of her alarm clock, to check the time. It was five-fifteen a.m.

The pounding of Natasha's pulse raced even more when, suddenly, she remembered that Isabel was in London and that she had been expecting Sebastian home last night. What is more, both of them had to make the morning meeting by seven-thirty for, everyone knew, it was professional suicide to partake of the pleasures at a party with colleagues the night before, then fail to show up at work, and on time, the following morning. Throughout the blur that had been December, it had become apparent that arriving at work sweating and shaking from alcohol poisoning, falling asleep at one's desk, being heard snoring in a lavatory cubical, or simply being of absolutely no use to anyone, was forgivable, however, not arriving at work at all, was NOT. Sebastian had to get up; now. Natasha had to get up in less than an hour's time. She propped herself up on her elbow and, adoringly, looked into her lover's sleeping face. Inspired, she leant down to kiss him, tenderly on one closed eyelid, then the other, to become, immediately, intoxicated by this simple intimacy, before she whispered, gently, "Baby it's five-thirty. You've got to get up. You've got to go home…"

Nothing. Gently, she nudged her Love and cajoled:

"Darling, you have to get back home. Please baby, it's late. You have to wake up."

Sebastian stirred faintly. Natasha rested her cool hand on his warm smooth shoulder and she rocked his heavy body, slowly, backwards and forwards. His eyes flicked open, their greenness accentuated by the red-tinged whites. He opened and closed them, several times, to blink away the last vestiges of sleep. Natasha stared into them lovingly, yet she became distressed to observe that they had begun to fill with full, wet tears.

At five-nineteen on a December morning in London, the dawning of the day was still hours away, yet it seemed that the terrible blood-orange dawn of Sebastian's predicament had arrived. Exhausted and snuggled up next to the warm, soft, smitten Natasha, Sebastian seemed unable to find the strength to do what he must. Instead, he gave a forlorn moan and buried his head, deeply, into Natasha's bosom and his arms gripped her, fervently, while he wept, almost inaudibly. His despair was so tangible that Natasha could taste its acridity. Sebastian just kept burrowing his head farther and farther into her chest, like a tiny child determined to seek refuge from some deep emotional trauma, back inside mummy. Tears pricked Natasha's eyes too, to see her Love so distressed. She caressed him, compassionately, and made 'Shhhing' sounds as she held his big warm body close to hers. She wanted to shoulder his suffering and she became immersed in the art of 'comforting', an activity that often provides greater solace to the one giving, than to the one in need.

Sebastian started to snivel and Natasha loosened her grip before, gently, wiping away the tears from his face. He sniffed some more, before abruptly pulling away from her to sit upright on the edge of the bed. He stared blankly at nothing while Natasha propped herself up to place her hand, reassuringly, on the centre of his back. Sebastian shrugged her off, embarrassed, and then started to look down at the rumpled heap, of black and white, that had so recently been his impeccably smart attire. He stared long

433

and hard at it, as if contemplating its lack of structure and sense, along with his own. Finally, Sebastian gave a morose sigh, before he leaned forward to tackle the heap and try to extract a recognizable item of clothing. Thankfully, for it postponed the moment when he would have to find the strength to stand, the first item he held up in front of him was a silk black sock. Sebastian then delved into the material molehill, once again, and managed to retrieve the second one. He remained seated while he put them both on, before he stood up to reach for his boxer shorts.

With the slow mechanical movements of a defeated fighter, Sebastian deconstructed the black and white pile, item by item, until he was almost fully dressed and it had disappeared altogether. He then picked up his beautiful Patek Phillippe watch, from the bedside table, and put it on, before doing the same with his knotted solid-gold cufflinks. He gave a giant yawn, stretched his shoulders back and cocked his head to one side, then the other. Finally, he pulled his trousers up by the waistband, donned his cummerbund, buttoned up his jacket then popped his bow-tie into his pocket.

Grim-faced, but ready, Sebastian stood still, for a moment, as if preparing to leave then, all of a sudden, the strength streamed from him as fast as air from a burst balloon, and he dropped to the floor, heavily, where he crumpled into a foetal position, and wrapped his long arms around his knees. To Natasha's horror, Sebastian began to sob, uncontrollably, as he rocked himself, repeatedly, backwards and forwards in self-comfort like some lunatic. She became paralysed as she witnessed his overwhelming overture of grief, for his agony was far too core and acute to cuddle away with soft cooings of comfort. In short, Natasha knew not what to do. Aghast, she knelt down next to him and put her hand onto his back, once again, in an attempt to alleviate his suffering. Anguish-ridden, she listened to Sebastian repeat through his snivelling, in a tiny, frightened voice that she did not recognize:

"I can't go home, Natasha. I can't go home, I can't go

home. Natasha, please, don't make me go home…"

After an interminable time, the strength and regularity of Sebastian's sobbing began to abate yet, with every sporadic heave of his chest, Natasha's heart winced, as she tried to swaddle him with her gushing love. Oh, what she would have given to rescue him from his torturous, private pit of emotional purgatory.

It was five-minutes past six and, at last, Sebastian was silent, as if the worst of his despair had been spent. By now, Natasha was curled up behind him and hugging him, her naked skin tight next to his black dinner jacket. Without uttering a sound, he pulled away from her and sat up with his broad back facing her, for a while, before he finally stood up. He walked the couple of strides over to his black Berluti dress shoes, slipped them on and then, in an instant, his tall frame was standing by the front door. Sebastian reached for the latch, hesitated for a moment, and then, quickly, opened it.

"I have to go." he said softly, under his breath, without looking back.

He left, and closed the door behind him with a soft click. Natasha was still naked and sitting up on the floor as she stared after him, shell-shocked and dejected. Now that she was not cuddling him, Natasha suddenly felt freezing cold. She struggled to her feet, and then slumped straight back into bed. She was so hung-over, so exhausted and hurting so much inside and out, that she just pulled the cool duvet cover around her, to snatch a moment of warmth, comfort and rest.

Lying there, all alone, Natasha rolled onto her back and, with the back of her hand resting on her forehead, she stared up through the skylight. It was still dark outside and she could just make out the North Star, which twinkled, tentatively, in the sky. It seemed silent, but the longer Natasha stared out of the window, the more she became aware of intermittent tweeting. Sunrise was almost two hours away, yet the birds seemed impatient for first light, for several of them had begun to chirp, gaily, warming their voices for the full symphony of dawn chorus. It seemed so strange to hear birdsong in such darkness. Even in her semi-catatonic state, a little voice in Natasha's mind muttered, repeatedly, "Fifteen-minutes and then I have to get up, fifteen-minutes, then I have to get up, fifteen-minutes, then I have to get up..."

Natasha was not sleeping. Natasha was not even resting. Natasha just needed to STOP and she had fifteen-minutes in which to do so. STOP. Stop, before she had to wrench herself out of bed. Stop, before she had to stagger down the stairs, grab a shower in the scummy shared cubicle, and pray the hot gushing water could wash away the fogginess of her head, and sooth the soreness of her heart. Fifteen-minutes to stop, before she had to get ready, get to work, face her colleagues and face HIM. Get ready to be in the same room as HIM, in public, after this. Get ready to be in the same room as HIM and not be allowed to touch HIM, or betray her eternal longing for HIM, after this.

Her head was so sore now, that the tweets and chirps coming from the garden square, painfully pierced the chaos of the overwhelming emotions that coursed through her confused mind, while her consciousness continued its wilful chant: "Fifteen-minutes, then I have to get up, fifteen-minutes then I have to get up, fifteen-minutes then I have to get up..." before she flashed a look at her glaring alarm clock, "Fuck, ten-minutes and I have to get up, ten-minutes and I have to get up, ten-minutes and I have to get up...

* * * * *

It was seven twenty-eight when the shiny U.C.B. lift door opened with a hollow "PING!" and Natasha stepped out. It was seven twenty-nine by the time she reached her desk. She was still a bit drunk, her mouth had a revolting metallic taste, and she had a splitting headache, but she had arrived. Natasha dumped her handbag on the top of her desk and then, quickly, grabbed her thick, scribbled on, sales blotter, the top pages of which were already becoming curled over through use. Conveniently, a black biro had been jammed into its white plastic binding. Hugging it to her chest, for scant comfort, Natasha strode down the corridor in between the back-to-back desks, unceremoniously shoving stray swivel chairs out of the way as she did so, before she stepped off the trading floor to waltz down the grey carpeted corridor, and then straight into the morning meeting at seven-thirty on the dot. She had made it.

Everyone was there. Even Sebastian was there. Everyone was grey, tired and waxy looking, but everyone was there. Their hollow-eyed faces turned to look at her as she entered. Natasha had cut it fine and everyone knew it, but she had made it. She gave an uncomfortable smile, trying to disguise her vague sense of triumph. The only penalty she paid was that she had to remain standing, for all the chairs were taken. Pouting with juvenile disappointment, for if she had ever needed a seat it was this morning, Natasha leaned against the wall, next to a pale-faced Keri.

Everyone's attention soon returned to Sebastian, and Natasha was free to study him closely with increasing awe. His attire was fresh and impeccable. He was clean-shaven and, astonishingly, he looked the most bright-eyed of the bunch. His composure was assured as, effortlessly, he started to articulate the axes of the day, just as confidently and succinctly, as was his habit. There was even a mischievous smile that lurked behind his lips, as if he had just gotten away with something secret. Just looking at him made Natasha feel perplexed, and even more exhausted than the previous evening's events justified. Simply, she was flabbergasted by this presentation of him, and she could not reconcile it with the broken man that had shaken and wept on the floor of her bedsit, only hours ago. Natasha's mind launched into an insane spin, 'On what reserves did Sebastian draw? What "will" allowed him to continue, as if he had not flirted with a nervous breakdown earlier this very day? Quite simply, how did he do it?'

The more Natasha dwelt on Sebastian, and compared his current condition with the sorry state of her own, the more exasperated she became and her thoughts raced on, 'Where, oh where, did he locate the switch that turned his emotions off, in an instant? What lever did he flick to so effectively fashion himself a machine?' The longer she thought about the phenomenon that was Sebastian, the more gormless her expression became. Sebastian, in contrast, was full of beans. In fact, he seemed to struggle to contain his enthusiasm and the light of hope shone from his eyes. Natasha continued to try to fathom his apparent mood, 'What on earth could have changed in the last two hours? How was it possible that, when Sebastian looked at her now, all she could see was his jubilant heart and rapturous soul?'

With an abrupt clap of his hands, Sebastian shocked Natasha from herself and concluded the meeting. The tired, bedraggled traders and sales people then pulled themselves away from supporting walls or, grunting, pushed themselves up from their chairs. Listlessly, the herd shuffled out of the room as they started to ruminate on the objectives for the day. It did not take long for many of them to conclude that Sebastian's directives were far too challenging, for the Friday following their Christmas Party. Come to think of it, getting to work had been challenging enough and he demanded more of them? Greedy bastard! Natasha was just about to leave the room too, when she heard Sebastian speak her name.

"Natasha, can you stay behind? I need a quick word."

She gave a nod, and tried to appear as unmoved as possible. She stepped aside from the doorway, to allow the others to pass, and waited for Sebastian to enlighten her. Finally, once the last person had left the room, Sebastian shut the door behind them. Turning to face her, he took Natasha by the arms, impulsively, and he held her, firmly, in front of him. He was grinning madly with excitement and his face emitted an astonishing glow. Natasha looked up into it, with confusion. He squeezed her arms, once again, and then, continuing to hold her, he began, "Natasha, my Love," Sebastian gave her another firm squeeze, on her upper arms, as he cocked his head from one side, and then to the other, while he stared into her puzzled face, "it has become abundantly clear that we cannot continue like this."

Natasha became rigid, terrified by the words that might come. Sensing her fear, Sebastian laughed out loud and shrugged his shoulders, with nervous resignation, and then, suddenly, he let her go. He averted his attention as if to concentrate fully on what he was about to say. With a determined expression he began, randomly, to pace around the room while staring down at the toes of his beautiful Berluti shoes, as he announced, in a formal voice:

"Tomorrow I leave for India…" He then raised his head to catch sight of Natasha's increasingly ashen complexion. He looked down again before adding in afterthought, "with the family."

A lump formed in Natasha's throat. She felt like her guts had just splattered all over her suede high heels. Sebastian continued to stare at his feet, as he paced around the room, with his arms held behind his back, in his usual posture of a nobleman. She was paralysed. He went on.

"We shall be spending Christmas and New Year in Goa." he continued.

Natasha's mouth became as parched as Thar Desert sands, while the colour drained from her face, completely. Sebastian stopped his pacing and glanced over to her, smiling insanely as he announced in fanfare:

"Natasha, while I am there, I am going to DECIDE. I am determined to DECIDE! Once and for all!"

He gambolled over to her and held her, firmly, by her upper arms, again. He stared, penetratingly, into her eyes, searching far beyond the tiny reflected panes of white light that bounced off them. Sebastian managed to locate Natasha's quivering soul, and he spoke to it, with certitude.

"Oh, my darling one… I can never again go to the place I visited this morning. I have to do something. I do not believe it's possible for me to be without you and, I have to work out what I'm going to do about that. Don't

439

you see?" Natasha's rigid body began to relax, and she nodded her understanding, tentatively, as she allowed fragile hope to trickle into her breast, while her eyes began to brim with full, hot tears. He smiled, indulgently, and said:

"I will not see you for the next three and a half weeks and, my darling one, by the time I come back, I will have made my decision."

Sniffing, Natasha blinked to stifle her weeping. She was speechless. Not a thing had changed, yet just the prospect of resolution had made Sebastian as joyous and playful as a puppy. Not a thing had changed, yet Sebastian's studied words had furnished our heroine's heart with Hope and, with strong, white-feathered wings Natasha's soul now soared high up above, among the angels. With the arrival of dawn, the deep darkness of Sebastian's earlier despair had been obliterated, and the embryo of 'future happiness' implanted, firmly, into Natasha's fertile womb. Time, and Sebastian's courage, would bring forth its birth.

And so it was, Sebastian's determination 'to decide' had given him much needed relief, while Natasha was rocketed beyond the stratosphere. In just over three weeks' time she would know, once and for all, if Sebastian were to be hers. Surely, no mortal deserves such blissful possibility? Yet, at the epicentre of Natasha's being, she knew they were destined to be together...

****

**TO BE CONTINUED.
WATCH OUT FOR THE
UP AND COMING SEQUEL
OF FALSE GODS
at www.cyblack.com**

4395234R00244

Printed in Great Britain
by Amazon.co.uk, Ltd.,
Marston Gate.